Western Alliances

ALSO BY
WILTON BARNHARDT

Lookaway, Lookaway

Show World

Gospel

Emma Who Saved My Life

Western Alliances

WILTON BARNHARDT

ST. MARTIN'S PRESS
NEW YORK

First published in the United States by St. Martin's Press,
an imprint of St. Martin's Publishing Group

WESTERN ALLIANCES. Copyright © 2023 by Wilton Barnhardt. All rights reserved.
Printed in the United States of America. For information, address
St. Martin's Publishing Group, 120 Broadway, New York, NY 10271.

www.stmartins.com

Photos courtesy of Wilton Barnhardt, Robert Patrick Doyle, Gabriele Merlino, and James D'Emilio.

The Library of Congress Cataloging-in-Publication Data is available upon request.

ISBN 978-1-250-09000-3 (hardcover)
ISBN 978-1-250-09002-7 (ebook)

eISBN 9781250090027

Our books may be purchased in bulk for promotional, educational, or business use. Please
contact your local bookseller or the Macmillan Corporate and Premium Sales Department at
1-800-221-7945, extension 5442, or by email at MacmillanSpecialMarkets@macmillan.com.

First Edition: 2023

10 9 8 7 6 5 4 3 2 1

To
Denis Baresch
Davide Bova
Christina Gerstgrasser
Alexander Luckow
Kai Maristed
Christian Pervilhac
and Annette Smith,
my Europeans

CONTENTS

PART II: 2019, TEN YEARS LATER

PART I:
2008–2009

New York System

U pon reflection, it was an ingenious way to keep a bright six-year-old occupied and out of one's hair, to set down *The Wall Street Journal* or the business section of *The New York Times* before him, select a crayon of the day with much pretended interest and debate as to the color's importance, and task the child to circle *each and every* instance of his father's name appearing in the pages. And won't Daddy be proud when he gets home?

Roberto Costa, for uncounted hours, scanned the pages concerning foreign exchanges and dividend rollovers and pork-belly commodities in hopes that his father might be quoted—since his father knew everything, and American business could hardly function without him. There were datelines from Frankfurt and Strasbourg and Brussels and an array of less pronounceable locales from where his father, one minute in the door, suitcase in the foyer, would empty into the designated bowl his pocketful of foreign coins for his son's collection. The unrivaled treasury of coins would make for a definitive show-and-tell at school. (One day, from a park bench in western Russia, Roberto would determine that his numismatic show-and-tell was the first in his series of ambitious international projects that would not be seen to completion.)

By his eighth birthday, the jig was up. Roberto had figured out that only the headlines featuring BONDS or MUNICIPALS led to the possibility of a paternal mention. Still, what joy to find Mr. Salvador Costa quoted and to take the crayon and fill in the circles of the *a*'s and *o*'s, create a halo around his own last name. Then how, lying in his bed, Roberto would fight to stay even half-conscious, 10:00, 10:30, 11:00 p.m., attuned to the percussion of the front door opening and gently closing. His pages had been placed specially on the foyer lamp table next to the outgoing mail so his mother wouldn't forget to present his work . . . which she invariably failed to do. Gratification often waited until breakfast the next morning:

"You found me again, Bobby!" his dad would say, waving the illuminated manuscript, before reading the article, before grumbling, "I see they misquoted me as usual."

"You gonna fix 'em, Dad?"

"You bet I'm gonna fix 'em."

As an adult, Roberto Costa now understood that the name-finding exercise was emblematic of his mother's approach to child-rearing, a chore usually delegated to house cleaners and nanny services, but when minions could not be found, when no one could be drafted, anyone, anyone at all, to give her children a hint of supervision, there was always the *Wall Street Journal* assignment.

He had never entirely given up the exercise. Throughout his twenties, in some European train station café, in a Florentine piazza or a Viennese coffeehouse, nursing a too-pricey miniature soda, he would check the financial part of the *International Herald Tribune* and fill in the *o*'s and *a*'s for a paragraph, hoping for a spark of childhood joy.

"I am also starting to have the thought," Liesl said quietly in English, darting a glance to their fellow train passengers, "that you have not to have been so . . . so honest with your Liesl. I think . . ." She studied a sleeping businessman and then a stern, skeletal, middle-aged man reading a thick novel. "I think that you are a very rich boy."

He said nothing.

Liesl tucked a strand of white-blond hair behind her ear, then tapped the *Financial Times*. "You fill in the circles on the name Salvador Costa—he is head of something enormous. Some bank, yes? It is your father?"

He nodded, shrugging. "My father is well-off, yes."

"And you too? You never do talking about working. I never hear you to have a profession, hmm? And the hotel in Ettal we stayed in. You must, perhaps, a thousand euros there spent?"

"I have money now, but maybe not for much longer."

It was August of 2008, and *The Economist*, the *Financial Times*, all were gathered in his lap, emblazoned with panicked headlines; even the unexcitable *Frankfurter Allgemeine* had been allowing the headlines to span five out of six columns. Only the end of the world would get all six, Liesl clarified, noting that it happened once, after 9/11.

"Hmm, yes, but it is a rareness," mused Liesl, "for any rich person to become un-rich, I think. We live in a world that the centuries have organized around giving those with money the protection of the state, yes?"

Roberto wasn't sure whether a Marxist tirade awaited from the gorgeous blond graduate student, but the train was applying its brakes and the diesel burnt-hair smell was faint in the cabin. They were in Frankfurt.

Roberto snapped a picture of the modern skyline as they decelerated; Frankfurt was one of the few European cities you might mistake for an American one.

Soon Roberto and Liesl were off the train, retrieving their backpacks, and standing in the busiest train station in Europe, the largest in Germany, with a football stadium's worth of fast-walking commuters who would mow down all in their path to board a train that left precisely when announced. Roberto and Liesl looked up at the enclosed space, the hangar-huge steel arches and begrimed glass in the ceiling above, which prepared one for a rainy, gray German day even when, like today, it was sunny outside.

"Okay, Baron," Liesl purred, "I go away so you don't have to introduce me to your Vati and explain to your father who, *who* must be this mysterious girl . . ." With this line of dramatics failing to catch hold, she became more like herself again. "Oh, I do want to see your father, from a distance, though."

"Twenty guesses, and you still wouldn't select him from the crowd."

"Please. I marry your father instead, ja? If he is the rich one."

Roberto thought he saw the silver-steel coiffure of Mrs. Santos . . . Yes! His heart warmed to see her again, though she had been, historically, a source of terror. Talking into her phone, she marched through the crowds of German commuters, and sure enough, Roberto's father was behind her. Where was Sam the Intern? Usually he scurried ahead in advance and prepared things for his father, like a cross between a harried high-society caterer and a Secret Service agent.

Salvador Costa and Mrs. Santos tarried at a newsstand in the heart of the station. Mrs. Santos was exasperated about something and had her finger raised, a sign of imminent wrath, but it wasn't guessable who was the recipient . . . Maybe Sam the Intern was in trouble. Roberto would have liked that. Mrs. Santos now wagged a finger at Salvador, her boss of twenty years, and then strode toward a station exit, talking into her phone.

Liesl was saying, "—because older men love me, for some reason—"

"Meine Baronin," he said, cutting short her ingratiation into the family fortune. "See if you can pick out my father. He's among the businessmen by the newsstand there."

"This will be easy . . ." She studied the men aswarm the newsstand. "He will be tall like you, maybe good-looking like you too—I hope more so since, yes, I am to be his next wife . . . I say the man in the brown. That is an American suit, I think."

After four guesses, he put her out of her misery. "The man in the plaid coat, the magenta tie."

"Mein Gott," she marveled, swatting him on the arm. Was he a dwarf, Liesl asked before putting a hand to her mouth, astonished by her own rudeness.

"He's a foot shorter," Roberto laughed. "I took entirely after my mother's side in looks, and my sister got the short, Portuguese genes. My father did give me his bad-heart issues," Roberto added, pointing unnecessarily to his chest.

"Oh yes. The . . ."

Roberto smiled good-naturedly.

"He appears to be a kind man, but does he . . . does he not know how to dress?"

"Yes, look—you see—someone is stopping him—he has a TV program in the United States, and businessmen recognize him. He is famous for his tasteless sports coats and loud ties."

Salvador Costa played to the ingrained caste system of Wall Street; he was the off-the-rack Men's Wearhouse–wearing little guy, the bond trader in Short Hills, New Jersey, in the strip mall peddling unexciting municipals, five o'clock shadow by 11:00 a.m. He may have offered amusement to the WASP and Jewish swells in the glass boardrooms, but he was the hero of muni and commodity traders, hollering for a living in the Stygian world of the trading floor. Roberto Costa's sister, Rachel Costa, would deny outright that she was related to the Sal Costa on CNBC's *Costa: Doing Business!* Fortunately for her, every other Portuguese American was named Costa, so she had deniability.

Roberto claimed his father every chance he got! He would search the cable TV menus in hotel rooms with a hundred channels hoping the European cable systems ran his dad's half-hour CNBC segment at 5:30 U.S. eastern standard time, the lead-up to Jim Cramer's *Mad Money.* Cramer may have been playing up his antics for the camera, but Sal Costa, preaching the gospel of low-yield but dependable securities, dressed out of some 1980s thrift shop, was the real Sal Costa. No playacting involved. It was a pure delight to sit in a hotel room in Brussels or Warsaw or Stockholm and let the sound of his dad's flat Rhode Island cadences comfort him, even if Roberto had no clue what his dad was talking about.

"When I am his wife, he will not wear that tie." Liesl then gathered up her yellow canvas backpack. "Okay, okay, na ja, you have your wonderful family moment, und ich gehe nach Kaffee. Text mir wenn du am Ende bist. Tschüss."

Roberto watched as she sauntered away unsteadily, the backpack swaying once in each compass direction before steadily settling onto her back.

Roberto steered his own backpack and suitcase-on-rollers toward the central Imbiß, the German sausage, kraut, beer, and french fry stand. He got to see a caper in process: lurking from behind a kiosk, Sam the Intern now joined his father hurriedly, rattling two grocery bags. His father patted Sam on the shoulder, good man, attaboy, and began rummaging through the contraband. He removed a paper container . . .

"Hey, it's Bobby!" Sam cried out, spotting him.

"Bobby!" his father cried out too, abandoning Sam's purchases to come hug his son. They hugged strongly but quickly, his father's head at his chest. They were always faintly aware of how comical they must look (Roberto was six foot five, Sal was five foot four). "I'm getting shorter or you're getting taller—cut it out, whatever it is! Looking good, son."

"You too, Dad. Hey, Sam. What have we here?"

Sam had been dispatched secretly to the Kleinmarkthalle, arguably the premier wurst emporium of the Hessians. Some ruse had been enacted to distract Mrs. Santos, Sal Costa's personal cholesterol-policewoman.

Sal unwrapped some butcher paper around a paper plate and whispered confidentially, "The weißwurst is a Munich thing but, lo and behold, you can get it at the place I sent Sam to . . . It's almost noon, and you don't eat one of these after twelve," he said, pointing with his plastic knife to the spongy light gray sausage.

Roberto knew all about the weißwurst, but he let his dad enjoy telling him something about Europe, as if Roberto hadn't lived there for nearly a decade.

"Bobby, you go inside this establishment and get us some beer—you know what's good over here. I don't want 'em yelling at us for using their tables without buying something. Sam, you stand there, block me from view when Mrs. Santos comes back."

The food stand had Darmstädter pilsner on draft; Liesl was from Darmstadt. He got that for his dad, and for himself ordered a bottle of bock to go with a Bockwurst and Rindswurst, the local fave sausages. Roberto's passion for foreign languages (credentialed by his happily useless double-major bachelor's degree, French and German, from Brown), as ever, swarmed his thoughts: Surely, there wasn't goat meat in a Bockwurst, or anything goatlike about the bock beer. *Der Bock* could be a ram or a stag too, depending on where you were in Germany. Odd, the Chinese also had a ram / billy goat confusion, one word for both animals there too . . . We probably got the English word *buck* for male deer through the Saxon Bock. Buck was always feisty, for sure—bucking broncos and being buck naked, always something masculine, to buck up was to man up, the antiquated racist slang for an African American laborer, buckaroos, pirate jargon—aye, me buckos . . . or maybe that was just Hollywood pirates. He'd have to do an entry in his Notebook and consult with Liesl about which word she used for goat—

"Ohne Pommes frites?" the cook asked him.

He said yes to the fries, knowing his father would like to steal a few. Roberto, subtracting a year or two off both their lives, paused at the condiment table to pump a small hillock of mayonnaise on the plate beside the fries.

Sam was a twenty-three-year-old MBA from Sloan. Roberto had crossed paths with him many times before: boyish, slim, enjoying fashionable dark suits of European cut, spiky hair, big brown eyes, probably Jewish but maybe Middle Eastern (Sam for Samir, say), from New York . . . Roberto hadn't inquired. Sam hung on his father's every word and clearly had seen past the yuck-it-up CNBC *Costa: Doing Business!* routine to gauge that his father really was unusually intelligent about finance. Roberto tried to tamp down the jealousy.

"Oh, you got french fries with mayonnaise!" said Sal Costa, barely able to enunciate for the food in his mouth. "Now, first sign of Mrs. Santos—"

"I run for the trash can," Roberto said, nodding. "Dad, we could relocate inside the Imbiß. Standing out here, we're sitting ducks."

"I told her I was going to have a beer and swore an oath not to eat sausages *from* the train station—which, technically, these were *not*."

"As good as a Buckett's wiener with a warmed-up can of B&M beans?"

His dad pretended it was a tough call, the great German wursts versus the hot dogs of Providence. "Only goddamn reason to go down to Riverside, lemme tell you that."

"People are crazy down there, Dad—that's what you always say."

His father nodded. "The sweet onions, the celery salt—no use in going if you're not going to get the celery salt. Saugy-brand franks. Get a coffee-milk to go."

"'New York system,'" Roberto said, racing his father to the term. Though nothing like Rhode Island–style hot dogs existed in New York, anywhere.

One would have been sad without the other one prompting the rote back-and-forth Providence shtick that reminded them who they were, the chouriço from Mello's over the line in Fall Riv', the grilled octopus to kill for at the Riviera Inn, right there on North Broadway when you get off the Henderson Bridge. Get yourself down to the piers for a stuffie—chopped and breaded quahogs, baked up with a mince of onions, celery, and peppers sometimes.

Roberto's sister and his mother anathematized Rhode Island, sneered at the homey comforts of Providence. Rachel gave out that she was a New Yorker and claimed to be Jewish to throw friends off the track, though she was less brave around actual Jews. Their mother, Madalena, had concocted an elaborate tale of life as an ambassador's daughter and being, truly, a citizen of the world . . .

"Your mother's here," Sal Costa said, now beginning to attack a container of still-warm, mustardy potato salad.

"I know. She's in Cologne."

"No. She's *here*, in Frankfurt. Heard that I called a family conference and said she would get off her sickbed, unplug all the tubes and wires . . . disappoint all the Indian swamis and African shaman gathered around her bedside."

Roberto laughed; Sam pretended not to listen in.

"She'll show up in one of those bubbles they put those kids . . . those kids who have no immune system, whatever that's called. That's why I set the meeting inside the train station. Figured that would slow her down, having to breathe some train exhaust like the rest of us normal folk. Besides, I got to be in Zurich by tonight. This is a weekend jaunt—Stephanie's got the broadcast tonight, but I gotta get back to New York by Monday so I can do the show." (Stephanie Velazquez, his regular substitute host on *Costa: Doing Business!*, could match Sal Costa with Wall Street trash talk and her own South Bronx charisma.)

Sal examined the giant pretzel next to the mound of soft, oniony cheese. "I know we're supposed to bow down before France," Sal Costa said to his son, "but I think German food is more my speed. Germany's just as classy."

"Dad," Roberto said, smiling. "That cheese is called Handkäse mit Musik. The cheese is brined and so flatulent-making that you can't help but fart up a storm after you eat it. That's why they say, 'With music.' The country that gave us Bach, Beethoven, and Brahms—that's how classy they are."

His father put down the pretzel. "Eh, I got to be on my best behavior in Zurich. Can't be farting away the company. I'm over here to see if our foreign partners looked out for us any better in Frankfurt and, like I said, Zurich."

"Did they?" Roberto asked.

"What do you think, Bobby?" Sal asked wryly. Wry was his resting expression.

Pooled Viatical Settlements

The most treasured moments of father-son time for Roberto had been when Sal Costa, now, dazzlingly, improbably, CEO of Hightower Wiggins, tried to teach his boy anything about finance. Roberto could spend money, make money last, work out who owed what in his head on a restaurant check, and so on, but when it came to committing his allowance to fiduciary vehicles or applying the whims of economic law, he wandered as a lost child.

"So big demand and low supply?" Sal would prompt.

"The price goes up."

"And eventually when the supply catches up?"

"Then the price goes down."

Sal's smile dimmed. "When Krispy Kreme came to New York City—lines round the block for the hot glazed, right? People like us waiting hours, remember?"

In 1996, father and son had visited Twenty-Third Street to spend a lunch hour participating in the mania, just to say they'd had one.

Sal: "Now there's no lines. Anyone can get a Krispy Kreme doughnut when they want it, okay? But the price didn't go down, did it?"

"I think it went up."

"It did go up. The initial lower price helped drive the demand. That's what MBAs and the smart guys and gals from the business schools do. Make sure the supply is right and the price never goes down."

There had been a series of those smart guys and gals who had come between Roberto and his dad through the years: new hires, trainees, Sally from HBS, Luis from Wharton, and now Sam the Intern from Sloan. Sam was super-friendly and, in any other universe, Roberto would have tried to charm his way into a friendship, but that would have given away his seething life-envy of the stylish smart guy from MIT who was his father's young confidant. Roberto could have been one of his father's interns, but no sooner did he imagine the life of yields and rates, the tedium of MBA coursework, than that desire receded. His dad, Roberto knew, probably enjoyed giving extra fatherly tutelage to Sam the Intern to compensate for rarely seeing his son, and whose fault was that?

Oh, but Roberto tried. Whenever anything financial dominated the news, he offered up an opinion he had read in the newspapers or *The Economist* that he'd only bought to research a manufactured comment—which usually backfired.

"I was reading all about it," Roberto ventured, meeting his dad in Strasbourg in March. "Those credit-default swaps ruining everything, which made for all the trouble."

"Eh, hold your horses there, Bobby. Nothing wrong with a good credit-default swap! We bond people use them all the time; it's part of the landscape."

"But I read . . ." Bobby went quiet.

"You know how they work?" Sal Costa's eyes had that gleam, familiar to his TV viewers who loved his explanations. But he and Bobby had their own pedagogical method familiar from childhood.

"Okay," said Sal Costa, picking up the salt and pepper and little jar of mustard. "Bank of Dad"—he scooted everything to his side of the table— "and the Bank of Bobby." He scooted a paper napkin toward his son. "The law says I can lend out only so much, right? If I have, say, ten billion at risk in investments, then I gotta have one billion left in the bank as reserves. The government insists."

"I'm surprised to hear banks had any rules. I thought it was the Wild West."

"Oh, there are rules. Anyway. The Bank of Dad is out of money to lend, if I want to follow the law. But what if I could get *you* to insure my ten billion? Then my risks wouldn't be my risks anymore, would they? They'd be *your* problem, and I could lend out that one billion collateral, free and clear." Mr. Costa reached over for the napkin in front of Bobby. "What if I buy a policy from you covering the billion? I'll give you a down payment of a hundred million."

"I say no to the Bank of Dad. Why do I want to insure any of your risky investments that will sink both of us?"

"Nooo," sang Salvador Costa, his eyes smiling. "I want you to insure my safest blue-chip, can't-lose-in-a-gazillion years investments. My holdings in Microsoft and Apple and Siemens and Mercedes-Benz..." He tapped the mustard pot. "Triple As from municipalities like Hamburg and London, rock-solid stuff from Transamerica, BlackRock, et cetera. You can insure me and there is *no* chance, short of world cataclysm, that you would ever pay out."

"Okay," Bobby said slowly, wondering what the trick was. "I'll take your money." He reached for the saltshaker. "But aren't you throwing your hundred million away insuring something that doesn't need insuring?"

"Not at all. Now that my ten billion is insured and not at risk, I can now lend out that billion collateral I was supposed to hold back. And the Bank of Dad will make millions off the billion. And I won't spend a hundred million—I'll borrow it, put down ten percent, some bank will commit, on paper, to guaranteeing the rest, wanting a piece of this action. Meanwhile, Bank of Bobby gets a hundred million richer." Sal Costa scribbled *Bobby insures Dad's billions* on the napkin, then tucked it in his son's shirt pocket. "What went wrong is that all the houses secured insurance for the worst investments in the portfolio. The rating services were corrupt too. Now those rotten mortgages, those tranches ... by the way, you might appreciate this as a French studies guy, but anytime in American finance they have a French term for something? Tranche, municipal bond arbitrage, banque d'affaires offerings—read the fine fucking print."

"Mortgage is a French word."

His father pointed a finger at him. "What'd I tellya?"

The next time he saw his father was in Amsterdam in May. Sal was doing his show that week from the Netherlands as one of his theme weeks on *Costa: Doing Business!*—How the Dutch and Their Tiny Country Took Over the World, Sal Costa peeking around too many vases of tulips, while yukking it up. This kind of traveling circus theme show was soon going to be at an end because Salvador Costa had just been named the CEO of Hightower Wiggins.

In June of last year, 2007, Richard Culp, the CEO of Hightower Wiggins, told the board that three subprime hedge funds were at zero; the panacea of collateralized debt obligations, that heralded salvation of Hightower Wiggins that the old fuddy-duds (like Sal Costa) couldn't get their heads around . . . well, they were approaching worthlessness. Culp explained that one Cayman Islands–based SPE—a special-purpose entity, a satellite limited partnership that issues securities back to the mother ship—had sold them securities that were not only unsound (the tranches of mortgage-backed securities, rated from super-senior to dog-poop residual, had all, every last one of them, lost their value) but also, Culp said, now that we're mentioning it, another SPE set up on Tortola in the British Virgin Islands had sold Hightower Wiggins additional collateralized debt obligations that were an elaborate second investment, banking on the blazing success of the first investment. This was known as a *CDO squared.*

Culp said as if he'd missed a putt, dash it all, it didn't work out.

"Dick Culp," Roberto brought out with the sharpest possible enunciation of the consonants.

"Culp resigns," Sal narrated, "a one-man band of bad swaps; Havner goes next, then Dudley, then Franklin Martin, who—what did I always say?"

"A buffoon for the ages."

"That buffoon for the ages resigns."

The CFO, Morris Maynard, was asked to step down, as were the senior executives who had leveraged Hightower Wiggins at a scarcely credible twenty-nine to one (for every $29 billion risked in these worthless-on-their-face subprimes, only $1 billion was held back as collateral). The accounting officer who covered up the disaster, even from the board, stepped down. Well, not "stepped down." These gentlemen leaped from the turn-of-the-twentieth-century building on William Street, launching from the spires and gargoyles of the seventeenth floor, floating gently to the sidewalk with their golden parachutes with sapphires on top and a diamond trim. Severance packages and lavish payouts and, as their contracts specified, reimbursement of their losses, which took priority over the investors' losses. Use of the corporate jet was cut off, naturally, but the car and driver would be kept on for a suitable transition period, a calendar year.

There was a raid on the collateral. Some $1.15 billion needed to be disbursed to calm the panicked investors . . . Of course, the suckers weren't offered actual money but other financial instruments, like some more CDOs that were lying around, real and synthetic, and a showcase of fiducially flimsy, semi-illegal, and possibly made-up-on-the-spot financial vehicles: pooled viatical settlement funds, foreign-bank-backed promissory notes, securities composed of swaps of all varieties, mortgage swaps, interest swaps, credit swaps, money-in-a-brown-paper-bag swaps—tied to forward rate agreements and insured by financial insurance firms chartered the week before and staffed by nebulous, mysterious entities . . . who having insured this mess offered additional securities that made money *if they themselves defaulted,* which top executives of Hightower Wiggins also bought for their own portfolios . . .

"Was this on-paper one point fifteen billion dollars wrenched from the collateral holdings of Hightower Wiggins, Bobby?" Salvador Costa asked.

"I'm going to guess *no.*"

Correct. It was borrowed. Of course it was borrowed. The firm just wasn't leveraged enough, apparently. The billion was advanced on a transfer of $100 million, courtesy of some bank called Bahrain Capital Ltd., which hadn't been in existence three months before. Within a month, five major law firms representing investors as well as hedge funds papered Hightower Wiggins with lawsuits and requests for repayment. A Saudi sheik, one of the emirs from the Emirates, and three Russian oligarchs respectively sent threatening-looking men to the office for personal appointments with the geniuses in the boardroom. Hightower Wiggins now had around-the-clock security.

The credit rating of the firm went from AA to A.

"How was it even an A?" Sal Costa asked rhetorically. "Not even Standard & Poor's, still in denial, wanted to think the unthinkable."

The major hedge funds at Bear Stearns collapsed the next month.

Lehman Brothers shut down its mortgage lender.

Citigroup headed toward a loss of $5 billion for the quarter.

Merrill Lynch posted a nearly $2 billion loss.

So. After two more executive forced retirements and another accounting office indictment, the board offered Salvador Costa the CEOship in June. Sal showed up in the boardroom, 10:00 p.m., after every senior clerk from every division (except Sal's moneymaking bond division) had read to the bigwigs the bad news in red ink. The bigwigs were facing annihilation, humiliation with a laugh track. They were a grim-faced lot, contemplating selling the home in the Hamptons, taking the Jaguar back to the dealer, their children having to abandon the Ivy League for a state school. This was their Hail Mary pass: let Salvador Costa, beloved financial guy on TV, the funny man, the character, that comforting fellow who couldn't possibly be a front man for such naked larceny, take the reins. Could his antics buy them a little time?

"I am under no illusions," Sal Costa said, "about why they put me where they put me. You heard of the glass ceiling? Women and minorities can get so far up the ladder but not through the glass ceiling. But there's another phenomenon known as the *glass cliff*. The company is tanking, so they go choose some poor Black guy, some woman VP of something or other, some maluco from the alleys of East Prov—they let *that* guy take the company down all the while getting brownie points for diversity. When they restructure, it's back to business as usual."

"They turned to you, Dad, because you're the only honest one on that board."

"They turned to me because I haven't lost anyone any money, have I?"

The sole profitable page left in the tattered Hightower Wiggins portfolio was the boring old bond division, due to a decade of leadership by Salvador Costa. By the spring of 2008, his once condescended-to 2 percent gain was a lifesaver to a drowning company that had to make minimal payouts to investors who were jumping ship. There would have been no passengers left on board were it not for his comforting appearances at shareholder meetings—not to mention his laughing, cheery predictions on his CNBC half hour.

Roberto didn't understand all his father was telling him, but Roberto was proud, he couldn't stop beaming—his dad was in charge of the whole storied Wall Street investment firm! Roberto had from elementary school claimed that his father was a titan of Wall Street, but now it was true.

But Sal had conditions before he'd do it, and they were severe: He and he alone would decide which bonus and severance arrangements would be paid out. He and he alone would be CEO, COO, and CFO combined into a single omnipotent position, so there would be no end run around his company-saving policies. He and he alone talked to the press, and anyone leaking scuttlebutt (e.g., Hightower Wiggins was flat broke) would be terminated immediately, with all negotiated pay packages out the window and a nasty lawsuit to follow. The board looked elegantly ruffled, rumpled in their tailored suits and dresses, awake for twenty-four hours of worry and misery. Sal wore a University of Rhode Island T-shirt and his frayed blue jeans. They drank from Dick Culp's desk supply of Pappy Van Winkle bourbon; Sal held a forty-four-ounce Big Gulp of Diet Coke from the 7-Eleven on John Street. As they contemplated his terms, his straw found the bottom of his soda, letting the swells and masters of the universe enjoy the noise of him sucking air, gurgling from the bottom of the Styrofoam cup.

A Situation

Back in the Frankfurter Hauptbahnhof, visible to all, Salvador Costa was ready for the family meeting, just after one more pretzel bite—

"Aha!" It was Mrs. Santos, moving toward them with an accusing index finger.

Most of the wursts and condiments had been disposed of by Sam and Roberto, who scarfed down the last of the forbidden goodies over the trash can, stealthily dropping the evidence into the bin. The pretzel and cheese, least harmful of the contraband, survived to distract Mrs. Santos from the more forbidden items. Avoiding the reckoning with Mrs. Santos, Sam the Intern slipped away to prepare a table at Starbucks for the family meeting.

"Both of yous, covered in grease!" she pronounced.

"Nonsense," said Sal, his eyes widening with innocence. "We just had a beer—"

"Don't take me for a fool." She aimed her hair helmet at Roberto, her silver coif held together by a ferrous hairspray that no jet blast could dishevel. "Wanna know how you fuck it up big-time?" she fired at Roberto. "You wanna end up like your father on the operating table? Do what he did for fifty years, eat a diet of fat and grease."

"You see what happens when you abandon me, Mrs. Santos."

(Forty years working together, and Sal never called her by her first name or permitted anyone else to. He did nothing to lessen her authority or the terror she dispensed to the rest of his staff, which included his pretense of being scared as well of his own office manager.)

"We had your numbers down low, Salvador, and then you come to Germany, and what do you do? You fuck it up."

Mrs. Santos was a prim, mass-attending Catholic woman who, for all her personal conservatism, her merciless meting out of puritanical judgments, had not been taught that the F-word was a bad word. Roberto reflected that, growing up where she did in Providence, she might yet be unaware that the verb had a second meaning of *copulation.* Roberto had seen her hold forth on who *fucked it up* while the matrons and patrons of high society listened grimly. If the pope himself were to lose the Host in the Communion wine, she would say, "Eh, you fucked it up there, Holy Father." Roberto and Rachel, at their childhood dinner table, loved to insert Mrs. Santos into an array of historical tableaux ("Hey, Bob Lee, what did I tell you about Pickett's Charge? You *fucked it up*, is what you just did . . .") and then not be able to eat for their laughter.

Now Mrs. Santos was scowling at her phone. "Miss Westmore. She wants to move the location of the family meeting. The family she is in no way a part of."

Merle Westmore, who had dropped out of Penn Law a year before achieving the degree, had compensated for her lack of credential by passionately threatening litigation wherever possible. And where Rachel went, Merle went—there was no separating them.

Salvador Costa sighed. "Sweet Jesus, I could get Jean-Claude Trichet and Angela Merkel on a conference call before the week is out, but my own family I can't get to meet me at the Starbucks . . ." He pinched the bridge of his nose. "I hope you made it clear—"

"I made it clear that Miss Westmore is not invited to the meeting. She said it may 'prove doubtful' whether Rachel will attend."

And then Sal's phone rang; it was his ex-wife and Roberto's mother. "Lena," Sal began, "you mustn't trouble yourself to attend this meeting, this meeting you were not invited to. I . . ." Roberto could hear the essence of the call since his mother's Providence yawp cut through the roar of the train station. Lena was proposing a change of venue. Not fifty meters across the Poststraße was the Steigenberger Metropolitan Hotel, a very nice hotel, real class. Sal and Bobby could ask the desk for the tearoom reserved by Madalena van Till in which she was prepared to offer everyone a light lunch, should Sal consent to the change of venue, since the Hauptbahnhof would have deleterious impact on her health . . .

"The Steigenberger," said Sal to Roberto. "See how poor she is? What is that—four hundred euros a night over there?" And to his ex-wife, he said, before hanging up, "We're not meeting at the Steigenberger, so forget about it."

Mrs. Santos said to her boss, "And you won't be meeting in front of this den of cholesterol." She reached for Sam the Intern's abandoned scrap of mahogany-brown pretzel, dipped it in the tub of brined cheese, and popped it in her mouth. "That *is* good. Now let's move it!"

Mrs. Santos marched them into the greater melee of the Hauptbahnhof; it was necessary to dodge a tour group, someone running for a train, pulling a suitcase behind them with rollers that weren't functioning. Bobby and his father stood stupidly in place for a moment. Mrs. Santos skipped through the crowd to join Sam the Intern at the table he had claimed at Starbucks' "outdoor" café even though everything was enclosed by the giant steel arches and glass planes of the Hauptbahnhof above.

Salvador, walking slowly with his son, asked, "How's the ticker?"

"Fine, Dad. Haven't had any angina in several months. Of course, my blood is about one-half nitroglycerin. If I trip and fall in here, I might blow up."

"Tell me about it," his father said, patting his own heart.

"How's Rosie?"

"Rosie's still in the picture." Rosario D'Ambrosio, Sal Costa's consort for the last three years, sassy, rich with her own money, twenty years younger in her forties, famous in the family for her giant, elaborate, New Jersey dyed red head of hair—well, more maroon, more purple than red. Rosie got Sal into ballroom dancing as heart exercise, which he first hated and then loved. Sal had a bypass operation in 2003 and danced his way back to health. "Rosie, and a million pills," he added, "keeping me alive. That's what doctors are for, right? We junk it all up, clog the pipes, and they clean out all the gunk, and we pay 'em the big bucks."

Mrs. Santos, arranging folders and papers on the Starbucks table, caught the last of Sal's health philosophy. "You are *done,*" she said, "fucking it up for one day, Salvador. No pastries for you."

Just then, her phone buzzed again: a new round of negotiations with Merle. Merle let it be known to Mrs. Santos that Rachel Costa, for whom she was authorized to speak, preferred the requested meeting be conducted at a hotel conference room at the Jumeirah, where Merle would be in attendance for whatever her father had to say, where the proceedings could be recorded and a later transcript agreed to and seconded, just so there would be no misunderstandings, unlike the *last* such family meetings that had distressed Rachel in the past. Was Mrs. Santos aware of a problem with Rachel's Hightower Wiggins ATM bank card? It would seem that—

"Thank you very much, Miss Westmore," Mrs. Santos said. "Now. Tell Raquel Malfalda Costa she has five minutes to get her little Portugee behind over here and sit it down in a chair at the Starbucks across from her father, or what was intended for her hands will be put into her little brother's. And if I see *your* sorry face, even catch the merest hint that you are in the train station lingering like a contagion in the air, Rachel will know the joys of a nonworking ATM card for the rest of the twenty-first century."

Thus began fifteen minutes of radio silence from the Rachel faction.

The next phone contact revealed that Rachel Costa, Merle Westmore, and Madalena van Till had, somehow, joined forces and were camped out, waiting for his attendance at the Hotel Steigenberger, really, no distance at all, a mere fifty meters from the north exit of the Hauptbahnhof. Tea had been ordered, a table had been set. Come, this was how civilized people did things in Europe. Why should Salvador Costa pretend they were all back in Providence at an Amtrak platform, meeting at a Dunkin' Donuts?

This time, Sal Costa took Mrs. Santos's phone. "Hello again, Merle. I'm going to Zurich in an hour, and you tell my daughter she will find it most unpleasant financially if I get on that train without conferring with her and my son both. And do pass my regards to Rachel's mother. Maybe you can sit there and have tea together while we do this business."

Five more minutes of radio silence, while Sal Costa checked his watch. "I got my foreign-language-genius son sitting here," said Roberto's father. "I might as well take advantage." Sam was then dispatched for today's issue of the *Frankfurter Allgemeine.* Sam returned in under a minute with the newspaper, already folded to reveal the business section. Roberto, ashamed of himself for blushing proudly over being called a genius in front of Sam, raised the newspaper to hide behind and started scanning the pages to see if his father's name popped out anywhere . . .

"Read me anything, Bobby, about Hightower Wiggins or some cold, clear-sighted assessment of how the American financial world is about to go belly-up."

Roberto translated a deprecatory essay or two, while his father nodded serenely. Sam the Intern busied himself, delivering several coffees; in spite of Mrs. Santos's prohibition on pastry contraband, he also set down a plate of biscotti, small rhubarb tarts, that tooth-breaking spice-brown plank they make in Aachen.

"Hello, Daddy," said Rachel, appearing out of the station mob.

Roberto was struck, as he always was after not seeing his sister for a bit, by her diminutive stature, five foot one—she seemed to come up to the Germans' midsections, in danger of being taken out by a passing briefcase. She had steadfastly refused to alter her look of adolescence: a shaggy bowl of lank black hair around her face, round Harry Potter–style eyeglasses that magnified her glance confrontationally.

Mrs. Santos poked Sam, and they decamped to the Starbucks interior to leave the Costas to their family business.

Rachel allowed herself to be hugged lightly by her father. "You look just like you do on TV, Dad. Do you never *not* go with the tacky neckties?"

"My health is fine. Thanks for almost asking." Then Mr. Costa smiled his familiar sideways smile, which showed something facetious was coming. "Sorry to disappoint. I know you hoped to get your inheritance sooner than later."

"Oh, Daddy, please." She decided on a redo of that hug, leaning in and giving her father a meaningful squeeze. "I was going to push you in front of a train later today, but not until we have a proper visit."

"I would," he began, "love to see my own darling daughter without an hour of negotiations with Miss Westmore. Do you think we can ever come to that understanding?"

"Really?" Rachel asked. "Was she being a pain? I don't know what she's up to half the time."

When Roberto snorted his disbelief, she finally redirected her attention.

"Bobby," she said, nodding. And after a moment, "I'm pushing you in front of the train too."

"But what's the point? Nothing could induce me to put you in *my* will."

"I'd get your share from Dad, dummy," she said, tapping her head.

"How nice to hear my children give a thought to their financial future," said Mr. Costa, settling back in his chair. "So as I was telling Bobby earlier—"

"How long have you been together, scheming?"

"I just got here, Rach. Jeez."

"You could have been here earlier," said her father, "if you hadn't sicced Merle on me for an hour. I would have bought you a *weißwurst*."

"I'm going to assume that is some hash of slaughtered-animal organs, so I would have declined." Rachel's stare bored holes through her father's briefcase. Roberto felt pure annoyance—she would prefer to grab the money order and run for the exit.

Sal Costa asked about his ex-wife. "You teamed up with your mother? That's a surprise."

"Only by phone. She had a number of questions for you, only one of which interested me: she wants to know why you haven't bailed on Hightower Wiggins and made use of your parachute of gold—or whatever they call it. She wanted to remind you that that was what self-respecting, greedy executives do in times such as these."

"I'm fighting to save Hightower Wiggins. I'll let the crooks jump overboard."

"To quote her . . ." Here Rachel performed her uncanny imitation of their mother's unreconstructed Rhodie: "'You just watch, Rach. That man is gonna stay to the bittuh end outta loyalty.'"

Sal nodded appreciatively. "Loyalty. Another thing your mother wouldn't know the first thing about. I'll get out of the building before it burns down, so none of yous two has to worry."

"Hoo boy," said Rachel, distracted by something.

Salvador Costa turned to see what she was looking at. "Good Christ," he muttered.

Roberto assumed Merle Westmore had decided to stage an assault, but he turned around to see it was Madalena herself, arriving in theatrical splendor. There was a lab-coated doctor by her side, out of central casting, fatherly, wise, supervising the progress of a motorized medical transport chair, painted white with a red-cross decal. The Germans couldn't help but gawk. Lena wore a shimmery turquoise gown with a golden silk turban. It was an entrance worthy of a silent film star. Oil-black eyeliner, blue mascara about which Nefertiti might have wondered, "Eh, too much?" on aggrieved eyes that looked out accusingly over the face mask. The medical attendant strolled beside her with an IV tree with a clear tube leading to some portal amid the folds of the gown (it wasn't attached, of course—

Lena was too lazy to fully commit to her imposture), and there was some EKG-like device beeping and whirring away.

Sal Costa shot an accusing look at his daughter.

Rachel shook her head. "For fuck's sake, *I* didn't invite her."

Madalena waited for her solicitous prop doctor to "unplug" her from her medical drag, and then she rose out of the compartment as if on wires. She weighed nothing, true, but her moving as if she were made of air was impressive. The silken gown was full length, and Roberto hid a smile because she was, a little bit, fabulous. The doctor, a handsome fellow, must be Italian, because Lena excused him with a "Grazie," and he bowed in old-world fashion to the other Costas and absented himself to the interior of the Starbucks.

"Lena," said Salvador, with faint warmth. "There was no need to convey yourself in from your bed of pain. They must be missing you back at the hospice."

"Don't tease us, Mother," Rachel said. "Having us fantasize about the cozy warmth of your deathbed."

Roberto raised an eyebrow. "Who is this getup for?"

"Oh, Bobby, you know train stations—there are those CCTVs everywhere, recording my every goddamn move."

Lena had three main pretend charities. The restoration of a Providence mansion, the Hezekiah Williams House, for which a million had been raised without any trace of improvement in the property.

Then there was the Roma Holocaust Memorial project, which had led to a several-year pretense that "she had Gypsy blood" (arguable, at least, in anyone Portuguese) and was useful in guilting her German acquaintances out of small checks that had, to date, not gone to any substantive memorial to the Romani genocide. Perhaps she would have had more success in her fundraising, if she could have stopped herself from calling the Roma "Gypsies" at every turn.

And then her miracle-cure scams. During her tour of German spa towns and health clinics, she constructed her most recent persona, the Dying Lena, sick with a mystery illness that was badly understood by doctors but was more common than realized, Constança (her middle name) Syndrome unsearchable on all databases. Peddling a mystery illness to cranky old European women who felt they were long suffering from something or other too turned up some of her greatest profits but, alas, as of last year, a federal audit, plus a class action lawsuit from American donors, plus an investigation from the U.S. attorney from the district of Rhode Island, had slowed down the intake of money.

"I have to appear sick," she explained, settling in at their table. "The attorney has his spies everywhere waiting to catch me dancing a jig. Well, I am genuinely sick. I do have Constança Syndrome, but it happens to be . . . in remission."

Roberto began, "What precisely is—"

Rachel: "Oh God, Bobby, why would you even ask?"

"Just wait 'til you get it, pumpkin," their mother said, not really up for battle. "It runs in families." No one could or would say anything for a moment, so Lena carried on. "Speaking of family, if this is a 'family meeting,' then I should attend, because like it or not, I remain 'family.'"

"You *were* family," said Sal.

"If what you have to say involves my children, how wouldn't it involve me?"

Rachel broke her biscotto in half, saying without passion, "Since when were you remotely interested in our lives?"

"Pumpkin, you shouldn't be so jaded, and at such a young age . . ." She smoothed out her spectacular gown, which was, as she had hoped, still turning heads of every businessman who walked by. (Was she a countess? A soprano singing tonight at the Alte Oper?) "It is I," she said, through a sigh, "who should be offended . . ."

That spurred a triplicate of groans.

"Lena, you may listen," said Sal, "despite none of it concerning you. Hightower Wiggins, as you children may be dimly aware—I have no idea if you read a word about your native country in the papers—is in trouble. Stupid decisions were made, cover-ups have been attempted, money is being quietly transferred hither, thither, and yon. The SEC . . . Hmm, maluco that I am, I don't know why I even ask, but can either of my children venture a guess what that stands for?"

"I'm sorry," said Rachel, "what does what stand for?"

"SEC," said Roberto. "It's a banking thing. Security and Economic . . ."

"Control?" Rachel guessed.

Sal offered a flat smile. "The Securities and Exchange Commission. They investigate financial shenanigans."

"Obviously not very thoroughly," Madalena said, "or the continuous Ponzi scheme of Wall Street wouldn't be one flush away from the East River."

"The SEC," Sal continued, "has frozen all liquid assets of Hightower Wiggins—all of them. To keep the more disreputable among my colleagues from accessing ten-million-dollar liquidity accounts while stiffing investors."

Madalena: "But you're the big boss now, Sal, am I right? There is no reason at all that you can't pay yourself an executive bonus at any time. Isn't there a bag of diamonds in a safe-deposit box in Russia? If you need a name, an account where the money could be deposited secretly or with little publicity—"

"Lena, please, there are actual laws."

"Like there's any law for those crooks you work with! Don't be noble, Sal. Just clean out the accounts into your own Christmas bonus and shut the light behind you."

Sal fought to get to the point. "Since I can't raise you kids by phone or email—"

"Daddy," Rachel said pleasantly, "half of what you send out is that unreadable newsletter."

Roberto: "It's not exactly unreadable, Dad, but . . ."

Rachel: "Stop sucking up, Bobby; you don't read it either."

"I don't hit Delete the second I see it, like you."

"Ooh, you give it all of—what?—*three* seconds?"

Salvador Costa leaned back in his chair as if to observe them from a distance, his countenance stern. Soon they trailed off, aware of their father's silence.

"Sal," said their mother presently, wanting to be on someone's side, "don't be mad at the children for not reading your gobbledygook newsletter."

"It has," Sal said in a small voice, before finding volume, "a subscribers' rate of over four million. Folks pay two hundred eighty dollars for a two-year subscription, so don't worry your head there, Lena, I'll have plenty of money if Hightower Wiggins goes bye-bye." Sal's ego was genuinely small for a man of his power; nonetheless, his children could tell they'd offended him. "A number of people in the global economic bond community hang on its every word," he added.

Rachel now playacted enthusiasm. "Yes, what do you call your cult followers . . . Costa Heads? Costa . . ."

"The Costa Nostra!" Bobby rang out, just remembering it.

Sal Costa's legion of fans called themselves the Costa Nostra. Guys who've been up since six working at trade or commodities, who head to the dives on Stone Street, Pearl Street, where they wait for their hero, Salvador Costa, and his show to come on.

Rachel volunteered, "I did play your drinking game once."

Sal Costa was only recently aware that his CNBC happy-hour audience, watching him in taverns in financial districts throughout the world, agreed to knock back a shot every time he said his trademark, "*That's the cost a doin' business!*" Recently, Patrón Spirits began advertising on his show, hoping that close-ups of sweating glasses of chilled tequila would subliminally steer the Costa Nostra toward their product.

Sal allowed himself to be diverted. "You, Rachel, have actually watched my show?"

"You were on in that Irish pub in the Gare du Nord. Place was full of Brits waiting for the Eurostar—I don't know why CNBC was on, but it was. I asked why they were doing shots, and it was all explained to me." Her father's expression was unreadable. "You were very parsimonious with your trademark line. No one got very drunk, I'm sorry to report."

Sal began again. "Along with the newsletter I sent you were other more vital attachments, pertinent to your situation."

"We have a situation?" Rachel wondered.

"A situation?" Roberto echoed.

Madalena: "What kind of situation? Now, Sal, don't be mysterious. I mean, do I have a situation too, Sal, or is it just the children?"

Sal folded his hands on his small belly. "Have you kids begun a portfolio as I suggested?" Silence. "Along the lines of the plans I laid out in the . . . Rachel, did you not see what Mrs. Santos sent you two months ago?"

"If I delete you on sight, Daddy, why on earth would I read something from Mrs. Santos?"

"I laid out some very painless investments, all available in the online self-regulating accounts I set up for you. Oh, sweet Jesus, have you even been to the site since I set it up?"

Roberto looked at the train station floor.

"I forgot the password," Rachel brought out.

"As for your money, and—of course, again, I am beginning to suspect the answers to these questions before I even ask—but did you open accounts in the foreign banks I recommended so there could be an avenue through which you could continue to draw money?"

Roberto did remember seeing some email about that, and it sounded like a good idea, to circulate his money in the wider world beyond his Hightower Wiggins checking account, the single ATM card and associated credit card (which functioned everywhere as he traveled the continent). But he hadn't done it.

"I have bank accounts in three countries," Madalena volunteered. "The only sensible thing, Sal, is to deposit any money you intend for them with *me*, and I will distribute it in such a way that no regulator can know what's happened."

Rachel snapped to her old self. "Mom, I wouldn't let you look at *a photo* of my money, let alone hold it for safekeeping."

"Bobby . . . ," his mother pleaded.

"I haven't trusted you since you said we were going to the Salem Maritime Museum as a special treat and you dropped me off at Brockton Academy for boarding school. I thought I was going to be a day student."

"So, children," Sal asserted, "you don't have other accounts and savings in a variety of dependable banks, the ones Mrs. Santos wrote to you about."

Again, silence.

"What on earth have you done with your savings? You have trusts generating one hundred twenty thousand each year, which even *you guys* can't spend down every little cent."

Rachel sighed. "I do spend every cent of it. Indeed, I've been strapped lately—"

"If you weren't supporting yourself *and* Merle Westmore, you might not be so strapped. What about you, Bobby—Mr. Backpack and youth hostels. You can't possibly be spending one twenty K."

"No. I don't."

Rachel glared in big-sister disgust.

Roberto added, "I guess it's just sitting in the current account, not getting spent."

Sal frowned at hearing his son call a *checking account* a *current account*—somebody had been in Europe for too long. "That money makes what? Point oh five percent interest? You could have thousands of dollars extra, a weekend at the Ritz in Paris, off the interest you could be making, if you just made the dimmest of investments. Good God, what is the point in talking to you ingrates?"

Mother adjusted her turban. "They're just awful children—really they are. The only solution is for me to dispense money to them, but only if they deserve it, Salvador. One hundred and twenty thousand, my God . . . Why, it's just shameful—I had no idea my children, who tell me regularly they can't contribute a *dime* to their poor old mother in her illness, all this time were living like Jackie Onassis on Skorpios."

"Stop babbling, Lena." Salvador Costa put his briefcase on the café table and opened it. He produced two envelopes, and from the two envelopes removed what looked to be money orders. Rachel looked at the rectangular pieces of paper longingly; she attempted a smile, hoping to sway the father she used to have wrapped around her finger. Roberto expected the worst—that whatever money their father had prepared for them would have to wait until they had jumped through the hoops that Mrs. Santos had held aloft.

"These teller's checks," he began in a voice fearsome in its intensity, "were for you to deposit in your happily waiting, long-established alternate accounts. Money that could in no way be traced back to Hightower Wiggins and therefore could be yours free and clear. But what I am now hearing is that you spoiled brats have only your checking accounts and ATM cards through Hightower Wiggins, accounts that you can neither access nor, even if you could access them, withdraw from. Sweet Jesus, what kind of international ATM fees do you kids rack up in a year? It would almost make for someone's monthly salary!" He sipped from his coffee and then dabbed his forehead with the napkin. He was calmer. "You may have noticed you can't withdraw money with your ATM cards, or if you haven't, you soon will."

Rachel, still trying to look light and charming, began, "You could . . ."

"Just what could I do, Rachel? Bobby, what do you think I should do with these teller's checks, which can't be deposited?"

Roberto stirred uneasily in his cold metal café seat. "Um, I guess we could take those checks and open a new account—today—with it at say

Dresdner Bank or . . ." Roberto feebly pointed to a bank kiosk in the train station within view. "Or Deutsche Bank."

"You won't be doing any banking business on a Saturday in Germany. I don't think you could open an account in Germany, anyway, with this sort of teller's check. You'd need a wire transfer that showed the trustworthy source of the money. Plus you need a German address."

"But I live in, you know, Paris," Rachel said. Never had a declaration of Paris living sounded so forlorn.

"Fine, no prob. You just need a lawyer to attest to your identity."

"Well, Merle could—"

"No, a lawyer," said Sal, "not a law school dropout."

Madalena's color had returned to her face; she must have thought victory was as close as it had been in years: "Of course, I have a German address, children, in Cologne. My accounts in Milan, in Guernsey would also work. I could deposit both orders into my passbook account—"

Sal then tore up the checks. Rachel gasped. Roberto stared in horror.

Madalena looked like she might faint. "That was . . . money that . . . money we could have—I could have . . ."

"Lena, you're babbling again." Salvador Costa stood up, slammed his briefcase shut, looked at his watch. As if by some magical dog whistle, Mrs. Santos and Sam appeared from the Starbucks, ready to accompany him to the train bound for Zurich. Lena's handsome doctor stood behind them, looking on.

It seemed Sal Costa might walk away with no further explanation, but he turned and concluded, "I have failed to make you decent, functional adults. I think I did a pretty good job of raising you as kids, giving yous two all that you could need or want, even with your mother walking out on us."

Madalena began, "Oh now, Sal, I . . ." But she cut short her self-defense after meeting the eyes of her ex-husband.

"You children have become the worst sort of American rich-kid flotsam. Not even responsible enough to read a few emails, devote a few hours to protecting your money. Do you somehow think money is just always there on a countertop? Cyprus. Argentina, where I saw money collapse for myself. The ruble tanked under Czar Nicholas, a quarter trillion in today's dollars wiped out in a week, and lookee there, here comes Lenin.

Hell, right in this very city several generations ago, where you're sitting, the most powerful currency of Europe once upon a time, was being exchanged at four point two quadrillion deutschmark to the dollar in the Weimar Republic. Money can disappear"—he snapped his fingers, and dramatically, it seemed loud enough to be heard across the Hauptbahnhof—"like that. Everything I encouraged you to do in those newsletters—"

"Oh, not the newsletter again," mumbled their mother.

"—and emails was to increase the odds that you might, just *might* keep afloat in a crisis, in which the suspicion is beginning to dawn, that there is forty-some, fifty-some trillion dollars out there in bad paper—much of it sold by Lehman and Bear Stearns and Merrill and Hightower Wiggins. And you couldn't even do me the courtesy of reading my warnings and, the joke is, the person you did the least courtesy to was yourselves. If Hightower Wiggins ceases to exist in a few weeks and the shares of the company aren't there to feed your trusts . . . what happens to you layabouts, hmm?"

Rachel stood too. "Dad, what do we do?"

"Guess your pal Merle can support you for a while. Fair's fair, right?" Then he turned to Roberto, looking a tad bit more concerned.

"I'll be all right, Dad. There are a million couches I can sleep on."

Salvador Costa nodded. He gestured to Sam and Mrs. Santos, and they turned and began to make their way through the crowd to the Zurich train.

Roberto knew that his father hated this—he hated all episodes of discipline or tough love when they were growing up. But the larger truth was that right now he didn't have time for his kids (insert Mrs. Santos: *Kids, Sal, who are always fucking it up*).

"We'd better go after him," said Rachel.

Their mother sighed, looking up at the pigeons squabbling in the great girder arches. "Well, it's never worked for me. Begging and lowering myself."

"How do you imagine, Mother," Rachel said, automatically, "you could possibly find a lower plane to exist upon?"

"No, don't run after him," said Roberto. Among other things, he didn't want to put on more of a show for Sam: Bobby, the worthless son who has to be paid off so he can go away and play with his mountain of money and keep out of Daddy's hair while Daddy saves the financial world for the Western Alliance. "It won't work," he told his sister. "Not when he's mad at us."

"What am I going to live on?" Rachel sat back down again.

Salvador Costa and Sam and Mrs. Santos had reached the entrance to the train platforms. Roberto wondered if his father would turn back and look upon his family. He did not.

"Maybe Dad has a point," he said to his sister. "Maybe Merle can contribute and stop living off you, for a change."

She shook her head as if to fling that thought to the farthest reaches. "What a waste of time to come here."

Rachel abruptly launched herself toward the nearest exit of the Hauptbahnhof without any gesture, not even a goodbye pat on the arm. Roberto followed along behind her. This had the merit of abandoning their mother, who couldn't break her ruse of being too ill to give chase.

"I got your Würzburg photos," he called out. "Still working on the trompe l'oeil article?"

In the era before the "cloud," no matter how they annoyed or hated each other, they sent copies of their latest work by email to each other; they were each other's human hard drive. She stopped with her back to him; he could see her body becoming less tense. "Losing heart on that one. It will only be worth something if I can find examples not done to death. No one needs another monograph on Andrea Pozzo. I know there are chateaux and palaces all over Europe with trompe l'oeil rooms . . ."

"In the Palazzo Barberini—"

"Yes, there and the Palazzo Spada, Villa Farnesina, Palazzo Labia—see if you can name something that isn't on every postcard tree."

They had divided up the European arts: his terrain included music, hers included painting; they seemingly agreed to share literature and po-etry, which left the carcass of European architecture for them to vulture over.

Rachel was a completist. If you could see all there was of something, *then and only then* could you write a scholarly paper about it. 1999 was her Year of Vermeer (there were only thirty-four certain paintings), 2000 was her Year of Piero della Francesca with eighty-plus paintings, occa-sioning a reluctant pilgrimage to Williamstown, Massachusetts, which somehow had gotten a hold of a Piero. In the days before Merle's regency, Roberto would cross paths and join her for part of her annual quest, like 2001's Year of Caravaggio (with only forty certain, undisputed works). Roberto recalled how they cajoled, begged, and eventually bribed a sex-ton to fetch a key to get into the church of Santa Maria degli Angeli in Messina, after hours, to see a final Caravaggio on their list, which, once accomplished, led to a wine-soaked evening at a portside trattoria, cel-ebrating their victory against that most implacable of enemies: Italian church-closing hours.

Roberto said as lightly as he could, "If I need a place to crash—"

"You can stay with me in Paris only when Merle is away. Too much drama otherwise. What happened to that Hélène what's-her-name?"

"She might not be speaking to me. I guess Rupesh is in Spain some-where."

A sudden light sparked in his sister's eyes. Roberto considered tickling her, as if to add, *C'mon now, admit it, you know Rupesh and you and I had fun in Spain, back when you actually permitted laughter and sang along to bad French pop on the radio.*

"What about," Rachel suggested, "that egomaniacal monster you dated, Lucrezia Borgia? Go stay with her."

"I may be desperate, but not *that* desperate."

Rachel was already walking away.

"See you in Paris?" Roberto called out.

"If you see darling Rupesh, tell him La Generalísima said hi."

They stopped at the entrance. What do you know, Roberto thought—it actually remained a sunny day beyond the overcast air and gray light of the train station.

Okay, thinking of temporary lodging, where was Liesl? Maybe they could meet up in Darmstadt; maybe he could be consigned to the family basement? He brought out his phone and turned it on. He texted her:

YOU MISSED MEETING YOUR FATHER-IN-LAW. WO BIST DU?

He checked his phone for the text:

ES TUT MIR LEID, MEIN LIEBLING . . . it began.

A series of small texts came in with the *ding* of a triangle. Liesl was indeed on her way home to nearby Darmstadt and hoped he would understand if they did not commit to a reunion. They were "a hostel hookup," and it had run its course. Soon the fall academic term would be here and she'd be back at her marketing program, and he would be God knows where.

Oh well, he thought. Liesl was being kind. After the dressing down he had gotten from his father, he was in the mood to wallow and sink all the way to the bottom. He texted back in German, for her to be honest. Was it the sex?

There was a long pause. And then a ding.

WENN WISSEN DU MUβ, JA.

If you must know, yes.

He sort of figured.

Drittennacht

Liesl had been such a delight, a several days' fling that they both were enjoying until, of course, the inevitable. She was unselfconsciously beautiful, always a few centimeters from laughing, a perfect travel companion with just the right amount of combativeness for Roberto, when they tried to think of something in the region they could sightsee together that neither of them had seen.

Wasn't there a fine art museum in Basel, Switzerland? Liesl pantomimed gagging herself with a finger. All right, neither of them had seen the bell tower of the Ulm Minster, highest in Europe.

"Ullllm," said Liesl, exaggerating the gloomy name.

"We could climb the tower—good exercise."

"And throw ourselves off?"

"Einstein was from there," Roberto prompted.

"And he left."

How about the biggest glacier left in the Alps, the Aletschgletscher?

"Some friends and I were going to hike there on Deutschen Einheit. We use the national holiday to get out of Germany, of course. You must come with us!"

Roberto had smiled at that, wondering if he would have a cent to spend by October. If he would still be a millionaire's kid.

"I will take you to Walhalla," she said next.

Roberto assumed, as much of their banter suggested, that sexual paradise was being offered but, no, just Valhalla.

In the 1830s, King Ludwig (not the crazy one, but his father) decided to build a temple to the greatest of the Bavarians and Germans of consequence: Walhalla, a Parthenon look-alike built with an Olympian stone stairway leading up from the Danube. They took a fast train to Regensburg. Green fairy-tale-village Bavaria camped it up beyond their window. From where the bus eventually dropped them in Donaustauf, they walked along the Donau/Danube banks so they could climb the stairs of Walhalla. They attempted to jog briskly up the 358 stairs but were halted by a guard. Something like that *did not* befit the dignity of the Great Personages enshrined within Walhalla.

"You know," Liesl reported, trudging up the final steps by his side, "there was on the TV a program where they got the most famous historians in Germany to walk through here on camera and try to remember who these people were . . . and most had no idea."

It would amaze someone from the past, Roberto reflected, sounding it out for the eventual Notebook transcription, that we think of Germany as the most efficient, organized, competently managed society in Europe. Despite so much twentieth-century enmity, most EU members in poll after poll think that if anyone has to run the show, it had better be their old enemies, the Germans. But for centuries, the concept of Germany was associated with comic disorder and chaos. Hundreds of different gradations and titles of tin-trumpet nobility—emperors, a half dozen

kings, dukes and grand dukes and archdukes, counts of the empire and of the Palatinate, barons and baronets, Reichsritters and lords, landgraves, burgraves, margraves, altgraves, 350 ministates and satrapies, some no bigger than half of a village.

"We are still a raging chaos," Liesl said when consulted. "We just disguise it better than anyone else. It's the Scandinavians who have everything organized. And we hate the Swedes."

Walhalla's interior was a high-ceilinged faux-Athenian chamber where miniscule busts and hard-to-read engraved inscriptions identified the grandees. In the twentieth century, a more sensible roster of personages was added—Heinrich Heine, Gregor Mendel, Richard Strauss—but Liesl and Roberto preferred the temple's original inspirations: Feldmarschall August Graf Neidhardt von Gneisenau. Generalfeldmarschall Gebhard Leberecht von Blücher. Christoph, Duke of Württemberg.

"Yes, Christoph," Liesl brightened. "I think he made my hair in Darmstadt before Fabien started cutting. Oh, look!" Liesl skipped ahead to a bust of a woman. "They let inside a lady by mistake."

Liesl had demanded they buy a guide, in which they looked up Amalie Elisabeth of Hanau-Münzenberg, later consort, regent, and Countess of Hesse-Kassel. Roberto made an on-the-spot translation: "She was a countess; her first husband was one of six Bohemian nobles present at the Second Defenestration of Prague."

Liesl provided a sound effect of people being thrown out of a window and going splat. Two prim elderly tourists turned their head in disapproval. "Which every schoolchild over here knows," Liesl continued, "began the Thirty Years' War."

"There was a First Defenestration, and they let the Bohemians back in for a Second Defenestration? Seems a little naive."

"I think there were centuries between the two Fenstersturz."

Liesl took her temple brochure and brought it up to her cheekbones, like a coquette peering over her fan at the opera. "*Mein General*, I understand you were present at the Battle of Schwänzespritzen. You have my earnest devotion."

"Ah," Roberto said, taking her hand to kiss it, "Baroness Scheißenstrümpfe Graf von . . . von Furzenpoopsen, Margrave of um . . ."

"Margrave of Kuhfladen. Mein General, I understand you are fucking my chambermaid, my stable boy, *und* my schnauzer."

"Mein Gott, Baroness, the schnauzer said he vould not tell."

The guard hissed at them: "Ssssssssssh!"

Other Bavarians, dislodged from their solemnity, were not enjoying their theatrics. "Fah," said Liesl, "let's get away from these Mäusemelker . . ."

Mice-milkers. A great word to describe the legions of the petty . . . one for Roberto's Notebook, his unfinished project of many years. The French speak of people who would *enculeur de mouches,* sodomize a fly.

"Baron," Liesl continued as they left the temple. "Your Notebook simply must be destroyed. The compromising stories of sexual conquest will make for *Skandal.*" They were flirting again, and sex was in the air, so tonight, right on schedule, Night No. 3—Drittenacht—would prove either glorious or another wince-making reckoning.

Most of Roberto's hostel hookups ended around Night No. 3.

Night No. 3 was when some explanation had to be made about the sexual nonperformance. But Roberto had become expert in stalling that conversation for seventy-two hours.

Night No. 1, the physical exhaustion ploy.

Roberto had wanted to take in Linderhof, collecting the Mad King Ludwig castles and palaces that had bankrupted the kingdom of Bavaria, and had decided to walk the trails of the grounds to the prominence known as Ammergebirge. He passed her on the trail, then as he was flagging, she passed him, then conversation, then flirting. So he proposed joining forces for the trails leading into the mountains around Schloß Neuschwanstein, the grandest of Ludwig's proto-Disney kitsch piles. Up, up, and farther up they went until a magnificent array of alps (all of them Austrian) presented themselves. By the time they reached the lake, Roberto and Liesl had legs of gelatin and could barely stand upright. Would Liesl like to leave her youth hostel in Garmisch-Partenkirchen to share his room in the pricey baronial hunting lodge in Ettal? She did not ask what he was doing in a hotel only the rich could afford; he was on vacation, simple enough. He sneaked her past the censorious hotel concierge who spoke twenty languages, all in an accent appropriate to an old Dracula movie. After a sexy, hot shower to heal the screaming muscles, they fell into bed affectionately but too exhausted for anything else. Night No. 1.

Roberto's plans for Night No. 2 included an equally grueling hike with the added sex-impediment of a big meal. After going halfway up the Zugspitze and snapping selfies at the waterfall, they returned in time for dinner at his inn, a delicious Bavarian bloat of every organ of a veal calf, pickled root vegetables, brined meats, Dampfnudeln, and creamed sauces and spätzle forming an anvil in their stomachs. All the alpine mushrooms, handpicked by the teenaged children of the owners, the Pfifferlinge, the Steinpilzen, the monstrous parasol fungi—Liesl and Roberto ate them compulsively, greedy for every sliver, in a velvet sauce over Schweinefilet. After a rich gooseberry strudel, they sought recourse to digestives, strong shots of Kräuterlikör that, in principle, would act as drain uncloggers for the body, and they tried two before the waiter soberly brought out, on the house, two phials of Unterberg that, when not being used for stripping paint off rusting barges on the Danube, invariably made you feel not so full. Possibly because you have died.

They undressed and rolled around fondly but to little sexual effect—too full. As Liesl nodded off to sleep, Roberto slipped from the bed in gastric distress. Roberto shouldn't eat or drink like this. He gently left the bed and sought his little mint container. He hated to walk around with medical pills—that was an invitation for too-friendly fellow backpackers to steal, hoping they were painkillers. Plus, having a prescription container at hand made him appear geriatric. He carried his heart medicine with him in a Smint dispenser. He took a pill with some pricey five-euro farty-tasting water from the mini-bar. Night No. 2 was in the books.

After Walhalla and Passau and a day of Bavarian tourism, they made their way to Regensburg, where her friends Elise and Rudi had an apartment they were lending her throughout their own vacation; Liesl and Roberto were welcome to stay, providing they kept the plants watered.

Liesl clung to his arm as they walked from Regensburg train station to Rudi and Elise's. Roberto begged a momentary delay to snap a Romanesque gargoyle or two on the sooty twelfth-century façade of the Schottenkirche so he could send it to his sister.

"How sweet," she said, a little insincerely, "that you share your travel photos."

"Oh, but you misinterpret, meine Schatz," he said, photographing some mermen. "My sister despises me. She wanted desperately to be an only child and never forgave me for being born. Tourism for us is blood sport, a competition." A photo or two more. "My sister, Rachel, hasn't seen the façade here, and I have. Sending her those lovely mermen above the door will constitute an act of aggression."

Rudi and Elise were packed for vacation and, being Germans, were ready to go at the appointed hour just as Liesl was there to take their keys at the appointed hour.

Roberto held his hosts' eighteen-month-old son and made funny faces until it was diaper-changing time; endured their dogs aggressively pawing at his crotch. But soon Rudi, Elise, toddler, dogs, all piled into their battered VW Jetta and began their journey to the cold beaches of Nordfriesland.

Liesl hogged the hot water for a while, then it was Roberto's turn in the odd shower stall no higher than six feet, built under an eave, not wide enough for him either, a spray nozzle midway up the wall with sufficient water pressure to conduct placer mining. A strange sharp quiet then fell over their actions; nakedness, intimacies, irresistible things were approaching. The dread Night No. 3.

She presented herself in a towel to Roberto, now down to his under-wear. Before the high-pressure shower, she explained, she had feeling in the outer layer of her skin, now she was not so sure. After abandoning the towel, Liesl positioned herself astride him; Roberto leaned back into the sofa, permitting whatever indelicacy she had in mind . . . but things were slow to rouse.

"*Entschuldig' meine Gräfin,* but it takes a while," he said.

"Mmm, Baron. Your *Landbesitz* is so vast."

Soon, they had switched positions, and Roberto had expertly, magnif-icently devoted himself to oral sex on her behalf, and though there was ample physical proof of her enjoyment, Roberto also knew, with lover's telepathy, that Liesl was still determined to make intercourse happen.

"Baron," she whispered, switching to German—which (actually) made what she proposed sound a whole lot dirtier—"do you want me to bind up my breasts with a mesh bandage, put on a T-shirt . . . I tuck my hair into your sports cap, and I be your little boy . . . your little stable hand, Jens, hmm? You take me as you would take a boy?"

Roberto shrugged resistance to that, and so she slapped him lightly, again playfully, then a nice stinging pop across the cheek—did he wish to be commanded? It was nothing for her to make him crawl! Where had gone the leash for Rudi's Pomeranian, since you are lower than a dog? He should not be shy with his Liesl . . . Or maybe the other way? Elise's silk scarf hung from a hook by the door. Should she get it so he could tie her wrists? Why, she would be powerless to prevent him entry anywhere he liked . . . think how she would be his toy, his doll . . .

Which of the many excuses, Roberto was thinking, should he give for this lack of genital enthusiasm? Roberto had his pick of reasons—medical, physiological, psychological. His rotating Wheel of Sexual Mal-adies spun wildly, and telling the tale of his heart issues was the safest way to go—and it generally occasioned sympathy from the unsatisfied lover. But after many years of not being able to sustain an erection for more than the first rush of engagement, there was a weight of history; even when things were looking promising (and occasionally they did!) the gravity of the inevitable failure ahead worked its dampening effect. He tried not to look too pathetic as he brushed her hair from her face, his Lotte-Luise-Lulu, incomparable Liesl.

She was a sport about it. They traveled and hiked and museumed around Bavaria a few more days—with a foray into the Czech Republic putatively for hiking but mostly for beer—before their train ride to Frankfurt and Roberto's family conference. But on their final day, on the train journey to meet his father in Frankfurt, she was not in the usual jovial mood. Not even the renewed appearance of the Baron and Baronessa revived her spirit.

Roberto's laptop dinged; Rachel had responded.

Rachel's subject line on her email read: REGENSBURG IS NICE, MURRHARDT IS BETTER. Liesl peeked around to see what she'd sent.

Liesl leaned away. "Both of you, collecting and capturing every inch of Europe, making the categories and pinning us poor Europeans to the board like insects, making to preserve us in Bernstein."

"Who is Bernstein?"

"You know, *Bernstein*. The insects become stecken in the . . . the Harz des Bäume."

"The German word for *amber* is *Bernstein*? Boy, English won that one, I think." *Bernstein* meant "bear stone." He thought of his mother's great complaining buddy and fellow chain-smoker from Providence, Sylvie Bernstein. Her name meant "forest bear-stone" or "forest amber"— entirely too grand and indigenous a name for Sylvie Bernstein.

Prompted by their visit to Walhalla, Roberto had become obsessed with the Thirty Years' War. What a waste of lives and fortunes, impoverishing every nation that committed to it. Half the men in German provinces died; nearly twenty thousand towns were wiped off the earth. The Seven United Nether Lands, Sweden, Prussia, of course Brunswick-Lüneburg, the Scot, the Turk, Russians against Spain, Bohemia, the Danes—switching sides— the Pole, and of course, what of France, who had had her own thirty-years bloodletting, slaughtering three million of her citizens in Protestant-Catholic strife. The country of Catherine de' Medici and Cardinal Riche-lieu would surely enter on the side of Rome? No, they threw in with the Protestants because that's just what France does, keep everyone guessing. Lots of hate for the Habsburgs. Bernhard of Saxe-Weimar from the Elec-torate of Saxony—who else to take on Feldmarschall Gottfried Heinrich Graf zu Pappenheim? (Pre-twentieth-century German history was an old Mel Brooks routine, Roberto concluded.)

"How does your strategy work?" she asked, barely audible.

Roberto was confused, thinking she referred to their discussion of the Thirty Years' War.

"You pursue women with passion, with charm, but at the same time, you know, your . . . your condition will make for an embarrassment along the street . . ."

"Down the road," he corrected without malice.

She waited for an answer.

"Um, sometimes . . . ," he began, looking comically at his lap. "Some-times it works, and I hope each time that this will be the time that every-thing again works properly."

His last fully functioning affair was with Valentina from Madrid; he often thought of his life as A.V. and P.V., ante- and post-Valentina. After Valentina, Liesl had no idea how many affairs and flings Roberto had launched, only to founder on the seawall of the harbor, the voyage over before it really had begun. Witty Katje from Amsterdam, the incandes-cent Branca from Coimbra, the riotous Siobhan from Cork. The same promise of laughter and rollick and touristic adventure, all to fade and falter after too many nights of nonperformance. His victims tended to be united by their good-heartedness, the gentleness of their retreat and breakup, all kind souls. Roberto tended to choose his audience for his failures wisely.

"And yet," said Liesl, not at all negatively, just curious, "you go back and try to take the castle again and again. Some men would . . ."

"Would withdraw from the battle, I know," he said. "But I fall in love a little bit and . . . how else would I ever get to know you well? Maybe it ends in friendship, but is that so bad?"

She shook her head; it was not so bad. "You do not have a typical male ego, I think. Which is lovely."

Roberto smiled. Of course he had a male ego—a shallow American edition!—and each spotlighted episode of impotence was humiliating, but wasn't he allowed to pursue love like everyone else? Maybe deep down, he hoped that Roberto Costa, without the functional fireworks, would be enough for some women. Here, enacting his tic for nervousness, he had been filling in the *a*'s and *o*'s on Salvador Costa's name in the *International Herald Tribune*.

"I am also starting to have the thought," Liesl said quietly in English, turning left and right to survey their fellow train passengers, "that you have not to have been so . . . so honest with your Liesl. I think . . . I think that you are a very rich boy."

Les Incidents du Marais

Perhaps the Merle-Rachel Maginot Line would give way and Roberto could at least invade their sofa in Paris for two nights with a longer stay to be negotiated, certainly, with exacting demands and tributes. He began ambling toward her rooftop rental in the Fourth, the Marais.

It had been a year since he had last visited Rachel in Paris. He remembered the medieval quest to get past the all-powerful concierge, followed by the trial of the soiled cage that was the lift, big enough for two Frenchwomen or one Roberto stooping a little. One pressed the 6 especially hard (there was a crackle of connection after a moment), then there was a shudder, a mechanical exhale perhaps announcing its final ascent, some low groans and scrapes that gave way to high-pitched keening as one passed the fourth floor, metal on metal. Roberto suspected that a single jump up and down would unhinge the floor of the lift, depositing him in the shaft's abyss. If he had crashed to the bottom, his last visage would be the stern face of the concierge looking down at him without empathy: *See what your inelegant American proportions did to my precious lift?* Then at the sixth floor, the lift would halt—often before making it that final inch or two to where the manual door was permitted to open. Roberto had in this circumstance usually taken the lift down to the fifth and walked up to the sixth, but once was successful in reaching through the bars, grabbing a beam and performing a chin-up, nudging the lift up a few more inches to where the door could open.

Once past the concierge, he saw the FERMÉ tape across the lift's door. The benighted lift had finally died, and so would he die too, walking up six sweltering flights. He tapped his inner jacket pocket and felt the candy container that held his nitro pills. He would sit and rest on the landings, he decided, in order not to be seen panting, providing a near-death tableau for Merle's pleasure.

Odd. Three major pieces of drama played out in Roberto's life in the Marais; the dramas had not had the decency to spread themselves out around Paris, whereupon more of the city could be suffered in, reminisced about during long, brooding walks.

Les incidents du Marais . . . #1. Roberto and his first homosexual experience.

It was 1992. It was the long-awaited Brockton Academy summer trip to Paris. They had gone with Ms. LeFevre (French instruction) and Mr. Sidney (history instruction), who babysat them to death, certain that the rich scions and heiresses of New England would be daily plunging before the wheels of the Métro, the boys succumbing to the geriatric whores of the rue Saint-Denis while the girls were undressing for the local séducteurs.

Rupesh Doshi, his roommate on the trip, proposed playing sick in the morning—and their tender stomachs had been acting up, so that was quite credible. Once left behind in the hotel while the other students marched to Les Invalides, Roberto and Rupesh bounded into Paris on an adventure of their own. Rupesh had a route planned; they were going to the Marais, which was the gay area. Gay Paree! They lingered around the closed-at-this-morning-hour Le Depot where actual gay men patronized; they found a viewpoint for the Quai des Célestins where, on the stone banks of the Seine, male nude sunbathing was plainly visible, as were unashamed acts of affection between the lovely jeunes hommes. (Eventually, as Roberto would confide to a future Notebook entry, Paris put an end to this well-attended frolic with $4,000 fines.) After an eyeful from the street above, they moved for a better angle from the Pont Sully, but some of the garçons spotted their interest and beckoned for them to join—*Quel est le problème, boys? You know you want to!* Some of the Frenchmen were mocking them in English, so Roberto and Rupesh (who had acquired a beret) had not persuaded Parisians they were French, a fantasy they both had cherished. They sped away like Frédéric and Charles at the end of Flaubert's *L'éducation sentimentale,* where the "Turkish" brothel's madame displays her female wares to the terrified fifteen-year-olds.

Roberto and Rupesh burrowed into the Île Saint-Louis and hunted for the famous ice cream. They had gone in search of adult sophistication and ended up licking ice cream cones like the school-group youngsters they were. Rupesh put Roberto up to buying a bottle of expensive dessert wine in a tiny Saint-Louis shop that simply billed its aromatic contents as DÉLICES. Truth was, teenagers did not usually present themselves in six-foot-five versions in France, so the shopkeepers assumed he was well past eighteen. And the boys had no wine sophistication, thinking an expensive Sauternes was best because it cost the most. They sat on the quai on the Saint-Louis side and stared back at the Marais and drank the bottle in paper cups bought less excitingly at the Monoprix. Having not eaten anything but ice cream, the sticky-sweet dessert wine sent them into hyperglycemic head-spins. They raced back to precede their schoolmates and resumed their ruse of being sick when Ms. LeFevre came to look in on them. Rupesh, much smaller than Roberto, now really *had* become sick and went to their small bathroom to vomit. Ms. LeFevre put a hand to her heart, so concerned.

"You're glassy-eyed, Roberto," she noted, shaking her head in sympathy. "Perhaps you will be better tomorrow. I'll have them send up some yogurt."

When she left and Rupesh got cleaned up, they were giddy. What an adventure the day had been! They hugged and . . . well, two drunk fifteen-year-olds, in T-shirts and boxers, Paris, the Marais, the array of *exhibitionniste* French youth . . . And come to think of it, it was a double bed, not two twins, which was still relatively rare in modest hotels then. It would have been a failure of adolescence had they not rolled around and then slipped a hand into each other's shorts. For Roberto, it was hormones and wine, curiosity and experimentation; for Rupesh, it was a long-suppressed secret crush come to fulfillment. There would be drama concerning that ahead.

Les incidents du Marais . . . #2. Hélène and Roberto break up publicly because of the Musée d'Art et d'Histoire du Judaïsme.

It was late 2003. They had returned from a month at Hélène's family's country home in Provence, with the specter of Lucrezia, a Milanese model, and her designs on Roberto understood between them. Back in Paris for another week together, they decided to play tourist. Having seen, repeatedly, all of Paris's major sites, they were circling the second-tier but worthy attractions, each alternating control of the itinerary for the day. Hélène had picked the Natural History Museum, which set them up for a look into the Grande Mosquée and its teahouse, a hazy orientalist den, all tile and hanging verdure, glasses of scalding mint tea, a side street in Marrakech dropped whole into Paris.

It was Roberto's turn, and his choice was the Jewish cultural museum. Two blocks from the entrance, Hélène declared that she didn't want to go, she said she had been dragged as a collégienne, back in her cinquième—why not the Musée Picasso instead?

"You have *not* been dragged there when you were twelve," Roberto corrected, since it had only opened four years ago. He had prompted, "There'll be art. Chagall. Soutine, Lipchitz. Modigliani."

Hélène said she didn't want to spend a depressing morning reviewing her perfidious countrymen conspiring with the Germans to wipe out French Jewry. That heartbreaking book of photographs with two thousand pictures of French children, some eleven thousand of whom were shipped to the camps by the Vichy French. *Le Chagrin et la Pitié,* Claude Lanzmann, and *Shoah*—of course she had seen these films; of course it is all true, but it is a sunny day, and she did not want to rub her face in this wretchedness again. The Jewish lawyers would never give it up, she went on, down to the last hundred-year-old man, they will keep searching for the Klaus Barbies and René Bousquets—yes, execute them all, they were masterminds. But teenagers who would have been shot themselves for not following the orders of the Milice? We must empty out our retirement facilities and put them all on trial? It was a Paul Touvier associate who offered up names of youth around Sisteron, who had helped with all his little extermination projects—one witness ratting out another who ratted out another who eventually said her grandfather's name. God, the endless trials!

"'Endless' trials? Just a handful of Vichy functionaries have ever been tried."

"Perhaps if the Americans had not helped so many collaborators to escape to South America, there might have been more trials, n'est-ce pas? You helped Klaus Barbie hide out in Bolivia for thirty years."

This was a sensitive, worn-raw subject in the Disse family since Hélène's eighty-five-year-old grandfather (the surly old patriarch, on her mother's side) had come under an investigation about the elimination of the Jews in Haute-Provence. Roberto had calculated; Auguste Disse would not have been a "teenager" but a man in his midtwenties during the war. It was family lore—and known throughout their ancestral village—that her grand-father was, Hélène insisted, a terrorist for the other side, a Maquisard.

"The Damascus Affair," she groaned. "A whole floor to Dreyfus, I imagine."

"I read that the museum's displays stop before the Holocaust. Dreyfus, yes—he'll be there. There's a Modigliani I haven't seen."

"Hmm, now I understand all. You told Lucrezia she resembled a Modigliani painting—oh, how that pleased her. Perhaps you wish to buy the postcard in the museum store and send a little sexy note on it to your new lover. All the better if it is a Modigliani nude." Hélène would raise her voice about trifles (e.g., not consuming snails in front of her), but when she was truly upset, her voice grew cold and still. "Her peasant blood was designed to be fat, turning out baby after baby for some stink-ing fisherman in . . . Naples. I know Naples is not in Sicily, I could not come up with a Sicilian city. Do not correct me."

"Naples *was* in the Kingdom of the Two Sicilies, so technically, you are correct."

"Techniquement, you should fuck off." Hélène turned to walk back to the Métro, mumbling, talking to herself.

"If you have something to say . . . ," Roberto cued her.

"I say nothing could have pleased that future porcinée more than say-ing she was like those emaciated figures in Modigliani . . . You—perhaps, of course, how could I not have seen it. You have fucked her already in Provence, yes? When my back was turned?"

Roberto thought this set some kind of couple argument-escalation re-cord to manage Dreyfus, Vichy France, the Holocaust, and if he'd fucked an Italian model behind a cork tree, within a single minute. There were two or three less dramatic encounters ahead, but he and Hélène had more or less broken up on the cobblestones before the museum, and his planned autumn in Italy therefore would not be canceled, so yes, he was fleeing to Milan, where Lucrezia happened to live—which Roberto even then, pull-ing out of the Gare de Lyon, morose and looking at a rainy Paris retreat from view, knew would be the setting of a loud, ludicrous, short-lived affair.

He sat down on the top step of the fifth (sixth? fourth?) floor. A cleaning lady with her bucket and mop emerged from an apartment, saw him, gri-maced, and muttered something about the broken lift, the management of the building, such criminals . . .

"I was middle-class longer than you," said a voice from above. Rachel leaned out on her landing to confirm that her brother was a floor below, and out of stamina. "I went to public school and was inevitably bullied—for looks, for smartness, for deigning to be alive. My travails prompted Lena to send me to Sacred Heart—you remember that phase?—where new tormentors appeared—namely, the One True Holy Roman Catholic Church. Nuns don't like a smart aleck. We were wealthy enough for boarding schools by your adolescence." Rachel was giving this speech as she walked slowly down the steps to join Roberto.

Rachel, Roberto recalled, became one of those boarding-school girls who never wanted to come home, who would cadge invitations from other girls over holidays rather than endure her own folks, the forced marches to Vó Costa's and all the paltry family traditions. At the Walsh Academy, she could perfect her alter ego, her claim to be Jewish (non-observant, from atheistical parents, should someone follow up with questions, not even a bat mitzvah!), a New Yorker really, temporarily waylaid in Providence, Rhode Island, related to people she barely knew . . .

"So," Rachel continued, sitting herself beside him one step up, so she could be eye level with her foot-taller brother, "I, having achieved the incomparable, unlikely gift of never having to work, of living on a trust fund from the labors of others, of being a white-privileged plutocrat's daughter despised justifiably by the coming revolution . . . hear as I say unto you, little brother, that I *do not* want your sorry, too-tall self cock-blocking the flow of *my money*."

"I'll try not to. But that's mostly up to Dad, isn't it?"

"Dad needs reeducation too. He is loyal like a Boy Scout. He will follow Hightower Wiggins down the drain."

"That's who Dad is."

Rachel announced to echoes of the stairway: $172 a share. "That's Bear Stearns a year before they hit the skids, before JPMorgan Chase offered them the pity fuck of two dollars a share this spring. Let's say dear ol' Dad worked at Bear, and not Hightower Wiggins, and had given his baby boy a trust fund with a modest hundred thousand shares at one seventy-two. That's seventeen million, two hundred thousand—or as it's known on the street, *never working again the rest of your life.* Ah, but what's this? Bobby looks up from his café table in the Barceloneta, filling his little Notebook with crap about Dutch diphthongs and, oh look, realizes Bobby, at two dollars a share, 'I have only two hundred thousand dollars now.'"

Roberto frowned. Rachel had a way of framing things.

"Two hundred K," she said, knocking lightly on his skull as one would a door. "Back to the U.S. to teach foreign language in a nice public community college. What else is your degree good for? I bet between security deposit, furnishing your apartment, buying a car . . . I'd say you're gonna go through that two hundred K pretty quickly. But don't worry, that five-five load at Warwick, twenty-five kids a class, will net you a cool thirty-two thousand salary a year. Maybe you can find another teacher and be roommates—"

"Okay, enough with the horror stories."

"C'mon," she said, nudging him. "One more staircase. Merle's got some ideas about how we can shake loose some of Dad's other assets he is being disingenuous about. Your big sister will handle everything, like always."

Roberto pulled himself up on the banister, standing. His sister had *not*, he thought, always handled everything.

Les incidents du Marais . . . #3. The rescue of Rachel in 2002.

Roberto had been the focus of attention through his teenage years because of his health crises, and Rachel had shrugged off all concern or supervision, proceeding through an unchaperoned, invisible European existence, far from the declassé rabble of Rhode Island. Rachel had had a Yale girlfriend the family had only met a time or two—limp, silent Gwyneth—but to the family's surprise, in her first year at the Sorbonne, Rachel took up with a man and (also a surprise) a fellow American.

Michael McCord was one of those bearish bearded Midwestern white-guy clones you couldn't pick out of a police lineup if he'd robbed you at gunpoint. Firm handshake, a backslapper, would go on endlessly to Roberto about some delicacy or fine wine that he alone had discovered—the tarte au citron, Châteauneuf-du-Pape, galettes versus crêpes. Who knew such splendors existed, Bobby? (Everyone who had spent three days in Paris, that's who . . .) That's when he wasn't roping Roberto into "men's talk"—what hottie was Roberto dating now, the women of Paris, ooh la la. And there were sports—what about them Tigers? A total bore, but steady. Salvador and Lena and Roberto all figured Rachel was using him as a porter, a hauler of photo equipment and heavy suitcases, the large lump of a man who would glare threateningly when diminutive Rachel was being dismissed by administrators or sneered at by hotel managers.

Yes, Rachel's thesis sounded narrow and obscure—"The Surviving Paleochristian and Byzantine Mosaics of Europe"—but in truth it was too big a topic for a thesis. There were forty-some major survivals from Rome and Jerusalem and Ravenna, from Sicily to Aachen, from Istanbul to the Italian Riviera, Cyprus, from Kyev, Ukraine to Poreč, Croatia. Rachel would rent the car, book the hotel, and Michael would be laden like a peasant's oxen cart, advancing with difficulty several yards behind her. There was a time Roberto and his parents felt sympathy for Michael, so sublimated was he in his role.

But then one spring day, their mother made a surprise visit to her daughter's little flat on Passage Saint-Paul in the Marais—hoping for a loan from her daughter, most likely—and found Rachel elusive and incoherent, sallow and way too thin. When Madalena barged up the stairs, insisting on seeing the apartment, she was appalled. Filth, insects, food scraps, dust . . .

"There are crack houses that are better kept up," Lena told Roberto, "not that I've been in a crack house."

"Have you not, Mother?"

"Bobby. *Everything* was broken or smashed. Why would Mike even want to live like that?"

Rachel, probably knowing her confessions would somehow bring an end to her predicament, told Lena that Michael controlled everything. Michael McCord of Holt, Michigan, didn't have to rob Rachel at gunpoint. She turned over her life to him voluntarily, her accounts, her money, her personal freedom, when she could go outside, when she could use the toilet. It broke everyone's heart. She wasn't who they thought she was, Roberto reflected as he staggered to the doorway of Rachel and Merle's lair. The Costas had mistaken her unpleasantness for strength. Lena, Sal, and Roberto rallied, though, and sent Michael packing.

Sal devised a plan, requiring a rare moment of family unity.

Lena hovered in a car close to Rachel's apartment; it was parked there the day before the secret operation to assure her a space amid Paris's parking miasma.

Mr. Costa made common cause with the concierge, a woman who

gossiped liberally about everyone in the building and had a sympathetic sense of Rachel's predicament. The concierge hoped that, as a father, he would rescue his daughter—providing there was no interruption in the rental payment, of course; these things must be maintained. The concierge and management company were notified and were supportive: locks were to be changed, the furniture was to be sold, the lease contract was paid off (with a little extra for the concierge's trouble, d'accord), and a bit more for all repairs and refurbishments after they left.

Mrs. Santos discovered that Michael had secured total access to Rachel's trust fund and her money, and indeed, she was only given what he allowed her. He had spent lavishly on himself. Mrs. Santos, in a matter of a few days, detached Michael from all accounts with his cessation timed to become apparent on the day of the secret plan's execution.

Roberto's job was to "run into" Michael as he was coming back from whatever leisure activity he had been enjoying and propose a late lunch / early dinner, Roberto's treat, and Michael, not being one to turn down free anything, accepted. What in God's name had they found to talk about? Roberto barely could remember anything but the food details. Michael got the most expensive entrée on the menu, then the priciest wine, then a series of liqueurs and brandies, narrating like Orson Welles in a wine commercial, holding forth about whether the street café's bargain brandy was as good as the one he had in 1998 when he and Rachel visited Cognac . . .

Back at the apartment, Rachel was panicked and a little offended by what her father and Mrs. Santos were doing—disassembling her life and pulling the plug on Paris and Michael. After some initial resistance, her will collapsed, and she was helpful in packing up her essential things. She then was guided by Mrs. Santos to the waiting car with Lena. Rachel's belongings fit in four suitcases. Lena and her defeated, sullen daughter sped away to the Porte d'Orléans where a suite in a businessmen's hotel awaited.

At that point, Sal made a phone call to Roberto, who pretended it was a girlfriend who demanded his presence. Michael, of course, having had his free meal, was happy to let Roberto go at it. Roberto walked Michael back to their building and said goodbye. This next hour was where the plan could falter. Sal and Roberto felt the idea of Lena babysitting Rachel at the hotel was doomed, given Lena's tendency to judge and Rachel's lifelong resistance to maternal commentary, so it was thought best that Roberto show up and see to Rachel's distraction and entertainment. Sal had cleverly asked for Rachel's phone and hadn't returned it; he didn't want his daughter to call Michael in the dead of night and reconnect. Yet if Roberto could rewind the videotape of life, he would have stayed put and followed Michael up the stairs to see how that little eviction scene played out. It was re-created for him by Mrs. Santos and Sal . . . but still, to have seen the denouement in person!

Sal bade Michael sit down. Mrs. Santos recalled, with her cackle, how Michael's lip was trembling and he was barely audible when he spoke. Roberto could imagine with what cordial intensity his father had explained the changed situation to Michael, who nearly broke his neck nodding and acquiescing. Michael's abuses, proof of which were a drawer full of Polaroids of outrageous degradations, had been shown to the police. If he did not wish to begin a long conversation with the Police Nationale resulting in domestic abuse charges, he had better leave France at once for the United States. Michael tried, reportedly, to stammer that many of their collected things were his, a laptop, his CDs and books, there was a Pierre Cardin suit . . . *All purchased with my daughter's money,* Sal reminded Michael. As a last generosity, he had purchased Michael a ticket to Detroit.

Rachel, within days, went back to the family's New York apartment, where Sal intermittently could look in on her, and yet—thanks to his ten-hour workday—she would have privacy and space to regroup. When Roberto ran across his mother in Europe or when his dad was overseas for business, the conversation turned inevitably to their central stupefaction: Of all women! Of all people to submit herself to a mediocre, controlling, toxic man! Rachel, who would hold up an airplane's departure if someone was being annoying next to her assigned seat. Rachel, who would work her way up the chain of command in a department store until she spoke to the CEO if something went amiss at the acne cream counter. In private, how had she been so . . . so weak, so broken?

Lena would sigh, shrug, and say, "Well, she's not a great beauty, Bobby. You got all of my looks. She took after your father." The stocky frame on a five-foot-one woman, the faint mustache, the hairy arms . . .

In the Marais of 2008, Roberto had now summited. He was within the Rachel-Merle compound.

"Shall we have tea?" Merle asked after setting up her PowerPoint presentation on the central room's coffee table.

Merle was back presently with a porcelain teapot with a linen cloth to grip the too-hot handle, cups, saucers, an array of petit écolier cookies. She fished out of the teapot a metal cage packed with tea, some larger leaves, little aromatic flowers. Of course, the tea was delicious. The key to Merle's indispensability to Rachel's life was this, a constant assault of caring servitude, the making of tea, the folding of fragrant and pressed laundry, the paying of bills, and the chores of daily life in their most deluxe version; anyone, once acclimated to this Dubai six-star-hotel treatment, could scarcely be expected to deny themselves and expel the invasive species from the garden.

"Let us talk about your father's very dark past," Merle began. "With the CIA. Surely you have worked that out for yourself."

"In your last PowerPoint," Roberto said, glancing at an impassive Rachel, "you assured me he was insider-trading. So now he's a spy?"

Merle now sat, hands together sagely, fingertips touching. "Was he not? He was part of the 1977 delegation from Merrill Lynch who, at the invitation of the shah, was part of an attempt to capitalize Iran and bring it into the Western markets. After that, he took over the Buenos Aires office for a consortium of American investment banks. In that office building was the World Finance Corporation, the CIA shell bank founded by the leader of the Bay of Pigs failed coup. Also in the building was his eventual employer, Hightower Wiggins, in 1978."

Roberto saw she wasn't using notes. How much research had she done, had she memorized? "Yes." He nodded seriously. "I recall as a lad, my dad bouncing me on his knee, fondly recalling what fun it was to lead paramilitary operations to overthrow leftist regimes."

Merle said, impervious, "extraordinary measures had to be taken by the CIA to keep the shah in power, Perón in power. Rachel showed me a stack of postcards sent back to the family; he apparently was in Santiago in Chile too, helping to bolster Pinochet, no doubt."

"Or sightseeing?" Roberto offered. "He was in his twenties. Those foreign assignments were low-man-on-the-totem-pole assignments, and he didn't have kids yet. When Rachel came along, he was moved back to the Providence office. Are you happy, Rach? You were the reason Dad had to stop being an international secret agent."

Merle: "By the time you will visit again, I will have examined the great leaps forward of your family—the big house in Providence, which in no way could have been afforded by a strip-mall-office retirement account manager for middle-class customers. The move to New York. Seems unlikely a bond trader for a chain investment house, working out of a cubicle in Providence—"

Roberto nodded. "Maybe you're right. My father on three-month assignments, in his twenties, was the linchpin of American subversion operations worldwide—a wonder that I didn't see it. But he spent much more time in the Montreal and Brussels bureaus. Hmm, who could we have been looking to overthrow? Queen Mathilde?"

"That type of ambitious young man with a chip on his shoulder was precisely who the Central Intelligence Agency in those days recruited and used for their foreign interference, idealistic and right out of college—"

"What chip on his shoulder?"

"He was playing in a world of Ivy League–educated experts, relegated to the butt end of finance, municipal bonds. He was seen, much as he is now, as ethnic comic relief. Plus, he had to endure it being known his business degree was from the University of Rhode Island."

Roberto said, "If you had spent any time with my father instead of creating PowerPoint fantasies about him, you would know that he lives and breathes pride in his URI association. He no doubt has left more money to them than to us in his will. He wants a building named after himself there. You do not understand the first thing about my father."

Rachel: "Bobby, there's some smoke to this fire."

"How do you intend to"—he grasped for a word—"monetize this theory?"

Merle wrapped it all up with a bow. "It would be very inconvenient in the midst of his high public persona at the moment to be revealed to have committed crimes in his youth. It might be easier, simply, to tap into one of many personal accounts he has access to and restore the flow of money to Rachel's trust. I know from my law school training that the regular remuneration from the trust fund can be said to constitute a contract, a contract which he is currently breaking—"

"Did you stay in law school long enough to learn," Roberto interrupted, "that as the trustee of our fund, Dad has the power to increase or decrease the flow of our trust money at his merest whim? That's why they call it a *living revocable trust*. In any event, as he told us, there's an SEC freeze on accounts set up through Hightower Wiggins."

"Do we even know that's true?" Merle asked. "How convenient that the SEC is investigating Hightower Wiggins, so he can manipulate his daughter's trust."

"Yes, in the midst of a world financial crisis, while trying to save a century-old brokerage house and the investments of millions of Americans, that's what he's really up to, isn't it? You sniffed it out. Dad's priority right now is sabotaging his daughter's checking account." Their bland reaction to this suggested they might think he was, at last, seeing the light. "Are you both fucking kidding me?"

"Oh, stop playing naive," Merle said, her exasperated tone barely different from her welcoming, smiling tone. "Of course, you do not even have to play—you are naive. Your father's associations to fascist regimes will prove embarrassing."

Roberto settled lazily into his chair, affecting something akin to boredom. "You are not going to shock me or horrify me—or anyone else in the financial world, for that matter—that my father has dealt with Russian oligarchs and corrupt sheiks and emirs and dictators. Providence is full of mob bosses and mafiosi—their portfolios contain mutual funds with a solid base of bonds too. No one in the financial world forbids sales of financial vehicles to people because they are bad or got their money from doing bad. You are the naive one if you think that information will cause a ripple on the water."

Merle was speedily taking notes. "Mob bosses in Providence?" she checked.

Roberto sighed. "You have expressed before your extreme distaste for the profile of the United States in the world. Abandoner of the Palestinians, placater of the Saudis, partner of any number of juntas and strongmen and genocidal regimes. All the money my father has made for this family are from bonds, including American and European treasury bonds that fund the entire Western Alliance. Rachel lives off that money, is bathed in it, drowning in it. And you leech off my sister, so you are also in the hog pen too with your mouth ever craning, thirsting for the great satanic sow's teat."

Merle pursed her lips, perhaps not ready for this particular feint.

"I will help you write the letter this afternoon," Roberto continued. "*Dear Mr. Costa, Due to your visible importance in the funding of the obscene American national enterprise, do not trouble yourself to return us to the flow of such tainted money from Hightower Wiggins as supplies your daughter's trust fund. We prefer to be pure and make our own way in the world, free of imperialist entanglements. We wouldn't want to be privileged hypocrites—we could not bear* that *for a moment. Sincerely yours, Rachel and Merle.*"

Merle glanced at Rachel with a look that said this conversation had deteriorated just as she had imagined. She stood and said simply, "I'll get some more hot water."

After Merle left the room to refresh the teapot, Roberto whispered to his sister, "So I can't stay on the couch tonight? She'll forbid it?"

Rachel faintly smiled. "What do you think, genius?"

Les Disses

Roberto had hoped to avoid a reunion with Hélène Disse, whom he left on bad terms in 2003, and also her mother, who may have turned against him in solidarity. But desperation suggested he needed to scrounge a canapé-lit—and quick.

But before his fall from grace, though, Roberto Costa had been number one with a bullet.

Hélène's sole motive for dating in her early twenties was to appall her respectable mother, who was the chief purchaser of dresses at Galleries Rochambeau on the rue de Rivoli in the heart of Paris. Hélène brought home Senegalese would-be hip-hop artists, North African hunks with previously sired children . . .

"You want to live with another woman's bawling infants in the banlieue, be my guest," her mother informed her.

There was a range of inappropriate ages, from dreamy schoolboys to silvered men older than her late father would have been, before Hélène arrived at her most ingenious offense: an American, a big, tall, unemployed one too. But this was "une erreur de calcul."

Madame Disse was given an assignment in New York soon after he and Hélène were a thing. Bloomingdale's was seasonally featuring the merchandise of the Galleries Rochambeau in a cozy corner of their women's floor. Lots of shop assistants in berets, Arc de Triomphe and Eiffel Tower plastic replicas amid the clothes, purses, clutches, gloves. Clementine Disse was fawned over, treated like Bourbon royalty, deferred to . . . Why these New Yorkers weren't so bad, after all. And the food! As good as Paris! (Well, it's often the same French chefs, the same bandied Michelin stars.) She must have done a little research on Roberto Costa while she was stateside, that regrettable nobody from Providence, whose father turned out to be delightfully well-off. Commencing upon her return, Roberto and the United States generally were celebrated. After all, he was the rare young American who could speak French quite well (though she would insist that his accent was frequently inadequate, to keep him on his toes).

And, from this détente, Roberto could chart the waning interest of Hélène.

Madame Disse, whose number had survived in his phone, was delighted to hear from him! And what good fortune to catch her before she and her daughter and her newest petit ami made their way south to their holiday home in Provence!

"Vous êtes la chanceuse," he said, insisting she was the lucky one, speeding away to paradise, the serenity of Mas Disse, oh how he enjoyed his invitation there in 2003 . . .

"So you must visit us this summer," she said.

The impossible-to-refuse Clementine Disse demanded that Roberto join them for a week; he pretended to be torn, but he had no intention of refusing free accommodation. Maybe, with charm, he could stretch his time there to several weeks and beyond.

Madame Disse proceeded in English confidentially. "Our Hélène will be there with her . . . her newest love. Mon cher, it was all down to the bottom of the hill after you. Un homme sans promesse—I hate for to say—one disaster after another!"

He next, dreadfully, called Hélène. To his relief, she was delighted he would join them again—did he remember the fun they had had back . . . when was it? Ah, 2003. She had missed him utterly! Why had they not been in touch?

"Mas Disse was wonderful," Roberto said, "but we were not. We fought the whole time."

"Uhh," hummed Hélène. "I don't remember it that way . . ."

It was agreed that she, he, and her current lover, Marcel, would drive down together. To not have a car was to be trapped every afternoon in the arrière-pays provençale with the severe Aunt Sidonie and the other awful houseguests, Monsieur Hacquin—

"He is *still in attendance*?" Roberto nearly cried it out.

"He will outlive us all."

"The Speedo," Roberto murmured.

Hélène wanted to meet Roberto that very evening after work, without her mother or her boyfriend around, so a few hours later, they met at one of her neighborhood cafés near the Métro Alésia, Roberto arriving on time, Hélène twenty minutes late.

"I had forgotten how tall, tall, tall," she said, pressing her cheek against his. Always the best perfume, just a suggestion . . . The advantage of having a mother who no doubt had a suitcase of eau de parfum samples to dispense. Hélène was only five years older from their last encounter but so much more beautiful. There was nothing anymore of the cherub-cheeked perpetual student whose eyes nearly shut when she smiled; she had grown angular in a French-favored way, sharper eyes and cheekbones than her mother's. And she was thin in the way of an actress or model who did not perhaps have an eating disorder, but on occasion enacted some of their methods.

She saw the faint amber in the glass. "Un pastis?"

"A Suze, since we're going to the South."

"That's my mother's drink. Regarde toi, you are sucking up to La Clementine even now, even when she cannot see you to do it."

Hélène once accused him of "wanting" her mother. Roberto imagined scenes at the country house out of Feydeau: Hélène abandoning her current lover snoring in his bed to sneak down the hall to Roberto's room, while Madame Disse, in flagrante, panicked, bolting from Roberto's bed to hide in the giant eighteenth-century oaken dresser . . .

"Suze," Hélène was saying, "tastes like mouthwash, if mouthwash were to decide to taste like hand soap." She ordered a pastis, and a single ice cube. If Clementine Disse's grand master plan was to use Roberto to break up Hélène and her latest beau, she needn't have bothered. "Marcel and I are breaking up," Hélène declared. "So you need not lecture me that he is unworthy or become jealous—whichever occurs to you."

Roberto settled in the chair. This was the Hélène way: to speak in headlines, accusations, pronouncements.

She toasted him with her pastis. "It will be so, so, so much less dramatic than how you and I—" She swam around for an American phrase she used to know.

"Called it quits," Roberto supplied. "We did not break up officially. You abandoned me to Lucrezia."

She switched to French: Don't act like that was unwelcome! I tried to sleep with her myself, you will recall.

"I assumed you had."

I believe we let you believe that, trying to make you jealous, trying to shake that insufferable American complacency.

Roberto joined her in speaking French: Lucrezia and I lasted barely a few months. I thought you were too dramatic, but that was before I spent time with la sicilienne. Mt. Etna erupted less often.

I'd *prefer* to say I never hear from her, Hélène said, but my mother and she are Facebook friends. They chat about fashion. Sometimes I say hello—we used to heap abuse upon you for not having the sense to choose one of us.

Roberto reverted to English: "So. Why are you ditching Marcel? Has your mother started to like him?"

"He is un peigne-cul . . ." One of Roberto's favorite French insults, an ass-hair comb, more exquisite than merely saying someone is an asshole. "He is detestable—you will see."

"Does he mistreat you?"

She stared at him. "He annoys me—which I find more contemptible, yes? Too much energy, which is good for his career in children's entertainment, but is intolerable out of that context. He is bouncy like a cocker."

Roberto must have look bemused.

She smiled. "I was not referring to his cock . . . um, le chien cocker."

"Cocker spaniel."

"Yes." Another sip. "But his cock, since you insist, yes, is very nice. I will be sorry to see that go away." Another sip. "I was sorry to see your cock go away too. If only"—she shrugged—"the great cocks weren't attached to such hommes exécrables. What is a woman to do?"

After a moment, Roberto began, "You were wise to trade me in. My swordsman skills are on the wane." He reached into his jacket and shook his heart medication like a rattle. "My circulation issues, you recall, have worsened to compromise the full . . ."

"Éclat. Oh, what a shame. I never got to make love to you enough. I needed two or three more times. Did you feel that way about me?"

"Mais oui, bien sûr."

Despite the prediction of mutual hatred between Marcel and Roberto, within an hour on the autoroute drive south, by the first stop at the commodious French rest area, the two fellows were laughing like they were old friends. Hélène found nothing they laughed at funny and seemed to regret chauffeuring the boys to Provence so many hours away.

"I see," sang Marcel, "we have not passed the toilet equator."

The toilet equator, where the sit-down toilet gives way to the "Turkish" pit toilet one had to squat over. That was a skill that Roberto at his gangly height had never acquired; you had to be brought up using them not to encounter grief.

"*Toilette d'oil* versus *toilette d'oc,*" said Marcel seriously.

Returning from the rest area's sumptuous convenience store, loaded down with French *chips* ("sheep") and Volvic fruit-laced waters, Marcel began a scatological story about two old men arguing near the toilets. He would stand to the left to say one man's lines, then hop to the right to face his former position to say the other man's lines with theatrical voices. Marcel was always "on." He knew how to "commit to the bit," as the comedians instruct. And he was surprisingly big, that kind of rounded bigness of the provinces, barrel chest, thick thighs, meaty forearms, which made his ease at physical comedy, his sweeping gestures occupying the space a meter above and around him, a bit surprising. Roberto could see how the kids loved his clowning and ventriloquy; they loved *him.* Hélène must prefer outsize guys, Roberto surmised. Her waifish petiteness wished to control and command a vast tract of male real estate.

As Hélène resumed driving, the boys returned to their vital topics. Toilets, worst ones ever, Germany's "continental shelf," where one's stool was on display, misadventures while squatting, then the inexhaustible subject of pissing, where one had been forced to piss, how to sneak a piss in a city in midday . . . there was not time and world enough for these puerile topics as Hélène grew steadily more annoyed.

The viaduct at Millau was all it was hyped up to be. The bridge, with the world's highest bridge towers, achieved the impossible: augmenting the beauty of the valley with a highway bridge. *America,* Roberto thought coldly, *is no longer capable of doing one magnificent thing like this collectively.*

They at last arrived in Cuges-les-Pins. All of the Disse clan habitually arranged to arrive from the west, so as not to slam into the traffic at the grand prix racetrack to the south (which, when not hosting the Formula One event, was being used for something else automotive and noisy) and OK Corral (a Wild West theme park where one could watch the bad guys outgun the good guys—in French!—on the dusty main street of a faux Texas town).

"What about *my* heritage?" Roberto demanded. "I insist we go to OK Corral."

Marcel concurred, "Oh, please, Hélène! We go so we can laugh."

"In no universe will I go to OK Corral," she said, barely audible.

They stopped at the Carrefour for some staples—milk, eggs, some almost acceptable baguettes since the boulangerie they liked in the tiny town was not open past 2:00 p.m. and the sun was in his last hour. Marcel, Hélène, and Roberto also conspired to have a secret stash of candy, cookies, and alcohol that would remain in the trunk of the car and selfishly not be shared—not shared with the hefty great-aunt, who would offer their precious treats to her intolerable old acquaintances when they came to call, not shared with Monsieur Hacquin, who would spend the day circling around the kitchen, like a hawk riding the thermals, picking and fingering and nibbling and depleting the supplies of anything tasty.

"I cannot believe," Roberto said, depositing an overpriced package of American Oreos into the shopping cart, "that Monsieur Hacquin is still—one—alive and—two—invited. It has been five years since we were all at Mas Disse together, and I sensed even then that he was universally detested."

Their supermarket detour allowed a full unpacking of their detestation of Maurice Hacquin, the three of them eager to land the vilest description. His skin was sallow to a remarkable degree, deep trenches of purple under his sad eyes, skin the color of bruise around armpits and groin and, invariably, day after day, his Speedo, which gave décolletage to the ass crack in back and tormented anterior observers with an unseemly bulge that threatened as he craned this way for the drink just out of reach, as he lumbered in and out of his chaise longue (the blue chaise was ceded to him), to expose itself or, at minimum, the pubis. Every time Roberto looked at him, there was a suspicion of an erection as he lay oiled and engreased by the pool, inert, a human sloth limp and slumped on his branch, staring at everyone with disapproval or with furtive lusts.

"You have no knowledge of summer protocol in French country houses," said Hélène. "I have spoken to my mother about getting rid of him. We both find his conservative politics odious. But my late father, a century ago, invited him."

Marcel shrugged. "Once invited, it is for life. It would be a social breach to not invite."

"So breach away," Roberto said.

All strategies to sneak down to Provence without him were useless because Maurice Hacquin's Paris acquaintances formed a virtual tracking system of Clementine Disse's progress south. It was likely what he lived for, Hélène informed Roberto, his greatest social triumph. "I'm sure he is in love with my mother," Hélène declared. "Probably lives for the summer show of breasts during the sunbathing matinee."

Marcel: "Yes, he retreats to his room to touch himself, to touch that monstrous, oozing slug between his legs . . ."

Thank you for that, Roberto said in French. I am thoroughly revolted now. No need for a light dinner.

The Disses advertised Cuges-les-Pins as their summer residence, but the actual house was up in the dry aromatic hills to the north and closer to the village of Lo Bordac. A deader Southern settlement could not be discovered in France; no one ever thought of heading into it for shopping since it seemed to be inhabited by villagers who made it a point of honor to go bankrupt (for their stores were never open) and to roast alive in their houses (since all the windows and shutters remained tightly closed).

From this ghost town began a twelve-kilometer winding ascent upon the chalk-white roads known to the Bouches-du-Rhône high country— switchbacks so severe, a lane so narrow, lurches so nauseating, that it ensured once you were in situ at Mas Disse, you would only begrudgingly leave it. The driver had better have a good memory too, since no amount of practice could build confidence with the four identical intersections. Directions were always kept in the glove compartment; rarely was an ascent from Cuges accomplished without having to reverse for a missed turn.

At Mas Disse, there was one large dining room / kitchen with the designated living room half defined by weather-wracked chairs and a dried-out leather couch with a kilim thrown over it; the other ground-floor room was a bedroom that remained in crepuscular gloom on the north side of the house. Not able to mount the stairs for an upstairs bedroom, Clementine Disse's eighty-seven-year-old aunt Sidonie had annexed the only truly private bedroom in the whole house. Aunt Sidonie eschewed the sun, never took meals with the rest of the group (nor was there any insistence that she do), just puttered and moped around the ground floor continually, left dishes in the sink for others to wash. She invited an also-loathed set of visitors, old ladies from the town who paid her court, a former house servant, the neighboring farmer and his wife (retired, but they looked after Mas Disse when no one was around and kept the place from becoming a shambles), and two or three indistinguishable spinsters who spoke of old times—old times when all sorts of people were alive who now were not.

"Maman, s'il vous plaît," Hélène had said before switching to English so Aunt Sidonie would not comprehend: "This spectacle of sitting with my grandfather's gardener and that horrible fat cleaning lady like they are our intimates . . ." There was that classic French shudder, no doubt learned in the crib. "How can you bear it?"

"I like to hear them reminisce about my mother," Madame Disse said evenly, "who barely troubled herself to know me."

The rest of the visitors were assigned one of four bedrooms upstairs. Roberto's was the most rustic—a mattress on the wooden floor, the cast-off junk of the house instead of furniture, a child's floating toy for the pool, a bicycle missing a wheel, winter blankets. He was five inches longer than the mattress provided. But, Roberto reminded himself, free accommodation.

There was the pool, which, all stoically assumed, had never been cleaned. Leaves and needles, dried browned petals, a yellowy film of pine pollen floated upon the surface. I am scared of it, Hélène confided in French: They will have to remove my gangrenous vagina if I swim in it. For once, Roberto thought, the French didn't pretty up the grotesque: *vulve gangreneuse*. Good name for a punk band, he decided.

"Be not afraid!" Marcel declared, moments before peeling off his jeans and revealing heart-covered boxer shorts, and taking a flying leap into the murky waters. "But cold!" he proclaimed, bobbing quickly to the top.

There were three pool-seating possibilities: the blue chaise (tainted by the suppurations of M. Hacquin), a second chaise that was La Disse's by seniority, and a sun-cracked plastic chair that for all its ugliness was much contested. Madame Disse moved her chaise away from the pool, dragged it with a scrape over the concrete, to the grass away from the shade of the trees. This was her sunning station.

That first morning, Roberto observed, Madame Disse was walking around the kitchen, singing to herself, wearing a loose chemise attached by a single button. The strictures of Paris were behind them, it was the south, it was summer. One declaration followed another: she would have everything "tout liberal, tout ouvert, toutes nues." She chided the others encased, imprisoned in their clothes, as she stepped gingerly over the spiky dry grass to reach her chaise. Roberto's hostess, her back to the house, removed her chemise for the ritual sunbathing.

Marcel by the pool, Mas Disse

Roberto discreetly turned to see if Maurice Hacquin was fixed on Madame Disse, only to see that he was preoccupied with his pâté and toasts on a paper plate. How he brought each morsel to his mouth as a cephalopod, a tentacle furling and unfurling . . . Madame Disse bathed in the southern sun, her arms fixed on the arms of the chaise, eyes closed, like a statue of Anubis.

You could hear everything in Mas Disse. The old plaster walls served somehow as amplifiers for whatever was afoot—the ritual honking of sinus clearing from Monsieur Hacquin at bedtime, the tinkle of bottles upon Madame Disse's toilette table, the creak of the bed with Marcel and Hélène, the tuba-like passing of gas of Hélène's great-aunt . . .

"There is no way to make love in this house," Hélène mumbled to Roberto at breakfast, having made a face at the taste of the coffee that Aunt Sidonie had made.

"But I recall you and I doing it when I was here five years ago—"

"And apparently our every movement was heard and discussed."

Roberto poured himself a cup. "Oh God. No wonder your aunt stares at me like I'm a fiend." He sipped. "And she is trying to avenge herself by poisoning us with this coffee."

"She is so senile," Hélène whispered. "She probably put potting soil in the cafetière a piston."

After some indistinguishable sunbaked days, it clouded up. That was the cue for a round of necessary visits: Madame Disse would go see her eighty-five-year-old father in a nursing facility in Aix-en-Provence. And they would take his sister, Aunt Sidonie. It finally became clear that Monsieur Hacquin had a use: after lunch, he would bring his sputtering Renault around to the side door of the house and load Aunt Sidonie into the front seat, while Madame Disse took the back. Monsieur Hacquin was the uncomplaining chauffeur for a long and winding progress to Aix. Roberto wondered why a care center had been found so far from Cuges-les-Pins—even Aubagne or Marseille would be closer—but Hélène stared holes in him. "An hour there, an hour to visit, an hour back—it is the only freedom we have here. Do not talk my mother out of it!"

Indeed, what could have been a three-hour round trip often stretched to five or six, and the sputtering Renault returned around sunset, everyone clutching shopping bags from fashionable Aix, a trunkful of groceries, delicacies unknown to the Carrefour in Cuges, a new scarf for Madame Disse, which she would model as an exhausted Aunt Sidonie moaningly staggered to her cave without dinner.

Madame's departure was the only time Marcel and Hélène could make love without an audience, so they begged pardon, taking their leave of Roberto, who stayed with his book by the pool. Of course, true to the house, every squeal and laugh and grunt was audible, broadcast to the poolside. Auditory engineers who design concert halls should study Mas Disse's construction to replicate such aural fidelity.

OK Corral

M arcel stuck his head into Roberto's bedroom. "Are we still committed to . . ."

"Oh yes."

Roberto was not sure what would be reckoned the worse offense to
Hélène—he and Marcel planning an outing, just the boys unmonitored,
ready to get up to boy things, crude talk about women, crude talk about
her . . . or the offense to her French sensibilities that was OK Corral, the
Wild West USA theme park, itself.

"Go," she said simply, staring straight through the windshield, dropping them in the dreary Lo Bordac, farthest reach of the Cuges-les-Pins
public transport bus. She sped back to the house, sending a plume of dry
white Provençale dust into the air for them to inhale.

Marcel and Roberto stayed near the bus stop for a few minutes, then
wandered around to the one plaza of closed-up buildings. It was like a
tombstone, perhaps like the original Tombstone, Arizona, whenever there
was a main street shoot-out. They practiced quick drawing and gunning
each other down with their phones as guns; Marcel, ever the ham, played
out a death scene as drawn out as Massenet's *Werther*. Marcel's throes were
so loud that Roberto ssh'ed him—surely someone was alive and being dis-
turbed in this necropolis.

"There is no one here. Halloooooo," Marcel called out, creating an echo
in the plaza. In French: Will one of you bastards show yourself! Nothing.
Next, Marcel turned his back to Roberto and undid his trousers, dropped
them with his underwear. He stepped out of his fallen pants, then peeled
off his T-shirt. "Je suis ici, Lo Bordac! Naked for you to behold . . ." Roberto

had thought Marcel a little chubby, maybe even fat, but out of clothes, it was evident that he was merely large-framed, barrel-chested, and sturdy, good peasant stock. And now Marcel shook his member at the village, offering to bed any woman, no matter how ancient—any man, then . . . farm animals? He made a quite good cow noise, but no nearby bovine appeared to accept his offer. Marcel shrugged to Roberto and began to dress himself.

OK Corral, for the love of God. By design, it was mostly for kids. Low-impact rides, a few acceptable roller coasters, water slides, all with a Territorial West theme. American flags everywhere, signs in Franglais to keep the illusion of Provençale Arizona extant. That afternoon, there would be a spectacle, six-horse teams barreling into town with a stagecoach, a holdup, some politically incorrect Indians, and Zorro was promised. There was a bar for adults, and after fifteen minutes, Marcel and Roberto parked themselves there. And when it appeared they might miss the *Le Spectacle Western Days*, halfway across the park, they had just *one* more beer, and missed it.

Well, the important thing was to defy Hélène and be appalling, so mission accomplished. They caught the bus back to Cuges . . . where, look, another outdoor bar-café beckoned. They continued with beer. One waiter was decrepit, dating from the days of the Avignon papacy, the other a twentysomething gay guy who kept eyeing them and posing, pouting. After an excess of the La Minotte local brew, they got up to piss.

When they arrived in the men's room, the gay waiter was there taking his sweet time to finish up at the urinals. Marcel openly flirted, while Roberto turned slightly protectively so as not to be on display. Eventually, the waiter sulked off, and Marcel laughed.

"I thought he was lingering," he said, showing his cock to Roberto, "for a taste of this."

Okay, thought Roberto, that was *two* appearances of Marcel's penis in a four-hour period. Roberto rarely gave in to making sexual brags, but after the beers, he had become festive. "No," he said, "I think it was *this* that piqued his interest." Roberto let Marcel see himself before repositioning and zipping up.

"*Mon Dieu*," said Marcel. "It is as Hélène reported."

They returned to their table outside. Marcel was now meeting his eyes in an entirely more intimate way, so Roberto tried to tamp down his enthusiasm. "And Hélène told you that it is not reliable."

"My American friend," Marcel said, leaning into him, "there are pills for that sort of thing."

"And I might die if I take them." Roberto hadn't told the story in a while, so he told it to Marcel:

When he was eleven, he began a growth spurt that would not stop. At eleven, he shot up to six feet; by thirteen, he was six-five. He looked like someone in a refugee camp, his body outpacing his ability to fill in proportionately. The kids in the public school called him Skeletor and Auschwitz, but, despite the abuse, he was assured that once he got to middle school, he would be pressed into service on the basketball team—there was even a visit from an assistant coach or two. When he complained to his dad that he wasn't good at basketball, that he was sure to fail before arenas of frothing fans, the idea of a prep school was floated. Was there such a prep school that emphasized academics and barely bothered with athletics—so the temptation to indenture his son to some team or other could be again resisted? Brockton Academy was such a place, top ten private preps in New England, big enough (nine hundred students) that one need not be a part of any clique or athletic impulse, recently coed, a springboard to the Ivies . . . but it was a boarding school forty miles north of Providence. Roberto assumed that his parents would never let him live away from their beloved sight . . . and so he thought, up to the day when his mother dropped him without preamble at their gates.

Throughout adolescence, there were tests, of course, for thyroid and pituitary problems; there were ugly procedures and scans looking at his aorta, which was enlarged. The doctor thought it might be Marfan syndrome. His blood pressure was through the roof, and he had to be put on hypertensive medication at fourteen. His arms and legs were long, like his long fingers, a little out of proportion. At fifteen, they detected a heart murmur; his sophomore year at Brockton, he had to stop playing during a casual volleyball match because of angina, which he assumed was a heart attack, though it was not. He was whisked to the hospital by ambulance; soon his mother appeared at his bedside, then Salvador and his business associate Gehrman van Till, driving in from a corporate meeting in Boston. Then Mrs. Santos clutching her rosary—all hands on deck, apparently.

Marfan syndrome manifests itself on a spectrum from mildly health-compromising to early-death-dealing. A cardiologist said that they would monitor him and that one day, inevitably, they would have to resect his aorta, which was developing an aneurysm and must not be allowed to burst. To Roberto, lying in the ICU, living until thirty seemed unlikely. Marfan runs in a family. Lena confessed that she had some cousins still in the Azores who were overly tall and yes, one who died young, but she was certain that had more to do with drinking and driving . . .

"But it works, yes?" The only interest for Marcel in this narrative was the state of Roberto's penis.

"I'm good for a few minutes. But I'm approaching the day when it won't work at all. And again, Viagra is off-limits."

Marcel grew pensive.

The next day was gray and, therefore, another pilgrimage to Aix for the older denizens of Mas Disse. Roberto, sprawled in his bed, was reading Gilles Leroy's *Alabama Song* in French, and struggling a bit. It was about the Fitzgeralds, mostly about Zelda and not so much F. Scott. Roberto thought it would be good to see what a French author made of America's most famous expats.

He put the book down. Marcel and Hélène were going at it down the hall, unaware he was upstairs. He listened to them for a bit. Yes, that had not changed, Hélène's little breathy squeaks. He reached for his phone and his earbuds, but they were in his day pack downstairs. So as not to embarrass them, he stayed very still. But the astringent lavender smell of the sheets, mixed with some floral fabric softener, made him sneeze. They stopped . . . before resuming.

Hélène, once showered and redressed, leaned into his room. "Marcel swore you were not in the house. But now I see he wanted you to hear us."

"I tried not to make a noise."

"You should listen more often. Marcel was never better."

"He likes an audience."

"He likes you as an audience. He will consider it a defeat if he does not sleep with you before our time here is over."

Roberto returned to his book. "I think defeat is in the cards."

There were dutiful days where Hélène, Marcel, and Roberto behaved, washed up in the kitchen, took their turns preparing the food, made small talk with whatever guests popped in to see Clementine Disse, read books, slept too much. And then there were the sex days, when Monsieur Hacquin hauled the ladies away to Aix and sex was in the air for a few fevered hours. Roberto took his expected position in his bedroom while the lovers now made as much noise as possible. At one point, they stopped . . . Roberto craned to listen . . . and Hélène appeared naked in his door, Marcel a moment later, just as naked, slipped beside her.

"They will be back soon," Hélène said. "You must take the opportunity to play with yourself."

"We are here to watch," Marcel said, stroking himself as if Roberto might not know how it was done.

"We insist," said Hélène, running a sharp finger around Marcel's left nipple.

Roberto was a little turned on. As he reached into his shorts, Hélène touched her breasts, exhaling deeply. "There is no Wi-Fi signal here for porn," Roberto said. "With my arousal issues, what is there to excite me?"

"Marcel has forgotten how to fuck," Hélène said breathily. "Would you help him to enter me?"

Marcel and Hélène lay down beside him and remained passive while Roberto manipulated them . . . while they both, with free hands, helped him along.

Hélène was much leaner than when they were together. She had conquered any chubbiness she feared—her diet of raw vegetables, coffee, cigarettes had proven efficacious. She was small breasted and had often, when she first dated Roberto, delighted in binding her chest to pass as a guy, to go to gay bars with Roberto, to strut down the streets as a pretty boy and see what that life attracted. Another fiction of that era was that Hélène was open to women and that she insisted her boyfriends be similarly polyvalent. Roberto passed that qualification, and apparently Marcel did too, but Roberto had never known Hélène actually to have a female lover. It was something she liked to announce and say about herself, but it was not something she had ever followed through with. Perhaps she had changed. The current premise, Roberto acknowledged, was what she most longed for, two men whom she would command for her pleasure, direct to make love to her and each other, obeying her whims.

Each day when the elders were gone, there would be sex. But that bled into the days when the elders stayed put. Sex then would involve waiting until they were unobserved, when one's finger would probe the other, when a hand was thrust down into another's jeans . . . small little attacks of depravity not far from the others, risky, stupid . . .

How long would it be before Madame Disse would go to Aix again? Hélène would suggest it. No, not today, her mother would say. "I cannot take that miserable road, that horrible drive. We will give Maurice a rest."

Conferring under a tree in the surrounding woods, Marcel and Roberto would plan what position they would try at the next opportunity. Hélène would have demands, but the boys united to withhold them until the act *they* both wished *her* to perform was undertaken. Of course, they all three had to work around Roberto's flagging arousal—but he was good for five minutes, when inspired. Marcel tore through the ancient desk on the ground floor, a sepulcher of dead pens and little bottles of baked-solid glue and tape without adhesion. "Aha," he said, holding up a desiccated baggie of rubber bands.

They waited until the Renault pulled out of the driveway—oh, the minutes like hours, the elders' circling back into the house, having forgotten something, having decided not to take this hat after all, Sidonie, do you need the toilet, and well, might as well go now . . . endless bother and flutter, then at last the turn of the ignition, the crunch of the gravel. Marcel would fling his bathing suit off, impatient and ready to play.

"Perhaps I will have sex with myself," he threatened. His erection, he explained in French, was too good to waste on sex with others.

Hélène held back. "Wait until they are miles away. They might still turn back." After twenty minutes, they were safe. Anyone who wound their way to Lo Bordac would not turn back for a trifle.

That Tuesday afternoon, Roberto was working himself up to almost full tilt when Marcel raced over with his rubber bands. "We make the tourniquet, non?" He found a thicker band to wrap around the base of Roberto's organ while Hélène helped adjust it—it was all very clinical. Was it too tight?

"If my penis turns blue . . ."

But the rubber bands were ancient and dry and snapped when stressed, which prompted peals of Hélène's laughter. They tried to find a thick rubber band, but only the thin spindly ones were left and, when Marcel stretched them, they too snapped. A series of three thinner ones seemed to hold fast, although the prime phase of Roberto's evanescent erection was waning. Marcel barked out orders: Roberto, you take the front! Hélène had shown reluctance for any anal penetration, but this morning, to humor them, had cleaned herself in preparatory anticipation. Marcel took to the rear, Roberto did his best to invade the front, resulting in one of those sex escapades more conceptual stunt than desired goal . . . but then Hélène found she really liked how it felt. And the men had the curious sensation of registering each other's thrusts through that septum wall that divides the vagina and the rectum.

Thursday, it was Marcel's turn to follow orders. Hélène and Roberto presented themselves to his face and demanded simultaneous oral sex, grabbing his hair and pulling him one way, then another . . . After a number of permutations, they lay in Hélène's assigned bed upstairs, hot, filmed with sweat. They were curious about each other's bodies, touching each other without permission to weigh this or feel the pressure of that, inspect a mole, put one's tongue somewhere unlikely . . . Circumcised (Roberto) versus uncircumcised (Marcel), pros and cons.

"Most Americans and North Africans, of course, are circumcised," Hélène announced. "Having been mutilated at birth—"

"Vache," Marcel broke in, "some African boys have it done at local fairs with all the world watching! Can you imagine? Not just the embarrassment but the pain at having your foreskin snipped once your penis has grown to adult size?"

"As I was saying, that is why Americans and North Africans are rougher lovers. The sensitivity of the tête du pénis has lessened, meaning the men must use it as a battering ram in order to feel something, without nuance." She paused. "Which is why I tend toward both nationalities, I suppose."

Marcel claimed first dibs on the weak shower, scrambling for the bathroom and the noncommittal hot water. Hélène lay there, nestled with Roberto; the electric fan blasted them from its spot at their feet.

"Your attendance at OK Corral has made for a demotion in my eyes," Hélène reported. "You are now no longer our registered dilletante."

He thought a moment. "Hélène, is *dilletante* a negative word in French?"

"A little bit," she said. "But you have to remember—and I think this is true throughout all of Europe—that to do nothing, to sit in cafés, to write in journals and sightsee and sleep with the local residents . . . that is an ideal. If you can arrange to have a life like that—what European would

not envy you? Most of us live like that after university, and then somewhere around thirty, the game is up, oui? At some point, la fin, time to
work, time to play our part in lovely capitalism."

He sought out her hand in bed. "Is the game up yet, for you?"

She squeezed his hand back. "Yes, I think. I will dump Marcel, say goodbye to you, and probably ask for a permanent place at Deslauriers-Rhône,
where I had an internship and was generally adored, worshipped. I think . . .
But the autumn is weeks away. Let us not speak of it. Embrassons-le." Roberto kissed her as requested, a pact to pursue escape until they had to
grow up, commencing the day they left Mas Disse.

How treacherous French was. *Embrasser* meant "to hug" as well as "to kiss."
A kiss was *un baiser.* The verb "to fuck" was also *baiser.* That would have been
a very useful place to choose a different word. The phrase *passer a la casserole*
is sort of like "let's get the sex show on the road," literally to "move on to the
pan" . . . but no American can divorce his thoughts from the ideas of Aunt
Sarah's green bean casserole with cream of mushroom soup—the opposite
of a sexy thought. *Pine* ("peen") is one of the many words for penis. But that
must amuse the French, to see the amount of English poetry, the country and
western songs, place-names that make use of the penis-word. Whispering
Pines. The lodgepole *pine*—not a bad thing to have. There's nothing better
than the smell of *pine* in the house at Christmas. Look at the beautiful *pines*
nestled among the Grand Tetons (the big breasts) . . .

Saturday . . . would there be another visit to the retirement home in
Aix? No, not today. Aunt Sidonie's wonderful former retired gardener is
popping in. Won't that be fun?

Sunday. Clementine expressed interest in the Galleries Rochambeau in
Marseille. Were they performing up to standard? What of the big windows on rue Henri Barbusse? Just when it was looking good for the older
housemates to speed off to Marseille . . . the sun came out. Nothing would
prevent Madame Disse from ascending her throne and taking the sun.

Monday. It was gray; there was a brush fire burning somewhere, making
the air dingy. Lying upstairs, the threesome heard the car shuffle the gravel.

"It's too hot for the bedrooms," Hélène commanded. "To the pool!"

She still had yet not risked the sepsis of the aquamarine pool that was
never once cleaned. Marcel and Roberto peeled off their bathing suits
and jumped in. Oh, it was so cold . . . "Look," Marcel indicated, "we have
shrunk down to nothing."

There was an earlier discussed plan of doubly entering Hélène, both at once. It was ruled out since Roberto's size and Marcel's width was already troubling when presented solo. But maybe the genitals fresh from the ice bath would allow the acrobatic feat to occur. Positions, everyone! Quickly . . . while the shrinking phenomenon obtains! Everything conspired against it. To lie on the cement apron of the pool meant ants, who began a parade up and over a leg or arm. Marcel and Roberto had to form a scissor formation to unite their genitals, and laughter kept breaking out, with their legs colliding. Hélène speedily tried to mount the unmountable tangle . . . when there was a cupboard door closed in the kitchen. With lightning-strike adrenaline, all three rolled immediately into the pool. They paddled to the side of the pool nearest to the cottage so it would not be so obvious that they were naked. Aunt Sidonie. The others had left her behind. She was shuffling around, scavenging for food. She was too short to have seen successfully out the kitchen window . . . How many times had she passed by the open door? She stood in the doorway with a piece of baguette and a plastic cup of wine, squinting at them all, wondering who was swimming—oh, just the kids—before she padded off to her cave and closed the door.

They looked at each other.

Hélène said simply, "We have become animals. And now I get to be infected from swimming in this piscine septique."

Tuesday. "Where are you going?" Madame Disse asked the threesome on their way to the car. "I thought we could all be together today." It was explained that Monsieur Hacquin hoped to play belote, and two compos mentis people needed to be on hand to participate, since Aunt Sidonie's attention wandered fatally for card games.

"Today is Pieds et Paquets Day," Hélène protested. They simply had to have real pieds et paquets, the Provençale specialty: sheep hooves (for which a special hook of a fork was provided) wrapped in tripe.

"I do not believe for a second you will eat a bite of it," Madame Disse said, taking their daily escape personally. "Even if you find it on offer."

"I love it. I have it every year," said Marcel.

"Liars, both of you," mumbled Madame Disse.

On the way to Cuges, Hélène turned instead down an unused lane to a closed-up farmhouse. A copse of trees appeared, and the road was wide enough for a car to pass; she pulled over. "I have nothing on under this dress," she announced.

This episode was not ideal. It was one hundred degrees, even in the shade. Gnats, flies, other flying things usually content to stay in the tall grass menaced and buzz-bombed them. Marcel was out of his clothes in record time, his head up Helen's skirt, his bare ass to the road. "What if someone . . . ," Roberto began, but that question answered itself before he could bring it out; these two were thrilled by the risk of being seen by a passing car. Roberto slapped Marcel's ass repeatedly. For a man with a strong shaven beard, wild ink-black hair to his shoulders, he had a remarkably smooth body as well as a smooth posterior. Roberto offered him a spanking, reaching between his legs to rub whatever came to hand of Marcel or Hélène . . . this caused enough ecstasy that Marcel's devotion to working on Hélène began to flag. Only Marcel seemed to enjoy this encounter, standing to deposit himself upon Hélène's dress, the seat of the Renault . . . and the dashboard, how did it get up there? Hélène found a rag in the trunk and tried to clean it all up. Like acid (which it was), Marcel's exuberance bizarrely discolored the sunbaked dashboard material as she scrubbed. Meanwhile, Roberto slapped at a mosquito. He had believed the wives' tale that there weren't mosquitoes in France until this moment.

"Soon," Hélène reported, back at the wheel, Cuges-les-Pins ahead, "I will have to make my annual pilgrimage to see my senile grandfather in that horrendous facility in Aix-en-Provence. It will become a point of family commentary otherwise."

"Pauvre toi," Marcel said. "A nice hour drive," he went on, "with Clementine and Sidonie. You can sit on Oncle Maurice's lap the whole way."

"I may drive my mother," she said, "leaving Oncle Maurice behind for you and Roberto to play with. You can peel back the Speedo to reveal your new toy for the afternoon."

They had been too personal with each other, too undignified, and their intimacy was entering its final phase: contempt.

Roberto had gained the telepathy about his partners that seeing all sides of them bestows. He knew Hélène would hate the thought of Marcel and him doing something without her; she would like to forbid it, but that might make it all the sweeter to Marcel when it happened anyway. Marcel was thinking of getting Roberto to himself; every time he looked at his new friend, he smiled back, one eyebrow raised, as if to say, *Put your mouth on me now.* Hélène and Roberto certainly enjoyed sex, but Marcel,

Roberto had decided, was a sex addict begging for round after round, his batteries always recharged, the tank never empty. And as for Roberto . . . to have two lovers who didn't seem to care if he brought an erection to the proceedings, in a summer house in Provence: this was about as good as it was going to get for him. And as for Hélène . . . this was a fantasy, for the woman who viewed *Jules et Jim* twenty times and didn't find the antics in *Les Valseuses* reprehensible. This was the sort of halcyon episode that would allow her to graduate to her thirties, to settle down with the next boyfriend she had, who would be a bit more bourgeois and propertied this time, no more shocks to Maman, someone who would provide a respectable pattern into which she could trim herself agreeably to fit.

There had been a bit of drama when they returned to Mas Disse. Hélène's grandfather continually rambled about the men, the men who wanted to know about the war, who came to talk to him all the time, because he was very important . . . all of which could be dismissed as his elderly confusion and high self-regard. But Aunt Sidonie was able to learn from one of the attendants, that yes, someone from the L'Office Central de Lutte contre les Crimes contre l'Humanité had been to the care facility, asking questions of several of the patients and residents.

"*Salauds,*" groaned Aunt Sidonie, waddling toward her room with a glass of cognac. Unspeakable grandstanding, Sidonie spat out in her provençal accent: *The Jews, the Jews, how they will not let it go . . . They want to see someone punished even if it is my brother, a wrong person. He was with the Maquisards!*

Roberto had found out what he could about Vichy France's Nazi collaboration, and local antihero Paul Touvier, on the internet. The eager helper of the SS had been housed and hidden for decades by the church. He had twice been sentenced to death in absentia for war crimes. In 1989, authorities found him in Nice, under the protection of radical schismatic priests, whose conspiracy showed that the hyper-Catholic church-state combo favored by Marechal Pétain, including the elimination of Jews, still had its adherents in the 1980s. It was learned that Touvier was hidden in more than *twenty* religious houses; sympathies could be traced as far up as the office of Pope Paul VI. Later, President Pompidou quietly pardoned Touvier for all crimes, but public outcry was ferocious. Pompidou then allowed Touvier to keep all his various properties, stolen from the Jews he had killed. Touvier was the sole Frenchman, in a nation full of Vichy atrocities, convicted for crimes against humanity.

But there were many reprisals for those aiding the enemy, much vigilante justice, with collaborators coughing up names of neighbors, old friends, old enemies. Now, perhaps just for the official record, the writers of French history wished to know what Auguste Disse was up to in 1944. Roberto felt none of this was his business and tried to edge himself out of the conversation, sidling toward the stairway.

Hélène stopped by his bedroom before she turned in to say she would go the next day to Aix to see her grandfather. Actually, the old patriarch came alive when she visited. Maybe she could persuade him not to talk to the investigators.

Roberto smiled from his too-short mattress and threadbare blanket. "Marcel and I will not do anything without you."

She smiled a little sadly. "You are moving on, probably not to be seen for another half decade. And Marcel is getting dumped. Soon I will be out of your lives, so do as you wish."

All was quiet the next morning with the women and Monsieur Hacquin departed, with Marcel sleeping in. Roberto made coffee and was determined to add to his Notebook. He had gone too long, in his mind, without producing one cultural thought amid the orgies and debauch . . .

Mas Disse had collected a pile of yellowed bestselling French paperbacks, comprising a discouraging number of American schlock writers translated for the international market. There was a ratty *Blue Guide* to France, so much like the one Roberto had lost years ago. Most study-abroad hosteling youth clung to their *Let's Go*s and their *Rough Guide*s, but when you wanted an exhaustive assessment of every village altar, cobblestone, doorknob, and scrap of woven cloth, then it was time to put aside childish things and graduate to the *Blue Guide* . . . well, the *Blue Guide* of the 1980s, if you could find it. Roberto hoped against hope it was the ill-tempered Ian Robertson edition, a man (British, surely) who carried on the tradition of the Murray Red Guides and John Ruskin's or Henry James's travel writings in which narration mixed with author prejudice to celebrate and condemn. A model for the *Notebooks of Roberto Costa*, once he attained that cultural confidence.

Indeed, it was Mr. Robertson! He riffled at random . . .

Lourdes: *Non-Catholics will be appalled by what they see at Lourdes, most of which is an affront to any instinct of veneration, and would do well to avoid the place entirely.* Lyon's Notre-Dame de Fourviére and Paris's Sacré-Coeur? *Both are equally hideous. It is only of interest for the meretricious splendour of its marble and mosaic decoration in a depraved taste, which should be seen to be believed.* Roberto liked the easy dismissals of little roadside villages one might have thought worth exploring . . . Quillebeuf (*a decaying fishing port*), Monaco (*this toy enclave*), Alès (*dreary*), Carcassonne (*some have said looks its best when seen from the motorway*), Rocamadour (*many would prefer the distant view, the closer merely provoking disillusion with its Saint-Sauveur restored out of all recognition or built in a bogus Romanesque style*). The newer *Blue Guide*s had softened and sweetened, coddling France and its treasures.

Roberto contemplated stealing this copy of his old friend. He opened the cover to see a name inscribed at the top right: his own. He must have lost it here, amid the daily conflict-management with Hélène back in 2003 . . .

Brushing against the topic of France's medieval treasures reminded him of his duty to out-culture his sister. Though he had not visited Moissac on this particular trip, Rachel would not know that, so he decided to goad her with a monument that he knew she had yet to see. He texted: YOU SEE WHAT AWAITS YOU, A WANTON WOMAN OF LUXURIOUS VICE. YOU MIGHT ENDURE THE VIPERS ON THE BREASTS, BUT SERPENTS UP THE VAGINA?

His phone dinged. Rachel was answering.

NOW NOW, THE SNAKE UP THE VAGINA MIGHT HAVE ITS MERITS, Rachel texted.

Moissac, she texted, was an unfair sucker punch, given her yearning to go, given her poverty to not, but he had yet to go to the immense trouble to drive to Conques, which rules supreme among Romanesque tympana. She texted: CHECK YOUR EMAIL. PERHAPS YOU IMAGINE YOURSELF THE YOUNG MAN AT THE DIVIDING LINE BETWEEN HEAVEN AND HELL, BEING NOTICED BY THE DEMON AS HAVING BARELY MADE THE CUT . . . BUT IN TRUTH YOU ARE AMONG THE DAMNED, BEING FED INTO THE BEAST TO BE CHEWN AND DIGESTED AND SHAT OUT INTO HELL .

He texted back: THE ONLY TORTURES AHEAD FOR ME ARE 1) YOUR COMPANY, AND 2) MERLE'S AND 3) YOUR RACK-LIKE SOFA.

And now Rachel was calling. "About that," she began. "This staying on my couch at the end of the month? Merle has forbidden it."

"Hmm. She canceled her trip to stay home and make sure I did not enter the sacred precincts?"

"No, she's still visiting her mother in Tours."

Rachel didn't add any explanation, so Roberto prompted her. "And . . . and I can't stay there even when she's gone?"

"It will mean drama for me. It will take us weeks to get back to normal after defying her. You should have at least pretended to play along with her CIA theory for my benefit. She'll try to blackmail Dad, he'll laugh her out of the room, and she'll try to contact journalists, and they'll laugh her out of the room, and then it *will be over.* But now she's furious, determined to prove you wrong, staying up and not sleeping, trying to add to her dossier."

"Her insanity is only rivaled by yours for staying with someone like her."

"Merle knows a lot, young one, about what's happening in New York. Hightower Wiggins is going *down,* and there will be *no* money but what Dad can grab on the way out the door and what we can grab from him. You're either with us or against us."

"Really? You're quoting George W. Bush?"

"Go stay on Rupesh's couch," she concluded. "He'll take you in."

Spain, 2002

The trip to Spain in 2002, right after the Michael McCord incident, did not seem to Roberto to promise any fun or pleasure whatsoever. Rachel had returned to the United States; she had started some therapy at their father's insistence, but was mostly climbing the walls, declaring she did not need further babysitting or imprisoning. The only cure was for her to be allowed to go back to Europe and continue her monographs, her thesis, her researches in art history. Sal Costa relented, but he had one more demand: that she and her brother spend some time somewhere other than Paris with its bad memories and toxic life patterns. Roberto was in Barcelona that summer, so that meant Spain.

"Look," Sal said to Roberto by phone from New York, "I just wanna make sure she's all right and won't start up a similar relationship again with someone new. Take her around Spain, let her look at Romantic architecture to her heart's content."

"Romanesque," Roberto corrected quietly.

This project would be subsidized by Sal Costa. Rent an apartment somewhere, an automatic car, eat all the kinds of *jamón* (Rachel wasn't a vegetarian yet), drink all the wines! Maybe Rachel would open up and the Costa siblings could be friends at last. Roberto did not want Rachel opened up; he wanted her sealed airtight in an impermeable container.

His summer was looking like one long list of obligations. He had also promised Rupesh that he would meet him in Europe. The Rupesh-Roberto friendship had been, admittedly, an awkward history with their Parisian sexual antics always in the air between them:

Rupesh had asked to be roommates their prep school senior year at

Brockton, and Roberto couldn't think of an inoffensive excuse not to. Besides, there were two other guys in the suite. Rupesh never made any overt passes, but he stared longingly at Roberto when depressed, collided with Roberto in the small hallway when drunk, stealing the slightest and least consequential of physical contacts, yet Roberto sensed he was fed by them. And then, one day, like a switch was flipped, Rupesh got over it. His last half of senior year at Brockton was spent chasing after some sophomore dweeb, whose blond physiognomy (and body shaving for the swim team) rendered him perfectly prepubescent. Roberto, for the rest of his prep school days, was off the hook.

Rupesh was one of those guys who was smart without seeming smart in the least; he had never been caught studying—there were not even rumors of him working—yet he aced all his classes. Rupesh did not seem even to care for knowledge, learning, human attainments; his public persona was notoriously philistine.

"Why do you want to study foreign languages, Bobby?" he would ask. "There are plenty of people who speak them already, better than you ever will."

"I dunno, Roop. Lots of Study Abroad and drinking high-quality beer in Europe. The girls who major in foreign languages are the hottest, scientific studies have shown."

Yeah, there had been a bit too much of that hetero performing back then, hoping to short-circuit any master plan Rupesh might have of following Roberto to Brown for romantic reasons. But Brown was his friend's choice, for which Rupesh had to cajole his father considerably because Mr. Doshi had never heard of it. Rupesh had first applied to Amherst under the impression that it was solely a men's school; that's what some yellowed U.S. college guide moldering in the Ahmedabad public library had informed him. His father urged Harvard, Yale, Penn, but Rupesh lied and said he did not get into any of them, which he did. Rupesh had no intention of breaking a sweat in his university years—Sloan, Wharton, HBS, the schools urged by his father would certainly require a work regimen that would interfere with his Game Boy time on the sofa.

Roop and Bobby, inseparable at Brockton, went their separate ways at Brown, past a few freshman-year tours of Roberto's personal landmarks of Providence—chowder from Mort's (Roop: "Like drywall made into a soup") and Olneyville hot dogs (Roop: "This would be better in a roti with curry sauce, but then it would not be American, because it would possess flavor"). They did not really reconnect until their senior year, when Roberto was taking his spring classes in Europe and came back stateside on rare occasions. Over beers at the Wild Colonial, they hatched a plan to meet up in Europe. Who better than Roberto Costa, honorary Eurotrash, speaker of five or six languages, as a tour guide?

"And we should put it on our list to have lots of sex," Rupesh said with great earnestness.

Roberto was about to answer when Rupesh broke in:

"I mean with Spanish people. Not you and me."

Roberto said, "Oh, I knew what you meant." So, Roberto thought, it really *was* over, whatever was teased and tortured between them.

Roberto had uncharitably decided the promised trip for Rupesh (which, now that it was upon him, he was not enthusiastic about) and the dreary dealing with his depressed sister could be one and the same chore, combined, gotten over with. He would present it to Rupesh as a fait accompli so he couldn't agitate about his sister's presence beforehand. In the meantime, Rachel—hours before getting on her transatlantic flight—had texted: GIVE ME ONE REASON TO SHACKLE MYSELF TO YOU FOR THREE WEEKS. HAVING SECOND THOUGHTS ABOUT YOUR COMPANIONSHIP FOR LONGER THAN A FEW HOURS.

To this, Roberto sent her email account a photo:

Then he texted, UNCASTILLO—AND THERE ARE FOUR OTHER 12TH C. CHURCHES IN THE SAME VILLAGE. WE'LL PROBABLY BE THE ONLY TOURISTS THERE TOO.

He added, I LOVE THE GUY HOLDING BACK THE JOWLS OF THE MONSTER.

And with no response, he texted, OR WAS YOUR INTEREST IN ROMANESQUE ANOTHER FRAUD TO MAKE PEOPLE THINK YOU'RE CULTURED?

Finally Rachel texted: JUST SEE IF YOU CAN NOT TALK TO ME FOR THE NEXT THREE WEEKS. SEE YOU TOMORROW IN SARAGOSSE.

Roberto smiled. His sister didn't know it, but she was going to fall in love with Spain, an open-air Romanesque museum, its twelfth-century life frozen in the sleepy mountain villages. He'd have her trading in her French (*Saragosse*) and properly lisping away like an aragonésa: Zaragoza, *Tharagotha*.

Roberto met Rupesh at the Barcelona airport. A taxi ride back to the city passed an appalling number of road prostitutes flagging the passing truckers for some semi-visible-to-all action behind the bushes.

"A glimpse of India," Rupesh said solemnly. "I am always a little bit happy when I see that Europe or the United States is not so terribly different from my country in its demerits."

Rupesh slept off his jet lag on the train ride to Zaragoza. Roberto sat opposite him and could take the time to stare at how his school friend had changed. Rupesh, in his Amsterdam phase, now attained a high level of grooming: sharply defined eyebrows, a beard shadow managed exactingly at its edges, some skin treatment that made him glow golden in the bleary light from the train window. His oil-black hair had strands that gleamed collectively at the beginning of their curl.

Rupesh remained semiconscious on the trip to Zaragoza's jungle gym of an airport to pick up a rental car and await the arrival of Rachel Costa.

"The airport code for Zaragoza," reported Rupesh through a yawn, "is Z-A-Z. So that's something."

Roberto warned his friend, as the Arrivals board showed Rachel's flight was ATERRIZADO, "Rachel is likely to be morose, pessimistic, nihilist, belittling."

"Then we are destined to get along just fine. You might as well know, Bobby, I am done being the good-natured, smiling Indian minstrel for American people's amusement. From here on out, you must prepare to deal with the real me."

"Okay," said Roberto without any emotion. "I never thought of you as smiling and good-natured. I thought of you as malcontent and petulant."

"Really?" He was briefly disappointed. "Well, I am more so now."

Rachel appeared last among the passengers, dragging two large suitcases and burdened by a knapsack nearly her size. Roberto inserted an unreturned hug and took the larger of the suitcases.

"Who's the extra person?" Rachel asked, barely giving Rupesh a glance. "Is he helping with the baggage?"

Rupesh arched his eyebrows but wasn't really offended. "Oh, because I am Indian, I am here to be your baggage wallah, following your orders."

"I thought you might be Ecuadorian. They usually do all the scut work in Spain. You do appear Indian. On second look." Rachel then looked at Roberto. "Are you two fucking?"

They were stunned silent for a moment, then Rupesh said no, and Roberto said yes simultaneously.

Now Rachel looked more critically at Rupesh. "Nice pull, Bobby. You always could get the hotties. Okay, pretty boy, get the other bag."

On the way to the rental car, Rupesh whispered his question to Roberto: Why did he say they were a couple? "She's a fag hag from her earliest years," Roberto whispered back. "She'll treat you much more nicely."

Roberto had planned nothing much for the first half day, and sullen, silent Rachel did not appear capable of being entertained on the drive from the airport. Roberto figured they'd settle in at the two-bedroom apartment on the main square, part of Sal Costa's deluxe vacation subsidy. The crushing gigantesque Basilica of Our Lady of the Pillar was right there, so they walked the several football fields of pavement to go inside and abase themselves before the pillar where the Virgin appeared to St. James, the first Marian apparition . . . which was even more amazing given that Mary was still alive back in Palestine. She must have been burnishing her teleportation skills for all the future apparitions to come.

"Her feast day is in a few weeks," Roberto noted.

"Let's clear out of town before that shit show," said Rachel.

The basilica was a high-ceilinged stone box with a central closed-off choir, no aisle, no nave, no transept, the compartmentalized way the Spanish built cathedrals in the Renaissance, in Sevilla, in Grenada, and so on. Rows of side chapels were either unused and forgotten or kitschy with bleeding saint statues and attended by the proliferate elderly ladies in black.

"Monstrous," Rachel mumbled, looking around inside. A two-minute look-around was enough; Rachel was back out on the plaza.

On their way to dinner, they passed the church on the opposite end of the square, La Seo, and its intricate tile-and-brick wall courtesy of Islamic influence.

"Here we go," Rachel said in her debut of approving of something. "We will have to have a Mudejar Day."

"Mother's Day?" Rupesh wondered.

"Mu-de-jar," Roberto clarified.

Rupesh asked, "And why must it have its own day?"

Rachel: "There will be many *themed* days as we see all there is to see. I will plan and declare the themes, plot the itineraries, and you will willingly come along and be enlightened. I control the itinerary for two days, then, I suppose, Bobby will get a day."

"What about me?" Rupesh asked.

"You do not get a day. It is your greatest privilege and honor to be allowed to come along on my days. You will be obliged to suffer through Bobby's day—and we saw how mediocre his trip planning was by his making me go in the basilica of the stupid pillar."

They stopped while Roberto used an ATM. "I thought," Roberto said, defending himself, "that you'd be tired from the flight and we would have a light day."

"An under-ten-church tourism day in a place like Spain is malpractice. We could have left the airport, made a run for Daroca, and still made it back here before sunset to sit around and have tapas."

"Who made you the boss of us?" Rupesh asked, before Rachel's expression caused him to shrink into himself.

"Because I have . . . *der Koch*."

Rupesh's mind went *very much* the wrong place.

Roberto helped. "She has the bible that every European art and architecture student venerates and learns everything from, Wilfried Koch's never-to-be-equaled book of drawings. Everything built by the ancient Greeks to the moderns, all drawn in meticulous diagrams by Herr Koch himself and his children." Who, judging by the immense effort, must

have never had a life outside their father's masterwork. A German ideal.

At the restaurant, Rachel went into her knapsack and brought it out, held it like one would the tablets fresh from Mount Sinai. Wilfried Koch's *Baustilkunde*. Not merely were there diagrammed drawings of every significant building in Europe—Parthenon and Pantheon, Ravenna to

Reims, dimensional floor plans—but also impossibly researched maps where each of the thousand dots represented a church in which some remnant of Merovingian or Carolingian or Visigothic or Romanesque architecture survived—all waiting for the One True Tourist, the Completist . . . Roberto knew his sister. They would see every dot.

Rupesh: "I take it the Costa family does not go to the beach and just enjoy it?"

Rachel said, "To lie on rocks, burning in the sun, with the prospect of swimming in the swill of the Mediterranean?"

Roberto was lost for a second, thinking of his great love Valentina and their sex-sodden holiday in Málaga, but he nonetheless chipped in, "No, we don't do beaches."

"We grew up on the sea; it's no big deal," Rachel said.

"What," protested Rupesh, "is a bigger deal than the sea?"

The next morning, they were roused at seven, unlike anyone else for a hundred square miles, apparently. No time to mess around for a breakfast. Spain had no takeaway coffee culture in 2002; Rupesh had to make do with a tiny paper-cup espresso from a gas station.

"These travel conditions are already intolerable!" Rupesh cried from his backseat exile. "You are like a dictator!"

"Generalísimo Franco may be gone, but there is now *La* Generalísima." She paused as if there might be rebellion. There was not.

Roberto instructed, "All sibilants are *t-h*'s. Make the *g* a guttural *h, cch-eneralíthima.*" Rachel never said it the anglicized way again.

It was Cloister Day, and nearby Huesca was worked over, top to bottom. Often these sites forbade photography, which made Rachel only more determined . . . lining up Roberto and Rupesh as human shields while she snapped unobserved the best of the Romanesque capitals atop the columns. One column in the shadows needed the tripod, so she sent Rupesh to the museum guard's desk to jabber at him in Gujarati and create a distraction while she worked.

If the boys thought languorous lunches and lazy siestas were going to constitute a respite, here too they were wrong. Rachel assigned *readings.* Like Mary Poppins's portmanteau, no end of Penguin paperbacks, xeroxed stacks of papers, pamphlets, art books could be produced from her luggage and knapsack at a moment's notice.

Rachel returned from the WC. "I don't see anyone reading," she said.

Rachel directed Roberto to read aloud a marked passage in *Mont-Saint-Michel and Chartres* by Henry Adams: "*Young people rarely enjoy the Romanesque. They prefer the Gothic . . . No doubt they are right, since they are young: but men and women who have lived long and are tired—who want rest—who have done with aspirations and ambition—whose life has been a broken arch—feel this repose and self-restraint as they feel nothing else. The quiet strength of these curved lines, the solid support of these heavy columns, the moderate proportions, even the modified lights, the absence of display, of effort, of self-consciousness, satisfy them as no other art does. They come back to it to rest, after a long circle of pilgrimage—the cradle of rest from which their ancestors started.*"

"That," Rachel said, closing her eyes, aligning her face to the sun, "cannot be improved upon. Do you or do you not, Mr. Doshi, understand the difference between the Romanesque of the 1100s and the Gothic of the late 1200s?"

"Gothic is the pointy arch, and Romanesque is the rounded arch—"

"Gothic," she sneered, personally affronted by the Gothic period, "is the beginning of the Disney-fication of religious art and observance. From Burgos in Spain to Amiens in France, Cologne in Germany, anywhere you care to look from the 1200s onward, the statues are stamped out of a mold. Famous artistic families, guilds, for lucrative centuries-long contracts, cranked out Marys and Matthew-Mark-Luke-and-Johns for church doorways, one indistinguishable from the other, the regional, local, pagan roots erased utterly for church conformity."

"You sound like you would tear down all the Gothic cathedrals," Rupesh ventured.

"It's an eventual project. After I raze all the boring-as-shit Renaissance buildings from existence."

"Hear, hear," Roberto said to be agreeable.

"The figures on a Romanesque doorway were a collage, an effort of hundreds of unknown anonymous artists, sometimes crudely amateur. You see the pagan gods, mythical monsters that were believed in—griffins, phoenixes, dragons. You see the horrors of hell, you see raunch and porn, like the Celtic sheela-na-gig exposing her mermaid vagina—she shows up all over Europe. You see the medieval imagination, produced by artists who believed in it all."

"And you believe in God too?" Rupesh checked.

"Of course not, but I'm moved by the fact that they believed. On Notre-Dame in Paris, you can wander the roof, and you see stone faces, gargoyles, monsters, saints that no one could ever observe, before the days of guided roof tours. The artists put them there because they thought *God* was watching. He would see their work and be pleased."

There were two bedrooms in the rented apartment, one with a queen-size bed (which Rachel claimed against arguments that Roberto, the driver, the largest and weariest, should have the biggest bed). That left Rupesh and Roberto with the other bedroom with its two twin beds, and Roberto having to sleep diagonally with his feet hanging off the end.

"I thought you said she was a basket case," Rupesh said from his own bed. "Weak from a bad breakup."

"I guess she's worked through those issues," Roberto said, looking at Rupesh, shirtless with his pajama bottoms. "Roop, you had those pj's at Brockton. How old are those?"

Rupesh stirred in the bed. "They have been washed."

Crypt Day proved more adventurous than it sounded; many crypts had narrow, steep passageways under the church altar, some were at-your-own-risk, some were forbidden entry—not that that stopped Rachel, who set aside barricades and unhooked chains with such authority that even the sextons humbly accepted it. Aínsa, then the monastery at Leyre, San Esteban at Sos del Rey Católicos . . .

Then came the Road to Santiago Day. Roberto drove them to Jaca for a thorough tracing of the pilgrimage route to Santiago. The gray arched nave of Jaca was the first-ever Romanesque church in Spain, from 1063. The porch and outer doors, which time had softened, were plain, unrenovated; this was more or less the very bare, simple church that the eleventh-century pilgrim to Compostela prayed in, gave thanks in for surviving the snow of the Pirineos. Roberto, now reading *The Tragic Sense of Life*, quoted from Miguel de Unamuno: "*It is with landscapes as with architecture, nakedness is the last aspect you learn to appreciate.*"

Rachel paused. "Send me that. That's my epigraph before my future book on Romanesque."

"I was going to use it in my Notebooks."

"In my book, it will stand a chance of actually being read by other human beings."

Jaca was before the monastery of San Juan de la Peña, tucked spectacularly into a cliff, and then Santa Cruz de la Serós, then Ares, then Ruesta, then Sangüesa, where, when Rachel's back was turned, Rupesh mouthed, "Make it stop," to Roberto. Later to Rachel, Rupesh braved, "We have done Romanesque Day. Let us move on to, say, wine country and the sampling of wines."

She was quiet a moment, gauging the degree of necessary punishment for that remark. "Every day," she said, "is Romanesque Day."

Yet for the surface show of resistance, Rupesh made a great assistant to Rachel. Setting up and steadying her tripod, fetching rolls of film from her bag, marking on the film canisters which portal of what church in what village resided on the exposed film, even delicately, charmingly asking people not to walk into Rachel's shot as they came and went to their sanctuaries for mass.

At a gas station on the drive back to Zaragoza, Rachel relinquished her passenger-seat privileges and hopped in the back with Rupesh; they began to discuss life matters, only some of which Roberto could overhear. Roberto reflected on how Rachel, who generally hated all his friends, and how Rupesh, who generally connected badly with women, were getting along. Roberto wondered if Rupesh was faking his wide-eyed enthusiasm and—for that matter—if Rachel was being gently patronizing. But no, they were bonding, bonding over art and architecture.

Rupesh pulled out his iPod from his pack to show Rachel the Dharmanath Temple in Kerala. "And Dilwara, you see? Famous for its interior. You see that we have amazing carvers too, you know.."

Roberto peeked at his backseat passengers; Rachel was actually smiling.

At dinner, Rachel and Rupesh competed with their personal trainwreck lives, trying to outdo each other, unified by their world of awful men on offer. Occasionally, they would both look at Roberto as if it were his role to answer for pathetic masculinity worldwide. And what despicable families they both had!

"I'm sitting right here," Roberto reminded her.

Back in their rented apartment on the Plaza Nuestra Señora del Pilar, Rachel gathered up Wilfried Koch's tome to take to her bedroom to strategize the next day's itinerary, but she paused and looked at her companions.

"For a pair of young lovers," she said, "you two barely touch each other. C'mon, kiss in front of me."

Roberto and Rupesh did so. But Rachel squinted, not convinced. "Not very passionate."

"We've been a couple for a while," Rupesh said.

"The thrill is gone," Roberto said, shrugging.

That night, Rupesh sat restlessly for a few minutes on his bed, grabbed his blanket and bathrobe, and told Roberto he was going to bunk with Rachel for the night. Roop and Rachel would cuddle . . . which might do them both some good. Rachel and her pet boy. Roberto contrarily loved the crisp solitude of the old-fashioned Spanish bedroom, the sere, starched sheets, the heavy, oaken, black furniture from some aristocrat's estate sale, the simple crucifix above the bed. Driving and wrestling the steering wheel of the SEAT Ibiza on the mountain roads had made Roberto's chest tight. He popped another nitro tablet and fell into a catatonic sleep.

Rachel arrived at breakfast with two small boxes: Family Tree home-testing DNA kits. "I *know* I'm some part Jewish," she said. "This will prove it. I got the family pack, one for you, and for Lena and Dad too."

"You want to be Jewish?" Rupesh asked, coming to this topic late.

"We Portuguese are a jumble of North Africa and Spain, Semites and the Celts. How unlikely is it that I make the twenty-five percent cut, which qualifies me for the Ziffer-Katz Fellowship at Tel Aviv University? They pick lots of non-Jewish winners, of course, but only the Jews get to be on the kibbutz, and *I want the kibbutz!*"

"Our genetics will come out more or less the same," Roberto said, eyes closed, sipping espresso.

"Wrong again, Bobby. Sibling results can vary widely." She spoke to her brother like a kindergartner: "Now if you'd listened to Ms. Da Silva in biology class, you would know that. What if you're twenty-six percent Jewish and I'm seventeen percent? I bet Dad is Semitic as fuck. Lena, who knows—probably all the rubbish DNA of New England in one trash can."

"Oh, I wonder what mine would say," Rupesh enthused. "It would destroy my father if I could prove we were Pashtun or Balochi, actually Muslim, so of course I would very, very much like for that to be the case."

Rachel relented and let Rupesh have one of the kits.

Rupesh at Tudela Cathedral, Navarre

Navarre, the little province next to Zaragoza's mighty Aragón, under-touristed except for when the bulls are running in Pamplona, yet a region once powerful enough to claim the French throne. The trio parked outside the old city of Tudela and walked the alleys to see the cathedral's famous doorway with a hundred-plus figures from the Bible arranged on the arch of the sanctuary doors. On the left side (the right hand of a judging Christ), the saints; on the right side, the damned. At the base they were vertical, but as the arch came to a point, the figures were aimed head-to-head.

"Nyeh, late Romanesque," pronounced Rachel. "Better than a poke in the eye, but one feels the taint of Gothic on the horizon."

Rupesh sputtered, "Did you notice the storks on all the chimneys? Wait, you guys, I want to take a picture . . ."

Rachel's military campaign did not permit time for storks. "On to Soria. Onward!"

After a frustrating hour trying to find a working ATM in Tudela, and a scorching commute across the red flatlands of Castille, they arrived in Soria at siesta time. It was depopulated, another city of the dead. The doorway of Santo Domingo was remarkably uneroded and intact; surprisingly detailed figures representing biblical episodes . . . some quite obscure. Rupesh helped Rachel set up her tripod, and then went in search of a Coca-Cola.

Rachel excitedly read from Cees Nooteboom: "*What, I wonder, is so attractive about all this? I stand in front of the Santo Domingo . . . Is it the simplicity, if that word is at all justifiable? The piety? The unshakable totality of a world view? . . . The idea that this was ever new! New! Just finished, hewn out of those almost golden blocks of hard stone! How proud the makers were, how everyone in the province crowded to see the sight! Is Nooteboom still alive, Bobby? I may have to sleep with him.*" But Rachel trailed off at the sight of Rupesh, walking hobbled from the tangle of streets to the right. He had a young girl affixed to his leg; he was dragging her, she was wailing and begging.

Rachel sighed. "I'll get my photos quick. The Gypsies are in town."

Roberto decided to stand nearby—he would be giant and hulking, lest any of the girl's compatriots appeared to make a run for the camera and tripod.

"Por favor," the young girl keened, her voice filling the square in a mix of Spanish and English: "Please, just some money, a euro, two euros, you can afford it señor, good señor, por Jesucristo, they beat me if I don't bring the money. I am such a poor girl, so sad, so sad." She showed a burnt place on her palm, as if it had been held over a candle. Rupesh did not speak Spanish enough for her appeal to make sense to him; one hand he kept in his pocket where his wallet was . . . he knew the trick of someone distracting you with their hands at crotch level, while they slipped their hand in a back pocket for your wallet. Roberto looked around the plaza—was anyone seeing this? It would be unpleasant to disrupt the afternoon siesta, but the locals would have no sympathy for the girl. It would be even less pleasant if her relatives, lurking in the plaza shadows, were watching—watching to see that she gave a proper performance, either coming to her aid, or punishing her harshly if she failed to produce a coin from her target.

The girl was defiant. Five euros, she demanded. Rupesh, veteran of the indefatigable beggars in his own land, would have dragged the Romani girl to Barcelona and back without paying a tenth of a rupee, but he wanted his friends' photographic mission to continue, so he surrendered and brought out a five-euro note. He held it higher than she could jump for.

Someone in this siesta-dead plaza must have heard the commotion, peeked from their shutters, then called the police. A police car cruised into the street before the church, pulling up quietly. When the girl saw the officers, she turned and ran, without the five-euro note.

The photography reestablished itself, but everyone was more somber about it. Rachel read from Nooteboom again, but the original enchantment had slipped away. There had been an idea to stay in Soria, have a little night away from the Zaragoza plaza and the monstrous basilica whose offense magnified for Rachel each and every day, but they decided to return, after all, to the Aragonese capital.

"Bobby," Rupesh asked, slumped affectionately against Rachel in the back seat, "didn't your mother have a Gypsy charity among her scams?"

"Yes," Rachel answered for her brother. "She raised quite a bit for that one—a memorial to the Gypsies lost in the Holocaust. That'll be my luck, right? The DNA test will come back one-third Gypsy and no Jewish, whaddya bet?" She sat up straight to accuse Rupesh. "The Roma are Indian in origin. What do you have to say for yourself?"

"She was dirty," Rupesh noted, "but her hair was lustrous, like an Indian's. We have the world's best hair. We make all the wigs."

That night, Roberto was so exhausted he could barely make a fist, and as he burrowed down into his crisp sheets, there was a faint knock at his bedroom door.

Rupesh hissed, "Bobby, it's me."

Roberto let Rupesh inside. He was wearing only his pajama bottoms.

"I am back in here tonight. Do you mind?"

Rupesh suggested they push the twin beds together, which they did.

"Did Rachel throw you out?" Roberto asked as they scooted the beds toward each other.

"Yes, sort of. I asked her each night about Michael and if she has recovered, and she always says a little something, then shuts down. So I began my series of prying questions again, and she pushed me out the door."

Roberto mentioned that all attempts at therapy in New York had been derailed as well. "It was nice of you to try to be her friend. Few have succeeded at that."

Roberto returned to the enlarged bed. "I'll snore less if I sleep on my side . . . like this. You have room?" As they jostled, Rupesh's knee hit Roberto's lower back in transition. "Ow."

Rupesh reported, "That was my erect penis."

"Felt like a knee. Is your penis erect? Will this be an issue?"

"My ardor for you has long cooled. Go ahead and check. You'll see I'm completely flaccid, even pressed up against you."

Roberto decided to call his bluff. He was hard as a rock.

"Ha-ha, fooled you. Made you touch it—yes!"

"You've got me going a little bit too," Roberto said, realizing what he was inviting.

Rupesh reached over . . . "The proportions, Bobby, I well recall." After a moment, he let go. "I wouldn't exactly say that was hard. Story of my life. Inspirer of semi-erections."

"No, you should be flattered. More and more, that is as hard as it gets." Roberto turned so he wasn't molestable; he nestled into his pillow. "My circulation is getting worse. I have mild neuropathy in my feet and fingertips. You remember at Brockton, that casual game of volleyball where I was killing it, making every point, and then I fainted?"

"Oh yes. Bobby, I—who am not Christian—went and prayed in the chapel for you. Then I went back to my room and asked the Indian gods. It's probably why you are alive."

"I was told if I had penis reduction surgery"—Rupesh was already laughing—"that I might get myself fully hard again."

"Well, why not? It'd still be big at half the size."

"That's all we need, something to go wrong with surgery like that."

Rupesh then asked, "You think about dying young?"

"Several times a day."

"No one's given you a timeline or anything, right?"

"I have to have the aorta resected sometime before I get too much older. Doctors are all full of pep talks. I feel like a doomed Henry James heroine, being told to go live, live all I can, follow my dreams, while they shake their heads at the nurse the second I'm out the door. So I live. I travel and do as I please, fill the Notebook with observations about languages and culture. Make friends, attempt intimacy from time to time."

Rupesh put a gentle hand on Roberto's shoulder. "You and your sister need to back away from all things to do with Henry James. Such is my suggestion."

"My dad's got the bad heart too. Although I'm not sure if he has the sexual component. I sometimes wonder which of us will go first. I can't think of a world without my dad, but it would be worse if I went first." Roberto wondered if Rupesh, whose breathing had turned regular, had fallen asleep. "You still awake?"

"Henry James . . . We were eating the ham . . ."

Nope, he was falling asleep. Roberto rolled to his side again, aware Rupesh's penis was still straining against his underwear, trespassing upon Roberto's lower back. Wow, Roberto thought, hard *while asleep*. What he wouldn't give! Roberto adjusted himself and soon fell into the well-deserved sleep of those who march in the service of La Generalísima.

Art Museum Day.

Frescoes Day (which edged them into Catalunya).

Monastery Day.

No breakfast or lunch was allowed to proceed without chores related to Rachel's many projects. One day, Roberto and Rachel wrote recommendation letters for each other, for Rachel's dreamed-of kibbutz residency, for Roberto's perpetual attempt to get into the Camargo Foundation, an artists' colony atop the white cliffs of the Calanques on the Côte d'Azur—Rachel even wrote his rec letter in French.

"It can mean nothing, surely," said Rupesh. "A brother writing for a sister, a sister writing for a brother."

Rachel wrote under Raquel Malfada (her second last name, in Iberian fashion, technically legal); Roberto Costa stayed Roberto Costa. They wrote glowing recommendations from the East Providence Center for the Arts . . . a bogus not-for-profit created by Lena. When it was refused 501(c) (3) status, Lena gave it up, but there was a gross of stationery to be used.

"You should write me a letter, Roop," Rachel said, not looking up from her typing.

"But I am nobody anyone should listen to."

Roberto: "Use some big, long Indian name no white person can pronounce and claim some dreary provincial polytechnic. No one, I promise, will ever make the long-distance call to a place asleep while we are awake to follow up."

Rupesh crossed his arms. "You make fun of your mother, but you are as corrupt as she is. You both understand that, do you not?"

On day fourteen, day fifteen, whatever it was, Rupesh detected, at long last, a certain exhaustion setting in among the culture-a-holics, and he struck at this moment of vulnerability and demanded a day where drinks by a hotel pool would be the theme. Rachel momentarily weakened; her hip travel guide had mentioned a lesbian night held at a downtown Zaragoza gay club. Only elderly Cees Nooteboom, alone among men, had a shot at her modest favors; all other males on the planet were off the list. But they must see one architectural treasure to assuage her guilt for playing hooky. So they went to Alquézar.

Here, after trudging up a mountain in the little village where the monastery was perched, they found the mother lode for a paper Rachel wished to write but felt had too little evidence—medieval, doctrinally correct representations of the Trinity. Here the medieval artist showed the creation of Adam, perpendicular across the lap of God, who had three heads—Father, Son, Spirit—with angels holding open the circular border . . .

What was it? The womb of the world? The stone around the tripartite god and his creation was dyed red, the paint having lasted for centuries in the arid desert plain.

"Holy Mother of God," Rachel mumbled, moved, her mind writing the monograph in her head on the spot.

"That is so good!" Rupesh even agreed, helping her with the tripod. "Of course, India has gods with many heads, many arms. Again, we invented that."

And that put an end to any notion of lollygagging by a pool, long sleep-ins at the apartment, staying up too late at clubs. Nope, their bible had fallen into disuse, the spectacular scholarship of Wilfried Koch had been ignored, his disciples had turned away from their god just as the Israelites had abandoned Yahweh and built a calf of gold . . . Rupesh later saw Roberto and Rachel poring over Koch's compendium, open on the hood of the rental car as they decided where to go next. Rupesh leaned in to see the innumerable small dots, each dot representing a church, and this map just the early Romanesque, with other pages of maps with even more dots, for the late Romanesque, the Mudejar . . .

"No," he asserted, actually stomping a foot. "I will not go to all these dots! You are going to lose your wallah! I will get on a train and leave you behind."

They stared at him, a little annoyed they had to be diverted from their planning with the map.

"You are *not* normal human beings! You cannot see everything there is to see in Europe! After you polish off this whatever-it-is, this old dead road to Santiago, then there is Andalusia. There is every village in France with a church. And Italy, Germany, everything—and you cannot see it all! Why are you being ridiculous?"

They weren't listening.

"Baños de Cerrato," Rachel mentioned, "was misidentified as Visigothic for years, and there's a shelf of scholarship attributing the horseshoe arch to the Visigoths rather than the Muslims—"

"Since the church is 690 and the Muslims didn't get to Spain until 710."

"Though founded in the 600s, the nave's arches are 900s."

"But we still have to see it," Roberto prompted.

"Of course we have to see it," she said.

Rupesh's attempt to gang up on the Costas was once again futile. "Do you hear yourselves? You have a . . . a compulsion, you understand? You must beware not to become too refined for the world in which you must make your way."

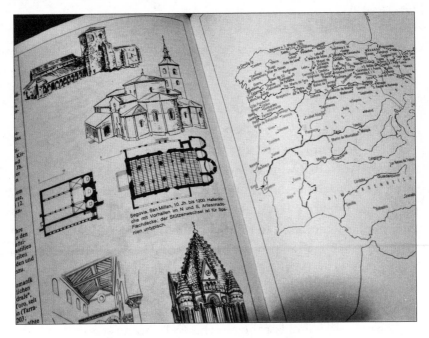

"Oh, Roopisimo," Rachel said. "That ship sailed long ago."

That night, Roberto returned to the apartment after raiding the one late-night Zaragoza convenience store they had been able to find. He found tiny bottles of rioja, little screw-top bottles, one of which he passed to Rupesh.

"What else," Rupesh asked, seeing the bag of toiletries, "do you have there?"

Roberto cagily, making a show of it, brought out some kind of oil, a fleet enema, some sanitary wipes . . . and a box of condoms.

"You have found someone for a date tonight? I will not give you the satisfaction of being jealous and playing some torrid scene—"

"Roop. It's for you and me."

Rupesh stared for a moment, unreadable.

"You are versatile, yes? You do both, topping, bottoming?"

Rupesh's eyes widened, and he quickly worked through his stupefaction. "You want me to . . ."

"I've been thinking. One day, perhaps, this . . ." Roberto made a clutch of his genitals through his underwear. "This may give out entirely. But there are other ways to explore the body, other ways to receive pleasure. If you're up for it. You have said I am too big to do *you*, so that leaves one choice, doesn't it?"

Rupesh nodded as if this were merely a logical procession of normal events. "Yes, I suppose we must . . . must do the other. Am I the first to do this to you?"

"Yes."

"I know when you lie. I am not the first."

"Yes, I was lying. But I've only been passive a time or two."

"We will pretend I am first and that we are in love."

"I do love you. That will not require pretending."

A brief trip to the bathroom to prepare, and Roberto returned to the room to find Rupesh naked in bed waiting for him. Rupesh, with hands and kisses, helped himself to his much taller, broader friend—there was almost too much man to process properly. But between kisses, he whispered, "I do this on the condition, Bobby, that we do not travel to every dot in Mr. Koch's book."

Roberto kissed his neck, whispering, "No dice. It is not just Rachel. I want to go to every dot. For the Notebook, I want to see and experience it all. And as long as there are more dots, my heart will keep beating until I see them all. It is my formula for cheating death."

Rupesh paused in the dark and then resumed. He would have to share this victory with Wilfried Koch, after all.

Lucrèce

Roberto often thought of the Spain trip in 2002 and the innocence of it, the silly obsession to see everything. Much had worked like that in his life. Music—he had bought and researched and sought out so much classical music to his taste . . . but now listened to no more than a few of his favorites, often content to let the Euro-pop station be his companion for days at a time. And reading. Oh, to regain the thirst for reading of his early twenties! You had but to mention an important book, and he got his hands on it. He was voracious in those days, Victorian novels, Nobel winners in translation, poets, critics, thinkers . . . And culture itself. The European Union would declare a city the summer's culture capital, and he would flock there for the dance, the sculpture in the plazas, the specially curated art exhibits . . . And now? He spent a lot of time watching British and German detective series on the hotel TV. His enthusiasms remained, of course, but they had faded, too little attended to, like souvenirs confined to a shoebox on a closet shelf.

Given the unceasing warfare between him and his sister, the searing Spanish afternoons of hyper-tourism loomed as a warmly preferable memory. But back at Mas Disse in 2008, the one blast from the past he thought he could remain free of was nonetheless steered by fate to their door: Lucrezia Pappalardo.

From the moment Monsieur Hacquin returned Clementine Disse to her summer house, she was uneasy, upset. Roberto thought more drama had occurred at the care facility with the police and her father . . . but it was something else.

"Roberto," said Madame Disse, "I have done something on accident, something maybe foolish. This may perturb you, which of course I did not wish."

"Mother," Hélène said, quietly dreading whatever it was. "What are you—"

"It involves someone we all know," she brought out.

Clementine Disse had been in Marseille, not Aix, and she had availed herself of the competent internet signal in the café on the top floor of the Galleries Rochambeau. There, Clementine Disse posted sparkling pictures of herself, amid the racks of fall designs and the new North African scarf collection on sale in Marseille. She posted a picture and some text— already liked by three hundred of her sycophants. Translated to English it, more or less, said, *Oh, what joy to be in the South, with my friends, my darling daughter, Hélène, and her former beau Roberto. It seems like 2003 all over again when summer knew how to be summer!*

"So why is this a problem?" Hélène asked.

Because it was seen. Because vacationing in Noli, visiting Ventimiglia, and then driving west to see friends in Menton, were . . . Lucrezia Pappalardo and her husband, Ludovico Something-or-other.

"They want to drop by Mas Disse," Hélène's mother finally confessed.

Hélène looked momentarily pained, but the next moment recovered and broadcast icy indifference. "So. Let her come. If she wants to steal my lover again, she can have Marcel. I brought extras."

Might they cancel? No, the next morning, Ludovico Marchesini called Madame Disse for directions, and it was agreed that there was no possibility of successful navigation up the tangle of rutted lanes from Lo Bordac, so Hélène volunteered to go down in her car, meet them, then they could follow her car back up. She asked Roberto if he wanted to come with her. Yes, he said. Maybe better to have his Lucrezia-reunion hug and cheek kiss without Madame Disse studying it, without Monsieur Hacquin's drooping moue as part of the scene. Marcel announced he would stay behind, as if anyone had thought to invite him.

In the long, silent, sullen drive down to Lo Bordac, he and Hélène barely spoke.

"I have spent two weeks," Roberto said presently, "ministering to your sexual whims. You can't imagine I want anything to do ever again with Lucrezia."

Hélène was impassive for thirty seconds. "I let you back in my bed. Maybe she will too."

"You must tell her how unsatisfactory I've become as a lover."

"Your limitations make you more inventive. She might prefer you this way."

Roberto spent the rest of their descent thinking how they all met:

February of 2004. Clementine Disse was girlishly excited by her yearly triumphal pilgrimage to Milan to bargain for dresses for the Galleries Rochambeau. She stayed in a deluxe suite at the Grand Hotel et de Milan, sprawling with brocade and gilt and fresh flowers in enormous vases and an entire second bonus bedroom. She insisted that her fashion-antagonistic daughter accompany her; Hélène countered that she would never go to anything as empty ("as the voids of space") as a Fashion Week . . . but, well, maybe if she could bring her new American boyfriend, Roberto . . . So there they all were in a bower of nineteenth-century luxury. Madame Disse was continually courted by mid-level designers or mid-level executives for world-famous designers; she was ecstatic, giving off light. Hélène, naturally, did her best to disappoint, hiding her original beauty in worn sweatshirts and ripped jeans; her mother would have despaired, but she didn't have time, running from event to opening to reception to after-party.

On a whim, Roberto decided to pretend to be fashionable that morning and was fitted for an Armani double-breasted coat in double cashmere, perfect for the winter blast blowing down upon them from Ticino. Hélène and Roberto sat down unannounced beside Madame Disse before a runway show; Madame Disse sat for a minute before she glanced over and only then cried out in surprise, finally recognizing him—the American backpacker who had only been seen heretofore in a denim jacket! Was that Armani? She was so thrilled with his purchase—she could not stop stroking the material and praising his taste . . . which led to Hélène disgustedly decamping for "deeper companionship," heading to a bookstore near the university. Lucrezia Pappalardo, talking with a group of models who, like her, were walking later that afternoon in the Zara show, came over to join in on the adoration of Roberto's tailored cashmere.

"*È stupendo*," she said, pressing her cheek against the material. "And the coat is nice too," she added, with a wink.

Madame Disse cutely wagged her finger—*This is my daughter's boyfriend, Lucrezia, so hands off.*

Lucrezia mockingly enacted a tragic face and wiped away fake tears, before being called back to her herd . . . which is when Madame Disse leaned into him excitedly and said, "Do you know who that is?"

Lucrezia Pappalardo at her career apex. With her projection of desperate sexual need sharpened by some resident cruelty in the eyes, Lucrezia was all the rage in the early 2000s, capturing a cover of Italian *Vogue.* That winter, there was a financial flirtation in which Lucrezia was on the brink of being paired with Gemma Ward, a brunette paired with a blonde, to be the brand image for the spring-summer line of Prada. Nothing, apparently, came of that (or came of any of her almost-deals) because of her notorious behavior.

"Lu-crazy," was her industry nickname. She was unstable, she required medication. She was bipolar, at least, with a few uncharming personality disorders on top of that. Her mercurial nature, the mystery of whether she'd rip the dress she was supposed to wear and sweep all the assembled makeup backstage to the floor or weep with joy when it came time for the models and designer to take their bows . . . it was a mystery too few in the empires of fashion were willing to contemplate.

Lucrezia insisted that Roberto and the departed Hélène join her after the show for a drink. A trendy Milan below-ground club, she promised— all the models would be there! Hélène pretended that she was being dragged, but both she and Roberto were curious to have such an evening. If it was fun, well, then, good; if it was self-satirizing and empty, then they would savage the participants for eternity.

They arrived at the texted address; it was one of Milan's severe pitch-black clubs where one could barely see not to stumble into the black onyx-topped tables and black velvet beanbag chairs. There were wandering lasers of intense primary colors that crossed each of their faces every few minutes.

"So, Hélène," Lucrezia said frantically, "you see that I must decide quick!"

Lucrezia showed off her new business cards, which, on one side, reprinted the *Vogue Italia* cover in sumptuous color, and the other side simply read: LUCREZIA.

She sought their advice, nearly crying over it, whether she should continue on in the business by a single name like Veruschka or Iman.

Hélène strained to say anything pertinent. "Pappalardo," Hélène noted, "has a musical quality to it."

Roberto, thinking he was being helpful, said the syllable *lard* was not so euphonious in English.

Lardo was a popular cold cut, she wondered aloud. "Everybody likes that, yes? What does the *lard* mean in English?"

"*Strutto*," explained Roberto.

"Oh, so when I get a little fat," Lucrezia raged, "the gutter press can make the joke, say my ass is full of lard! *Pappalardo è tutta lard!*" But, said one model friend, who was really a rival and not a friend, "Lucrezia will make people think of Borgia, who poisoned people." Better a murderess than someone whose ass was filled with lard was the general consensus. Roberto remembered being relieved when the party left that club; one kept receiving the wandering lasers directly in one's retina, probably assuring blindness in later years.

Back on the winding white-dirt lanes down the mountain, Roberto tried to lighten the tone. "So a five-euro bet," he offered. "Lucrezia looks just the same, if not better. Your predictions of her becoming an overweight peasant crone in black will be found to have been . . . ill-conceived."

"I will not take that bet. I, like Maman, have seen her Facebook page. Do you think you will desire her again?"

"Will you?" Roberto's best ploy was to humor Hélène's sense of being polyamorous and unpredictable.

And neither of them said anything else until they pulled into the emptiness that was Lo Bordac, where a silver Audi TT roadster idled in the desolate main square. Lucrezia's husband, Ludovico, an architect, sprang from the car. Five inches shorter than Lucrezia and not bothered about it, bald (by design, an expertly shaved head) with a graying, impeccably trimmed goatee, dressed in light white linen trousers, calfskin sandals, a patterned loose silk print shirt with geometric diamonds . . . what? Two thousand dollars, minimum, out of an Ermenegildo Zegna window. "So you are Roberto?" He clasped Roberto's hand. "Yes, just like she said, shaking the hand of a . . . of a skyscraper." Lucrezia tarried in the sports car with its tinted windows and offered no hint of what was to come. After Ludo kissed Hélène's cheek, they all turned to the Audi.

Ludovico sighed. "She wait, even here, to make a grand entrance, no?"

And then the door flung out, and perfectly tan shapely legs set down on the unworthy dirt of Lo Bordac. Lucrezia Pappalardo presented herself in a big sun hat, sunglasses, a tissue of a scarf above an even gauzier sundress—her entire ensemble did not weigh eight ounces. She made her way to Hélène first for their perfunctory kisses before stopping to assess

Roberto. "You are the same," she said, with something between a shrug and a smile on her face.

"You are not," he said bending down for the cheek kiss, during which she was immobile. "You are more beautiful."

And so she was. Any trace of the swollen, lusty Sicilian girl who looked as if she could be squeezed like ripe fruit had been tempered by age and the rigors of posing for a living. She was cut glass, precise, perfect, as if computer generated from the best parts of Italian models over the last decade. The wildness in the eyes, the spontaneity of an appearance that rarely held still and allowed you to assess it . . . those engines had ceased to function. She was cool perfection now, almost not human enough to desire, Roberto thought.

And so they rumbled back up the mountain, leaving trails of white dust that hung in the air.

Marcel, after being introduced, excused himself for the upstairs bedrooms. Hélène busied herself in the kitchen, finding clean-enough wineglasses for the watercolor-faint Miraval, the local rosé.

Madame Disse, having engineered a meeting she feared would blow up in her face, soon became convinced that things would, after all, swim along agreeably, and she began to display her most charming self, laughing and free. She asked if Lucrezia wanted to see some of the fall line exclusive to Galleries Rochambeau, and Lucrezia clasped her hands together, "Oh please, oh please . . ."

Madame Disse called up a series of dress photographs on her Modbook tablet while Lucrezia hummed assent. Surely, Roberto thought, Lucrezia's enthusing over the matronly department store offerings was a charity on her part, she who had debuted Versace on a Milan catwalk. The earlier Lucrezia, the darting eyes, the erratic gestures, seemed to have at last been pacified. Perhaps it was attributable to the love of a good, indulgent man, Ludovico.

Ludo stood off to the side and cleared his throat. "Will Signora Disse permit?" he asked, with an open, silver cigarette case in his hand, offering one to Roberto.

"She sneaks them herself, but out at the edge of the property . . ."

So let's go where she goes, Ludo's face said. They began walking to the cork trees. Ludo lit up, and Roberto declined . . . but he felt that familiar pang of wanting to smoke.

"Hélène, she is very pretty, a little like a boy, yes?" Ludo asked. "You sure she is a woman . . . ?" He nudged Roberto, chuckling without any encouragement. "I do not judge! And you are a couple?"

Roberto explained, "The man with the big black hair, who ran away? That is her man." Ludo nodded. "I am also Hélène's ex, in addition to Lucrezia's ex. Vuoi parlare italiano?"

"No, no, English is nice." He smiled, breathing smoke out from his depths. "Ah, that's right. Lucrezia said you speak a million languages. Will we be so fortunate to see Hélène and Lucrezia slap each other, to make a fight over you . . . ?"

"If they fight, it will be about who gets to hit me with that shovel first." Roberto nodded to the rusted shovel propped against the side of the house.

"Lucrezia will come after both of us, amico."

"Lucrezia is so much more . . ." Roberto waited for the right word to occur to him. ". . . *serene* than when I knew her."

Ludo savored his cigarette. "That is the wonder of medicine. Many, many bottles." Ludo was chuckling again. "And therapy, but that . . . un peccato, was not so effective. She make the therapist herself go into therapy—I no make a joke." There was a lone cigarette in his case. "I am almost empty. That little village. Is possible for the purchase the cigarettes?"

"No, that is a ghost town. We would have to go back to Cuges—"

"It is difficult, yes? To have to observe the beautiful Hélène and your replacement, the boy with the big hair?"

"Not at all." Roberto quickly met Ludo's eyes before looking away. "We are all three sleeping together."

Ludo laughed loudly, which momentarily turned the heads of those by the pool. Madame Disse and Lucrezia returned to the iPad and the dresses; Monsieur Hacquin sipped from his rosé, astride his blue chaise. Hélène stared death rays at Roberto.

"Well," Ludo said, "when you are to visit us in Milano? I have a big, very big house."

"I do not think Lucrezia would like it if I visited."

"It is my house. I invite who I wish to invite. My childhood friends I have been loyal to, but all they wish to speak of is sports. I wish to talk of art and architecture, world politics, books, music. Lucrezia said this is your neighborhood too."

Squealing like schoolgirls, Madame Disse and Lucrezia declared they

would sunbathe topless while the afternoon sun was so strong . . . Would
Hélène like to join them? The three graces! Hélène said no, not about
to reveal her modest chest for the pageant of platonically ideal breasts.
Ludo and Roberto walked toward the Audi, calling out their mission for
cigarettes. It seemed Hélène wished they would take her, but Ludo billed
this "man's work, the fetching of cigarettes."

Ludo took the white-dust roads with immense speed, expertly shifting; Roberto glanced at the side mirror to see a plume of white dust shoot
behind them as if from a rocket ship.

"You do not," Roberto noted, "have an Italian automobile."

"I make the choose . . . choice?—the word? I *chose,* yes, on the beauty
of design. I could not do anything other." He smiled. "You will find many
Milanese look to the north for our treasures, not to the south."

Roberto asked if there were buildings Ludo had designed that he had
seen, and discovered he likely had, in the Porta Nuova business district
that had a fair share of César Pelli and Cino Zucchi. There was the famous
Bosco Verticale, a residential high-rise overcome with vegetation from
each ledge and balcony, resembling a thirty-six-story piece of shrubbery.
Ludo waved these masterworks aside; he and his firm had a few modester
projects standing in Porta Nuova, but they had great things portending.

Roberto had never been in such a nice automobile; he ran his finger
along the leather armrest, the decorative stitching. "I was just thinking of
the Balkans. That was to be Lucrezia's and my great vacation. A trip along
the Adriatic, ending in Greece. Now, the only way I would go is if I could
ride in a beautiful car like this."

"Well then, let us to do it, yes?"

As they rode back up the mountain to Mas Disse, again at top speed,
Roberto thought Ludo the friendliest man alive. Wanting to be instant
pals, wanting him to visit him in Milan, wanting to go on a road trip
with him along with his partner—who was Roberto's ex. Perhaps I am in
a Henry James plot scenario. Some wily European aristocrat is trying to
separate me from my American money. *(You and your sister need to back
away from all things to do with Henry James . . .)* Roberto, unknown to
Ludovico, was determined to accept *any and all* hospitality that involved
a guest room and a bed.

Upon their return to Mas Disse, Ludo distributed cigarettes among the
smokers (amid elaborate declarations of everyone being a nonsmoker,

but just this once). Lucrezia, ready to get back to Menton, scolded Ludo for going away and dawdling . . . but then she stayed for another half hour commiserating with Madame Disse about her cat that had to be put to sleep. There were almost tears . . . Lucrezia whimpered without any moisture to follow. Perhaps her cocktail of antidepressants needed some adjustment. Her volcanic qualities had been substituted for simplicity, in love with everything, oohing and aahing over flowers and birds that landed near the pool and over clouds, which looked like shapes.

So much excitement was followed by collapse. Aunt Sidonie and Monsieur Hacquin retired with a snack to their bedrooms. Madame Disse sat in a chair, reading and nodding off, her head bouncing with each near descent into sleep. No sign of Hélène or Marcel. Roberto skipped dinner and took to his room for an early evening. Roberto, an hour later, headed downstairs when the house was quiet and the lights were off, for a bite of something . . . only to see Marcel stretched out on the sandpapery cracked leather couch, his face turned into the sofa, snoring. His suitcase was beside him.

Around eight in the morning, Roberto was aware of the crunch of gravel. Later in the morning, when he went in search of coffee, he saw that Marcel was gone, as was Hélène's car. She did not return until late in the afternoon when she said she had been, at long last, to see her grandfather.

"Were you able to talk to him?" Roberto asked.

"Yes, I learn everything. But first. Roberto, it is time for you to go, if you don't mind my having to say. I have disposed of Marcel—forever, actually. I took him to the station in Aubagne for the train to Paris. I will make it easier for you. I will take you to Marseille for the TGV so your commute to Paris can be the more quick."

Roberto assented with a nod.

"I wish to have a day or two with my mother, just her and I, before our time is over here."

She knocked on his door to his room almost at sunup. The rest of the house was asleep, and Roberto silently resented her choice of the earliest possible departure, and his not being allowed to thank Madame Disse personally as he left. He would send a thank-you gift and note or visit sometime in Paris. Roberto and Hélène tiptoed to the car.

Hélène was taciturn and moody, which she was often anyway, but Roberto sensed there was a cause. "Marcel was not as bad as advertised," he said, to stir up some kind of conversation.

"My mother and Lucrezia were sunbathing without their tops, you remember? Oh yes, you went with Ludo for cigarettes. I walked upstairs to find him, and I saw he was masturbating to both of them, looking out the window from above. To pleasure yourself to my mother is bad enough, but Lucrezia? How many men will I lose to that Sicilian peasant? Well, that was the final thing. Enough, I said. He has a problem, I think, a compulsion."

Roberto decided not to follow up about Marcel. "And you saw your grandfather?"

"I got the names of the investigators, and I will call them and tell them to leave my grandfather alone. He told me what happened. Outside of the town, there were camps of Gitans. They had been warned to move along, but they did not. The Milice rounded them up, and they were shipped to some camp in Germany. My grandfather went with the party of men with the guns . . . So that should be the end of it. They were not Jews."

"They will not investigate further?"

"No, not for Romani. The Jewish organizations would keep asking, keep prying until some clue of the names of the Jews could be found in the records, what families, what camps. But for Romani, it is over. They do not have prosecutors or advocates."

Roberto learned from the newspapers that President Sarkozy did not like them, or any number of people he considered rabble, speaking frequently of urban neighborhoods that needed to be hosed down, people who were dregs, scum of the earth. Didn't he just say Africans had no part in history? And he wants something done about the Romani, but they are EU citizens with the right to cross borders . . . The Romani have no champion in contemporary Europe any more than they did in the Nazi era. And of course, Madalena van Till is pretending to raise money for their European memorial—a final insult upon centuries of insult.

Soon Hélène and Roberto were winding through the street of Marseille, the sunny ochers and yellows of the alleys, the lavender and aquamarine closed shutters, locking in the aromas of a thousand seafood stews for midday. Roberto had the car window down and felt his right arm bake in the Mediterranean sun; he felt he could hear the Van Gogh–thick paint job of Marseille crack in the heat.

Roberto really needed to be taken to the airport, but Hélène's sufferance was not to be tested by a longer drive; he would hop out and thank her for the taxi ride. But then it was off to an internet café where, with his phone and a humongous international phone bill to come, he would investigate a long-lost forgotten bank account that he only recently remembered when thinking of Rupesh. He did have an ATM card back in 2002 when he was in Spain, right? There had been fun-delaying searches for an ATM all over Spanish towns while Rachel and Rupesh complained. Banco Santander, he thought he remembered.

As they approached the drop-off lane at the Gare de Marseille-Saint-Charles, Roberto tried to turn on the charm, but she wasn't in the mood. "I will not stay away five years this time," he said, gathering his bag from the trunk and slipping on his backpack. "We will catch up more frequently."

"As you wish," Hélène said, just pleasant enough. She kissed his cheeks and then hopped back into the car.

Her window was down, so he said lastly, "Give Monsieur Hacquin my best."

At last, she smiled. "I will steal his Speedo and send it to you."

"It will always remind me of you."

The Continental

Neither the flight nor the shuttle from Gatwick had been cheap, so Roberto made his way to an economy hotel, the British franchise Sleep Tight!, a few blocks from the King's Cross St. Pancras rail complex. A single twin bed for £130, in a two-star family hotel, in a room the size of a closet—London's idea of economy. He was now reunited with at least three of his suitcases from the Gare du Nord; Roberto couldn't swear where all of his suitcases were, parked in stored baggage facilities in an unmemorable array of train stations.

What was the obsession the British have with fire doors? In going down the hall, he had to lift his heavy suitcase over an inside stile every five meters, while propping open a fire door with a tight spring determined to gnash itself closed, catching his suitcase or his ankle or both. There were four of these obstacles . . . and a tiny half flight of stairs to pull his suitcase up, another bear trap of a fire door, then a new flight down again, before the room. It was stuffy from the day's heat and the lack of air circulation. There was not a hotel room with air-conditioning in London until you got to the five-star joints and often not even there. The assumption has eternally been that hotel rooms, being in England, would cool off each night. The Republicans in the United States and British hotelkeepers are the last two groups on earth to be unconvinced it is getting hotter globally. There was a window, but it had been constructed to not crank open more than eight inches, and none of the advertised coolness of the evening could be seduced through this crack of an opening. Why the barely opening windows? What was the fear here? Suicide? That someone would throw themselves from the second floor to their death on the rosebush two meters below? There was a little electric teakettle and two bargain-brand tea bags, so that luxe awaited.

He called the front desk. Was there, say, an electric fan, perhaps? There was? But it was a fan assigned to a room on the other end of the hotel. Could the fan be moved, say, to his room? No, it could not. It was the fan assigned to that very room, but if he would come back to the ground-floor desk, they would switch out his keys. So it was back to dragging his suitcase over the obstacle course.

Next morning, the Breakfast Room.

Roberto was used to European chairs and tables not being conceived for someone his height, but the Breakfast Room in the basement of the Sleep Tight! had a Lewis Carroll quality to it, overcrowded with round plastic white patio tables and blood-orange tulip-petal chairs perhaps purchased from a 1970s American middle school lunchroom, adequate for humans who were 90 percent the size of real humans. The ceiling was low, with pipes (wrapped in yellow tape with accompanying notices to mind one's head) gurgling away, conveying the patrons' morning bowel movements to the sewers by way of the Breakfast Room. Roberto's legs didn't fit under the table; the chair crunched like it might break under him; it was impossible for the back of one's chair not to touch the back of the chair of the neighboring breakfaster. There was a constant thrum of British folk saying, "Sorry," "Pardon me," "So sorry" . . . and almost no other conversation, except a necessary breakfast detail or two whispered between couples.

Two uniformed women in their fifties presided (beige smocks, gingham trim, dark brown polyester trousers, a red neckerchief brandishing the red of the Sleep Tight! logo). Well, one of them presided, a stout tank of a woman, sturdy, butch cut, wielding a clipboard. The taller, skinnier woman (whose uniform was loose on her; it was clearly fitted for her predecessor) was meek, drab, silent, with an expression in expectation of being beaten.

The smaller one in charge said, "Before we can commence breakfast service, I should ask in which room you were accommodated?" (She tried to sound plummy with her rehearsed line of inquiry.) He told her his room number, but the in-charge woman's clipboard had him down for the first room that he'd been assigned, the one without the dedicated fan. "So sorry, we cannot proceed until this is cleared up."

The thinner exhausted woman was sent upstairs to ground level, bounding to the office to untangle this confusion.

"Is my name on your list?"

"Yes, sir."

"They moved my room, but clearly I paid for a room last night and am entitled to the breakfast."

"It very much matters to which room the breakfast shall be accounted."

"I'm in a hurry. May I help myself—"

"No one helps themselves, sir."

Roberto felt the eyes of all the British guests, crammed like sprats into the can of a Breakfast Room. Wouldn't you just know, the tall American was *causing problems.* Didn't have the right room numbers, and now wants to maraud, graze, defile the toast bar . . . Speaking of that, Roberto hoped something from the kitchen might emerge to justify why, by what rights, this had been dubbed the *Breakfast Room.* Of course, the low-budget philosophy of Sleep Tight! assured him there would be nothing cooked, no classic London fry-up, no stewed tomato, beans on fried bread, black pudding, the gorgeous bacon, toast soppingly buttered, best meal of the English day . . . No, he saw two toasters and some white bread in Sainsbury's sleeves.

The rangy woman dashed back down the stairs, through the fire door, to say that yes, Mr. Costa ("cost-her," she had the London twang that put *r*'s where they weren't and removed them where they were), was a guest indeed, ma'am, they had begun him in #244 but had moved him to, uh, what was it, #143, she thought . . . The senior Breakfast Room commandant examined her clipboard: "We have a Mr. Spittler who has been accommodated in room one-forty-three."

Roberto noticed a receding elderly man looking into the depths of his plate, aghast at being on display.

"One-*thirty-four*," Roberto supplied. "I was in one-thirty-four."

The stouter woman waved the thinner woman off to confirm this. "See that you remember it this time," she cautioned. Turning her face upward to Roberto, she smiled broadly. Someone must have told her that an ear-to-ear leer after being punctilious erased all annoyance. "I won't check off your name until she comes back, but we can begin with breakfast service," she stage-whispered like it would be a little conspiracy between them.

"Do I go up with you?" To the meagerest bounty arrayed since the World War II food shortages during the Blitz?

"No, sir, if you'll stay put. It is called *breakfast service,* and we will serve *you*. Coffee or tea?"

"Tea."

The tea was good, but he noticed when a neighboring table asked for another pot of hot water, and could they might possibly maybe if it would be no trouble have a new tea bag? The junior tall one dithered until the senior short one strode between the tables, brushing against each one, to say that no, no, the breakfast service offered by the Sleep Tight! was one tea bag to a customer.

Two pieces of whatever was the English equivalent of Wonder Bread were slipped into the toaster. A hard paper plate with a pad of butter, two foil-covered containers of jam, one inch by one inch (one marmalade, one berry compote), was set before him. There was a little foil-sealed tub-let of some potted meat extrusion calling itself pâté, and a three-inch-by-one-inch rectangle of orange cheese encased in a cellophane wrapper. After the junior hostess set down the plate, the senior was there within seconds. She picked up the cellophane cheese rectangle with her gloved left hand, produced a small pair of sewing scissors in her right, and snipped the end of the package and set it down on his plate, still encased in its wrapper. The offending bit of wrapper she had cut away was put into the hands of the junior, and the special scissors were returned blades-downward into a pocket on her beige smock that matched the *exact* size of the small scissors. Roberto knew as he knew nothing else that that pocket had been sewn onto her uniform by the senior waitress herself (probably in violation of the Sleep Tight! uniform maintenance bible) and that the privilege of wielding the scissors was the senior hostess's duty and hers alone.

Roberto saw one of his neighbors sawing into a hard-boiled egg with her plastic knife. "Excuse me, ma'am. How does one get an egg?"

"The egg can be purchased, one pound ten, sir. I regret to say that it requires an extra surcharge beyond the Sleep Tight! breakfast service."

Roberto nodded, passing up the extravagance of the egg. He would be heading to King's Cross Station where there would be no end of earthly bakery delights, sandwiches, French croissant makers, that Cornish pasty company one sees in English train stations, Krispy Kreme doughnuts, for

Christ's sake . . . Roberto was brought his lightly browned toast from the toaster by the junior hostess, holding both slices by a serviette. He began to peel back the foil tops to the jam containers, the potted meat, the berry compote. He might not eat any of it, but he had become a soldier in this war of parsimony, and he didn't want the senior hostess to repurpose his unopened condiments and offer them to a later diner, congratulating herself in exercising a splendid thrift.

Two silver-haired ladies came into the Breakfast Room, a look of mild pain registering on their faces. *Before we can commence breakfast service, I should ask in which room you were accommodated?*

They were not wealthy women (or they wouldn't be "accommodated" here), but they were educated. Roberto decided they were mother and daughter on a London weekend. For all the occasional botheration of English life, the bureaucracy, flummery, and pretension, there is an equal and opposite Monty Python energy that doesn't tolerate it—this work carried forward by an army of curmudgeons and malcontents, sometimes young and caustic, sometimes old and devastating. The mother barely moving a muscle on her face brought out so all could hear, "What a sordidly mean attempt at breakfast. I do hope some preposterous surcharge has not been added to the cost of our rooms." Then she added, delivered like any of the actors with *Dame* before their names, Dame Maggie Smith, Dame Judi Dench, in that magnificent British weaponized diction: "What did this paltriness run them, I wonder. A *tuppence*?"

The eventual battle between the stout hostess and these two breakfast warriors would have to go unobserved, alas, since his father was calling . . . and the signal in the depths of the Breakfast Room was not advantageous. Roberto made his way up to the street level. It was confirmed that his father could meet him near the Bank of England at three.

Strolling in London made Roberto thoughtful; one of his regular thoughts lately was the shape of artistic careers. There were the artists who attained Parnassus from more or less a single work—Ralph Ellison, Thomas Gray, Emma Lazarus, the sculptor Stefano Maderno, Grant Wood's *American Gothic*, Carl Orff, Pachelbel's *Canon*, Alfredo Catalani, who wrote that killer aria in *La Wally*. Sir Mix-A-Lot's "Baby Got Back."

These artists often produced (or attempted) other works, but the ages have sorted it out, and they stand pat on their masterpiece in the museum of time. And perhaps, one day, when *The Notebooks of Roberto*

Costa (better title to come), his bible of the expatriate, his snapshot and summary of the amassed goodies of the Western world striding into the twenty-first century, was published, he too would join the one-hit-wonder list. Having said all there is to say, why write further?

He only just thought of Pachelbel, because his inescapable "Canon" was on the noontime program at St. Stephen Walbrook, which, like many a center-city Christopher Wren church, had a concert series for the bankers' lunch hour. And then, Roberto sighed, there was the other kind of career, whose chief exemplar was Christopher Wren. After the Great Fire of 1666, he was given the commission to replace ASAP fifty-two churches in the center of London, plus, while he was at it, St. Paul's Cathedral, and he did, each one lovely, each one identifiable as his style. (Roberto had seen them all one summer, and St. Stephen Walbrook was Wren's most gracious.) What a dream assignment for an architect: here's a great city, now design a church architecture to represent the age.

Rossellino got to design a city (Pienza) in the Renaissance with so-so results; Frank Lloyd Wright designed the labs, factory, the CEO's mansion, and work campus of S. C. Johnson & Son in Racine, Wisconsin. Wright neglected to put women's rooms in the labs, capable of imagining the greatest American architecture of the twentieth century but not that women could be engineers. Niemeyer was given Brasilia to design with spectacular results, thirty-two civic buildings, from 1957 until the present day. He must be alive still . . . Roberto checked Wikipedia, and they had not filled in a death date—still going at a hundred. Wright dead at 91; Philip Johnson dead at 98. Note to self: next lifetime, go into architecture for the sake of longevity . . .

A few blocks away from St. Stephen was the Bank of England. For years, Roberto had assumed the grandiose Greek-style temple was the Bank of England, but that was the Royal Exchange. The Bank of England was the stodgy building across the street. A little after 3:00 p.m., as promised, there was Sal, open arms wide.

"There he is, the prodigal son!" he cried out, clutching Roberto. "I'm still such a tourist," Sal added, looking back from where he had emerged. "I never quite get over where my job takes me. That's the goddamn Bank of England. They built the East India Company and the British navy, which ruled the world for a few hundred years."

"With the help of armies to subdue the colonies, rape the natural resources with the help of enslaved labor—"

"I take it you and your pal Karl Marx don't want the filthy imperialist lucre I'm going to give you today."

"Um, Karl said I could have it just this once."

Roberto told his father that two blocks down Cheapside there was a Banco Santander branch where he had (painstakingly) retrieved and revived his account number.

"We sell treasury bonds and notes to accomplish our deficit spending," Sal began, feeling expansive as he walked. "The Bank of England sold 'subscriptions.' There was no securer investment from the 1700s. All through the Revolution, George Washington held paper from the Bank of England. When he had more money to put aside, he bought more subscriptions—while fighting the redcoats. And after the war, he cashed in nicely."

"Considering what the loss of the American colonies meant, I'm surprised the bank honored his payout."

"Of course they honored his contract. Business is business."

Roberto wondered if his sister had launched her attack yet. "I saw Rachel briefly in Paris. She forbade me to stay on their sofa. Or rather, Merle forbade it."

"Yeah. Merle says she has some fantasy about me working for the CIA," his father said, smiling broadly. "I ask you, Bobby: Who would ever entrust bigmouth me with the national secrets?"

"I told them they were nuts."

His father stopped walking a few yards from the Santander branch. "I'm sure I knew the guys who *were* CIA. Ford, Mercedes had men down there. The American guys in suits who didn't seem to be associated with any industry, who plied us with drinks at the Carrera Hotel. So overly friendly—or maybe they were trying to pick us up. I was hot in my day!"

"Dad."

"There weren't so many Americans in those locations back then. We weren't doing anything secret, just looking for business opportunities, right? Anyone asked, we told them what we were up to. I know that I rubbed shoulders with the CIA, but you know who was *everywhere* in South America back then? The Soviets. There was this guy Georgiye Gorki—you don't forget a name like that, all those hard *g*'s in a row. He would see me at the Carrera, and then the drinks would begin, and somewhere, after we were feeling good, he would ask questions about what investments I was overseeing."

"And he was KGB?"

"Yep. I confronted him about it one night. He shrugged and said he was just looking out for his country's interests." A lost look came over Salvador's face, maybe concern, maybe nostalgia, maybe both. "Helped the guy defect in 1983—that's another story. I should get in touch with him again, because thanks to Hightower Wiggins's rough Russian customers, I want to unwind our assets from Moscow and never see that town again."

At the Banco Santander branch, a check totaling $9,999.00 was deposited in Roberto's long-lost account. With the SEC "circling above me like a bird of prey," Sal reported, a transfer beyond ten thousand would attract official attention. "It'll have to do for now," he told Roberto. "Sorry it's not more."

"I'm the one who's sorry," Roberto said. "I mean, I'm sorry for my spoiled behavior—not sorry that it's not more."

"I understood what you meant," his father said, clapping his elbow. "Will that amount last awhile? Or is that one night on the town for you?"

Roberto confessed to a Hightower Wiggins Visa credit card bill of six thousand plus. They were strolling back toward the Bank of England. Mrs. Santos and a limo were due in another twenty minutes.

"Okay, okay," his father said. "Take six of the ten thousand and pay it off before you get interest on top of interest. I know, that only leaves you a few thousand, but I'll work on it. I'll get a Spanish associate to deposit something, and I'll . . . eh, that's probably a crime too. You let me worry about it. But. You get this installment on the condition you answer me a question."

"I take it it's not a Providence question."

"Indirectly, yes."

"Because you know I'm going to Olneyville when I'm home next."

"Yeah, of course—why wouldn't you?—with the celery salt."

"Goes without saying."

"New York system. But it ain't about that, exactly."

Roberto waited at the corner for the light to change.

"Look, Bobby, the writing's on the wall. If they don't rescue those SOBs at Lehman this weekend, then Monday, Lehman will go belly-up. Curtains."

"So it's really happening."

"Yeah, yours truly here figured Treasury and the New York Fed were just toying with them like a cat plays with a mouse, but no, I'm feeling it; they're going to teach Wall Street a lesson. And if they let a legend like that go down, who gives a crap about the con men at Hightower Wiggins?"

Sal bounded into the lane—and got a blast of horn from a cab. Roberto pulled him back. "Jesus," said Sal. "I will never learn which way to look in the UK."

"You look both ways, Dad. It's the only way to be sure." Roberto pointed toward a café ahead. With his longer gait, Sal's son couldn't help but lead the way.

"As I was saying, Hank Paulson can't let *every* house on the Street hit the skids or the whole investing economy of the United States starts looking shaky. By letting Lehman tank, it might, *might* just save Hightower Wiggins."

Roberto felt his breathing grow shallow. "But if he doesn't, will that mean our family could be cleaned out?"

"Bobby, even if the company and my stock and my so-called golden parachute turn to nothing, I got bonds, we got property in New York, Rhode Island. And the CNBC gig is fortune enough. But it will mean a change in lifestyle for us all, you understand? So here's my Providence question: If you had to go home, could you work? I'm not taking a shot at your dilettantish-like lifestyle; it's a serious question. Can you work?"

"I object to the term *dilletante*—"

"No, no, answer my question."

"Yeah," Roberto said, "I think so."

They entered a café on Princes Street, across from the Bank of England. They were the sole customers; Sal ordered a pot of tea, told the woman to keep the change on a £20 note, and they took a seat by the window.

Sal took a moment to text Mrs. Santos where they were. "I'm just wondering," Roberto's father went on. "It will help me sleep at night if I think, No matter *what* happens, Salvador, your boy can see to his feeding and clothing, a roof over his head."

"Yeah, Dad, I can teach foreign languages, conversational English."

"What? Thirty bucks a lesson, what are we talking about here? Only good-looking European girls signing up—" He nudged Bobby. "First the irregular verbs, then the bedroom? Oh, I know what you're up to!"

His father's caricature was distressingly close to Roberto's modus operandi, but Roberto continued, "No, I'd go and . . . I can finish the master's. Be able to teach in a college somewhere. More like a community college, maybe a private school. Maybe Brockton Academy."

"Yeah, they loved you there."

"They haven't forgiven me for being six-five in eighth grade and not any good at basketball. No, I'd teach in a college with pension plans, health care, retirement vehicles, all that. I wouldn't be like you, Dad—making a fortune somehow—"

"I made the fortune so you didn't have to make one. I still hope you get to do what you want. When you turn thirty, there's a . . . a thing you'll get, I'll tell you about that when the time's right. But what I leave you kids . . . well, instead of ten million, let's say it's more like one point five million. Sounds endless, doesn't it, a million dollars, but it isn't. It's great, however, when it makes for a *supplement* of your salary."

Roberto absolutely did not want to teach foreign language classes in America. He wanted to concentrate on his *Notebooks of Roberto Costa*; he saw himself reading at independent bookstores, the PBS and C-SPAN interview circuit, his work translated into most of the major European tongues—

Sal: "And that other thing we got in common. How's the heart?"

"No angina lately. I don't have much stress in my life, but you . . ."

"I suspect a doctor would say all this jet-setting and going from bank to bank getting one portfolio of bad news after another should be unhealthy for me, too much stress, too much adrenaline, right? Then racing back to tape a segment for TV. Between you and me: *I love it.* I wanted my hands on the steering wheel all my life, and now I got it." He toasted Roberto with his cup of tea. "Oh, you wanna catch your old ham of a dad doing a real dog and pony show? I have a press conference next Tuesday when my show would normally air, probably on the heels of the official announcement about Lehman going south on Monday. My presser is about Hightower Wiggins and whether we're going Chapter Eleven too. CNBC will carry it live, but I heard Fox Business, Bloomberg, friggin' CNN, Bobby, they're *all* carrying it live. Tuesday, 5:30 p.m. eastern U.S. Ehh, they probably won't carry it over here, so forget about it."

"You're not declaring one of those tactical bankruptcies?"

"The opposite! I've got a speech that's gonna keep Hightower Wiggins afloat for the rest of the year, if I play my cards right."

"You gonna fix 'em, Dad?"

"You bet I'm gonna fix 'em."

After a moment, Roberto asked, "Do you have friends at Lehman?"

"I do. Feel sorry for them all, even Fuld. I've been in Europe scrounging up a few billion to buy our stock back. Listen to this: Lehman, this spring, they got ten billion in loans; a few weeks back, they said they were working with *forty-five billion* in liquidity, and, Bobby, it was *still* not enough to cover those bad mortgages. Can you imagine? Forty-five billion— that's like Bahrain's or Azerbaijan's entire GDP, small oil-rich states. And Lehman couldn't bail the water out fast enough. Too exposed. They got eaten alive by the short sellers."

Roberto: "That's when people invest in you losing, right?"

Mrs. Santos walked by the window of the café and pointed a finger at Salvador Costa. She was inside in a moment. "Sal, the driver is here and illegally parked."

"He can be there another five minutes."

"If he drives on," Mrs. Santos began, "and we fuck this up . . . Maybe Bobby can walk with you—"

"Five minutes, Mrs. S. Go get a tea for yourself." Salvador had a look that Mrs. Santos recognized as a command from on high. Mrs. Santos went to the counter and stooped before the pastry display as well, deciding on a treat.

Sal patted Roberto's arm. They never had enough time to talk, for anything anymore. "Time for a lesson?"

"I don't promise I'll understand," said Roberto.

His father scooted the pepper shaker toward his son, and the salt-shaker toward himself. "There's lots of variations on this play, but here's a favorite of mine. Let's say you and me have, say, two hundred thousand shares of airline stock, and we know it's bound to go down. A big crash of a new model, say. Fuel prices through the roof. Bad earnings report."

"So we're gonna lose our shirts, right?"

"Nope. You're gonna loan me your airline stock . . ." Salvador scooted his salt toward Bobby. "Now forget about its value. It's a loan of so many *shares of stock*, pure and simple. I loan you two hundred thousand shares, and you loan me two hundred thousand shares." He slid Bobby's pepper back toward himself.

"But our shares are still going down the tubes when the stock sinks."

Sal cocked an eyebrow, eyes twinkling. "You sell all my shares I loaned you, I sell all two hundred thousand shares you loaned me. Let's say it was ten dollars a share, we each have two million dollars apiece." Sal handed his son two sugar packets, a million apiece, and he held on to two sugar packets for himself. "Down, down, down the stock goes, until it's five dollars a share. Now *we buy it back*. It's just worth one million now." Sal took a single sugar packet from his hand, and one from Roberto's, then replaced it in the sugar packet tray. "And now I repay your generous loan." He slid the pepper shaker back to his son and the saltshaker back to himself. "Here you go, like we promised: two hundred thousand shares of airline stock."

"But stock that's worth half of what it was."

"The loan was for two hundred thousand shares, and I repaid it."

"But I had . . . We . . ." Light dawned. He held up his sugar packet. "We both put a million dollars in our pockets."

"We both put a million dollars in our pockets. And are still holding our two hundred thousand shares of stock for when it goes up again."

"Holy cannoli. They let you play games like that?" Roberto asked, laughing. "A stock goes up, up, up, and I make money. A stock goes down—providing I have someone to do this loan scam with—and I make money. So how does anyone actually *lose* any money on Wall Street?"

The look on his father's face was intense enough to be fearsome. His father whispered, "Yeah, son. How *does* anyone lose money? How did Wall Street lose ten trillion in American wealth? The mutual fund guys, the corporate bankers, the proprietary traders. How'd they manage it? I'd have to work around the clock, never sleeping, devoting every second to making the worst possible decision about the worst possible investments, and I still don't think I could lose what Hightower Wiggins lost. And now my name's on the masthead, my name's stenciled on the glass wall leading to the boardroom."

"No one thinks you made this mess, Dad."

"I'm the CFO now. History will." He pinched the bridge of his nose.

Mrs. Santos was standing at the table. "Time to go, Sal. Good to see you, Bobby!"

"Good to see you too, Mrs. Santos."

Salvador Costa stood, straightening himself, grabbing his briefcase. "I'm retiring after all this! You too, Mrs. S."

"Counting the days," she said.

Before he left the café, he kissed his son on the forehead, which was only possible when Roberto sat and Sal stood. Roberto watched his father's shambling gait, Mrs. Santos's immovable silver hair helmet recede down the sidewalk, seek out the impatient limo driver so that they could be whisked to some regional London airport, some waiting chartered aircraft.

Roberto walked down Cheapside. He passed the beckoning Banco Santander ATM, but the big deposit would not be withdrawable until tomorrow. So he kept walking to the west, past Mr. Wren's St. Paul's Cathedral, circuitously heading for King's Cross St. Pancras where he'd stored his bags in preparation for the evening's discount-fare Chunnel Eurostar back to Paris. A late departure, second-class train car, all the best for making his money last. He passed St. Bartholomew the Great, one of the few Norman holdovers that survived the Great Fire.

There wasn't too much left of the Norman Romanesque with which to taunt Rachel. The Tower of London's Norman chapel looked built yesterday; Westminster Abbey was well-Disneyfied. But within St. Bartholomew's, they had kept the Middle Ages locked up, having imprisoned the damp and the gloom inside for nine hundred years.

He texted Rachel: I'M IN ENGLAND. SAW DAD. BY THE WAY, I AM FINANCED FOR THE NEXT TWO MONTHS. AFFECTION AND RESPECT—YOU SHOULD TRY IT SOMETIME. HOW'D MERLE'S CIA SHAKEDOWN PAN OUT?

That would be a shot across the bow, stern, quarterdeck, mizzenmast, forecastle, whatever parts of a boat you were supposed to shoot at.

Rupesh was, still, endlessly a student at an international business degree mill in Amsterdam, but he had a boyfriend somewhere in England and was frequently in London, if the Facebook array of drunken club and Royal Vauxhall Tavern shots were at all reliable. Roberto texted Rupesh a HELLO on the only number he had for his friend, Rupesh's old American phone, figuring he would get credit for trying to reach out but not actually make contact.

But as Roberto waited in a queue for a takeaway tea in St. Pancras, checking in for the Eurostar early out of boredom, his phone rang with a +31-20 prefix on the incoming call. Amsterdam.

"If you had told me you would be in London," cried Rupesh, "I could have arranged to be there, but you are again consistent—never making time to see me!"

Roberto explained his English invasion was only a quick visit to secure money from his father, like the worthless trust-fund failed playboy that he had sadly become.

"But you secured some funding, so you are *not* a failure. It is I who am a failure."

It appeared that the undying love of Rhys the Aristocrat, scion of an industrialist, stopped short of a marriage to Rupesh, so secondary to his money-sponging, his primary issue remained his visa, how not to go back to India when his student status at Amsterdam University played out. Amsterdam for Rupesh had been a continuous orgy seen dimly through the carbonized haze of substances illegal elsewhere, interrupted by several amyl nitrate-inhaled summers in Barcelona-Sitges. Roberto was wistful that his teenage boy-love had transformed himself into (probably) the only Indian circuit icon on the Eurogay scene.

"The only solution, Bobby," he said impatiently, "is for us to get married, which we can do in Holland."

"My visa is just a tourist visa. I don't solve your logistics problems."

"I will send you a photo like Rachel does, on your email. But it is something more fearsome than a Romanesque church, I promise you."

Roberto fished his iPad out of his backpack. In a few moments with Rupesh grouchily waiting, he called up a photo: a beautiful young woman, glamorous like a Bollywood star. "That is Ameesha," Rupesh narrated. "My father is on Ahmedabad's urban development authority, and so is hers. Two utterly corrupt Gujarati families intending to unite their corruptions. Ahmedabad is the boomtown—that's the word?—of Western India. The only thing standing in the way of my father rising further up the ranks of the BJP is that he has a very, very stupid son—that, Bobby, you are to understand, is *me*—who is dragging his feet and preventing the wedding of the decade, which will be attended by Chief Minister Modi, whom my father bows down before like he is Arjuna before Krishna, like Lakshmi before Vishnu. Do you have a wedding ring for me, Bobby? We can have an open relationship; neither of us shall be faithful anyway, so what does it matter?"

"Again, I will fail to be what you require. We Costas may be losing our fortune," Roberto said lightly.

"Your father is a plutocrat like mine, yes? Plutocrats always have money tucked away somewhere."

Rupesh thought of Mr. Doshi as part ogre, part buffoon, someone who scores of people wished would kick the bucket already and leave them their inheritance. It reminded Roberto of nineteenth-century novels where fathers and sons had little to do with each other and a young man had no "prospects" as long as his aged, wealthy father hung on, refusing to succumb to the ague. It was a lot more complicated when one's fate, fortune, future were dispensed by a father one loved, as Roberto did Sal Costa.

Roberto offered, "My problem—you know which one I mean—has gotten worse." Roberto raised his voice an octave, pleading like a melodrama's heroine: "We can't . . . can never have the children I know you dream of."

"Why are you being obtuse?" Rupesh snapped. "Of course your problem does not in the least matter to me."

Before Roberto could make another joke, Rupesh cut him off:

"You are too shortsighted to see the advantage of being with me. Bobby. We are rich men's only sons. My father will cut me off if I am gay, but he is an older unhealthy man and he will pass on, and my mother, who is from a much richer family, if the truth should be told, adores me, and she will eventually produce some money in my direction. And you will be rich too. Maybe less than you thought."

"A lot less."

"The warning I give is the same: you will never, ever know with any woman or man with whom you consort whether your money plays a part of their attraction to you. We will both be subject to romantic criminalities."

"Ah," said Roberto, understanding. "If you want an economic union, why don't you marry that guy from Brockton on the swim team—what was his name? His father was richer than mine."

"You very well remember his name. And until this minute, I did not gauge just how jealous you were of him."

Roberto prepared to huff about not being the least bit jealous, but okay, he had been jealous. Rupesh's love was *his* to mistreat and ignore, not that insipid little twink from Framingham. "I would, in principle, not mind marrying you," Roberto said at last, "if only to see Lena's reaction.

We'll take you to Thanksgiving at Uncle Vinnie and Aunt Bennie's—that will be fine entertainment."

"Lena did not like the looks of me."

Madalena, in a rare visit to Brockton Academy, visited her son's four-man suite (hastily cleaned up, on-the-floor underwear and porn and pizza boxes kicked under the beds). That day, Rupesh and the swim-twink passed through, acting as gay as possible.

"Bobby," she said afterward, "you should see about transferring to a different dorm if your suitemates are gay. That's how rumors get started."

Seventeen-year-old Roberto Costa stared squarely at his mother. "If I want to suck a guy's dick, I'll suck a guy's dick. I like women more, but I am following your example, doing whatever the fuck it is I want to do. Are you going to give me a lecture on sexual mores, Ms. Van Till?"

That was the last maternal visit and their last discussion about his personal life that was ever attempted. He had never been bothered by that exchange—it was one of the more efficient conversations in their troubled history.

"You do not love me as I love you," Rupesh announced.

"When did you get so goddamn dramatic?" Roberto said. "I will rescue us both. Give me some time to work things out."

Rupesh's voice faltered. "Rescue me, Bobby."

It was time for the train.

Most Americans' expatriation to Europe comes in one of two flavors: the Anglophile or the Continental. Roberto had never passed through the Anglophile phase. Too low a degree of difficulty. Same language (putatively), overlapping film and TV and pop music cultures, same screwed-up politics (workers voting Tory/Republican against their own class interests to the glee of the millionaire and billionaire oligarchs who reap the sole benefit). A shambling left wing that only gets in power when they imitate the Tories/Republicans. That's probably why Barack Obama won't win, Roberto thought wistfully: not enough obeisance to Goldman Sachs. Roberto had regularly touched down in the UK, a month here, a few weeks there, but it was almost like popping back to New England. He always had a good time, but it didn't really count as *foreign*.

The 9:55 p.m. train pulled out of St. Pancras, among the last to leave for the continent. St. Pancras Station was nearly empty, and so was the Eurostar train. This led the French-English-Flemish-speaking stewards to give him an extra snack, a second Coke Light . . . but soon even the stewards disappeared and the lights were dimmed. In an hour or so, they would be at the Channel Tunnel. Roberto had done this many times, but tonight, he felt nostalgic, regretful that he raced through his London visit. A light rain was now streaking the train windows; he absently studied the elongation of the raindrops on the glass.

In his decade on the European side of the Atlantic, he had become a late, very late, convert to the homey, shabby delights of England. The snug of a pub, the cold multidirectional mist that doesn't require an umbrella (which couldn't keep you dry anyway), the necessity of strong tea and biscuits (but English biscuits, that is, those inimitable brands of cookies, the McVitie's, the HobNob, the Garibaldi, Ginger Nuts, and Jammie Dodgers), the after-midnight search for food to soak up the stout and the bitter and the cider and the ale, the kebab van, the chip shop, a small gang of revelers not ready to call it quits at 11:30 p.m., at the height of good spirits, when the pubs inconveniently rousted them to the streets, careering back to the tiny worker's row house in a still-barely-affordable semi-gentrifying corner of London, led by a pale young woman, trying to hide her perpetual cold and runny nose with a ragged tissue, the space heater by the closed-up fireplace, the gas stove necessary to light a Dunhill now that the lighter is played out and the matches are wet, where stale bread is toasted, buttered, and spread with a film of Marmite . . . an island of cozy threadbare pleasures concluding with a single-malt scotch in a KEEP CALM AND CARRY ON coffee mug, a final sustaining sip before the freezing bedrooms where one plunges one's bare legs deep under the duvet to detect any warmth to be had, when it's clear that only snuggling with someone can prevent the arctic fate ahead—snuggling preferably with the pale young woman (after her friends have taken the hint and scurried off), who is quite lovely, but even cleverer than she is lovely, which, given the wit, the articulacy of Great Britain, means pretty clever indeed.

Funky Roller

As the money began to amass in Roberto's Santander checking account, Roberto decided to reward the country that brought his salvation—Spain—with his presence. Madrid itself was a city he had sworn to get in and out of quickly, lest temptation strike and he investigate the whereabouts of Valentina. In a life of indulging himself thoroughly, that was a promise he had kept so far: never to cross her path again.

Atocha Station in Madrid. Roberto particularly liked the interior tropical garden, which kept the station humid like a greenhouse, turtles on rocks in ponds lethargically surveying the commuters, all thirty of them plunging at once into the water from some secret signal. Al-Qaeda blew up the place, killing 193 people four years ago, through some Moroccan guy who bought his explosives from local miners . . . although they never really did find an airtight connection to Al-Qaeda. What was the prime minister's name? Aznar, who allowed himself to be led into the Iraq War quagmire by George W. Bush and Tony Blair. Tried to pin Spain's worst terrorist incident on the Basques so it wouldn't be seen for what it was, an Islamicist payback for committing troops to the Anglo-American Iraq War folly. A few days later, he was turned out of office in the election. God, what a relief to be traveling in Europe now that Bush's eight years were coming to an end. Surely, no president will ever be as embarrassing to Americans who are traveling abroad as George W. Bush!

Roberto's goal was to go to a businessman's hotel, where all the international financial shows about the CAC and the FTSE and the Nikkei and the Dow could be expected to appear on the hundred-channel cable offerings. He wanted a ringside seat for his dad's press conference. Already, Rachel had texted in a panic, wanting insider info—was bankruptcy in the works? Lena was pro-bankruptcy, because through that door beckoned severance and golden parachutes, cleaning out the china cabinet before the house burned down.

Having first ascertained that CNBC was among the cable offerings, Roberto lay there on the bed in his deluxe Hilton, but with hours to wait. On the hotel Wi-Fi, he searched for Valentina Garcia . . . of which there were way too many. Of course, she had a new last name now, but . . .

Fuengirola was a beach town near all the other indistinguishable beach towns near Málaga on the southern coast. And there he met Valentina Garcia: long chestnut hair nearly to her waist, shapely but lean in the manner of Madrileñas, a sly smile tactically let out between fierce expressions, a light butterscotch tan that piqued Roberto's appetite. They had met at Fuengirola at a beach disco called the Funky Roller (which is how the name of the town is pronounced). She was engaged. She and her girlfriends were having a last bachelorette fling and, dodging those friends for some variable hour of the day, she and Roberto got together in his oceanview hotel room—though the ocean was barely observed. They had quick, cut-to-the-chase sex, over in twenty minutes for both, followed by another ten minutes of postcoital conversation. The stopwatch on the whole affair never exceeded an hour, but it was better, more urgent for that, and the talk bolder.

"Someone," she said, wrote a Spanish twentieth-century historical account with a subtitle *The Silent History*. The Franco years were not secret, little has been successfully covered up—it is just that everyone has family members on both sides of this conflict and has agreed to be silent about the war, to never mention it. (It was Roberto who'd brought up the Spanish Civil War.) The atrocities, the outrages, the massacres, all of it never happened, and one's aunt, grandfather, great-uncle, Valentina assured him, will go unquestioned at the holiday dinner table. "The war would all start up again if we spoke at too great a length about what was done."

Roberto had read a magazine article about a woman who, through a nurse's deathbed confession, learned her mother was not her biological mother and that she had been given to another woman in one of Franco's most pernicious schemes. Women who were political prisoners, or married to leftists, or academics with Republican leanings, or whose families had once dared to criticize the fascists would wake up in the maternity hospital to be told their babies were stillborn. They were not permitted to hold or bury their dead children—they were all but shooed from the hospital, outcasts, pariahs. Franco reassigned three hundred thousand of these babies to his supporters, a grand experiment of swiped children who would be raised to revere the leader in patriotic pro-Franco households. Franco not only depopulated his opposition, but there was a bonus: the cruelty to his ideological foes, the heartsick mothers, the ruined fathers. Would those mothers ever want to bear another child?

Valentina said, not quite imagining it, "You find out you are not only adopted but that your parents participated in a cover-up, an unpardonable crime. You may love these people you once thought were your parents, but can you forgive them?" The Germans, Valentina noted, would have kept scrupulous records of their crimes; the Spanish burned all paperwork so no child could trace her long-lost mother, and yet with DNA kits, many children have made headway regardless.

"And yet no one apologizes," said Roberto.

Valentina gathered her shopping bags from the chair in Roberto's hotel room, her ruse to explain her absence. "Please, we have not apologized for the Reconquista and forced conversions at the stake. We have not apologized for the Inquisition. We have not apologized for the rape and subjugation of two continents. It is far too early to be apologizing for the Spanish Civil War—it must wait its turn!"

And after the very best wild afternoon they enjoyed, after Roberto's high watermark sexually, having no clue what was ahead for him on that front, she laughingly turned in the door and faltered just a second before saying, as she'd no doubt rehearsed, "Tomorrow, my almost love, there will be no time to meet. I am going back to Madrid the day after, to *mi prometido*, to my new marriage. You must not see me again. Not even to visit years from now. I will think of you, querido—perhaps you will think of me. But it is no matter. We make to finish right here, sí?"

Roberto concurred. But of all the accidental, whimsical European affairs . . . this was the one that really got to him. Because of the quality of the talk, the whole sweep of European history seemed to be at their disposal as they hurriedly dressed. He was in love; he would have married her if she'd have had him. And because he hoped she was perfectly happy, he honored their union by erasing her phone number, all social media contacts. So, not even in a weak moment, he could be tempted to say hello, guess who is in town . . .

Roberto resisted temptation to stalk her on the internet. Instead, he tried to watch a Spanish game show with answers so easy that even without knowledge of Spanish sports and culture, he was bettering 50 percent. And in the commercial breaks, he thought: *I can endure losing the sex life, the potency, the Valentinas, and the accompanying pleasures, but only because I thought money would be there to provide other compensations. My erection is dwindling? Here, wrap this roll of hundred-euro notes around it and use that . . .* (That had been a Rupesh joke at his expense, once upon a time.)

But maybe Roberto Costa, thought Roberto Costa, could lose everything.

And finally, over on CNBC, it looked like Sal's dog and pony show was going to begin. Maria Bartiromo began, announcing that Hightower Wiggins's CEO, and their own CNBC colleague, Salvador Costa, was about to take the microphone. A bustle, the click of cameras, murmurs . . .

"Good afternoon, guys."

It was his father, and a wave of heart-altering anxiety swept over Roberto.

"Usually at this hour, I am preaching the gospel of Treasury bonds and how they won't let you down when other equities are in crisis. So first off, let me say . . . *I told you so.*"

Mild laughter.

"Was I right? Didn't I tell ya? Doesn't two, three percent sound good about now?"

A pause.

"Lehman Brothers is gone. Can you believe it? Folks, we can keep panicking, keep short selling, keep bailing, keep selling at a loss, we can do all that and beggar ourselves into a great depression, if you want that. Our country's biggest savings-and-loan operation, Washington Mutual, is circling the drain—shall I give you Vegas odds on the order of future collapses? AIG, then Morgan Stanley, then a bank or two—let's say Bank of America and Wachovia—everyone's up to their chins in bad real estate derivatives. Then, hate to break it to you, Hank—Hank Paulson, you know, our treasury secretary—but your precious Goldman Sachs is on the ropes after that."

Heartier laughter at this audacity.

"I already hear—in just twenty-four hours—there is widespread regret in Washington about Paulson and Geithner letting Lehman go down the tubes. It's bad for all of us. My friends in Congress like to get up and speechify and say why bail out billionaires and millionaires who gambled stupidly with all our money? I agree somewhat. Not gonna BS you here— you know I never do. Some CFOs and COOs and CEOs need some jail time."

Whoa, that was heresy coming from a CNBC anchor.

"*But,*" Sal went on, now quiet and intense, "the billionaires and million- aires are not who's going to pay, are they? If they were the only custom- ers, then boo-hoo, let 'em take their licks. One, we got tens of thousands of employees in the banking industry, your mom or dad in the cubicle in the branch office right down the street. We got Bear employees who were paid in stock that went down to jack squat; Lehman's folks got paid in stock too, and so they're looking at zero; we're gonna lose thousands of banking jobs, and those are the people who had *very little to do* with decisions made at the top.

"Two, let's talk about *your* folks. Some of the lefty columnists who cheer at the losses of all the fat cats are going to soon wake up because they probably have parents with 403(b)s and 401(k)s and bank stocks. And all our retirement vehicles are vehicles that are *parked on Wall Street.* Everything's interconnected. Have you enjoyed your four percent return on your mutual fund? They bought CDOs from Lehman, from Morgan, from Bear, from Hightower Wiggins. They bought our stuff, we bought their stuff, we spread the risk around like good little boys and girls, except we were buying the same goddamn toxic thing, real estate derivatives. They tell me there's seven hundred fifty million in bad Leh- man paper in all our portfolios and retirement accounts. So, respectfully, Mr. Paulson, you can't let even one more of us go bust, okay? Or we're going to be in danger of taking the whole kaboodle down. So, to the Trea- sury, I say: Help us out. Give us a loan—you'll get your money back with interest. You can loan to Chrysler and Fannie and Freddie, you can loan to us.

"To the Congress, I say: If you don't like legislating a loan for us on Wall Street, if you senators hate the abuses, then they have this resource, some of you may have heard of it. It's called *regulating.* It's called getting off your backsides and *making laws.* It's called limiting the damage the system can do . . . but the wheelbarrows of cash from lobbyists meant that there *were* no laws, and I bet you very few people will head off to prison because although they were foolish, and reckless, and occasionally really, really stupid, I bet they didn't break any laws, because you know-it-alls in Washington *didn't pass any.* In fact, you tore up a bunch of laws. The uptick rule—could have used that, as the shorts are eating good companies alive like vultures. Glass-Steagall worked for sixty years, keeping banks on one side and investment brokerages on the other—nope, the lobbyists and Mr. Clinton got rid of that for us. So, Congress, make some laws, why don'tcha? You might feel good about yourself, feel justified in your six-figure salary.

"To the press, including my pals at CNBC, I say: Stop with the hysteria. I heard the other night a reporter do a remote in front of our door on William Street. The screen said: HIGHTOWER WIGGINS—colon—THE DEATHWATCH. Jesus Christ. We may be in the NewYork-Presbyterian waiting room, but we're nowhere near the ICU. Which brings me to our investors.

"To our investors at Hightower Wiggins, I say: Hang in there. Our stock's down to twelve dollars from thirty-one dollars. Morgan's down, Merrill's down. I promise you this is nonsense. All our companies have billions in good assets. They used to call economic downturns 'panics,' and that's what this is—*panic,* pure and simple. So I'm here asking our Hightower Wiggins investors to hang tight. You gotta ride it out somewhere. We hear there's a government plan being drawn up to take a percentage of our toxic assets and pay them down. Meanwhile, we got a line of credit, four billion, which we used to buy back our own stock so the shorts can't get us. Some of the other houses have too much stock to do that; we don't. We're leveraged now eighteen to one. Lehman was thirty-six to one, Bear was twenty-nine to one. Plus, a lot of our bad stuff is insured. I've been bouncing all over Europe like a Ping-Pong ball lining up loans, Bank of England, Deutsche Bank, Crédit Agricole, Credit Suisse, Societe Generale . . . I see you, Jim, laughing at my French—think you could say it better?"

Much laughter.

"I was in a Banco Santander this week . . ."

Roberto startled. His father, in mentioning that puny checking account deposit chore, looking right at the camera and winking, was hoping his son, Bobby, had found a way to watch.

"I'd negotiate a loan from an American bank, but I'm not sure there'll be any left in the coming weeks."

More laughter. Not really funny, but he made one of his trademark faces while delivering the line.

"You financial press have got your lede already: Hightower Wiggins is hanging in. Here's your headline: NOT DEAD YET. And you guys know me, you know . . ."

He paused. Roberto noted there wasn't a bit of ambient noise.

"I'm not CEO material, you guys all know that. I'm just a workaholic bond trader plucked from my happy cubicle in Providence, Rhode Island. I've spent my life balancing these high-flying risky portfolios for normal folk with good, solid, unexciting caches of bonds. Muni bonds. State bonds. Corporate bonds. Treasury bonds. Few derivatives—just bonds. And my heart breaks for the families, the small businesses, the retirement funds, who have—for the moment—lost some of their assets in a Hightower Wiggins portfolio. I said I wouldn't take the CEO job unless they met my conditions, which were that I get to allocate all money beyond negotiated salary. I am announcing that no bonuses, no supplemental pay, no so-called golden parachutes will be honored at Hightower Wiggins. Yeah, retroactive, meaning the fine economic minds that ran our little investment house into the shallows will not be departing with *The Price Is Right* showcase, after all."

Someone called out: "Starting with yourself?"

"You bet starting with myself. My new CEO pay package would net me four million, most of that being bonus. By the way, the only thing making money in Hightower Wiggins was *my* bond division. And I might take my salary if my job was just about bonds, but I'm CEO now, and I have a duty to make this right . . ."

If Roberto craned any closer to the television screen, he would have to crawl inside it. There were shufflings, crinklings, as his father was looking through his papers.

"To the Johnsons of Paramus, New Jersey. The Kolinskis of Duluth, Minnesota. The Darrows of Albany, Georgia. And, um, ten, thirteen, fourteen . . . sixteen other families, I am restoring out of my salary your principal investment. I have here"—more rattling, more pages—"former

CEO Richard Culp's eight-figure golden parachute. If he wants the money that was contingent—I checked our contracts—on 'good performance,' then he can sue for it. He can go to a court of law and explain how his loss of thirty billion in bad real estate derivatives is good performance."

There were hoots, claps, laughter. They came for a show, and he was giving them one.

"The retired teachers' fund of Malden, Missouri. The Sundown Investing Club—eight elderly women in Tempe, Arizona, meet weekly for cards and playing the market. I called these girls up one day. Talk about loving life, having a positive spirit. I'm reimbursing you gals' principal. The firefighters' retirement fund in Brannock, Colorado. All of you are getting your principal back. Now you can take it and run, sell your Hightower Wiggins portfolio tomorrow, but I would suggest you stay in and watch us rebuild as the markets rebuild. Nowhere to go but up, right? I have, for anyone interested, the names of the first hundred investors I can compensate with board member bonuses. I bet you got some questions."

The place exploded. Boy, his dad sure knew how to set off the fireworks. *What of Dick Culp's contract? Morrison too—you're taking his bonus? Isn't this all for show?*

"Ask Margery—I probably shouldn't be saying the whole names here—of Dillon, South Carolina, if she thinks getting her four hundred thousand back is a show. I have a list of investors who have agreed to be contacted if you want to talk to some *real* people. Be the first time for some of yous business reporters—I'm looking at you, Bob!"

But, but, but . . .

"Yeah, I'll only be able to help a few thousand of our hundreds of thousands of investors and only restore a fraction of what I'd like to. I have a few tens of millions to work with. But I ask you . . ."

And the mob scene fell silent again.

"Every house on the Street is busy with some seriously shady accounting so losing companies can give their bigwigs a royal jubilee send-off, the ones who made the mess, ten million here, twelve million there, before they get in their limos and drive away. As for mom and dad investor, in Indiana and Jersey, too bad for you! Well, we're not going down that path, okay? Not while I'm CEO."

"How long will you last?" someone cried out.

"Yeah, you *know* they're gonna try to fire me. Some of you are getting texts right now, leaks to smear me and cast aspersions on what I'm doing. You gonna publish it without really checking? Are you? Over the next few days, you can decide if you want to help the golden parachute crowd get their millions or"—more paper crinkling, fumbling with his reading glasses—"Sam and Esther of Troy, Michigan, who are getting their nest egg back. Sorry it's not more, but I'm gonna make sure those kinda investors have something to see them through."

More mayhem.

Roberto's phone dinged.

YOU WATCHING THIS? Rachel texted. DAD GIVING AWAY ALL OUR MONEY.

IT'S HIS MONEY, Roberto texted back.

THAT FOUR MIL HE'S GIVING TO MA AND PA YOKEL OF BUTTWIPE, KANSAS WOULD HAVE BEEN TEN MILLION BY THE TIME HE LEFT IT TO US. LENA WAS RIGHT ABOUT SOMETHING. THAT HE'D FOLLOW THE SHIP DOWN.

Yep, Lena was correct. But Roberto could not have been prouder of his father. Hell, give it all away! Do what no one else at the heart of American materialism would even dream of: make things right with the normal people who have gotten screwed. And now, as CNBC and the commentariat were heaping praise as well as abuse on his father, Roberto's phone rang. It was Lena:

"Bobby, we need to meet. I'm in Bern. That's in Switzerland."

"Mother, I think we have had several versions of this conversation before, in which I remind you that we cannot remove any money from our trust funds until the SEC says we can."

"But you can *borrow* against it. A loan is between you and the trustee— which is your father. A withdrawal violates the SEC freeze. Sal will let you borrow two hundred thousand against the trust." Lena then said, "When neither stocks nor traditional investments are any good, you buy property."

"Two hundred K won't get me anything but a shack in Europe."

"Rachel borrows two hundred K, then you do, then I sell my Cologne apartment and put in two hundred K, and with six hundred thousand, we can buy in Milan. And I have just the place, in Navigli."

Lena pronounced it to rhyme with *wiggly*, not as it was said by the Italians, *nah-veel-yee*. "Your father has decided he's going to be all twelve disciples and give away his worldly goods—your and Rachel's worldly goods, that is. That little trust of yours has already lost half its value, so time's a-wasting, sweetheart. It's time to let bygones be bygones and go in on a house in a place we can all use as home base. We won't have to be there at the same time, of course. We all travel, we all have projects. But we'll *own* something European, so we can belong here. Or maybe you'd like to apply for tourist visas your whole life, and Rachel can apply for a student visa when she's forty. Or maybe you will be going back to the States when the bottom falls out? Just let me know."

Now Roberto was twice as agitated as he was before his father's press conference. Navigli would be nice . . . but to be entangled with his mother and Rachel—and Merle in tandem too? He supposed it could be like their time in Manhattan; they barely saw each other in that apartment.

"I'll see you in Bern, quick as you can get there. If Ingegerd dies, the whole deal is down the tubes."

"What? The old crone with the porcelains?"

"Yeah, the old crone with the porcelains."

Ingegerd and Bothild

Ingegerd Stern had demanded complete obedience from her three children who, one by one, disappointed her. Her favored heir, Moritz, had attempted to secure his mother's blessing for his nuptials, but she did not approve of the fiancée (who Lena reported was from the best possible family, a brilliantly accomplished pediatrician). When they married against her wishes, begging her to come to the service and take her place as the materfamilias, she was unmoved and cut off her son. The daughter, Simke, had been failing her mother all her life, poor grades, poor results in school sports, a frumpish, unhappy girl who finally disappeared into Paris with some university friends and cut off ties with her mother . . . which left the entire eventual fortune to the youngest son, Mats, who then had to be forgiven most everything—a drug arrest, an assault on a policeman during that arrest, then refusal to pay Swiss taxes. But by this time, Frau Stern had begun to conceive of the joys of her role as scorned mother—the mother who loved only too indulgently, too deeply—whose children defied her. She had imagined and rehearsed (aloud for the benefit of the servants) the tales of each child's perfidy until her future listener dabbed her eyes, shook her head, empathized with the nobility of Frau Stern's new role of betrayed matriarch. Soon even Mats could not win back her goodwill and the break came. There it was—all three children, matricidally disloyal . . . Frau Stern had a nervous collapse, brought on by not eating, and her doctor recommended her for a rest cure.

Every other building around a lake in Switzerland is a place committed to the purposes of rest cures and mental rehabilitations of one sort or another. It was here where Madalena Costa van Till did her best work . . .

lingering with one of her pretend illnesses, consorting with the rich and debilitated, looking for contributors to her not-for-profit charities, cadging invitations to summer homes and country estates, where she could continue to play the role of supportive fellow aristocrat. Gehrman van Till, her second husband, was indeed from an established Dutch family, but *Van* is common in Dutch names and was not sufficiently promissory to the elite circles Lena would wish to be attributed. She was not above signing the hotel register "Von" Till. If anyone asked if she was related to the Von Tills of Marienstadt or any soundalike aristocracy, she demurred, "Yes, but we haven't been on good terms since . . . well, I'll be happy to tell you the long, sad story later."

Lena put her time in, sitting beside the grieving Frau Stern in the covered porch of the Hotel Santé du lac Neuchâtel. Lena played her role well, sympathetic crying, clasping the old woman's frail hands in solidarity, and of course, adding that her own children were just as disloyal, cruel, disobedient. How wretched had been Lena's fate (according to Lena), a philandering husband who had cut her off from the currents of a fortune that was half hers and children who contrived to despise her. To have a small select group of rich women think of her as a late-in-life close friend when it was thought the door to sympathetic human contact had closed—a godsend!

Months ago, for Roberto to participate in any of Lena's swindles would have been unthinkable. Now, maybe one could permit at least the *thought* of joining in. When Rachel got wind that Roberto and their mother would be together, discussing the Navigli scheme, she dropped her plans to make her way to Bern as well.

Roberto took a now-familiar position at an outside café table at the far end of the Brunngasse, waiting for his mother to emerge from the caverns of Residenz Stern.

"Bobby," Rachel said as if already annoyed, appearing at his side silently in complete stealth (her trademark) as she took her seat at the café. "It's coolish. Why aren't we inside?"

"When Lena gets here, she'll want to smoke, so we might as well claim a good outside table."

Rachel crossed her arms, perhaps for bad temper, perhaps for warmth. "You could have offered to share half of your ill-gotten gains from your London trip. We could arrange to split whatever either of us gets."

"Though I find you hilarious, your comedy routine is wasted in Bern. The Swiss never laugh. At least about the subject of money."

"Thought I'd suggest it." Rachel ordered a glass of wine in French. "You have actually met the woman on whom Lena has been running the long con?"

"The last time I was here," Roberto explained, "Lena tried to cast me in a little melodrama."

Lena had planned a little tableau vivant for the benefit of Frau Stern, in which Roberto would visit them both and play the role of the abusive, ungrateful son. "But," Roberto said lightly to Rachel, "I decided instead to pay Frau Stern a solo visit without Lena around to direct the scene."

Roberto relived the episode, pointing up the street to her building. Frau Stern's chambers faced north, in shadow all morning, and across the street were five- and six-story apartment buildings that blocked the sun again when it came around. No slant of light had ever penetrated the gloom of Residenz Stern. No light, indeed, had ever fallen upon Ingegerd Stern, whose pallor was kin to the underside of fish that live in lightless caves, a necrodermis . . .

"You are such a ham," said Rachel. "Get on with the story."

In Frau Stern's parlor, there were giant servers and china cabinets, stained darkest black. The wallpaper was a royal blue with a repeating lighter blue motif of a milkmaid carrying buckets of milk up an alp. The curtains, to keep out the chill of a Swiss winter, were also thick enough to protect against shrapnel should someone wish to set off bombs in the Brunngasse.

"Swiss taste is awful," Rachel said, waving the vision away. "Animal heads mounted on damson wallpaper beside a cuckoo clock."

Roberto tried to imitate Frau Stern: "So you have shamefyooolly come to beg moooney from your myooooother . . ." It was like Lady Bracknell saddled with peculiar Swiss vowels. Roberto narrated, that as his eyes adjusted, he could see the parade of figurines arrayed across the room in a variety of displays, clusters of rustic swains and dancing farmgirls, porcelain ladies of sixteenth- and seventeenth-century attire with great piles of hair atop their heads. Splendid examples of nineteenth- and eighteenth-century racist imperial kitsch, really—the Black figures in livery, the squinting, laughing Chinaman, an array of pajama-wearing Indians bowing before a white lady. His eyes further adjusted so he could take in Ingegerd Stern: a tiny woman, not a hundred pounds, in widow's black from head to toe, black stockings, black wrist-length gloves, she held a black hat with crepe but had not affixed it to her head.

"Hast du gern?" she had asked him, seeing him admire her collection.

Much as Roberto loved Kultur, here, here at last, was something of absolutely no interest, old-lady porcelain figurines. But he said in German, You have quite a collection. My mother has spoken highly of your figurines. Roberto only knew a few porcelain-makers to supply context for some bullshit—what was that place near Dresden with pieces in all the museums. Are these Meißen? he asked.

She tapped her cane to the floor, which was surprisingly loud. Yes, of course, one must have Meißen if one is to collect at all—anyone can have a Kändler, if you simply spend the money. But nowhere, nowhere in Switzerland, would he see greater examples of Zurich, or greater Nyon, the incomparable Swiss porcelainists, as fine as anything done anywhere!

Rachel: "Fun times. When did Lena show up?"

"Soon after. Panic in her eyes. I figured one of the servants tipped Lena off that her son was here and she came running." The servant, possibly, was an inside agent for Lena; perhaps the long-suffering maid was promised a cut of the hoped-for legacy when Frau Stern met her natural end. Or unnatural. Maybe the servant and his mother were intending to hasten this inevitability along. After his one audience with Frau Stern, Roberto was content to let his mother pilfer and extort. Frau Stern deserved what was coming to her.

"What's taking Lena so long?" Rachel asked, checking her phone for the time.

"Lena said Frau Stern was nearing the end." Roberto sighed, not about the passing of the old lady but that his glass was empty and he couldn't break the waiter's practiced avoidance. "Maybe it's a final deathbed push."

"I used to think," Rachel said, "that her greed was embarrassing, but now that the family money is about to disappear, I'm not sure I'm any different. I'd like to think I'd stop short of marrying a ninety-year-old viscount or something, but . . ."

"Just make sure his will is in order," Roberto said slyly, which prompted them both to laugh; it was the family's official inside joke.

Lena's fate would almost be funny if it had not provided such an unwished-for backdrop of farce and bother into her children's lives. Madalena Costa's first principle had always been the furtherance of her own bank account. Her money love stemmed from a psychological phobia of destitution; even their lunch and allowance money had to be prized from her hand. Lena had one, just *one*, chance at the big money, and she botched her play.

"She fucked it up," said Rachel, invoking Mrs. Santos.

"Yep, she fucked it up," said Roberto, invoking Mrs. Santos.

While Sal would have been content to put his feet up at Merrill Lynch, selling his bonds, looking out over Canal Walk from the One Financial Plaza building—second-tallest building in Providence, Bobby!—Lena had been quietly navigating a romantic course correction: tall where Sal was short, impeccably attired where Sal dressed like a car dealer, Château Pétrus at the Four Seasons in New York—an emblem of the life she wanted though she'd never eat five bites total, nor finish the single glass of thousand-dollar wine, seeing it as a source of calories—where such luxury stood in contrast to Sal's can of Del's Shandy and one of those goddamn hot dogs he was obsessed with. She focused her wiles on Gehrman van Till.

Sometime around the 1980s, someone from Hightower Wiggins had to be dispatched to Providence to clean up a corrupt bond operation where a salesman and a secretary had fashioned an embezzlement scam.

(For those who didn't know, Roberto was happy to inform foreign listeners, Providence is not only the most corrupt city in America, but it has additionally achieved the highest attainments in stupid, obvious, utterly *detectable* corruption, so life there is one long series of headlines about businessmen, the city council, mayors in succession, union bosses, the monsignor, governors, schoolmarms and florists and ditchdiggers, *everyone,* in court continually on racketeering charges, enacting grifts a child detective would have seen through.)

Gehrman, having been given assurances that it was temporary, reluctantly relocated from the filigree and marble mantels of William Street to Providence's 1970s box skyscraper that never had a fan from the day it was built. He lived out of a suitcase in the Biltmore Hotel and spent his late afternoons in the storied art deco businessman's bar, as did Sal Costa (a watering hole, take note, of Willy Loman in *Death of a Salesman*). The friendship was instant, a laugh-a-minute Vaudeville comedy duo that never was but maybe should have been: the Upper East Side Dutch first family of New York aristo who talked like William F. Buckley versus the scrapper from East Prov. The six-foot-three dusty blond fellow, elegant in a Brooks Brothers suit as well as tennis whites at the club, versus five-foot-four Sal and his loud ties, checked blazers, and a Thursday bowling night with the St. Joseph's church league.

Gehrman longed to be a partner, but he had been flung over to the bond division, from which he could not detect a path to career glory. Sal wanted a chance to evangelize to a larger flock for secure long-term bonds as an antidote for a roller-coaster stock market. Gehrman got Sal hired at Hightower Wiggins to turn the Providence office around—soon Sal was supervising in Hartford and Boston too—making the Hightower Wiggins bond division one of the true moneymakers for the oft-beleaguered investment bank. Gehrman took the bows, was made partner. Sal was soon imported to New York City, and the Costa family received all that one gets when the Big Apple summons you—the gleaming-chrome-and-black-marble apartment in a residential high-rise, the mid-six-figure salary that could touch seven when bonus time came around, an office on William Street that he could have put his and Lena's first Providence apartment inside of without touching the walls.

The move to New York should have been the very upward leap that Lena had spent her life waiting for, but she remained nervous, pacing, unhappy. What if it all fell apart and she had to work in a Fall River shop again, like she did growing up? What if she had to return to Providence to that Greek chorus (well, Portuguese chorus) of detractors who would laugh at her rise and fall?

Lena looked better at forty-three than at twenty-three when she married Salvador Costa. Spas, a great dye job, no exertions or work or life effort put forth year after year except in the service of makeup and fashion had made her a knockout. She would whisper her mantra to Roberto, "We got the looks in this family, and it ain't from Sal's side, believe you me." Rachel often posited that because she was not the kind of daughter whom one could dress up and accompany to spa afternoons, it had doomed their relationship. "Raquel Costa is not pretty enough for Madalena Costa to love," she'd say without emotion.

(Rachel was born Raquel Costa. Sal had hoped to keep the Portuguese lineage extant by not Americanizing his children's names, Roberto and Raquel. But the long, glamorous shadow of Raquel Welch, bombshell of the '60s and '70s, seemed to make for an unwanted comparison. Plus, "Rachel" was a better name for her steady assumption of Jewish identity.)

When Gehrman van Till was expressing his troubles with his second wife, Katrin (mother of their two adult children, his spouse of twenty-one years), Lena let it be known that she was in love with him. Unsurprisingly, the Costa marriage began to unravel. Roberto was still at prep school and Rachel had started at Yale, and except for the Christmas of 1994, where the children detected a parental chill in the domestic air, no telenovela slamming of doors, no broken dishes or screaming accusations reached their ears. Finally, with Sal gone on a business trip (by design, over their spring holiday of 1995), Lena broke the news that she was leaving their father to be with Gehrman van Till.

"Thought he *was* married," said Rachel.

"Not anymore," Lena cackled. "As of December first."

Of course, it was Roberto who was upset on Sal's behalf, though Sal seemed in no need of his son's sympathy or advocacy, perhaps looking for an exit ramp himself. All of Roberto's and Rachel's peers came from divorced homes, and the Costa children had been feeling left out, so now they could moan and self-dramatize with their friends. Rachel regularly petitioned Lena: "Gehrman's like ten times richer, right? I'll expect a bump in my allowance, lady, that's for sure."

So Lena left Sal. No alimony, no settlement—she was walking out for another man; she was now Mr. Van Till's burden. Vó Costa (Sal's mom) and the extended family had always cast Lena as the wanton adulteress Jezebel, so now here was definitive proof. It was a quiet New York wedding, fall of 1995, a city hall affair followed by a private dining room at Tavern on the Green. Neither child attended. Not that they minded Gehrman. Gehrman had been stopping by the house to confer with Salvador about business since Roberto and Rachel were kids. Until he annexed Madalena from Sal, he was the executive who plucked Sal from obscurity to the Wall Street fast lane, "the savior of the Costas." Having Gehrman as a non-parental, decorative family member was like having some dashing, retired black-and-white-era movie star for a stepdad, like Fredric March or William Powell (whom Roberto could never tell apart). Gehrman had a lovely, affable mien polished from years of making deals, slapping backs, meeting his enemies and friends alike at the Century Club for a scotch. Trying to buy the Costa children's goodwill, Gehrman gave *great* gifts, the pricey watches, the newest computers.

Lena, to the trained observer, was almost-happy, which was as happy as she ever got, always worrying a little, nervous cigarette after nervous cigarette, occasionally still frantic about falling through life's cracks. Lena moved to the Upper East Side and enjoyed the life of a Wall Street wife. Leisure, shopping, clothes from places that she no longer had to worry about affording or having to later endure a Sal lecture on frugality. This season of gold lasted about a year. In the autumn of 1996, Gehrman collapsed on the golf course, at the Westchester country club Lena was *just* getting used to, a massive coronary, dead before he hit the putting green. Somehow it had not registered that he was seventy-three—Rachel and Roberto didn't know his age until the obituary ran. And there was no proof of it, no witnesses, but Rachel and Roberto often imagined that after the shock wore off, Lena must have done a little dance around the East Sixty-Ninth Street town house—a widow! What to do with all the money coming her way?

But there was no money.

Not to her, at least. Gehrman, ever the easygoing, ambling scion of privilege and charm, had not gotten around to changing his will, which left shares to his children, his charities, his siblings, and of course his previous wife, Katrin. The one who was not Lena.

Lena obtained lawyers, she wrote letters to the powerful, she begged before judges, priests, then bishops, then archbishops, she wept, she performed . . . but the law is the law, and Gehrman's will left the whole shebang to Katrin van Till, who expressed mild regret in the courtroom that her husband had not been more efficient in updating his will for Lena, but since Lena stole her husband away in the first place, c'est la vie. Lena returned with a civil suit, but no jury was sympathetic; Katrin's lawyers made Lena look like a tramp and a gold digger and a bad mother, leaving her teenage children for Gehrman and his money.

"Should we testify for Katrin?" Rachel asked at the time. "We can back up the bad-mother deposition . . ."

And then began, like an outtake of *Bleak House* too incredible for Dickens to have written, Lena's descent into jurisprudence, trying to sue and sue again, Katrin, of course, but now Salvador too, demanding an alimony after the fact. She tried to convince the courts that she had been abused by Gehrman. Coerced into a second marriage so perhaps it could be argued that she was still somehow quasi-officially married to her first husband whom she had dumped. (It could not be argued, the court clarified.) There was only one thing the court would let her have—Gehrman's East Sixty-Ninth Street town house. Katrin was only too happy to let her have that old place, a money sinkhole, and when the property tax bill came due, Lena knew she had to sell. Upon selling, Lena immediately shut down the flurry of nuisance lawsuits; the house-sale money was now all the money she would ever see, and no sense giving it all to lawyers.

Then began her wandering years, always on the trail of Sal, stalking him around Manhattan and, for the last few years, Europe, so she could put in a good word for herself, attempt a rapprochement while simultaneously threatening innovative legal actions . . . and watch, watch helplessly, as Sal rose up through the ranks of Hightower Wiggins, watch as he signed a television contract with CNBC, watch as his millions, his pay package, his bonuses, his side deals, his investment-banker lecture tour ($1,000 a seat), his bestselling business title (*The Costa Doing Business!*), his subscription newsletter, watch as the money amassed, pooled, all smartly invested, all surfeiting and burgeoning geometrically, logarithmically, money piling itself upon itself, stacks tumbling over older stacks that had to be trudged through like snowdrifts, surpassing any fortune Gehrman van Till had tucked away.

And perhaps sensing she was being discussed, there she appeared at last, walking toward her children, the most elegant woman on the straße. You know, Roberto told himself, why does she not hook a new husband? She's really lovely, an elegant, regal woman who has shed any trace of her loathed past, the Seekonk Stink.

"Bobbikins," she said, after a cheek kiss, "you remembered to get an outside table. They're starting to make noises here in Switzerland about public smoking, so I should sit in the sun and puff away while I can." She looked at her daughter. "Rachel. Lovely that you could make it."

"Hello, Lena."

Roberto: "How was Frau Stern? You didn't let her bite your neck, did you?"

"She is on her deathbed. We have to move quick on this property of Bothild's, her dead sister's."

Rachel: "Haven't you inserted yourself into the old lady's will?"

After a bit of Swiss inheritance-law research, Lena now opted for a lesser goal. Switzerland (indeed, most smaller European countries) were exceedingly loath to letting nationals disinherit other nationals. Most judges assumed cantankerous fathers or embittered mothers could not be serious about cutting off their own children, and often divided the estate fairly between the surviving offspring, despite whatever querulousness was in the will.

"Mustn't be greedy," Lena explained with a shrug.

"I wish I had a camera to preserve for posterity those words coming out of *your* mouth," said Rachel.

"So I have centered my operations around securing her sister's Milan apartment."

It had been a distress to Ingegerd, Lena reported, that she had inherited her late widowed, childless sister's apartment in Milan. Why, if she were to die tomorrow, the fabulous residence might be lumped in with the estate and handed by a judge to her ungrateful children, mightn't it? Simke and her druggie friends turning it into a flophouse . . . This is when Lena persuaded Ingegerd, soothingly, gradually, incrementally pushing her a molecule at a time, that she should sell off this property, and therefore the money would be added to *her* personal trust—a trust that in no way could be infiltrated by her horrible, horrible children. There was no doubt a point where Ingegerd, persuaded that no one would want an overpriced flat in the seedy canal district of Milan, turned to Lena and begged her to buy it. *Could you do that for me, my dear Lena?*

"And you want us," Roberto hurried along, "to borrow against our trust and go in with you on this apartment. If we get Dad to agree to it, won't we owe taxes on that infusion of money? Would the loan constitute a gift?"

Lena looked to the heavens impatiently, sputtering. "You think the Waltons' kids or the Gates' children observe the twelve thousand gift limit? That's for the middle-class rubes who actually pay taxes."

Rachel: "But if Hightower Wiggins hangs on—"

"Oh, dear child, Hightower Wiggins is *not going to survive* if Bear Sterns and Lehman Brothers can't survive. For your own good, you and your brother have to borrow two hundred thousand apiece against the trust while it's still solvent and buy this property in Milan with me. The property will only gain in value, of course."

Roberto: "But then we'd have a giant debt. I'm not in a position to make regular payments on a loan—"

Lena could barely contain her impatience. "You don't pay *anything* back! You borrow it, invest in the property, and when Sal kicks the bucket, you and your sister become the trustees of the trust, in charge of overseeing your loans. *Which you forgive.*"

"That's legal?" Roberto asked.

"Bobbikins, I worry about you. Do you not know *how* to be rich?"

"Wow," Rachel said simply, suddenly educated as to what she could get away with. But then worry crossed her face. "But what about Merle?"

Lena: "Kick her to the curb. A few days' delay could kill this deal, so contact your father, ask him for two hundred K, which we will use as a down payment on our new home, our three-bedroom apartment in Navigli."

"Mom," Roberto said, "I cannot hear you pronounce that wrong for the next twenty years. *Nah-veel-yee.*"

"Nah-veeg-lee," she attempted, not conceding to kill off the *g*.

Sea House

It was almost October 3. The Tag der Deutschen Einheit, the holiday marking the reunification of East and West Germany. And Liesl said she would be with friends hiking along the Aletschgletscher, the biggest glacier remaining in the Alps. He had a sharp pang for Liesl, despite her frank conclusion to their frolics. She was the last celebrant from the historical era known as Life Before the Financial Crisis, when money did not have to be budgeted, before the age of scrounging and economizing. Her smile and company would be restorative. How could he happen upon them innocently? He couldn't. Maybe semi-honesty would work:

Roberto texted Liesl: STILL GOING TO BETTMERALP? I MADE PLANS TO GO WHEN YOU SAID YOU WERE GOING. SHOULD I CANCEL? WILL IT BE AWKWARD TO RUN INTO EACH OTHER?

Nothing appeared for half an hour. Maybe she had deleted his mobile.

So he texted again DIESE IST ROBERTO, DEINEN FREUND VON ETTAL?

ICH WEISS WER DU BIST came back the immediate reply. Then, as a charitable gesture, in English: PLEASE COME. YOU WILL LOVE ME FRIENDS.

The Swiss adventure would require capital; the village from which one hiked to the Aletschgletscher was only reachable by gondola, and the inns, enjoying a brief summer season, would be dear. He prayed that the credit card gods would permit him one more extravagance.

AUCH I HAVE A FRIENDIN YOU WILL LIKE, Liesl texted a moment later.

She knows a woman that adores guys who can't sustain an erection? Roberto wondered. A rarefied taste, but Roberto would not be talking her out of it.

IST SIE SCHON? Roberto texted back. With his British flip phone, he couldn't put an umlaut on the *O*, so Liesl might think he was asking if her friend was ready and willing rather than if she was pretty.

DU HATTEST DIE SCHÖNSTE VON ALLEN, she began—*You had the prettiest of them all,* meaning herself.

So from Bern, Roberto made his way by sleek, modern, punctual train to Valais.

What better place, Roberto thought, to dwell on the topic of money than in Switzerland? Switzerland's no-questions-asked banking practices made it the veritable high church of money, where four languages and twenty-six cantons and various ethnicities were united peaceably by the state religion of mammon, with cathedrals of worship—Raiffeisen, UBS, Credit Suisse, Julius Baer—nestled in the prosperous cities where the sacraments could be performed uninterrupted.

Roberto was just starting to care about money, but he was sure the rest of his family was much further down the highway of avarice. His mother had been corrupted by money long before it found its way to her hands. His sister and Merle, also too far gone. He liked to think money for his father was like a game he was good at; Sal did not exhibit outward signs of greed—no sports cars, no fancy Swiss watches.

And there was Uncle Vinnie, Sal's big brother. Now there was someone turned rotten by money, money he would never have. Like a cartoon character that spies a distant pot of gold and has dollar signs appear in his eyes, which would extend from his head while the sound-effects guy leans on a 1920s automobile horn: *ayoooo-ga!*

Uncle Vinnie and his plans for Sea House tore the family in two.

One desultory prong of the Providence waterfront was the Seekonk River, steeping itself against the factories and refineries of East Providence. Back in the old East Providence, if you didn't go to sea, you made paper at the Richmond Mill, a sulfurous, malodorous colossus.

"Imagine living here early in the century," his mother would say, meaning the twentieth century. "You either got a nose full of the paper mill, or you could turn your head this way and get a whiff of the canneries and fish markets. The stink survives. I'm still washing the Seekonk Stink off me."

The Costa family history threaded through the Phillipsdale neighborhood of East Providence: fishermen, mill workers, shopkeepers. Salvador Costa's parents had inherited from their parents—grandparents, probably—one of those mill-built bunkhouses. The Costas had Azorean lineage and island people, once getting land, never sell it no matter how shitty the neighborhood goes. The ancestral Costas subdivided the cramped dwelling even further and ran it as a boardinghouse for men (Sea House), up through the 1950s, with a few old pensioners who had nowhere else to go lingering into the 1960s. Both Roberto's father and Uncle Vinnie were confined to the smallest room and shared bathrooms and toilets with the aging bachelors, who had spent their youths in the Depression, who fought without complaint in World War II, who came home to work for too little money in the mills. No group of men ever looked more aged or weathered—and their last exhausted stand was Sea House. Sal and Vinnie remembered these men in their final throes a room away, struggling for breath, coughing up lungs, before silence and the eventual flurry in the house, the visit of the coroner, the taking out of the body, negotiating the narrow stairs with the bagged corpse . . . and, the next Sunday, a brief funeral service at St. Sebastian, ill attended, followed by, often as not, a lonely burial in the potter's field.

"Pee House," the teenage Rachel dubbed it, uncleverly.

There were cats. After their grandfather died, Mrs. Costa began collecting cats. At some point after her days of hard labor, she was persuaded that shag carpet was the mark of domestic elegance, which made the cat odor a permanent feature. All entreaties to Roberto's grandmother to give up Sea House and move somewhere nicer were useless, in part because the cantankerous Vó Costa had reverted tactically to Portuguese, "forgetting" whatever English she'd ever had.

It had become the Costa children's annual trial, the holiday trooping of the colors at Vó Costa's.

Rachel: "I'm not going. Nothing can compel me to go inside *Pee* House."

Lena: "Your mother's nose, Sal, stopped working in 1969. She doesn't care if we asphyxiate. Let's say the kids are all sick."

Their father: "Lena. What if she heard you guys talking this way?"

Lena: "She wouldn't understand a word of it. Or pretend not to understand."

Rachel: "I suppose I could curl up in the litter box, because that seems to be the *one* place the cats do *not* frequent in voiding themselves. Her carpet is like a tampon for cat pee . . ."

Their father: "Rachel!"

Lena: "She's always despised me, so it would please her if I didn't show up."

Historical photos revealed Lena was a natural brunette (like everyone Mediterranean for twenty square miles of Fall River), but when she dyed her hair blond, that tore it for Mrs. Costa: that no-good Madalena Malfada was a whore, pronounced *hoor.* That much English she knew.

An additional disincentive to these family conclaves was the presence of Vinnie and Bennie—that is, Uncle Vincent and Aunt Benita and their unpleasant children, the lump of a jock son (Vinnie Jr.), the rusty hinge of a daughter (Margarida) emitting a hundred whines, sighs, and shrieks of teenage discontent, determinedly uneducated as Rachel was smart.

"How are we supposed to talk to these simians?" Rachel would ask on the grim car ride to East Prov. "We should make up some picture flash cards to communicate like they did with Koko the gorilla."

Bad as Vó Costa's neighborhood was, there were rumblings of improvement. In the 1990s, developers floated meek notions of condos and a Seekonk River marina with a view of the green parkland of Baileys Cove. The Wannamoisett Country Club on the Phillipsdale side had a world-class golf course (reported Uncle Vinnie, who'd never played a link of golf in his life); the neighborhood got a historic designation that raised its value. People were going to start building mansions on the shore any day now! Sea House would be worth a fortune, Vinnie lectured the family, if we just could build a dock for watercraft . . .

"Vin, the whole area's zoned for industry," Salvador kept saying.

Of course, the sad sight of Sea House was the sort of view people on the other riverbank would behold, shake their heads, and go: *If only that eyesore was bulldozed into the river.* Nonetheless, Uncle Vinnie was alive with the idea that this condemnable shag-carpeted cat basket was worth $300K . . . maybe if they fixed it up, half a million. He would pace the soggy backyard envisioning the pier, the mooring bay, the yacht, the sailboat. Of course, Vó Costa could move to a lovely, classy facility—"I will die in this house!" she declared—or move in with one of her sons.

"No way," said Lena.

"No way," said Aunt Bennie.

Sal would try to inject some sense into Vinnie's plan: "Look, the plywood factory, the gas reservoirs, the ice house—none of that's moving. I could approach one of the industries on either side, and say, 'Hey, how would you like a guesthouse or an executive office right on the river? Buy it as is, quarter of a mil.' Then we walk away with a hundred twenty-five K apiece. Some payday, huh, for a run-down house that won't pass state inspection if we offer it as a residence, right?"

To Uncle Vinnie, that was lowballing. In fact, Vinnie speculated that his brother would love *nothing more* than to make a quick, cheapo deal, anything to deprive his little brother of the payday he richly deserved. Sal Costa had to be the rich one, Vinnie Costa had to be the poor one, wasn't that it? And it was a short distance from that accusation to both Uncle Vinnie and Aunt Bennie screaming about how Sal shouldn't be *any* part of the sale—Sal already had *his* money, Sal already had *his* big pile, Sea House should be for Vinnie, who didn't have the opportunities that Sal had. What opportunities? asked Lena. Going to a university for a business degree? Being smart and working hard? Lena and Sal gathered up their children, poured into the car, tore out of Vó Costa's driveway, and drove home before dessert.

In the next few months, through the lowest arts of cunning, Vinnie got his mother to alter her will and leave the house to him, cutting out Salvador. She wasn't in her right mind; her English may not have been up to comprehending what she was signing. This bit of treachery did not reveal itself until Roberto's grandmother died a year and a half later. Vinnie and Bennie looked ashamed of themselves in the lawyer's office, but they had pulled it off. Salvador (by this time, even wealthier) shrugged, probably with the foreknowledge that his brother would do as Mrs. Santos predicted, when she was brought up to speed: they were gonna fuck it up.

Vinnie took out a second mortgage on his own home and used the money to build his fantasy boat dock and pier, which was a little like affixing gold leaf to a share-cropper's shack. He contacted one contractor after another, and they all told him the same thing—Sea House was structurally unsound, rotted out from too many storm surges and the Seekonk at flood stage. There were termites, vermin . . . there were cats that, long after Mrs. Costa had passed, remained in residence, getting in through holes in the upper stories. It would never pass state inspection to be sold as a home again. To tear it down would cost $75K, to build something new and worthy would cost $400K, to decorate it and style it so rich people would consider living in it, another $100K . . . and it wasn't like the rest of the shabby street was improving. Why would a rich family want the lone respectable home on an industrial dead end? Couldn't Vinnie smell the chemicals from the plywood factory?

One contractor said he would not start any new construction there because the ground was too soft. When the original home was built in the 1910s, the river was more to the west; as Providence built up and paved itself, the rainwater flowed off in greater quantities into the Seekonk and widened the river. No state agency would permit building on that marshy ground . . . although he could build a house on stilts, which would be $600K . . .

Shamelessly, Uncle Vinnie turned to Sal and said that Sal "owed him," owed him money to help improve the Sea House tract, and this time, out of the goodness of his heart, he would cut Sal in on the deal. No thanks, Sal said.

Aunt Benita regularly took the bus with the parishioners at Our Lady of Fatima so she could gamble at Foxwoods, the Pequot casino. She always charged it. At some point, it was discovered this had become a five-figure obligation.

Then Vinnie Jr. had a skateboard injury that crushed a vertebra in his back. Sometimes he could walk, sometimes he couldn't. Attempts to get disability from the government dragged on and on, or perhaps had failed without Vinnie Jr. or Sr. realizing it. Physical therapy would be another five-figure commitment.

About the time they were talking to bankruptcy lawyers, Sal did what he always did: cleaned up other people's messes. Lena and Rachel threw fits, of course. *Let them get what's coming to them!* But Sal dipped into his bank account and brought his brother and his family back to being debt-free, with a little thrown in for goodwill.

Why was Roberto thinking about sorry old Sea House with such alpine glory around?

Pilgrims to the Aletschgletscher got off the train at the Talstation and boarded the gondola for the mountaintop. No roads led to the attendant village of Bettmeralp (well, not for the guests—surely there was some supply road for the locals) and from the upper gondola station, Roberto would hike to the Gästehaus, where Liesl, food, friends, drink, and presumably a roaring fire would be waiting.

"Guten Abend allerseits," he called out as he found his group, huddled around the predicted indoor central fireplace. Introductions, handshakes, salutary kisses from the men and women, a longer hug and kiss from Liesl, and the familiar stares of her friends scrutinizing him for his height before they all remembered their manners and pretended indifference.

Three women in addition to Liesl, and two men. So who was the woman Liesl was trying to set him up with? What would Liesl's matchmaking attempts be aiming for? He felt entitled to one last appraisal of Liesl—truly, the loveliest of them all, even more incandescent since their last encounter; her white-blond hair was spun gold in the warm firelight.

Roberto noticed the short-haired, quiet little mouse of a girl . . . she must be five foot two, Ferda, so surely that was not likely, unless the thought of more than a foot between them amused Liesl.

Then there was the fiery Italian (he assumed), Claudia, in her thirties and at peak looks, interrupting everyone, flirting with the men, leaning her head against the women on the sofa, full of kinetic energy. She wrapped her arms around her lovely, long legs scooped up into the overstuffed lounge chair. She would bring her forearms together and rest her head magnificently on her hands, her ink-black hair—a separate roiling entity—spilling around her face. There was a natural ballet to the woman merely sitting on a sofa . . . and from all Roberto knew about women, someone that sensual was *not* going to settle for his undependable sexual services.

Then there was the third young woman, Marthe. Pale white with facial freckles, a little horsey, barking out her German and laughing seconds longer at everything than warranted. Sturdy peasant stock. Marthe proposed getting up super early for breakfast, to be first on the trail—*What are we even here for, ja? Let's get hiking!* He felt zero attraction for her, and if this was the big hookup, then he would have to telegraph to Liesl that he wasn't interested. Maybe he should slip away early rather than make a social fiasco of things.

The two young men were college pals of Liesl's. Hans was shorter, compact, all ropy muscle and blond curls and smiles—a dreamboat, really. He was Tyrolean, a blend of the best of the Germanic and Italian looks. Jürgen was not nearly as handsome—skinny, pale, brown hair, and an undistinguished face with lots of moles—but it was Jürgen whom Liesl seemed to be wrapping herself around. He was as earnest as she was playful. Liesl was constantly shocking Jürgen, fooling him with her deadpan, making him laugh at her funny voices. She had found her ideal audience.

Roberto had interrupted them, all Germans, savaging the Swiss, which he understood was a fond German pastime (second to savaging the Austrians).

Marthe regaled them with the cleaning exploits of her Swiss sister-in-law, who gave public restrooms the once-over with wipes and sprays she carried in her purse before she let her children use them.

"How unnecessary," said Roberto. "Swiss toilets, at any hour of the day, are so clean you could perform a surgery on the bathroom floor, eat off the toilet rim . . ." It was strange to hear Germans complain about cleanliness.

Or, thought Roberto, the quiet. The insane pursuit of quiet in Switzerland has left many a foreigner shunned, fined, arrested. Housing associations who issue warnings when a tenant flushes the toilet after 10:00 p.m. Ditto draining of the bathtub, going up and down the common stairs, closing one's car door in the street, operating an automatic garage door—what kind of subhuman does these things after 10:00 p.m.?

But these topics were but antipasti to the main course of Swiss recycling.

The Swiss have garbage detectives (the Association of Swiss Recycling Organizations) to track down just who put the plastic-seeming polystyrene innocently in the plastic bin. Did you peel back the foil top (to be recycled separately as foil) to your plastic container of chocolate mousse?

Did you slip off the outer paper label identifying it as chocolate mousse—that is, for paper recycling. Did you *wash your trash* before recycling it so no bits of food remain? At some point, a citation appears in your mailbox relieving you of the equivalent of hundreds of dollars—ignorance or foreignness is no excuse.

"They can't be that bad!" shrieked Liesl.

"Wait," said Jürgen, back in English, "here is the definite Swiss story . . ."

His brother had gone nearly a month without running afoul of the Basel garbage police. He bundled his old newspapers and tied them up with a hemp cord. Anything other than the hemp cord will mean fines . . . but he did not tie the knot by the prescribed knot-tying regulation. The newspapers were picked up dutifully, silently, but in a few weeks, he had amassed thousands in fines for not tying the official knot. He went to city hall to complain, only to be presented with *photos* of his newspaper bundles showing his knots (tied as one ties one's shoes, harmless enough, but wrong). *How do you know these are my bundles?* he asked. Then more photos were produced of him in his overcoat, clearly identifiable, leaving his bundles. Only a neighbor could have taken the photos, a neighbor who must have noticed the illegal knot and *began compiling a dossier to hand over to the garbage police.*

"That is the Swiss way, like the Stasi," Jürgen said. "Secret reports, neighbors spying on neighbors and compiling grievances about noise or flushed toilets or piles of garbage leaning rather than standing up straight . . ."

Everyone nodded.

"Hard to believe," Marthe said, "that such nice people could steal billions in treasure from the Jews during the World War."

"Ach, I had family that were exterminated," said Claudia. "No Holocaust talk tonight, please."

Liesl stood and announced, "I will be the Schweizerin, ja? And order everyone to their beds, to be oh so quiet, to sleep. For tomorrow, der Gletscher."

Everyone did as instructed. Roberto made his way to his room. Only nine thirty—geez, he hadn't turned in that early since he was in elementary school. He watched Claudia and Marthe walk together . . . Ferda and Liesl shared a room . . . Jürgen and Hans shared a room. Would Liesl slip away and knock gently on his door and snuggle up next to him? It seemed she had her eye on Jürgen, but . . .

There were, Roberto surmised as the hours passed, to be no secret night visitors.

As Roberto let the coolish thinner air lull him, let the snuggled warmth under the duvet comfort him, he knew a supreme sleep awaited. Maybe that's all the Swiss were after: this pacific presleep bliss. After a lifetime of noise and chaos, the totalitarian quiet is welcome—Tina Turner, after all, retired to Switzerland. "Switzerland is for us older people, Bobby," his father always reminded him. "Young people can't take it!"

The next morning was beautiful, clear and sunny, prompting a rearrangement of proposed hikes so they could take advantage of the highest views. Over a thirty-item breakfast buffet arrayed by the Gästehaus, it became clear that Claudia had no interest in hiking or the glacier; she rejected all proposed group activities. She wore a light dress fashionable for the Roman summer and an inadequate ski jacket on top of it. She declared she would stay in the lodge and work on her article. "I'll be here when you get back," she promised, "with a tableful of snacks and open bottles of wine—just text me when you start down the hill."

Roberto had left his gloves on the nightstand, so the gang left without him, and he promised to catch up to them on the trail. In coming back from his room, he saw Claudia sprawled on the divan by the fire in the hotel's central room, making notes directly onto the pages of a textbook.

"Forgot my gloves," he announced.

"Aw, I thought it was to make an excuse to come see me." She patted the divan beside her, righting herself into a sitting position. "You can cheat and take the gondola to the same viewpoint and be waiting for them, perhaps?" Again, she patted the place next to her. "We are supposed to amuse the lovely Liesl by falling into each other's arms. Are you not part of this scheme?"

Roberto did sit, unbuttoning his down vest in the warmth of the firepit. "I am as innocent as you. Liesl did not say which of her friends I was supposed to seduce. I was pulling for you."

Pulling for you did not register as an idiom; she looked quizzical.

"Hoping it was you," he tried.

"How could I be flattered when the other two women in our competition are so . . . no, let's not be unkind. She said you were tall and, mio Dio, and it is true. And Liesl reported . . ."

Roberto decided to be direct. "She said I had some sexual issues."

"Normal and health-related. Nothing to be ashamed of. *My* issues are psychological, I fear. Far more of a tangle. But we should not even have a date here, where there is no air, where the food is appalling and under a blanket of greasy Swiss raclette." Her left hand was like a bird flapping its wings, waving away all whatevers. "Did you dine here last night? In the cast-iron plate was pickles, salted and peppered, covered in molten raclette. Now I ask you: What cuisine on earth has united the pickle with melted cheese?"

She finally looked away from her book to meet Roberto's eyes, and he met hers. There were a few seconds of recognition, recognition of a fellow traveler, two flâneurs, two curious drifters who didn't really belong anywhere, and there was attraction—they were definitely going to have to have sex with each other.

"Così ora, I am a visiting professor at the Politecnico di Milano. I know in your country, a polytechnic is a trade school, but—"

"I am aware the Politecnico di Milano is the best university in Italy."

"Well, I am there to spew sociology at the art and design students, to lecture about human tendencies, unhappy realities, truth. È il mio cavallo di battaglia. But," she was saying, "I have very few useful life skills—my apartment there in Milano . . . is shameful. I have turned it into a ruin. I am incapable of looking after myself. No, no, come see me in Rome in a few weeks where I will be in conference, some European Union–sponsored nonsense. They have me in a five-star, on the Piazza della Minerva, for which I will *not* be paying. We take it slowly and get to know each other. If you wish."

"I do wish."

She scribbled a conference name, a hotel, her dates there, her own full name—Claudia Ciobanu—and did not ask for his particulars. He would show or he wouldn't. Roberto, feeling politely processed, said arrivederci and headed to the trail.

On the last morning, Roberto woke before the sun came up, not able to get back to sleep. Roberto made use of the excellent Wi-Fi (yes, even here on the top of an alp, the Swiss offered an admirable signal) to browse the news and business sites to see the continued reaction to his father's giveaway of all of Hightower Wiggins's execs' perks and parachutes. Newspaper editorials praised him—at last, a Wall Street operative with a conscience! The business journals were less kind: Sal Costa's acting generous like Scrooge on Christmas morning was a stunt, an act, a way to throw the creditors off. Larry Kudlow on Fox Business said it set a bad example for Wall Street—if middle-class investors lose big, so be it, suck it up. The *Wall Street Journal* editorial page pointed out that even if he gave back a billion, that would be only a small percentage of what his customers were owed— and Hightower Wiggins clearly wasn't giving away a billion. Still, *Business Week* put Roberto's father on the cover. Who didn't want a feel-good story amid the collapse of everything? SAINT SALVADOR, the headline read. And in smaller print, HOW ONE CEO IS BEING MR. NICE GUY.

Lou Dobbs on Fox Business dubbed him "Softie Sal." Lou wasn't wrong. Not only did Sal rescue Uncle Vinnie, but he was reluctantly supportive of Roberto borrowing the $200,000 against his trust. What Sal couldn't process was how Roberto imagined he could live with Rachel and his mother—and God help us all—the ineradicable Merle, under one roof.

The sun was above the jagged ridgeline now. Roberto primped and shaved and moisturized, precious subtractions from his cologne and conditioner reserves, especially for their group's final breakfast, hoping for a winning goodbye impression on Claudia and having not entirely given up hope for arranging a future rendezvous with Liesl, before they all piled into the gondola for the real world below.

While Roberto was attending the vanities, Claudia had taken the dawn-departing gondola off the mountain and was en route to Milan. They could have gone together, ridden the same train, talked for hours . . . *But no,* he thought darkly, *I had to perfect my eyebrows.* As for Liesl, she and Jürgen were downstairs at the breakfast table, her leg touching his, her hand atop his as they finished off the pot of tea, laughing, flirting. Roberto, lumbering with his worldly possessions, his battered suitcase, duffel, backpack on his shoulders, stopped by their table for a goodbye, a kiss for both, a hope to hike with them again soon. Liesl was warm but eager to return to her incendiary topic—whatever it was—with Jürgen. As he left the hotel, he heard her familiar shrieks of laughter, whoops of interest, the musical play of her voice behind him, echoing off the rafters . . . Roberto had spent four hundred euros of his few thousands to earn a dutiful cheek kiss from Liesl.

Ugo and Enrico

Rachel texted, out of the blue: WHAT DO YOU KNOW? LENA'S ACTUALLY STUMBLED ONTO SOMETHING GOOD!

This started a series of photos sent regularly from Rachel of the living room, the balcony view, the canals, the local trattoria . . . Clearly, Rachel was sold on the place. At what point would it sink in that this was a house for three and not for four (Merle)?

In the meantime, as ever, seeking a couch or a forgotten bed next to a dog basket in the basement, he called Ludo with his oh-by-the-way, I happened to be in Mantova! Whaddya know? Maybe we could dine?

Ludovico Marchesini was overjoyed—Roberto must come by the house! (Lucrezia was in Milan, where she preferred to remain rather than mingle with Ludo's plainspoken family.) Ludo, and a school-days friend, were in Mantova only long enough to transport his grandmother to his parents' house in Bergamo. What good timing that Roberto passed through on their last day. "My parents feel it's best to look after Nonna when winter comes," Ludo explained, "but the truth not to be spoken aloud is that they much love her to cook for them when they are busy with the university, and it gets cold." He kissed his fingers.

Nonna, Ludo insisted, was an artisan of the region's adored buckwheat; she would make her pizzoccheri with the greens from his mother's back garden. And also her sciatt, the buckwheat cheese balls. And her risotto! The broth she made in the stockpot with chicken bones and skin, saffron, onion, before refining it . . . And if they were lucky, there would be the first frost and that meant, traditionally, the making of cassoeula, Ludo's favorite. It was like the French cassoulet, but one did not say that too

169

loudly to a proud Lombard—pork, organ meats, offal, some goose, some chicken, some sausage, held together by cabbage and fat . . . "Lucrezia refuses to eat it," Ludo explained, "since it is impossibly rich, calorical—you say that? The eater is condemned to two days of making farting."

"I'll eat her portion," Roberto offered.

Roberto now met Mira Visser, just returning from a run. Not even the baggy tracksuit could disguise the lithe, androgynous, athletic ideal that was Mira. She pulled off her sweatshirt to reveal the tank top underneath and the lightly muscled arms and rounded shoulders most fitness trainers would kill for. Mira was gamine, sporting a short bob of dark blond hair, a direct stare from gray eyes, features that held steady around an almost-smile that was pleasant enough but not inviting. Roberto had been told (by Rupesh) that everyone he was attracted to could read it on his face from the first second; he had no ability to play anything cool, so he tried looking at the ground. Ludo told Mira that Roberto spoke all of Europe's languages.

"U bent toch zeker Nederlander?" she asked him, wondering if he were Dutch because of his height. She exaggerated craning her neck upward.

"Ik heb een Nederlands Amerikaanse stiefvader," Roberto said, mentioning his Dutch-descended stepfather. "Perhaps that counts? And that's about the only sentence I can construct in Dutch."

The almost-smile again. "Oh, *was* that Dutch?"

Ludo explained that Mira was a classmate from when he went to Delft for architecture school. Mira had sensibly, Ludo narrated, abandoned architecture and had become an academic, specializing in something modern to do with gender studies, something, Ludo laughed, beyond his understanding. What exactly was there to study?

"Oh, for a beginning," she said, "remarks like that from threatened men."

Roberto was about to ask why Ludo went so far away to Delft to architecture school when right next door was Milan's Politecnico, one of the best architecture schools in Europe . . . when tact raced in from his subconscious: maybe Ludo had not been *accepted* for study in the Milanese program. Lately, Roberto had wondered just how successful or prolific Ludo had been in his profession. From the looks of his grandmother's country home, the second house in Bergamo ahead, his Milan town house, and of course his toys, the sports car, the clothes, Lucrezia . . . perhaps the architecture was a Potemkin profession for a life of leisure.

Nonna—in her nineties!—found the American giant Roberto Costa endlessly curious; she stared at him every chance she got. But she was charmed that he spoke such serviceable Italian. Roberto knew his value to the party increased by his ability to entertain the sweet but detail-negligent matriarch. With Ludo's grandmother worrying and fretting, the Mantova house was closed up and the two cars were packed (Ludo's heavenly Audi TT roadster, and Mira's deteriorating Golf). Nonna was delicately set down in the pillowed Audi passenger seat, enclosed with blankets, buckled in, handed a bottle of water for the trip. Ludo was surly, snapping about something at Mira, who was not the object of his scorn . . . she spat something back in agreement. They kissed socially, and Mira returned to her car.

The night before, Roberto had thought Ludo and Mira might be enjoying an affair, but though they seemed familiar, Roberto did not pick up on any forbidden-love electricity between them or even much in the way of friendliness. Indeed, Roberto's gaydar gave a slight reading; it seemed possible that Mira was a lesbian, which could explain her choice of academic specialty.

Roberto struggled to fit in the passenger seat of Mira's auto, but this was a familiar ordeal for him, endured throughout Europe. The Bastille's "Room of Little Ease" came to mind.

"Is Ludo upset about something?" Roberto asked Mira as they made their way toward the A22.

"Lucrezia rang. Hearing *you* were with us, she has decided to join us."

Roberto did not know if he could ask a personal question of Mira, so he asked no follow-ups about who was sleeping with whom.

The Marchesinis were delightful. The mother could have been on the stage, magnificent in bearing and hair (black and full in the manner of Susan Sontag) and clothes and clanking costume jewelry; the father, also a nationally famous academic, could have been confused with the grounds crew, a little shambling, mumbly, and content to while away his Tuesday afternoon in the garden. They were buried under university life during the week, but on Saturdays, they made a jailbreak. Please, they begged, stay until Saturday so we all might get to know one another! But Roberto had to be in Milan on the Friday to secure this house in Navigli. The chorus of approbation proved that no Lombard would fault him for that.

Last thing before midnight, time difference in mind, he called Mrs. Santos.

Mrs. Santos went down a list of things he had to sign and initial, papers that would be sent to the new address. Mostly, she wanted to know if he was crazy. "You sure you want to live with your sister and your mother? Who'll be coming into your room every night and sneaking bills out of your wallet?"

"I'll invest in a padlock," he said.

Lena's bank officer, Signor Ravoni, checked out, a senior bank officer at Banco Popolare di Lodi. Mrs. Santos: "Your father says Ravoni, like his bank, is probably crooked as the day is long. That's not a demerit for doing business in Italy, however." She emailed a cluster of information documents for purchasing property in Italy so Roberto could study up.

"I processed your sister's loan payment yesterday," Mrs. Santos reported, "so she's got her money. Yours will show up Monday. You have the weekend to run screaming from the whole thing."

"Thank you, Mrs. Santos."

The next morning Roberto rose at a decent time for a guest, downstairs by 9:00 a.m., he had nonetheless missed the Marchesinis, who had fled to the university, as well as Mira and Ludo, who had disappeared on some architectural mission. If it was to check out new architecture or historical buildings, that was the sort of excursion Roberto would *very much have liked* to have been included in. But it was now clear his role was to serve as Lucrezia's babysitter. The barking of the dogs around 11:00 p.m. had been explainable as Lucrezia's late arrival at the house. The Marchesinis' housekeeper had left out a breakfast that was mostly cakes and cookies.

"You are still going to be a writer, yes?" Lucrezia asked, sitting in the breakfast nook with her espresso.

"Yes, those Notebooks you made fun of still exist."

"I did not make fun, not really. You write about everything, do you not? Did you write about me back in 2003?"

"I'm sure I did," he said. (He did not.)

There was a cheese and a cured meat stick, a salami soppressata. What exactly was suppressed? The bane of Italian train travel is the echoey declaration over the PA in the cavernous station that one's train, *é soppresso*, is canceled. Could the soppressata ("annihilated, canceled") have been so delicious that there were moves to suppress it? Or did it have its roots in Spain, where pork was suppressed under Muslim rule? Another rumination for the Notebook.

"I too have an idea for a book." It was the most vivid he had seen his old friend. "You must help me to write it—you must! Here is the big idea, a big book of photos for the . . . how you say . . . you put out onto a table for all to see." Roberto told her she meant a "coffee table book."

"Photos from your career?"

"One or two maybe, but mostly me and cats. I love cats, as you know." That was news to Roberto. "I have an idea. I pose with a lovely kitten or cat from each province of Italy. Like for Liguria, I go to Camogli and I find a cat who lives near the fishing boats. I capture his life, where he goes, what he eats, I make a little story about him. And I wear clothes of a designer from the region or some kind of local hat or dress—I am not as important as the cat of the province."

"Any old cat of the harbor? It might bite you." Roberto pictured the lovely face of Lucrezia cuddling a series of unwilling, straining-to-escape, rabid alley cats all over Italy. "And you would write something to go with the photos?"

"I want you to help me do that! You can tell the story of how I met each cat, where we wandered . . . I think it will be very artistic. It will be a travel book, a cat book, a Lucrezia book. Popular too; people love cats. They used to love *me*," she added with a wink. "Oh, let us pick up where we left off." Roberto wasn't sure what that meant. "We had such fun back in Milano. You remember, don't you?"

Lucrezia and her beautiful friends, Roberto remembered. He learned that it was possible to be around so much beauty you didn't even see it anymore. Lucrezia dragged him to shoots (intensely boring) and runway shows (often exciting). Being tall and striking, Roberto was assumed to belong. There were the twins from Somalia; the daughter of a famous supermodel, who was an utterly miserable drunk; and who else . . . oh yes, Yuri, the gorgeous Russian.

Lucrezia one night, in some club, slid into Roberto's booth with some Russian male model: Eurasian eyes with black irises, cheekbones like arêtes, unblemished snow-white skin but with full lips lasciviously too big for his face.

"Yuri says he wants to kiss you," Lucrezia had announced. "And I told him he could."

"All right," said Roberto, "but you must kiss a girl I choose."

She had shrugged; that was barely a dare. Yuri mumbled something in broken English about his name being naughty, Yuri Yurkov—wasn't that naughty in English? He slid closer to Roberto in the booth but then seemed nervous. Roberto kissed Yuri . . . who was a much better kisser than Lucrezia, for the record. As he did it, Lucrezia cleared her throat. "Time is up," she announced, but Roberto let Yuri enjoy another three seconds.

Lucrezia launched herself from the booth, storming off. "I will let you two be gay! Buona notte, *froci!*"

Lucrezia had been talking about her cat book, and Roberto hadn't been listening. He decided to bail out early. "Lucrezia. You had so many artistic acquaintances in Milan. Surely there is someone in the arts who would be a better partner than I would."

Artistic acquaintances. No sooner had he said that than he remembered that Lucrezia had thrown an alarm clock at him because of an art opening he attended without her. They were to go to the opening of her long-time sister-like best, best, *best friend in the whole world,* then Lucrezia got cramps and canceled, but Roberto went anyway, socialized, praised the woman's quite excellent art, went out with the artist and fellow celebrants that night. "What, I am sick, and you go and try to fuck her? Did you fuck her in her artist's studio, on top of one of her bullshit paintings?"

Lucrezia was a thrower . . . shoes, coffee cups, once she beaned him with a book of Andrea Zanzotto's poems, which bounced off his head and over the balcony, gone into a Venetian canal . . . (Well, Roberto was struggling with the dialect anyway.) She was also a notorious canceler. That time they planned their road trip down the Adriatic. Reservations made, Croatian hotels booked . . . of course, she chose the night before departure, when no purchase could be refunded, to say that Roberto had been a trifle, some summer fun, goodbye forever. She treated many of her photo shoots the same way—waiting until everyone was gathered before announcing she was not even in the country of the shoot. Hence her career decline. Hence her long-awaited comeback clutching feral cats from Val d'Aosta and Molise . . .

"But I was so hoping you would say yes," she sighed.

"Well then," he said, smiling as broadly as he could. "I'll say yes." It wasn't like there was a prayer for this project to be realized. Lucrezia was so grateful he thought she might cry. Later that afternoon, she promised to take him into Bergamo's centro and show him her favorite cats. "You must meet Ugo and Enrico . . ."

Around the many-doored hodgepodge of the Duomo di Bergamo was a little-used back door of the 1100s, a marble porch with columns resting upon Romanesque stone lions.

"These are my kitty cats, see?" She petted their cold stone heads.

An Italian parishioner, leaving the church, began to stare at Lucrezia. He knew she was famous but couldn't place her . . .

"You are still world-famous," Roberto said, hoping to see her melancholy cloud lift for a moment. The compliment did not work; she smiled wistfully—her glory was over, the reckoning was in her eyes. But the next minute, she did beam again, intending to tell Roberto how and why she named the six stone cats of the Duomo di Bergamo. Let us walk around, she suggested, "so I can say *buongiorno* to them all."

Roberto humored her, and they made the tour from door to door. She reached out to take his hand. Nothing romantic or sexual registered for Roberto; it was like taking the hand of a winsome child.

Navigli

Lena had a five-by-seven cherrywood frame holding a sepia photo of an elderly lady, looking kindly and beatific, like a proper Italian grandma. Lena looked around the apartment for wall space, mumbling, "I'll be happy when the academic couple who Ravoni has let take the place moves out, and we can begin decorating." Lena settled on a wall that faced the entryway; when one came in from the stairwell, you would directly see the picture of this kindly grandmother. A moment later, she hammered a nail into the plaster and hung the picture.

"And just who is that?" Roberto asked.

"Why, it's Bothild Stern, our benefactress. I met her just once—the photographers must have worked all goddamn day for a smile this nice. She was a mean old thing like her sister in Bern."

The apartment on the top floor of a reformed warehouse on via Corsico was all that it was touted to be: one large bedroom (for Lena), two smaller ones for Roberto, and for Rachel, a vast living area with the kitchen nook to the side—and the roof! A whole separate plane upon which to garden, to arrange chairs and bowers, giant amphorae and trellises, to entertain and host weddings, to celebrate first publications. Roberto, last to arrive, moved into what had been converted to a guest room for a niece or nephew, and there was a child's bed waiting for him, where everything below his knees hung off the end of the bed. Oh well, that was temporary.

Lena gathered them all in the living room for a few pronouncements.

"I have an edict of my own," Rachel said. "No smoking in the house."

Lena, who was lighting up, paused . . . then lit up anyway. "I won't smoke inside often, but I *will* smoke on occasion in a dwelling that I'm sinking my life savings into."

Merle piped up to say that she wanted clarification about the deed. Who would be on it? Rachel should be on it. There should be a codicil concerning Merle as having certain rights and privileges; perhaps, in time, after residency of so many years—

"You are *not* on the deed," Lena barked. "This is a three-person house, and four is a crowd, Merle. You can rent your own place and visit on rare occasion. You and my daughter can meet at your place." Lena turned to Roberto. "You're not on the deed either, or Rachel."

Rachel was about to erupt, but Lena raised her hand.

"I am on the deed, and not you two, for some very good reasons. Frau Stern is selling to *me* because of my long-established story that, like herself, I am estranged from my horrible children. So I cannot buy a property from her with your goddamn names on the deed like we're one happy family. After the purchase, I will add a codicil to my will leaving the apartment to Bobby and Rachel—and you can come with me to get that notarized. Reason number two, thanks to the hovel I own in Cologne, I am an EU resident now and yous two are not. There is a three percent tax for me, which, if your American names are on the deed, goes to *ten* percent. Do you want to come up with another fifteen thousand apiece?"

"Lena, none of us trust you," said Merle.

Rachel asked, "Why did you and Roberto go to the bank, just you two, this morning?"

Roberto blithely answered, "There is a translation fee on an English contract issued for an Italian property. With me in the room, we can deal entirely in Italian, so we are avoiding that fee—or perhaps you would like to chip in for that?"

"I speak some Italian," Rachel mumbled.

"You speak tourist Italian." Roberto asked his sister, "Nessun privilegio, giudizio, o pagamento gravato può essere imputato al valore della proprietà." She stared at him blankly. "I rest my case."

Lena was impatient. "I will go with the nice Signor Ravoni to Bern first thing Monday to have Frau Stern sign the property over and receive our down payment of six hundred thousand dollars, but in Swiss francs. That'll keep the old girl in insipid figurines, for the time being."

"*Il rogito*," said Roberto. "That's what this process is called. As soon as she signs, the property is ours. If Frau Stern's heirs get wind of this, they can stop it and demand that their consent to sell be part of the contract."

"When did you become such an expert?" Rachel asked.

"Mrs. Santos sent me a booklet on buying property in Italy. These are my life savings too, you know."

Merle announced, "How are we supposed to trust this Signor Ravoni?"

Roberto interjected, "Rachel, actually, has met him."

Rachel was stymied. "Umm . . ."

Roberto: "You remember the man in the lab coat who walked alongside Lena in the Frankfurt train station? That was Signor Ravoni. I recognized him immediately."

"May I ask," Merle said with especial primness, "are you, Lena, and Signor Ravoni involved in a romantic relation of some kind?"

Lena paused a little too long, wondering if she should be offended.

"Oh, Mother," Rachel said, "so that's true."

"I like to leave nothing to chance," Lena stated with feeling, before turning to her son. "I have been working this plan for *months.* He came with me to Frankfurt so we could continue on to Cologne, where he is handling the sale of my apartment. Bobby, would you say Alessandro Ravoni is an attractive man?"

"I would."

Merle proposed that she and Rachel accompany Ravoni and Lena to Bern for the signing over of the deed.

Lena exhaled a long blue plume. "No, you will not. You're giving the lie to my story of being a lonely abandoned woman, racked with grief and heartache, who Frau Stern, out of the kindness of her heart, wishes to help find a place to settle. If she dies—which she could do any goddamn day—then this property folds into her overall estate and her kids will get this place, and fat chance we'll be living here."

Lena stood and paced in a frantic, intense fashion her children had long recognized. "And it is by no means certain," she continued, "that that witch, even with the money in hand, won't back out of it. She's greedy. And I ought to know, being greedier—but not by much."

Rachel muttered, "I would hope if you were seeing this Ravoni guy socially that it accrues some advantage to us."

"The notary fee is fifteen hundred euros, which he has waived. There are other complexities, which Sandro has been kind enough to help me with."

Everyone was silent, waiting for her to divulge.

Rachel: "Mom, what complexities?"

Lena: "If this was an agented rather than a private, friend-to-friend purchase, there would be something called the IVA tax. The tax will come to, oh, twenty-two percent . . ."

Merle gasped. "Christ . . . that would be . . . *one point two million more euros?*"

"Sandro says," Lena brought out carefully, "that one can apply for an extension in a sale like this."

Merle: "And why would they give you an extension?"

"Because a respected banker and *notaio* like Signor Ravoni is arranging it. He was at the very *center* of the Banco di Lodi scandal a few years back. He has a lot of respect in Lombardy."

Roberto said, "You'll still have to pay it, Mother."

"I'm gonna. With a loan against the property, which Signor Ravoni will be nice enough to set up."

Merle's head was spinning. "I cannot deal with a woman like you."

"No, sweetheart, you can't. I'm what you *wish you could be*! Someone who can work the system like a pro and not just flail about, threatening and sputtering and making empty demands. In a year, this property will be worth seven, eight million euros, and a loan against the gains in equity would be given by any bank on earth—and from that loan, I will pay the deferred taxes."

Rachel and Merle looked at each other.

Roberto asked, "And Signor Ravoni is party to this? What's his cut?"

Lena: "This is where our long-standing friendship comes into play. He is prepared to wait for his share."

Merle mumbled, "But that's fraud, and if it comes out—"

"DO YOU," Lena said at a volume to crack the plaster ceiling, "want to live in Milan in this fucking deluxe apartment in the heart of Navigli"—pronounced wrong—"or DON'T YOU?"

Again, her three listeners fell silent.

"Count me in," Roberto said presently. "It's about time your life of grifting paid some benefit to your children."

Merle hesitated. "I do want to talk to you alone, Lena. If I may."

Both Rachel and Merle stared at Roberto like he was an outcast.

Lena said, "I will discuss whatever arrangement you want to discuss, and then I will say no, throw you out, and that will be the end of it. All right?"

Now Lena, Rachel, and Merle looked in unison at Roberto as if he were an immense impediment.

"Okay, okay," Roberto said, and grabbed his jacket hanging on a hook and made for the door. "I'll call Dad and get him to wire the money to me right away."

From the Metro at the end of what would be his new street, via Corsico, he was seven stops later in the glorious Piazza del Duomo di Milano. He wanted a peek at the shuffle of humanity outside the Duomo, the newsstands around the piazza with so many international business titles (had his father made another of the covers?). It constituted a waste to be in Milano without walking by the most beautiful shop windows featuring the most beautiful clothes; a stroll through the Galleria Vittorio Emanuele II, the St. Peter's Basilica of shopping. He walked past La Scala—he could now have frequent access to the best of opera now. Beyond that, the Fabriano paper boutique, purveyors of the world's best papers since before the Renaissance. Michelangelo bought art supplies here, and he, Roberto Costa, in his pre-laptop/pre-iPad days, bought notebooks upon which he filled creamy, satiny blank page after page with his impressions, the pen floating atop the sateen stationery. Between the big names in fashion, the coming-up names in fashion, the discounted past-their-prime designers, the perfumers and the makeup houses, the sumptuous design stores for kitchenware and furniture—which no amount of Costa fortune would allow Roberto to own a stick of—there were the flower shops, with a confetti of stray petals on the sidewalk. He supposed Lazzaretto, with its bookshops and one great gelato bar, was too far to walk . . .

About the time he was sensing that he should call his father—it would be evening, after his television show in New York—his father called him.

"Just spoke to your sister. She wants in for four hundred thousand."

"I thought we were only going to spend . . ."

. . . and that's when Roberto surmised that they had wanted him away from the apartment so they could work out a deal that *excluded* Roberto. After one second of regret, of panic—and that's all it was, one second—Roberto felt relief. A home with his mother? With Merle and Rachel in permanent residence, competing over refrigerator space, who gets to sit on the rooftop garden when, whose music is allowed to be played . . . Just as well. His season tickets at La Scala, his Armani linens, his standing order of ossobuco from the legendary Macelleria Masseroni, right around the corner from the apartment, all blew away like smoke.

"I said I would approve no more than three hundred thousand apiece," Sal went on. "The trust is about under a million, and I don't think you kids should clean it out. After this 2008 dip, the market will correct, and I'm confident Hightower Wiggins shares will rise again. But if this is what you guys want—"

"Dad," he interrupted. "I don't think I *do* want in on the deal, after all."

His father was quiet a moment. "That's the right idea, Bobby. Geez. A house with Rachel, Merle, and Lena? It will be a race to see who poisons who first."

"I put my money on Mom as the last one standing."

All was suspiciously lighthearted when Roberto came back to via Corsico.

Lena was all little-girl laughter, sitting at a table with Merle, looking at a fashion magazine. Okay, fifty things were wrong with that visual. Rachel was nowhere to be seen—perhaps she had retired to her room to avoid what could be drama. So Roberto retired to his room—or what would have been his room. He sorted through his Alps and Mantova photos, waiting for the guillotine to fall.

Around 9:00 p.m., there was a quiet knock on the door.

"Yes?"

Lena stuck her head around the corner. "You and your father needn't trouble yourself any further." She smiled piteously.

"Let me hear you say it."

"Oh, Bobbikins. I am going to make this deal solely with your sister and Merle. When I thought of this, I thought it would be the three of us, but it is not realistic to imagine Rachel will do without Merle, so we were heading toward four people in this apartment with such small bedrooms. It's not really workable, is it, Bobby? You trapped with all these unpleasant women."

"If that's what you want, Mother. Hard to imagine you preferring to deal with Merle."

"I despise her—you know that."

"Well, how disappointing. I'll need a kill fee."

Lena crossed her arms, nodding slowly.

"I'm down to a few thousand left, and I spent a chunk of it to meet you here, with the expectation of housing. Just to breathe the air in Milan costs money. What are you prepared to give me as a peace offering? I would hate for this most recent treachery to . . . to come between us."

His mother pursed her lips. "I'll go check with Merle."

Roberto could hear the buzzing, voices intensifying but still whispery. In the meantime, he packed up his few clothes in preparation for his morning departure.

His mother knocked again. "For Merle to read the deed contract in English, we were going to pay the translation fee of five thousand dollars—rather, Merle was, since it was her demand. She will trust Signor Ravoni to deal honorably with us and give the five thousand to you. This is Merle's money, mind you."

"I will need ten thousand. I might ring up Frau Stern's children and let them know you are coming to Bern for the sale of their late-aunt's property, which could be potentially theirs."

His mother didn't seem at all fazed. Maybe she was even a bit proud. Look at her little boy, shaking someone down like his ol' mother . . . She got up and returned to the whispered negotiations in the living room. Then she returned.

"Rachel and Merle will each write you a check for five thousand. And you will make no trouble and try to—"

"Be nice about it?"

Lena shrugged. "You don't have to be nice to Merle. I certainly do not intend to be. It's good to see, after all her mooching, her putting some of her *own* money into something. But do not follow through on the threat to inform Frau Stern's children."

"Mum's the word. Merle masterminded scraping me off the arrangement?"

Lena took a breath and said, "No, Bobby, it was Rachel."

Roberto sat up a little. "Rachel."

"She didn't want you here. She said."

Roberto nodded. Rachel had always needed an enemy. Now her war was against the men in the family—himself, hated simply for his bothering to exist and divide her inheritance—and their father, who wouldn't give her all the money she wanted, who couldn't simply be a father who, after a million indulgences, now had to be cast as a CIA operative of the corrupt state, a Bond villain in a bad tie, a Mafia accountant, a totalitarian statue in the public square of capitalism that had to be pulled down by a righteous mob, led by herself and Merle.

But Roberto Costa was the author of the ten-volume *Notebooks,* the ultimate flâneur, wit, mordant observer, looking in keyholes where he shouldn't. Ha, to be a partial homeowner in pretentious Milan wouldn't have been on brand, non è così?

The next morning was a stiff morning, with Rachel fearfully checking his gaze and Roberto keeping his face impassive. Let them think he was crushed. They wrote him two checks for five thousand euros apiece. There was a Santander branch next to La Scala, where he had wandered the day before. Bank deposit, then the train station.

The train to Rome. Not the alta velocità deluxe businessman Eurostar, gleaming showcase of Italian design and engineering, but the standard second-class compartment on the InterCity Milano to Roma.

There was an art to not being joined in a European train compartment. With Roberto's proportions, he could sprawl over two chairs with legs extended into the opposite seating space, looking menacing, pretending an open-mouthed, ugly sleep to keep others from venturing into his compartment. But actually, handsome and unusually tall, he remained a figure of interest, and train-riding Italians couldn't wait to invade his sanctum and, at minimum, stare. A family of six—mother, father, grandmother, one older daughter, and two three-year-olds talking and moving so fast that they were a blur as to gender—invaded the compartment, as did the grandmother's picnic basket, out of which came plates, cutlery, thermoses of soup, cups for the soup, olives, Tupperware bowls of brined peppers, several sausages, cheeses, a crusty bread. Roberto straightened up and, defeated, made himself small.

"Soppressata?" The very first slice of sausage, cheese, and bread was offered to Roberto.

"Grazie, signora," he said, converted from grump to family member in an instant.

Amoral Familism

Roberto found the five-star Grand Hotel de la Minerve, swank and gilded in every particular, for which he was poorly dressed. But the beautiful attendants at the registration desk nonetheless pointed him toward the room where Dr. Ciobanu's presentation was being held. Moments later, the electric chandeliers were dimmed, the sizable crowd fell quiet, and Claudia walked out to applause. She was a knockout in a form-fitting chartreuse dress; a green-and-gold scarf held back her ink-black sprawl of hair.

"Thank you," she said, "for showing up for the sequel of what we began yesterday. To those just joining us, my team's assignment from Brussels has been an analysis of why our development projects fail from a sociologist's standpoint. It is easy to say, ah, well, there is *corruzione, la bustarella,* bribes were not paid, palms were not oiled . . . but there are more complicated social mechanisms at work. I have some stories from Southern Italy, but they are the same story . . . the story of what, back as far as the 1950s, was termed *amoral familism.* Not unique to Italy but practiced *here* alla perfezione."

Claudia's PowerPoint graphs appeared behind her—budgets, projects, money spent, projects completed. The European Union had, apparently, poured countless opportunity funds into the south of Italy—she had scenic slides inserted into the presentation—the billboard with the EU gold circle of stars on the blue flag greeting visitors to Bari, Matera, Cosenza, usually with some scurrilous graffiti added. No area of Europe—indeed, none of the EU's idealistic seed money to North Africa or the Caucasus—*nowhere,* Claudia reported, had EU money disappeared *into the void* as it did in

Southern Italy in the 1990s. Water treatment, electricity grid modernization, subsidized manufacturing, infrastructure—all that money delivered and absorbed, Claudia related with a finger snap, gone without a trace.

She had many amusing tales of outright theft, chicanery, scams, and cons, but her focus was on where money was desperately needed but there would be *one single family* attempting a bribe or grift, and that would halt the entire project, cause the whole community to lose countless opportunities . . . yet none of the locals resented the family for their attempt. In Basilicata, an EU representative had every door, window, stick of furniture, every pot and pan, every scrap of clothes in the closet stolen from his leased house when he was away on an assignment. The local water company, owned by a single large family, wished to hook the EU's representative's home up to their water, which the EU's man refused, because his family already enjoyed copious well water. So the water company cleaned him out. When he conceded to be hooked up for a great fee to the town water supply, his things were returned in the exact place they had been last seen. Claudia delighted in the incident's finishing touches:

"He had, five days before, poured a bowl of cereal but hadn't eaten it, distracted by an argument with his wife—it was there, just as it had been, on the counter. His crossword puzzle and his pencil, lying at the very angle in which he had left it. And one addition: a dessert waiting for him in the refrigerator, a *sanguinaccio.* Anyone had this? It's quite good. But it is a pudding of rich dark chocolate and pig's blood."

The crowd murmured; the Northern Europeans were amused and revolted.

"The theft, and the symbolic dessert, was a work of *theater,* of prestidigitation."

Her slides showed the restored mansion.

"The Italians"—she paused for a dramatic sigh—"understand, as no one else, the flourish, the gesture. This tendency has led to so much excellent design and art, but the tendency is also alive in Italian corruption and crime. The EU pulled its funds for another community, and that's when I came in to research. There was little to no objection in the town to the water-company shakedown. Had any of them owned the water company, they would have attempted the same thing too.

"Another story, from Calabria. There is a town, Bovala, that is famous for its lace. It is a quaint stone hilltop village—probably unchanged since the days the Greeks or the Saracens controlled it. There's a major high-way around it, but to enter the village itself is near impossible in a car. Narrow one-lane main street, no room to pass, no place to park. Old ladies and their intricate, exquisite lace, sit in their doorways, or in small niches of space on this main street, breathing vehicle exhaust and diesel fumes all day, hoping someone will pull into one of the few parking spots in the middle of town, a little plaza, treacherous to get in or out of, with maybe five places to park. Then a tourist would have to walk back to find the lace maker he spotted, sharing the tiny street with the traffic that forces you to press yourself against a wall as a car goes by.

"So our EU agent saw all this and proposed that they relocate the lace makers to a now-abandoned shop on the edge of town by the bypass highway. There was a parking lot for twenty. The elderly lace makers could work inside, in air-conditioning; each would have a cubicle and a table for their wares. Tourists don't often have ready cash—there could be a Bancomat in the store or a central banker who could accept a credit card. But, knowing that citizens do not value things like this unless they have a money stake, the EU project director said each woman (or the family of each woman) had to chip in one hundred euros a year for a space in the readily visible, appealing store property on the edge of town. Projections . . ." More slides appeared showing what each woman made, versus the projections of what they stood to make in the new lace center. "Yes, projections showed a tenfold increase in sales. Not to mention an improved longevity for the women coated in truck exhaust. So there was a vote."

More chuckles from the audience.

"You who know Italy know already how this came out. Twenty-one lace-making families . . . and the vote for this center was twenty-one to zero *against* the project. Amoral familism. Again, you don't understand Italy, certain Greek isles, the Balkans, if you don't understand this. This project would, indeed, benefit their own grandmother who sold her lace . . . but it would benefit the family next door and down the street, rivals and competitors. Why spend a hundred euros so that old lady two doors down might sell her lace on a good day while your grandmother has a bad sales day? Better that we carry on as we always have carried on. If there is no direct benefit to the family and *solely the family*, then it strikes many Mediterraneans as a charity to the other families. And if

Great-Grandmother asphyxiates from exhaust and perishes from lung disease, well . . . who is to say it was not her time?"

After some statistical analysis and graphs, she concluded to thunderous applause, a long session of congratulations and cheek kissing. Roberto thought perhaps he should slip away and leave her to her adulation, but she kept checking to see if he was still in place, and so he stayed in place.

"I know a joint," she said, meaning a restaurant still open for another hour. "Isn't that how you Americans talk? You call a restaurant 'a joint'?"

They settled into a pizzeria with simple fare, salads and pastas. Claudia pointed to a wine without even looking to see what it was, beyond its being red.

"I was dazzled by your presentation," Roberto said, filling her glass once the waiter opened the bottle. "I am dazzled by you. I could not help but think how my family should be studied by sociologists for the opposite impulse—immoral *anti*-familism."

She smiled but went right away to flirting: "If we are to have a little fling," Claudia began, tearing the scarf from her hair and freeing the wild mane, "we cannot tell Liesl. Think of how smug she would be."

Roberto asked how she even knew Liesl. Claudia and Jürgen had a fling when Claudia lectured at Technische Universität Darmstadt, and

through her tryst with Jürgen—doomed, as she declared all her recent relationships had been—she met Liesl, whom she could not help but like. "She is so blond and cheerful. I tried to resist, but one cannot hate her."

"How well I know. Yes. Even if you and I marry and have ten children, we will never tell her." (Meanwhile, Roberto wondered what kind of love potion uninteresting, moley Jürgen must use to enchant two of the most glamorous women he had ever met.)

Claudia, in post-presentation joyfulness, downed her glass of red in a few swallows. She murmured, "No children for me, though I accept your marriage proposal. My books, my public lectures are my children. Besides, I like going into the lion's den. Poking around Southern Italy asking about shakedowns and 'Ndrangheta. I am going to Slavonia to ask about how business contacts have flourished or not flourished in an area where neighbor turned on neighbor for genocidal purposes. Something might one day happen to me. Don't want to leave any orphans."

"Sounds like I may be an early widower."

"That will make you even *more* attractive to women—a young widower is catnip," she added as two plates of pasta arrived. This was the real carbonara, an invention of Lazio, the surrounding state of Rome. The black element was cracked pepper, seeming like little burnt flakes of coal—*carbonara*. Pecorino cheese and egg whites, some crispy bits of hog jowl. Not at all the cheesy cream-sodden egg-and-bacon breakfast dump, pawned off on Americans, four thousand calories a plate . . .

"Your being a widower will happen in any event. I am so much older than you."

"I skew older," Roberto said convincingly, though that was not particularly true.

"I take it that Liesl has shared information so that my stigmas and shames are somewhat known to you."

Roberto squirmed good-naturedly. "She was not specific. Liesl implied we should be well matched because we were 'similarly damaged.'"

"Damaged?" Claudia sacrificed her forkful of pasta as she shook her head, disapproving. "We are not damaged, we are nuanced."

"Nuanced." Roberto shared a last thought about Liesl. "Germans and their honesty."

"They drive in with a Panzer every time."

"But I *am* damaged," Roberto said after they shared a moment more of smiling. "My heart. I grew too tall too fast at puberty, and my heart could not catch up. I keep my misfit heart in rhythm with pills"—he patted his jean jacket pocket—"so, one day, a pacemaker. Or a heart attack, whichever comes first."

Claudia gently, under the table, rested her leg against his. Roberto showed no expression, although he noted that mention of his possible death resulted in her first intimate contact.

"And we know," he said, "what circulation can compromise."

"Ah," she said, nodding sagely.

"I am good for a few minutes, but, shall we say, my natural attributes will wither, however strong my desire."

She leaned back in her chair and appraised him, boring through him with her intelligent eyes. "But that has not stopped the women from climbing into your bed, I suspect."

He half smiled.

"No," she went on, "it is probably more appealing than the athletic lovemaking offered by your countrymen, I think. Women are perverse, sometimes preferring the wounded bird to the massive eagle flapping about. But, were we to become lovers, this would be ideal for me."

Roberto dipped the hard ciabatta slice in olive oil, though that did nothing to soften it. He chewed with effort, pretending such a clinical discussion of their future coupling was somehow usual lunch conversation.

She said, "My damage, so to speak, is my history. I had a relationship with an older man; I was too young, a teenager. It turned abusive. The lovemaking was an assault, with bruises and pain, very violent—once a broken rib. Not at first, but it is how he became—we became, because I permitted it by my staying with this man, too bullheaded to run home to my mother."

Roberto looked down.

"For years after," she continued, "I avoided men. I tried with women." She looked up from her recital to see if he registered this.

"And I tried men."

"Not bad," she said of her diversion, "but not what I really wanted." She now tore at the bread and dunked it in the oil. "So I became—I think therapists used to say—frigid. I suppose they have a kinder word for it now. A man would start his, um, motions, and I would break off, I would leap from the bed. Beg him to stop. I was reminded of the . . . my history. Even a gentle man reminded me of my mistreatment once he began to gyrate and search for pleasure inside me. Men, once they get started, like to finish—I know that. Most men that I would date were understanding, of course, but there were few second or third dates, as you might imagine. Now, very important question for you: Is it all physiological or psychological too?"

Roberto had just swallowed his bread; his jaw hurt from chewing it. "It's physiological. But after a few hundred episodes of losing my erection with women, it is a self-fulfilling prophecy. I begin, and sometimes it's promising . . . but I know what's coming—or not coming. So, yes, there is some psychological component at this point."

"But you can ejaculate? When you masturbate . . ."

Jesus, lady. Roberto cleared his throat and said, "Well, yes. I am never fully hard, and it takes a while, but it leaks out."

"We must speak of everything; there is no point in being embarrassed or, together, we will be another failure. I too have psychological issues. During the sex act, I tighten up, there is no"—she searched for a word— "ease, comfort. As if my body is trying to repel intruders."

"Fortunately, there's lubrication you can buy."

"And the erectile dysfunction drugs? They do not work for you?"

He explained that nitrogen-based heart medications and Viagra did not mix. She appraised him with a slight smile.

"You would not have any idea to look at you. You are most women's ideal, I think. Tall, handsome; Liesl says you are even rich. You're our American fantasy, you know. With one of those American big penises, Liesl was indiscreet enough to reveal."

"Big, but not so useful."

She smiled barely. "Rich, good-looking, well-endowed, but you can't get it up. You are American foreign policy since 1960."

"I'm glad I conform to the national characteristic."

"I would prefer you smaller. I fear my much traumatized sex will be further traumatized." She reached under the table to his thigh, sliding a hand up to his lap.

The wine and the abnormally hot autumn day and the haze of lust made it hard to remember how they left the trattoria for the Grand Hotel de la Minerve—who paid? *Did* they pay?—how had they manufactured the patience for the slow elevator to the fifth floor, then the preposter-ously long walk down the palatial length of the hall until her hotel room. Somehow they quickly prepared themselves, one after the other in the shower . . . and found themselves in the bed, the shutters pulled, the room made dark.

Roberto assumed she was midthirties, thirty-five at most? But with her clothes off, Claudia had that lean, streamlined look of a sexy woman in her forties, past the age of schoolgirl softness or pink blushing flesh. She had him on his back and urged him to be still. Ever so gently and slowly, she aroused him and it was so far, so good. He was to be like a corpse; again and again, she whispered for him to lie there unmoving. In time, she said, they could be more adventurous, but this first time, "Please, let me go at my own pace."

He was inserted, but not all the way. And she held still herself . . . Mo-ments passed, which Roberto could not interpret as being success or fail-ure, so he remained still, admiring the decorative plaster surrounding the lighting fixture, hearing traces of an Italian argument wafting up from the street, the revving of the Vespas. He looked back at her, and now she was looking at him intently, her hands were manipulating him and herself . . . and then she closed her eyes, looked upward, and shuddered. The next moment, she had collapsed beside him, breathing raggedly, tearful. Fig-uring he was permitted to move now, he cradled her and pulled her close. Within a few minutes more, she was asleep, which was surely as much an outcome from the presentation post-adrenaline and wine, but also some accomplishment for herself in their making love.

Some men might have felt like a prop or wondered when their own turn for an orgasm was going to happen, but given his limitations, Ro-berto enjoyed a triumph. And how many more afternoon siestas would be spent lying in Italian hotels with a beautiful woman beside him? Was an afternoon like this, with Roman magnificence as a backdrop, destined to be remembered as a last European hurrah when the money disap-peared? When he prepared his French 101 classes for the Community College of Rhode Island, and got up at 7:00 a.m. to fight the traffic to arrive at his paid-for parking space—*Oops, better renew my windshield sticker*—at the Liston Campus . . . Would this alternative almost-life he nearly got to live break his heart?

Termini

An invitation to stay with Claudia at the Grand Hotel de la Minerve was not forthcoming, though she commanded his presence between events she had to attend or emcee. So Roberto made his way to that bursting slum of bed-and-breakfasts, one-star pensiones, would-be hostels that swarmed around the Termini train station, all for the backpacker and the true budget traveler. Roberto stared at the outdoor buzzers of a shambling building—which establishment to select?

Roberto buzzed finally the Pensione Capri. Did they have a room available? Yes, the female voice crackled through the intercom, they did, thirty euros—would he be wanting a ceiling fan, since there was no air-conditioning—for a bit more, thirty-four euros. Rome with no air-conditioning, even in the autumn; in the seventies Fahrenheit outside, but it would be eighty-plus in the top floors of a stuffy apartment block. The pensione was on the fifth floor. Of course it was. He was buzzed inside, at which point, he saw there was no lift for the stairwell—the theme of his 2008.

Once Roberto trekked down the Viminal Hill and into the old city, he received a text that Claudia couldn't meet that day after all. Oh well.

Roberto decided to piazza-sit, sip something uniquely Italian—Alpestre, Cynar, Campari, Amaro Pasubio, Fernet Branca, something bitter and mouth-ruining in a tall glass with soda and three ice cubes. Roberto did not care about the cost of the overpriced piazza drink, he cared about finding a plaza that wasn't mobbed with Americans, loud teenagers, and Chinese tour groups. This was his goal in life, to be reading a book in a plaza with a beverage some waiter has brought to him. Today he was reading *La solitudine dei numeri primi* by Giordano Paolo, which was spectacularly written and unnervingly dark, filled with characters who were irreparably alone.

He settled on the Piazza Mattei and the low-glamor Café Tartarughe, in what was the old Jewish quarter. He understood Paolo's characters, their solitude like prime numbers, not combining or dividing, loners for life, much like that ultimate prime number: the expat. Roberto studied the trickling fountain of the square, and there he discovered his living ghost, haunting him from country to country, like the phantasmal hitchhiker that appeared in every town in that classic *Twilight Zone* episode, the expat that Roberto would become. Today's example was a sixty-year-old American man clutching the Penguin edition of Dante's *Divine Comedy*, retired schoolteacher, Roberto supposed, constantly arranging his wisp of white hair over his baldness, just for the hot Roman wind to un-arrange it . . . a tweed coat with elbow patches, smiling too broadly and talking too eagerly to the girls who asked him directions. Roberto wondered why he should detest him on sight. Because it was Roberto Costa in thirty years?

On this impromptu trip to Rome, Roberto decided he might as well finish off all Roman palaces, something that he had neglected on past visits. He trudged around the Palazzo Venezia (maps, armor, tapestries, zzzz . . .) and the Palazzo Spada, Palazzo della Cancelleria, Palazzo della Farnesina, Palazzo della Something or Other . . .

The next day was the day of Claudia's several-hour panel, and she had in advance ruled out that day for socializing. Roberto had some more palaces circled on his Rome map, but he abandoned that plan, lying in bed under the fan reading his own Notebook passages, and, out of curiosity, Rachel's notes for her trompe l'oeil piece, sent as part of her regular document exchange.

Humankind has been content to let art extend the notions of reality, stylizing and aestheticizing from the days of the cave paintings. But periodically, an obsession with reality takes hold—the painterly detail of Van Eyck and Vermeer, sculpted insects carved on leaves attached to flowers in the hands of a saint in the stonework of Lecce, photorealism in the late twentieth century. In the seventeenth and eighteenth centuries, the desire to perplex the viewer down below with the ceilings up above, to play with what was real and what was illusion, achieved a pinnacle of craft and whimsy. These trompe l'oeil ceilings were always glimpses of heaven, the beckoning luminous world waiting after death and judgment ... But was that afterlife real or illusion as well? Trompe l'oeil is an illusion upon an illusion, the central Christian interrogation.

Not far from Claudia's hotel were the two Jesuit megachurches, with showstopper ceilings courtesy of Gaulli and Pozzo, respectively, masters of trompe l'oeil. His sister had ruled out including these overly-written-about masters, but Roberto saw no reason to resist another look. Scores of international tourists stood still, looking upward.

Where does the gilded, plaster ceiling start and the fresco leave off? After a while, the eye works it out—or thinks it does—and you see how the illusion of the multitudes falling out of heaven (while some seem to be going up) seem also to be falling out of the ceiling itself.

Having seen Andrea Pozzo's trompe l'oeil masterpiece, he might as well walk a block away for his rival. These were the home churches of the

Jesuit order, trompe l'oeil appreciators, if there ever were any, themselves impresarios of statecraft and intrigues, conspiracies and false flags and forged documents. Their perpetual meddling in affairs of state prompted one pope, Clement XIV, to be brave enough to disband them.

Il Gesù was Giovanni Battista Gaulli's work, and here, Roberto remembered, one could see that bits of robe were sewn into the ceiling, draped over the outer edge of the fresco to suggest the subjects of the fresco were materially there. He had a clumsy photo from a former visit, but this time, he had his telephoto lens. He zoomed in beside the angelic figures above the altar, and there was the scrap of red cloth . . . waita-minute . . .

Roberto smiled, putting the camera down. He'd been taken in! The scrap of the red robe was also painted. It had the same shadow as the sculpture of the angel, from the window to the right . . . but it was opaque glass. The sun was not shining through it. It was all a fraud: the shadow of the marble angel statue was *also painted*, deceiving congregants for centuries and Roberto for a decade. This he would share with Rachel.

Roberto texted his sister, WHAT A MAGNIFICENT TRICK! THIS FOOLED ME FOR YEARS—I THOUGHT THAT RED CLOTH WAS REAL.

VERY FUNNY, she texted back. NOT IN THE MOOD FOR YOU RUBBING IT IN.

HAVE YOU BEEN FOOLED BY THIS TOO?

WERE YOU IN ON IT?

IN ON WHAT?

The phone rang, and it was a furious Rachel. "Mom's scam? Did she tip you off, all your little conferences in the bedroom?"

Lena had gone with Rachel and Merle to the bank, where they combined Rachel's 300,000 and her own 300,000 and waited for the international money order to be produced for the 384,000 Swiss francs. Signor Ravoni met them at a café (so Lena could smoke), brandishing the Italian contract, the various documents to defer the IVA tax, this, that, and the other. Ever-suspicious Merle photographed each document, then stalked Lena and Signor Ravoni to the train station to better assure that the deal-makers boarded the train for Bern. Merle insisted upon and was assured that she would be provided with an extra copy of the deed, to which, one day soon, Rachel would be added. *Maybe,* Lena mused, *you, Merle, may have to be on this deed as well, if you are to contribute to the upkeep, the bills.* Merle, Roberto suspected, could barely hide her pleasure. Lena hugged Rachel—she'd be back late that night, as the brand-new owner. Lena and her latest beau took their seats (first-class, of course) and waved goodbye through the window . . .

Never to be seen again, apparently.

No word of the finalized sale on Monday, Tuesday, now Wednesday . . . Rachel made an emergency call to their father. Nope, he was able to report, the property had not been sold. It remains in the hands of an Alessandro Ravoni and was used by him as a rental property. Merle and Rachel assaulted the lobby of the Banco di Lodi and demanded to see Signor Ravoni! After causing several scenes, Signor Ravoni was produced. He was not the man they had met. He did, indeed, represent the apartment in question, but he was not selling it, just renting it. He had never heard of Bothild Stern, and the property was his and unencumbered; it was not being held in a trust for anyone in Switzerland.

Lena had merely convinced them they were buying a property that she had a four-day rental upon.

At first, when Lena and Signor Ravoni did not return, Rachel figured the villainous Frau Stern had balked at the offer, but the light of truth finally shone down from the heavens, like rays of light on a Baroque trompe l'oeil ceiling. Rachel then railed at her father to engage legal services to hunt Lena down and get her money back. Sal managed to get someone important somewhere to check out Ingegerd Stern. It turns out Frau Stern died in 2007.

"Wow," Roberto savored. "Lena had us meet her in Bern down the street from Frau Stern's house, where she said she had been visiting. Frau Stern was already dead a year." Roberto admired her confidence game—now that he hadn't lost any money in it—and reviewed the brushstrokes . . . meeting "Signor Ravoni" in the lobby of the Banco di Lodi and decamping for a café so Lena could smoke. Her handsome partner did not actually work at the bank. Imagine that, the man pretending to be a doctor a few months ago was now employed by Lena to pretend to be a banker. And yet they fell for it.

After Rachel filled Lena's phone with abuse, threats, and murderous texts, Lena simply texted back: SORRY DARLING. YOU CAN GET ALL THE MONEY IN THE WORLD FROM YOUR FATHER. HE WILL REPLACE IT MANY TIMES OVER BUT THIS IS THE ONLY WAY I CAN GET IT. BUT IT WAS A SWEET DREAM WHILE IT LASTED, WASN'T IT? ALL OF US TOGETHER IN MILANO!

Their father, Rachel reported, had done some homework: Madalena van Till was indeed mentioned in Ingegerd's will. She had received Frau Stern's art collection. Roberto laughed on the phone with Rachel. "That's all Mom got? The figurines?" Probably upon learning that she had a crateload of milkmaid and flute-playing dandies with pink cheeks, Lena cooked up the sister-in-Milan plan. Another thing: Sal Costa had pulled a string or two to get a copy of the will and spoke at length with Frau Stern's lawyer. Frau Stern did not have a sister.

Roberto laughed. "Remember the old lady whose picture she put up on the wall? Wonder who that was?"

Rachel wasn't laughing. "Did you deposit the ten thousand dollars?"

"I did, Monday morning. It's already cleared. It will be delightfully spent at leisure, by me."

"You need to give us that back."

"You need to learn not to gleefully cheat your brother out of a real estate bonanza. You and Merle stuck a knife in me, and now you want me to give you the knife back." Rachel disappeared, and Merle was on the line next: "Bobby, that money was given under false pretenses."

"The only thing false, by which I mean conniving and untrue, was you and Rachel trying to scrape me off the deal with my own mother."

"You should send us a thank-you card for sparing you from being swindled."

"It's the thought that counts—or in your case, malice aforethought."

"We will sue you."

Roberto was calm. "It will cost you more than five thousand euros to go to some European court with a lawyer. You'll have to explain how you were made fools of by my mother and why you were so enthusiastic about scamming an old lady."

"I'm telling you as a friend—"

"Merle, you are not my friend."

"I'm saying something friendly nonetheless. You don't want to cross us. You want to write us a check this week, and bygones will be bygones."

"I like bygones. As in, wave good*bye* because your money is *gone*."

Trastevere

Claudia texted to say, at last, she now deigned to have an audience with Roberto.

Roberto dressed a little better for his second trip to Grand Hotel de la Minerve, but he understood his socks, their filth, the holes, would discourage any assessment of him as a responsible adult who could feed and clothe himself. On the way down the Viminal Hill, he ducked into Upim, the Italian department store, and bought their largest pair of men's socks, and it was as he left, as he passed the frames and photo department . . . that she appeared: Bothild Stern. Two or three of her. It seemed his mother had simply used the stock photo of the grandma that came with the five-euro frame she bought, passing her off as Bothild. He laughed about that all the way to Piazza della Minerva.

On this night, Claudia was more energetic on his behalf, but when it came time for her own pleasure, it was a repeat of the original process, he perfectly still, she satisfying herself with him in the role of inanimate object. He forgot to turn his phone off, and it dinged; he reached out quickly to the nightstand to extinguish it, and it broke her concentration . . . She startled, lost her breath.

"Your sudden movement . . . I thought you were . . ."

Going to hit her? he wondered. Was this the level of trauma she was dealing with? Poor thing, if so. He would cooperate without complaint with whatever she felt she could enjoy. Soon she had achieved what she wanted, and she fell to his side, wrapping both her hands around his bicep, snuggling.

"What's your next project?" he asked out of politeness. She told him, but much of it involved sociology terms of art he was not familiar with.

He stared at the ceiling politely while she worried about her project, her ever finding a permanent university home. After she ran out of steam, she asked, "Do you have a European project?"

He mentioned the several-years-in-the-making Notebooks, a commonplace book as the British say, notions and musings, a bible for the expatriate who had loyalty to nowhere and nothing on earth but his sensibility, heightened and tempered by travel and wonder.

"You will raid the junk-filled attic of Europe," Claudia examined. "Schools of art, trends, incomprehensible notions to the modern mind that came and went."

"Yes, exactly. Mostly, I write about language and what it implies about the cultures that speak them. I want the final draft to be thousands of pages but never dull."

"Mmm, good luck with that. I feel the audience fidgeting after a half hour of my very best presentations."

"I'm thinking of something like Walter Benjamin's *The Arcades.* A collage of splendid found objects. Musings, extrapolations, whimsies. Have you read W. G. Sebald's *The Rings of Saturn*?"

Claudia edged off the bed, then stood, then began to dress, retrieving and untangling clothes from the floor. "Just a friendly suggestion. Maybe you should have as your model a work that more than a few hundred people have read. I mean, the Benjamin, not the Sebald. A few thousand have read that one."

Roberto felt dismissed—not for the first time—concerning his Notebooks.

"Your family is from Friuli, perhaps," he said a moment later.

"Why do you ask that?"

"You are Claudia Ciobanu, not Claudia *Ciobano.* I wondered if you were Slavic. Or even Romani, some generations back."

She didn't say anything.

"Or simply Romanian."

She was concentrating mightily on putting on her shoes.

"You mentioned back in Switzerland that you had family die in the Holocaust—"

"You guess Gypsy but not Jewish. Interesting."

Roberto had felt the temperature of this conversational turn become chilly, but he pressed on. "You have a cross around your neck, so I did not think Jewish. It has been dangling in my face a few times—hard not to notice."

She patted the bed as if to say enough of the topic. "My father has Romanian roots, but no, I am no Zingale. You want me to be descended from the dregs of Europe? Would that excite you?"

New topic. "Are we dining?"

"Of course," Claudia said. "Where do we go for our last Roman meal?"

"I know a place in Trastevere that has never disappointed. Well, me at least."

Claudia's hair was in all directions; she must have decided to go out with it untamed and Medusa-like. She had put on a sleeveless light dress, white with a pattern of pointed green leaves; she was sylvan, something rustling from the jungle. "There are two kinds of people who find themselves in Rome," she said. "Tevere people, and Trastevere people. What is there across the Tevere for me? Nothing. A corrupted church, some slatternly altar boys and the geriatric cardinals who molest them, and a crumbling neighborhood that hides its poverty by copious gallons of ocher and orange paint. My retinas will turn the white pages of the books I read blue for a week after a walk there in the bright sunlight. I am the via Veneto, the Spanish Steps, Piazza Navona. Tevere, *per piacere*."

Roberto countered, "I am a Trastevere person. Tevere people are snobs; they walk among the Roman ruins and Renaissance palaces and feel Rome notices them, which it does not. It barely has noticed the Caesars, the popes. In the alleys of Trastevere, I can imagine a Roman life where one eats and sleeps and brushes one's teeth. I am not goaded there by Rome's monumentality; I do not feel my lack of . . . grandeur."

"But you are the future author of *The Notebooks of Roberto Costa*. And I too will find fame in what I publish. Grandeur is our destiny."

"Hmm. All the more reason to go out among the plebeians—while we still can."

It was pleasant enough to walk; they would take a taxi back after stuffing themselves. Claudia turned heads. Maybe it was the difference in height, but other couples smiled at them; men sitting outside in unfashionable cafés followed them with their eyes.

"The street has noticed us," Claudia said. "They are thinking, *Who is the rich signora who has purchased such a gorgeous gigolo? I bet he has a cock long as a python. Perhaps, she will bankrupt herself for her lover. Perhaps, she has a husband, back in Milan . . .*" Roberto enjoyed her scenarios as they aimed themselves for the Tiber and the old Roman bridge that led to the Isola Tiberina.

"Once I publish my Notebooks," he began again, "I will become a recluse. No sequels, no follow-up, no interviews. I will be like Thomas Pynchon. I will be . . . like Emily Brontë, one great work, but no death by consumption."

"Why not die young? It would make your career." She let go of his arm and took his hand.

"I will be famous for publishing a thousand essential articles. Future scholars will have to give over their entire lives to reading every word I have written."

Upon the banks of Trastevere, Roberto realized where they were. "We have four blocks to the restaurant, but do you want to see something?" he asked.

"What now?"

"Stefano Maderno's one-hit wonder. One of the greatest statues carved in the baroque era, but he could never equal it. After a while, he gave up trying. It's in Santa Cecilia."

Indulgently, she let herself be led a few blocks into the Trastevere tangle of alleys. It was not yet six, and the church was still open.

"Many of Rome's old monuments to the martyrs are wholly bogus," Roberto narrated, remembering the passage from his Notebook. "But there seems to have been a Santa Cecilia. From a good family with a big house. Forced to marry a Roman, she refused and was put in an oven but was not cooked—thanks to the angels."

"Angels used to come to a woman's rescue. They've been on strike for a few centuries, I think."

"So like in all the martyrdom stories, they beheaded her. She was like fourteen or something. Well, they started digging below the church in her honor and they found her tomb, labeled and everything . . ."

Claudia and Roberto walked toward the altar. There was a gilded glass-enclosed casket ahead that held Maderno's statue.

"And when the pope had the casket opened, Maderno, the sculptor, was in attendance. Like other saints, Cecilia hadn't decomposed. There was the twisted body of a teenage girl martyred fourteen hundred years ago. Her head had not been detached from her neck, though the blow was fatal. The scene so transfixed Maderno that he captured it perfectly in marble."

All alone in the church, they approached the sculpture. Roberto admired the young woman's just-maturing body somehow communicated through the marble robes, the hips, the new breasts . . . and the openness of the hands. "I think the hands," he said, "are particularly fine . . ." He turned in time to see Claudia fleeing from the church.

He found her out in the courtyard of the church, shaking slightly.

"His Cecilia," she said, "is *every* woman, every victim, passed around by a legion of soldiers, dragged forward to be raped or sold off—and if she refuses? You know what you do to disobedient women. What they do to them in conservative Islamic countries . . . Nanking, the women of the Balkans, every tribal conflict in Central Africa—right here, when Rome invaded Sabine and raped and abducted the women—ha, that is celebrated in works of art. Poussin, Rubens, David. It is as it ever was. Povera Cecilia," she concluded in Italian, composing herself. She slipped her arm into Roberto's arm.

Roberto spoke gently. "I wouldn't have brought you if I knew it was going to upset you—"

"A woman brutalized and slain for not fucking someone privileged who had power over her. No, why should you imagine that would disturb me?" She talked steadily, bitterly. "I was a teenager in Torino. I was cutting through the old center one night when two men grabbed me, laughing, shoving me back and forth, first to one, then the other. And each time I was thrown into one of the men, he would grope and plunge his hand into me, my breasts, put his filthy fingers in my mouth. You wonder why I have the sexual limits that I do—that incident is why. But, please, let us speak on anything else . . ."

She broke off holding his arm and chose to walk ahead of him for a block or two. When she was in danger of passing the trattoria he intended, he called out; she turned with a smile and was determined to find equanimity for the rest of the evening. Roberto, throughout dinner, let her caress him under the linen tablecloth. He was affectionate, reaching frequently for her hand. It did occur that she had previously explained that there was an older man who abused her, who was responsible for her sexual challenges . . . but both things likely happened. Both scenarios were not even unusual; if it was Wednesday, they were happening right now somewhere. If Roberto had learned anything about the precarity of being female, it was that all women—mother, niece, grandmother, sister, schoolteacher, professor, titan of industry—were simply doing their best to exist between manhandlings, assaults, gropes, molestations, rapes, liberties taken. A day without a hand where it shouldn't be, many women would declare a good day.

Ludo, hearing of the failed Adriatic road trip, wanted to re-create it with a new foursome—Ludo, Lucrezia, Mira, and Roberto. Or at minimum, they wanted Roberto back to socialize in Lombardia. They had texted him twice—when was he returning? Roberto had intended to call Ludo and beg off. He pictured instead a long, loud, smart, wild affair with Claudia, imagining books and art crowding their unmade bed, up at 3:00 a.m. doing shots of grappa and arguing the merits of Giordano Bruno as a cosmologist, Umberto Eco as a semiotician . . . but now, Roberto thought he might prefer the sillier, happier people to spend the next week with.

They taxied back to the hotel. Again, she did not invite him to stay over so the ascent of the Viminal Hill and the health-compromising staircase of the Pensione Capri was his fate.

"You will visit in Milan one day?" she asked so airily, it was hard to suppose that she meant it. She was leaving for there tomorrow. "As I said, my apartment may not be entered, but we can meet up somewhere."

She had a lover, Roberto suspected. "I am off to Milan as well," he said.

She offered no encouragement of them taking the same train, so he didn't push it.

He mentioned he would be with friends in Milan, visiting Ludovico and Lucrezia and their academic friend Mira. Claudia seemed to have no interest in an architect and a gender theorist, so the idea of a group dinner seemed out of the question.

"And this Lucrezia?" she asked absently. "What is she a professor of?"

"She's not an academic. She's a model. She was a lot more famous a few years back—"

"What is her name?"

"Lucrezia Pappalardo."

Claudia suddenly erupted. "My God, you *know* her? I have an addiction to fashion magazines—Italian ones, at least. To better perfect my self-loathing, I suppose."

Roberto mentioned how they had—admittedly, drunkenly—proposed a road trip through the former Yugoslavia to Athens, and the Greek islands beyond.

She laughed. "Perhaps I will come along! You can drop me in Belgrade for my Slavonia project research. How on earth did *you* meet Lucrezia Pappalardo?"

"I was with French friends, fashion week in Milan, and we met. She thought, given my height, I was one of the tribe of models. It was five years ago, so we were kids, staying up all night in some club—"

"You were lovers?"

If they all were to meet, then there was no point lying about it, but Roberto predicted the news would provoke something. "Yes."

Claudia's eyes seemed to cloud over for a moment. "Ah, one of the world's great beauties."

"And a train wreck."

"Perhaps she thought you were a train wreck too. If you could not satisfy her."

"I satisfied her. Five years ago, my problems had not begun in earnest yet."

"So this flawless creature knows what it is to be fucked by you."

"Yes."

Claudia regained herself, smiling again. "I am like a schoolgirl fan seeking an autograph. I would very much like to meet her."

Plesno Grozno

Lucrezia saw a cat. Her project had evolved: who cared about the provinces of Italy when the book could go international! *International Cat,* she pronounced, was the new title. She would make up little stories about each cat, who would have a name in the language of the country featured. *Children will love this book,* she assured Roberto. A clean, well-cared-for orange-and-white tabby was preening in the sun near a postcard tree in Pirano, and Lucrezia gave pursuit. *Here, kitty-kitty*... Soon Roberto was directed to block an alley and corral the cat back toward Lucrezia. But the mission failed as the cat energized and fled inside a nearby café, presumably its home.

Ludo emerged from the newsstand with a Michelin map of Istria; Roberto looked over his shoulder at the peculiar geography of Slovenia. This all used to be the kingdom of Venice, then it became the Austro-Hungarian Empire, then the Italians were allowed to keep Trieste on a narrow finger, with the amalgamated country of Yugoslavia owning the Istrian peninsula ... until its breakup, which led to its being subdivided again, between Slovenia (which got a twenty-eight-mile sliver of Adriatic coast) and Croatia, which got the lion's share, most of the Roman ruins, the seaside resorts, one of the world's best truffles by the metric ton. For those who thought crossing borders, collecting passport stamps, paying for toll stickers every few hours was "tres internationale", the Istrian peninsula was the road trip for you.

"You done playing with your cat?" Ludo asked, without interest. "Where are Mira and Claudia?"

They departed Milan the afternoon before, deciding to cross Northern Italy and call it quits here for Night No. 1 in Pirano, Slovenia. Lucrezia and Ludo got to ride in the two-seat roadster though Ludo said he wanted all the other participants, in rotation, to keep him company as the days wound on. Roberto longed for his turn in the gorgeous car with the gorgeous AC again . . . while the other car, Mira's Golf, tightly held Mira and Claudia in the front, and a very compressed Roberto in the narrow back seat, sealed off from all air circulation. Mira drove haltingly, a combination of the decrepitude of the model and her lack of finesse in gear shifting on hills. "I am a girl of the flatlands," she reminded him; there was barely a hill to practice on in Holland. There was talk of renting a larger car for greater comfort, but it was too much expense (and even steeper when one declared you were taking the car to the Balkans, insurance-wise), and so to keep the trip from collapsing, Mira had said okay, sure, they could take her car. Roberto assumed Claudia would change her mind about coming along given the travel conditions, but she was surprisingly serene.

Once everyone was rounded up, the party drove their two-car caravan up from Pirano to the ragged white Karst mountainscape of interior Slovenia, en route to Hrastovlje—a Roberto request, seconded by Mira— with one of Europe's best-preserved danse macabre, or a *plesno grozno*

in Slovenian, which was more fun to say. Predictably, Ludo would speed ahead and take the curves like Michael Schumacher at the Nürburgring; Mira would chug along on four cylinders and find Ludo idling at an intersection turn he didn't want her to miss.

Again today, Mira and Claudia were in the front, and Roberto was stretched out awkwardly in the back seat. The women went on about the baroque nature of German professorships—one had to have a national and a regional appointment, an impossible political chore for a foreigner . . . Speaking of teaching, Roberto decided that perhaps it was time to dust off his antiquated CV. Roberto had worked up a several-week conversational English class, the sort of thing one sees on flyers in coffee shops where you tear off a tab with the phone number. Everyone who had been taught by him seemed to like their instruction, his energy and commitment. Maybe that was a skewed sample. He ended up sleeping with every woman and two of the men he had taught. Maybe he would ply his trade in Malta, in Moldova, that Norwegian outpost above the Arctic Circle—an excuse to explore somewhere new, a region on his map yet to be checked off.

The tiny village of Hrastovlje was a few buildings, a big oak in what passed as a plaza (Roberto knew that *hrast*, in the village name, meant "oak"); one café, one restaurant, which seemed closed; and a winding path up to a walled fortification. There was a woman reading at the gate who was so startled that she dropped her book when they approached, losing her place. After the group contributed several euros and received a lecture in Italian about not photographing the frescoes, they were let in the late Romanesque church.

The danse macabre. An art subject found throughout Europe where death leads the locals on a jolly New Orleans-style parade to the afterlife. No one is immune, the merchant, the farmer, the pope and his prelates, kings and queens, all must follow the leering, mocking skeletons toward the waiting grave . . .

Roberto was thrilled to see Glagolitic script labeling the frescoes. He sneaked a few photos when the complacent attendant went back to her book at the front gate, but she had returned with a watchful eye. He took out a pen, but there was no paper—no one had any. He contented himself to feast his eyes. People attribute the Cyrillic alphabet to Saint Cyril and Saint Methodius in the 900s, but what they invented was the Glagolitic script, which, through the centuries, became recognizable as the Cyrillic alphabet used in the Balkans and Russia today. One could sort of see how the Ц became the Б, the ꝺ became the Д, but many letters remained unclear to the greatest scholars, and it was a fanciful set of characters to say the least: ⱱ, ⱳ, ⱶ . . .

"We didn't have breakfast," Claudia said, popping his backside. "We must go eat!"

The cat photographic mission had been a success; the cat associated with the town's one restaurant proved pliant, and Ludo had taken the picture of Lucrezia holding it next to the Slovenian signs for the tavern. Where the dance of death had made her nearly cry, the success of her cat-picture project had her giggling and throwing her magnificent head of hair back, nearly breaking into song.

They were the only customers of this family establishment; the tall, good-looking son, Žan, introduced himself. First, there was wine soup, with some meat stock, garlic, onion, and shallot, but all you could taste was the musk of the red wine. Claudia said it was like vinegar, but continued to eat; Lucrezia said she *did* have breakfast, her excuse for her habitual self-starving, but she tried a spoonful of wine soup from the others. Two pans of bread were brought out; the bread had crackling bits in it, and rather than butter, meat grease was brought to the table in a tub. Roberto thought: One nice thing about sampling restaurants with his European rather than American friends, was that no one in the party would dream of going, "Ewwww," or turning up their nose at animal parts, offal, organ meats. Which was good because in addition to the vast plate of Carniolan sausages and the prleška tünka (minced bacon and lard and garlic) came the bujta repa, the blood sausages stewed in a crock with turnips . . .

Ludo had ordered a Slovenian malvazija, one of the famous orange wines of the Julian Alps, the wines that looked like orange Kool-Aid and tasted like the inside of a clay pot. "Of course, I prefer the orange wines of Friuli," Ludo said patriotically, before savoring the glass of minerals, perfect for cutting through the lards and fats and suets and congealments.

Mira and Lucrezia turned up their noses and decided to order something else . . . maybe a local drink of some kind . . . Žan the waiter said they had fruit drinks, then he brought them some, then more; the count of fruity concoctions was lost track of. No one needed one more thing to drink or eat, but the elderly mother emerged from the kitchen to see if her work was satisfactory, and the table heaped praise on her . . . and this resulted in her directing Žan to put his tallness to use and take down a brown bottle, blow off the dust, and pour shots. Ludo and Roberto glanced at each other; maybe they should pass? But it was obviously a special bottle that this family-run gostilna wished to share with their best customers of the autumn—maybe their only customers. So they all threw back a shot of what had to be pure isopropyl ethyl wood alcohol paint thinner . . . the grandmother had poured herself half a glass of it and knocked it all back without a wince. Žan tried one too, and he had the reaction of his guests—an expression one might have if hit by lightning.

Roberto, feeling suddenly gifted in Serbo-Croatian, mangled a compliment to the grandmother. "Vrlo dober obled, gospo . . . um, gospa . . ."

The grandmother said speaking Italian was fine. Later, sober, he would realize he did not compliment her meal but rather commented on her being washed out and faded, unable to land properly on the word *objed* (meal). In Italian, he questioned the famous Slovenian national soup: How did the wine soup retain the flavor of wine once the alcohol was cooked out? It appeared the alcohol was in no way cooked out—they had consumed several bowls of red wine. The local fruit cordials that Mira and Claudia had had, one after the other, were *slivovka* (plum spirit) and then *višnjevec* (cherry spirit), not really cordials but 40 percent liquor; the industrial solvent at the end was *brinjavec,* a juniper berry moonshine—all homemade in her bathroom, the grandmother reported. (Which meant that they would all go blind before the evening was out, thought Roberto.)

How to proceed with many of the party too drunk to drive? Maybe, since it was the Mediterranean, you might risk it, but there was an international border with Croatia, and the passed-out passengers would be investigated and the driver would come under suspicion.

A drunken plan began to take shape: Ludo would drive his Audi to Poreč, Croatia, an hour away. He would take Mira, the drunkest, in the passenger seat. Given her Dutch drinking skills, she would be the least likely to be sick in his car. That settled, she stumbled to his passenger seat and promptly passed out in the sun.

Claudia was sobriety-wise all right to drive, but couldn't—no license, never learned how. Well, Ludo, concluded with a clap on his shoulder, Roberto could drive the Golf!

"I don't drive a stick."

This finally got a rise out of the unflappable Ludo: "You don't drive a manual?"

"I never learned. We have automatic cars in America."

Lucrezia had consumed hardly any food and had already been sick from her drinking, once subtly at the restaurant bathroom, and then not so subtly against the lovely town-symbolic oak in the main square. No one suggested Lucrezia drive or operate any machinery. Maybe Ludo would take Mira and come back . . . but no, he could only drive one of them at a time in his two-seater. They would be at it for hours. Was Hrastovlje big enough to have a taxi? No. The only solution was to hire someone local to drive the Golf (with Roberto, Lucrezia, and Claudia) to Poreč.

Roberto concurred, suggesting, "And then we'll give him bus fare back to Hravolso . . . Hrasovtoj . . ."

Ludo: "If you, the language master, cannot pronounce this godforsaken place, then don't look to me for help."

Žan was quickly petitioned back at the restaurant, but in the intervening time, he had gotten drunk too—trading shots with his grandmother. Jakob was turned up by Claudia, an old man sitting in front of his shop, half-asleep in the heat. He would be happy to drive them, but he did not have a license. No need to have one for local driving up in these hills, but he could not cross the border . . . Next was his grandson Jaka, who looked fourteen but assured them that if he could drive the tractor on his father's farm, the Golf would prove no difficulty.

"Why don't we simply push the Golf over the edge of that cliff?" Ludo mused, looking up at the Karst walls that surrounded Hrastovlje. "It will be faster."

Lucrezia, staggering, giggling, turned up a man in the only other business of the village. Nik seemed agreeable, but it dawned on everyone that he might be . . . simple, developmentally challenged, and spent his days in the watchful eye of his mother, who presided over the coffee shop—the business they had not selected to patronize, although now they repented and ordered strong Slovenian coffees for everyone. This chance to drive the Golf to Poreč had now consumed the village, and soon a volunteer came forward, Anže, a prematurely balding thirtysomething, who had tired of watching sports and came from his home, ready to make a little weekend money. He demonstrated complete mastery of the stick shift in a circular demonstration up and down Hrastovlje village's main street.

Five Stars, Ten Euros

The plan was to take a little boat out to one of the innumerable islets off the coast of Poreč, the otočići. A boatman would take them out, over the choppy harbor, into the swells, then pull up against an otočić and with the boat pitching and rolling, they would hop out on their own island and their own beach, to be picked up again at sunset. A picnic basket would have delicacies, and there would be prosecco . . .

None of that happened. Everyone lay in bed until noon. If they got up, it was to be sick or to think better of it and return to the bed. The idea of a bumptious boat ride upon the sea proved unpopular. Ludo texted everyone that he had secured a second night at the hotel, even though a day's delay wrecked the tight Balkan itinerary.

Around noon, Roberto abandoned the possibly dead Claudia in their bed, which smelled of alcohol sweat, and staggered from the hotel into the white polished limestone streets of Poreč, each boulevard a solar reflector. It seemed to Roberto the sun itself was making too much noise. Every sound of this Croatian resort made its way to Roberto's headache—the Jet-Skis, shrieking teenagers in swimwear, the Vespas, the shrill laughing devil-children, someone's loud radio blasting Yugo pop. Roberto was at that stage of gastrointestinal delicacy that anything—coffee, water, air— would only make things worse. He saw the steeple for St. Eufemia. He would throw himself on the mercy (and natural air-conditioning) of the old church from the 500s. After his insistence on seeing the church at Hrastovlje, he knew he would be overruled in his church-mongering from here on out, so he made the pilgrimage privately, to sit in the cool, to take in the glimmering mosaics.

He may have nodded off a bit, upright in the pews, but felt better upon startling himself awake. Thank you, Saint Eufemia, whoever you were. Back at the hotel, no one was around, not in the nearby outdoor café . . . he took this as a sign no one needed or wanted him, so he returned to the bedroom for more sleep. Which lasted until Claudia bounced onto the bed with the intention of waking him.

"We have two scenarios," she said as if it were time for another PowerPoint. "Either Ludo and Mira are having an affair and Lucrezia doesn't care or doesn't know. She is so medicated, perhaps they make love in the living room while she is sitting like a zombie on the divan a meter away. She is an empty shell. If she sits still too long, she nods off. It would be like sleeping with someone drugged, someone paralyzed. Though for many men, that would be their ideal."

Roberto, a veteran now of lying comatose while she manipulated him, was about to make a comparison but kept quiet.

"Or, opzione *due*, Mira and Lucrezia are an item. Ludo brings Mira along to occupy Lucrezia who, to him, is increasingly like a housecat that must be fed and petted from time to time."

"You don't think there is a threesome?"

"That is the one thing I do not think. Indeed, it is hard to see any of the three sleeping with any other . . . They are so cold, unromantic. Though

I think you are right that Mira is gay. I like her myself. The square face of the Dutch, the brisk blond man's cut, the upper-arm strength—she does work out. Would you like me to seduce her so you can have us both?"

Roberto was not baited into the trap. "You are sufficient for my needs."

Claudia unzipped her skirt, tossed her headscarf to the chair, lost the blouse, and snuggled in beside him. "But there *is* something between Mira and Ludo. I have seen them argue, in a very intimate way. They are conspiring."

"I have seen this too."

"I asked about his architectural portfolio," Lucrezia said "It does not seem to exist."

Roberto's final supposition on the matter: "Maybe we are misguided. Our traveling companions are simply friends."

"What a facile, simplistic American read on things," she said, poking him playfully. Claudia had behaved herself too long; the alpha female had to vent: "Mira is quite nice, but not my kind of academic. She posits some theory about gender and surgically grafts it to a topic, sensible or not—no data, no empiricism. Sociology is a loose, baggy discipline, but we do like facts, research. Of course, I have her email and number, and we will stay acquainted . . ." Claudia undid her black lacy brassiere. "My appointments in Milan, Stuttgart, Oxford, my conferences like this one in Rome, are of a higher tier than her work has invited."

"So," Roberto continued in that level tone that is the most provocative, "your worship of Lucrezia Pappalardo is at an end?"

"I'm sure you still want to fuck her. Your cock would be *adamantino* for your Lucrezia, wouldn't it?" She reached over to his boxer shorts ready to declare triumph if he were aroused at the mention of Lucrezia, but he was not. "She's infantile," Claudia continued. "Nothing more abominable than a woman—what is she now? Thirty? Acting like a teenager. It worked for her a generation ago, and she has not changed. What adult man would want to hear that little-girl voice: *Oh, come, my little kitty cat.* Think how grotesque that will be when she is forty, fifty! I am surprised Ludo puts up with it. Men can endure any female idiocy if there is some degree of beauty involved . . ." Claudia ranted for a good ten minutes, until she heard herself and felt exposed: her resentment was indistinguishable from jealousy, though it wasn't jealousy. "How was it when you slept with her?"

"Again, imagine her, imagine me, in our early twenties."

She pulled up his T-shirt to pet the hair below his navel, above his waist. "She must have been thrilled to find this." She made a more deliberate clutch of his genitals. "I bet she could sit right on it too. The Sicilian puttana—she probably can take bigger than this—two at a time perhaps."

Roberto reflected that Claudia's chief battle was with people who were happily sexual without complication.

"When she was young," Claudia speculated, "she used her charms, which only work on men, to connect herself to rich men like you. Yes, Liesl says you are rich; we needn't pretend that information is private."

"Not so rich anymore. Have you been reading the papers?"

Claudia was not to be dissuaded from her destruction of Lucrezia. "At first, she could get the handsome, rich sons like you, and now the men of middle age who are well-off, like Ludo, not so handsome. And soon, she will be attracting the old dissoluti."

"Ludo has something. Not on first look. But when he talks . . ."

"I agree, he is compelling. Probably a good lover, though his subtlety is surely wasted on Lucrezia. It is revolting how easily I see her flailing about, making little-girl animal noises, her hair whipping about like in a common pornographic film . . . Maybe that is what you like. Shall I squeak like a little girl and toss my hair around?"

Claudia returned to rubbing Roberto with one hand and the other hand arousing herself. The lengthy speculations about Lucrezia were—it was being confirmed for Roberto—merely foreplay for their own lovemaking.

Upon the next attempt to leave the bed, Roberto wandered to the shore, a vast, polished, white stone plaza with cafés and seafood restaurants, where the smell of fish—often overpowering in Italy—was trumped by the smell of garlic. The Dalmatians, Montenegrins, and Albanians formed a culinary axis of garlic. Garlic used in such profusion that even Southern Italians would back away from the table. He saw Mira reading a book and asked to join her. He had not gotten far in his *History of the Balkans.* For one thing, it was repetitive and depressing: everyone, when they got the chance, exterminated everybody else.

Mira, seeing him, put her book down. "Since we lost a day to wine soup, Ludo wants to skip the bulk of the Dalmatian coast and cut straight into the interior and get the four-lane motorway for Belgrade and Serbia. We have all seen Dubrovnik, yes? It will still be overrun, cruise ships and tourists. We are not here for that. We want to see what we have not seen. Kosovo, Macedonia, Albania."

Roberto nodded.

This was a pleasant break in the action, though. The autumnal sun was lowering, and the white rock of the offshore islands, the seawall, the piers . . . were yellowing. The shrieking of beachgoers had subsided; maybe everyone was resting up for the discos and lavish dinners the soft, warm evening promised. The plash of the Adriatic against the seawall was calming.

Roberto felt a hand on his shoulder. "Ah, my friend. You have heard of our plan—we go to Rijeka tonight and straight into Serbia tomorrow?"

Ludo had been speaking to an Italian truck driver (a sticker boosting the Inter Milan Football Club meant speaking was mandatory) when he went to put gasoline in his Audi. To drive down the coast was to hit the twelve-mile stretch of Bosnia and Herzegovina's finger to the sea. "A middle finger," reported the truck driver. The trucks were backed up for an hour, since one was leaving the Eurozone . . . and then twelve miles later, the same thing happened again—that is, if one survived the traffic snarl that was Neum, the sole beach resort town for a country of four million landlocked people. After Dubrovnik came Montenegro and a customs nightmare repeat. And one had to wind up perilous mountain roads for a corner of Serbia (border number four in a hundred miles) to get to an uncertain, often closed border into Kosovo. The Peja border crossing that Ludo had circled as a destination was a no go. Serbia, of course, did not recognize Kosovo's independence, and those crossings could be fraught. One had better come in from south Serbia . . .

"And Claudia asked me to give this to you," Ludo said, finishing up. He held a sealed envelope from the hotel stationery with ROBERTO written in her dramatic angular handwriting. How odd, thought Roberto. He had just left her in their hotel room.

Really I should die with one more kitty cat, one more pretension of this materialist Ludo and his sports car and his bratty model— what stereotypes they all are. Mira's interest is at an end, and if we are to see each other, fate will surely arrange it, my friend. I am taking a regional flight to Belgrade. A 600 km drive trapped in these cars — intolerable. You will see that for yourself.

No *Love, Claudia,* no perfunctory investment in any goodbye or *Hope to see you in Belgrade.* And he had been demoted from *my love* to *my friend.*

"I saw her with her bags for to go into a taxi . . . ," Ludo said. "I hope you are not too upset."

"We were not a real couple." Roberto shrugged, hiding away the note so his fellow travelers would not be tempted to read it and be unexpectedly insulted.

So, after a last coffee, they would stagger to the cars, Mira with Roberto in the Golf, Ludo and Lucrezia in the roadster, and wind across the Istrian peninsula this evening. Before leaving the comforts of the hotel Wi-Fi, he noticed that Rachel had been calling him. Then a Paris number, which was likely Merle. Still determined to get their ten thousand euros back. Come to Kosovo and get it, ladies!

And they were off. Mira announced she was made road-sleepy in no time, so they had to talk. What was he reading?

"I've got this *History of the Balkans.* Found it in that killer English-language bookstore in Rome's train station. Sort of a depressing read so far. I'm in the Middle Ages."

"It gets worse. I started a paper about what became of known queer people during World War Two in Yugoslavia. Nothing good, I can tell you. Did you know that Yugoslavia was a country where, in World War Two, more people died than survived?"

"No, I didn't know that."

"It wasn't from warfare either—Yugoslavia fell relatively quickly. It was all the ethnic cleansing. Hitler facilitated every side wiping out every other side. The Croat Utashe exterminated every single Romani in the country; they built five concentration camps for the Jews, then turned their attention to Bosnia, Herzegovina, and the Serbs. The Chetnik Serbs started out as resistance to the Nazis . . . but then they were given access to killing all the Muslims and Croats, and they outdid themselves."

Roberto was quiet a minute.

Mira changed subjects. "Get a load of this coast . . ."

The white limestone that made up the Istrian peninsula and the Dalmatian coast to their south, tamed and polished by the sea, now revealed more formidable cliffs and carbonate mountains bleached by centuries of relentless sun, getting even whiter as they headed east, unable to host even a blade of grass or a shrub. Roberto stared, mesmerized. It was as if someone tore up the moon into little shreds and dropped the fragments randomly into the dark blue Adriatic, a desolate scattering of dolomite, gypsum, broken travertine.

"I enjoyed meeting Claudia," Mira said good-naturedly.

"Hmm," Roberto said.

"But I am glad she is gone, to tell the truth." Roberto decided not to prompt her but very much wanted her to continue. "I am sure she gives marvelous academic presentations."

"I have seen one. She is like excellent theater."

"But she is performing for her personal life too. But here her acting is not always so good. We had not known each other very long, but she told me about her husband one night. Then forgotten she had told me the next day, and so she sang a rapture about being single."

"Husband, huh?"

"Some older man she knew from childhood. Her family, of course, did not approve."

"We had only just met," Roberto said, as much to himself. "I suppose I now seem very shallow, taking trips and sleeping with someone I barely knew."

Mira smiled wanly. It occurred to Roberto that he had never heard

Mira laugh or manifest joy of any kind. She had a Low Countries earnestness. "Please. Of course you'd have to sleep with her—look at her! She is electric, sensual . . ."

There was the winding drive to Rijeka and another hotel stop. But come morning, Ludo was reimposing military discipline. The four Balkanistas rose at the crack of dawn, reported to their vehicles, and wound their way toward the central motorway that was the main highway connecting the disparate parts of the old Yugoslavia—a two-lane commute stalled by diesel-spewing trucks that crawled on the hills, farm wagons that were even slower, and fleets of infamous Yugos, down to a cylinder of power, perfuming the highway with acrid blue smoke, struggling even on the level parts of the road, but there they were, models from the 1980s, still running . . .

Finally, the interstate equivalent. For fun, Ludo hung back and pretended to drag race with Mira's Golf, but about when it was looking even, he shifted into gear and blasted ahead at a speed more appropriate to the German autobahn.

"He will get a ticket," said Mira, "and we will have the last laugh."

At the last big gas station/rest area before the border, Ludo texted them to stop and confer where he was waiting for them. Lucrezia and Mira sought the ladies' room. Again, it was a subject of discussion, as on the French trip, whether Catholic Croatia would have commodes while beyond in Orthodox Serbia they would be condemned to the Turkish squat toilets, though this was sheer anti-Serbian prejudice not based on evidence.

"So," Ludo said, approaching Roberto. "Claudia asked for the hotel I had reserved in Belgrade, and she may be there." Roberto looked nonplussed. "I say we cancel the Belgrade hotel rooms," Ludo suggested sympathetically. "It is before 6:00 p.m., and there will be no fee. And we head on to Niš. If the border is not too bad, we will be there before evening. I take it you would rather not have a reunion with Signorina Claudia?"

"Belgrade is sophisticated and modern besides. Not the Balkans we came in search of."

"No," concurred Ludo, and he and Roberto shook on it. Ludo booked new hotel rooms on his laptop, set up on the hood of the Audi TT. "The best in Niš, and just forty euros!" he said. "Ha, wait until Albania! A five-star hotel for ten euros!"

History's Worst Brother-Sister Combo

Belgrade (and a hotel full of Claudia, somewhere) was jettisoned for the delights of Serbia's third-largest city, Niš.

Ludo texted to Mira that he would drive around town a bit, scoping it out, deciding where they might eat. The choices appeared to be kebabs and shish kebabs.

Mira nodded grimly. "Starting tomorrow, we will rebel. I do not think Ludo should set the pace without consultation. I would like to see something besides the interior of my Golf. Indeed, before we check in to the hotel, I have something I would like to see . . ."

Ludo was three cars ahead of them, idling amid the spare post-workday traffic. His Audi was turning heads, of course. The locals would shout out, "Juventus!" or "Milan!" seeing the circular *I* sticker and the license plate marking him from Italy.

Another text came in from Ludo: U SEE THIS INTERSECTION. I THINK UNIQUE IN THE WORLD.

Mira stared up, around . . . "Do you see what he's talking about?"

Roberto figured it out: "One intersection with offers to four world capitals on . . . no, five! Five world capitals from one intersection. Surely there's another place where . . . Maybe the Stans in Central Asia?"

They called up globes and atlases in their heads. "No," said Mira, "This may be the only such place. Of course, when I say, 'World capitals,' one thinks of Paris and Rome. We have our choice here of the boulevards of Pristina, the nightlife of Skopje."

(Was that humor-free Mira making a joke?)

Mira cruised by the Best Western where Ludo was unloading; she acknowledged them with a wave bye-bye. "I want to see the Skull Tower," Mira said.

In 1809, the Turks were reconquering the area, and the defeated Serbs decided on a Masada-like finish, blowing themselves and their fortification to smithereens rather than surrender. The Turks gathered up the heads, boiled them down somehow—it doesn't bear thinking about—extracted the skulls of a thousand or so Serbs, and glued them to the masonry of a tower. A warning for any future dissenters. They pulled over for the little park that had what was left of the Skull Tower. Mira relayed that she understood that many of the thousand skulls had since fallen off or been taken away as souvenirs.

"As one does," Roberto added.

Thanks to the one-way streets, they had to return to downtown by a different road, through a canyon of Tito-era apartment blocks. Roberto wondered when it would present itself—the grim misery of the communist architectural touch. All peoples have their slums, all cities have their run-down apartment blocks, but no ideology on earth ever excelled at creating such artless dead concrete human warehousing as did the commissars of public housing, whose work is still seen in profusion once one was behind the "Iron Curtain." Mile after mile of derelict buildings with signs of charring where there had been a fire in a few units halfway up the building, signs of abandonment (where windows were missing), signs of overcrowding, poverty, sometimes clotheslines—signs of squatters in towers long without electricity.

After dinner—shish kebab with the typical salad of cucumbers, tomatoes, onions, garlic, oil, and vinegar—Roberto took a walk outside and passed a postcard tree. Roberto was hunting for a Skull Tower card (*Merle, this is for you . . .*), but he saw cards for an archeological site with Roman floor mosaics instead, a ruin called Mediana, somewhere in Niš. Curiously, it didn't make his, admittedly, surface-interest travel guide, which compressed southeastern Europe and its eleven countries into a 350-page book. He asked the hotel reception about it, and they were very eager to trumpet its glories.

Roberto knocked on Mira's hotel room door. She called out for him to enter, despite her wearing only a bra and male gym shorts, sprawled on the bed, reading. He tried not to appraise her lightly muscled arms (which had been obsessing him) and nearly visible breasts, tried to look away from the floppy-loose gym shorts. He explained they had a chance to see a ruin as it was being uncovered, ancient floor mosaics, the workings of an elaborate baths . . .

"I'm in," she said. "We will get no cooperation from the Marchesinis.

Ludo wants to leave at 8:30, so you and I will go out . . . at 7:00 a.m.? See you in the morning. I will be up earlier for my run, so you do not inconvenience me."

"Wow. You can wake up that early?"

"I hope I can wake up; otherwise, I will have died."

(Roberto noted Mira was up to *two* jokes and counting.)

Roberto let himself out. Mira's lack of care in letting him see her nearly undressed was either a sly romantic escalation . . . or a sign of just how Roberto was in *no way* an object of her attraction, no more of interest than the furniture in her hotel room.

Roberto spent the too-quiet evening turning to the early chapters of his Balkan history book, which he had skimmed, wanting to race toward the modern era. This area was Illyricum, a Roman colony full of tribes; their conflicts, their temporary allegiances, their tedious double crosses. Julius Caesar, Pompey, and eventually Octavian (later Augustus Caesar) all exhausted themselves at Balkan pacification. Roberto turned to the index to see the many groups who thought they could hold their own against Roman might: the Ardiaei, the Avendeatae, the Bathiatae, the Bessi, the Cambaei, the Carni, the Carui, the Cimbri, the Cinambri, the Dalmatae, the Docleatae, the Glintidiones, the Hippasini, the Histri, the Iapydes, the Interphrurini, the Ligures, the Meromenni, the Moentini, the Naresii, the Oxyaei, the Palarii, the Perthoneatae, the Pirustae, the Pyrissaei, the Segestani, the Taulantii, the Taurisci . . .

Who were all these peoples? Their languages, their culture, their art, their centuries-old practices? Or was their only human mark that of being a notch on the victory post for Roman generals, mentioned once by the Roman historian Appian?

Roberto met Mira downstairs at the appointed time, and they sped all of two kilometers from town to a driveway, unmarked, that led to a field and a lot of dirt piles, lumber, haphazardly built sheds . . . A man in some kind of uniform and a gun in his holster met them. He shooed them away. Roberto mumbled, "So much for that," but Mira was impervious.

"We are here for the Mediana archeological dig." He did not speak English, but he surely recognized the name of the place he worked for. Mira, feigning impatience, brought out her faculty ID. "You see, Radboud University in Nijmegen. I am Dr. Visser. This is Dr. Costa."

Fortunately, he could not translate her Department of Gender & Diversity title, or that ruse might not have been so successful. Mira and Roberto were permitted through.

Looking at the scores of excavated rooms in an otherwise nondescript meadow, it did not seem to Roberto that anything had ever taken place here but the bringing in of the harvest, the milking of the cows, but this is where Europe surprises: almost no square of earth hasn't been soaked in history, particularly if it lies between Rome and Greece. The Emperor Constantine—the emperor who converted Rome to Christianity—was born in 280 in Roman Naissus, later Niš. Constantine built a lavish country villa for himself, named Mediana, which was left to his descendants, an array of relatives, emperors, and pretenders whose names are so similar as to cause scholarly offense: Constantine II, Constantius II, Constantina, Constans, Constantine III, Constans II . . .

Julian the Apostate, the last pagan emperor, who tried to put the Christianity genie back in the bottle, sunned and bathed and relaxed himself on the Mediana estate. Only a year and a half on Caesar's throne . . . one wonders what would have happened had he lasted and sent the church ayatollahs packing.

Emperor Valentinian I and his little brother, Valens, during some long soak in the thermal waters of Mediana, decided that their empire was too big to be managed by one emperor, so they got out a map and started dividing; if you ever wondered where that fateful East-West Rome division happened, it happened in Niš, Serbia, in 364.

The last emperor who got to rule over Rome in its entirety was Theodosius I, and his daughter Galla Placida, famous above all as the namesake of the most perfect building in the whole of Europe, the fifth-century Mausoleum of Galla Placida in Ravenna, shimmering with mosaics, although her body never made it to the monument. She was that rare woman who got to rule Rome for a while: daughter of, wife of, granddaughter of, cousin of, and brother of several different Caesars, no one objected that she be regent to her five-year-old son, the child-emperor Valentinian III. She also had a daughter, Honoria. Her kids, history's worse brother-sister combo, celebrated birthdays here in Mediana and would, between them, finish off Rome as an empire.

Roberto was mindful of Ludo's wrath. "Perhaps we should be getting back?"

"Ludo's entire joy on this holiday consists of driving his car on new roads," she said, while taking phone pictures of the mosaic patterns on the floor of the baths. "I predict Lucrezia isn't even out of the bed yet."

"Well, he said eight—"

"Doesn't Greek and Roman stuff make you horny?" Mira asked seriously. "It does for me. Baths, orgies, using slave girls as you wish. If you were privileged, you set up an estate like this where only the gods knew what heights of pleasure were attained." Mira met his gaze as if to say, *You won't dare say it, but I know you agree.*

When they returned to the Best Western in Niš, Mira had proven prophetic, and the Marchesinis were barely functioning. Mira went to hunt for more Skull Tower postcards—"I will use them as stationery!"—and Roberto checked his messages . . . eight of the ten being from Rachel, the other two from Claudia. Claudia would be awkward since they never arrived in Belgrade, so he got Rachel over with.

"I've been trying to get in touch *for days,*" said Rachel.

"I'm in Serbia now . . . not great on international phone service. Macedonia tomorrow."

"Mack-adonia? You're going with the hard *K*?"

"It *is* a hard *K*. I refuse to soften Greek and Cyrillic *K*s. Beware the shining Kiklades, not Cyclades. The Church Council of Chalkidon, not Chalcedon—"

"Oh, Bobby, shut up."

After a pause, he said, "What's happening in shakedown news?"

Rachel now sounded quivery. "Just to let you know . . . let you have a heads-up. Merle . . . well, Merle and I, of course, are putting a proposition to Dad, and we think he will have no choice but to release funds that we were promised. What is a trust fund, Bobby? It implies *trust*, and we trusted—I trusted that certain funds were going to be paid into it, and when they stopped . . . I mean, we are about to lose our Paris apartment."

"I wouldn't be able to gauge that loss because you guys never let me stay there, as you'll recall."

What was their Dad-shakedown move this time? Roberto darkly recalled his discussing the Providence mob, flippantly, with Merle when they discussed her CIA theory in Paris. It had been important for Roberto, somehow, to let Merle know that his father rubbed shoulders with all sorts of seedy characters and that it meant nothing, that Roberto even admired it a little in his father. Did she take that clue and research it, and was she now on the brink of revealing a mob connection? Uh-oh. His father in London had mentioned *that,* had hoped Merle wasn't looking into Providence mob stuff. Maybe his father was *still* beholden to the crime families in Rhode Island; maybe it wasn't something merely in his father's youthful past. If Roberto had unwittingly been the key to the latest extortion plot . . . Naturally, Merle would announce that: *We heard all about it from Roberto!*

"I can't work on all my projects without the Paris apartment," Rachel said, more weary than passionate. "We didn't want to use the nuclear option, but Sal is leaving us no choice. And you, of course. If you'd just return our ten thousand, then we could dial it back from DEFCON 5 . . . or is DEFCON 1 the dangerous one?" There was a pause where the siblings listened to each other's irritated breathing. "Hmm," Rachel concluded. "Don't say I didn't warn you. Nothing will be the same after this if Dad doesn't pony up what's mine."

Roberto got a killer-strong Serbian coffee (that is to say, a Serbian coffee) and tried to return to his history book.

Worst brother-sister combo in history whose pettiness ended the Roman empire:

The brother, Valentinian III, was beset with Franks, Vandals, the Suevi, Visigoths, and, most famously, the Huns. He had one general who could handle them all, Flavius Aëtius, honored in the east as "the last Roman," such was his honor and military finesse (i.e., the one Roman general who sent Attila the Hun back on his heels in northern France). Aëtius also put down the rebellions from the two rival generals who mutinied one after the other. His reward? Valentinian himself killed Flavius Aëtius in 454, jealous of his reputation. With Aëtius's death, Rome was wide open to the Vandals, who sacked and pillaged, raped and robbed. We got the word *vandalism* out of it.

His sister, Honoria, didn't want to follow through on her arranged marriage to an ugly old senator, so she reached out to anyone who could help, and she settled upon . . . Attila the Hun! She sent him a valuable engagement ring and begged him to invade Rome and save her from this loveless marriage, assuring her savior that, for services rendered, he could choose from a fine selection of the Roman Empire's western provinces. Attila took the wrong meaning from all of this and felt this was an offer of herself in marriage *to him.* Attila, with Honoria's letter in his breastplate, started his march into Northern Italy, destroying all the cities in his path. But by the time they got to the Po, disease had set in among his tribal hordes, and they would advance no farther—but here too was a silver lining: the elite of Grado, of Aquileia, and all the razed and destroyed northern Adriatic cities decided to elude Attila by setting up shop on the tiny islands of the lagoon . . . and from this grew Venice.

The reach-out to Attila—that was a Rachel move, Roberto thought, for sure.

Atrocità

R oberto was reading to Mira from the end of his Balkan history book. The core of Serbian identity was tied to this land since the 1389 Battle of Kosovo, which defined the Serbian nation. Kosovo was the home of the Serbian Orthodox Church; it was the motherland. After a few centuries of Turkish occupation and people moving about, there were more ethnic Albanians than Serbs in the motherland. As for the Albanians, the nineteenth-century Albanian National Awakening was centered in Kosovo, the League of Prizren—so it was vying for Albanian motherland as well.

"So," asked Mira, ever practical, "why not make Kosovo a Scotland or a Catalonia? Some almost-state that, no matter what it's attached to, has autonomy?"

Roberto kept reading: Starting in the 1980s, Serbian president Slobodan Milošević, not one to shoot second, started a slow cultural cleansing of the Albanian culture. The Kosovars started out doing the nonviolent, peaceful protest and civil disobedience stuff, but Milošević was unmoved by any of that, so by 1990, the Kosovar Albanians declared themselves a republic. By 1996, there was an organized terror/liberation group, depending on your point of view, the Kosovo Liberation Army; Albanians from Albania, armed to the teeth, swept across the border to help defend their brethren. The Klečka massacre. The Lake Radonjić massacre. At least fifty-six Serbians slaughtered. The Serbs take out fifty-eight Kosovars in a residential area; civilians running from the scene were picked off by Serbian snipers. The Račak massacre. The Velika Kruša massacre.

Ahead at a bend in the road was a big, white tent and men milling about. Was that the border?

"I think, for peace of mind," Roberto said, closing his book, putting it under the seat, "I will save the Yellow House story for after we're safely over the line."

Ludo, ahead of them, slowed down first. Mira was right behind him as they approached the compound at the curve. There was no Serbian customs, of course, since the Serbs did not think this was a border. They had company: only 98 of the 193 UN members recognized it either. Many of these non-recognizers (like Spain) didn't want to start breakaway-state-fever in their own fragile nations, which are held together by duct tape and string. The Kosovars had a tent, a shack whence smoke emerged (a fire for warmth or something cooking), a port-a-potty, and a flag askew on a telephone pole. No uniforms. All the unshaven, red-faced men wore the camo you could buy at a military surplus store.

"Nervous?" Roberto asked, since no one would ever know with her.

"I don't remember . . . did the Netherlands recognize Kosovo's independence?"

Ludo was waved through, after all the men stroked and knelt and touched the sports car. They were enjoying a look at Lucrezia as well, who had dressed down as much as she could.

"This," Roberto stage-whispered, "may be where my Americanness actually helps, for a change."

It did. When the armed men took the passports, one grizzled man called out, "Amerikan!" He gave the thumbs-up. "Beel Cleenton!"

When it was certain that Milošević had no interest in peace talks or intention of pulling back his forces, Bill Clinton pushed NATO to start bombing Belgrade and greater Serbia as an incentive. Eventually, Milošević said he'd withdraw from Kosovo to stop the NATO bombing, which resulted in another eighty thousand Christians sent packing at KLA gunpoint. Some two hundred thousand refugees—about half of Kosovo's population—showed up on Serbia's doorstep, with many Romani and foreigners in that mix.

Roberto and Mira, making a great relieved exhale, were welcomed to Kosovo and allowed to drive through.

So Roberto read her the Yellow House story. Three hundred Serb civilians were rounded up and taken by the KLA into Albania to the town of Burel and a place called the Yellow House. There, the people were told that they would be having their organs removed to be put on sale for the black market. Were they given a quick humane slaughter before the surgeries . . . or did the removals happen while they were still alive?

"All right, Mr. Costa," Mira said firmly. "No more from that book until we leave Kosovo. And maybe no more ever."

Roberto set the book under the seat, remembering that the fighting officially finished here in 1998—ten years ago. A little recent for comfort.

There was not a car on the road, eerily, from the border to Gračanica, where a medieval Serbian orthodox convent had survived.

When Gračanica's sprawl began, the road was suddenly overpopulated—sheep, a horse, a flock of goats being swatted to market, dogs, children with dogs, old men in baggy Turkish pantaloons walking and smoking down the center of the dusty road. There were no road signs, but one could see a church tower with the distinct orthodox cross, so both cars drove in that direction. None of their phone plans covered Kosovo, so texting and calling would have to wait.

Ludo parked near the armed fortress that was the cathedral. The church compound was surrounded by fencing and razor wire. Every few feet, a blue-helmeted UN peacekeeping soldier stood watchfully. This had been declared a UNESCO site, so the UN was spending the world's money to guard the place.

Lucrezia now had smartly put her head in a scarf. In part, this would prevent some of the catcalling and staring and kissing noises that the men were devoted to. There seemed to be very few women about.

Ludo flagged down Roberto as they parked.

"I do not feel I can leave the car unguarded," Ludo said, taking his handkerchief and wiping the dome of his head. Already boys were running their hands along the smooth silver sheen of it; the older men, spotting the Italian license, were calling out questions none of the party could understand. Ludo worked out they were asking if he was a fan of Lazio's soccer team, where Igli Tare played, a great Albanian player—very, very great—and a supporter of the KLA!

Mira and Roberto surrounded Lucrezia and swept her into the lobby with the metal detectors and UN crew. Seeing they were two Europeans and an American, the guards quickly allowed them inside the stone walls. It was paradise. One could hear the birds in the trees; the melee of the street outside was miles away. The church, though graceful and proportional with lovely ornate window settings, was best adored inside where from floor to ceiling it was covered in Byzantine painting and icons. The Turks had had their way with some of the images, erasing the faces, gouging out the eyes of the saints, digging into the plaster walls . . . which made the ancient images look even ghastlier and more devoid of mercy.

The souvenir shop offered the nuns' products. A treacly liquor, honey, some wafers baked there. One nun covered in black robes, except her smiling face, followed the threesome, hoping to practice her English.

Mira asked if the nuns felt the danger had passed.

"Oh no. If the soldiers were not here today . . ." She made a noise. "We would be gone. The locals would burn our home to the ground. God must decide to protect us another year."

Roberto and Mira exchanged looks.

Lucrezia came to life at that report. "Can you answer a question for me? Do you have a monastery cat?"

They did, and he was last seen by the refectory; the nun pointed, and Lucrezia freely went in search.

"They would not," said the sister, "merely send us to Serbia. There would be rape. That's what was done all over Kosovo. May we ask for your prayers too?"

Back outside, Mira suggested they cancel the proposed night in Pristina, capital of Kosovo, and speed for the Macedonian border. She and Kosovo were done.

"I agree," said Ludo, shooing yet another boy away from his Audi's side mirror.

"Pristina is perfectly modern," Roberto said. "Skyscrapers, hotels, bars. This is the backwoods. We probably shouldn't judge Kosovo on this place—"

"Too late," Mira chirped. "I have judged, and we should go."

Ludo said he wished to avoid the clogged, truck-delayed highways. He had found a backroad around the Pristina-Skopje main highway, one that went through what passed for a national preserve, a series of mountains and valleys in some of the wildest, most uninhabited regions of Europe. This was not exactly put to a vote. Mira said they would dutifully follow. Some nature would be nice.

Once they began their drive south, Ludo and Lucrezia were frequently out of view, he had sped so far ahead. As they reached a hilltop in some administrative zone that Roberto detected from the signs declared a national forest, the view spread out forever. Green mountains, like the Appalachians, mostly pines but with deciduous trees starting to yellow, bounded a valley with a straight road down the middle. Distantly, they saw Ludo's Audi opening it up full throttle and filling the serene valley with the sound of acceleration, audible from miles away.

"The man does not understand tranquility," Mira mumbled.

There weren't many villages in these woods, but Roberto was fascinated by the scene: the hamlets looked like the little villages in Bavaria or the Czech Republic, terra-cotta tile rooves, white farmhouses with dark wood beams, winding cobblestone streets, but in the center, where the church steeple should be, a minaret. This was Muslim Europe, had been for centuries. Roberto knew it existed but was nonetheless a little surprised by the sight of it.

Mira prompted, "So, about Honoria, inviting Attila the Hun to rescue her from a bad marriage."

"Nothing is known of her fate for sure. She was probably carried off as a slave to North Africa to sell to Carthage."

"No, they made a movie, I think. I saw late in the night on TV, Italian, I think . . . very old-fashioned—how you say?—cornball. You know how they made ancient Rome pictures and Bible pictures and Egypt pictures all through the sixties."

"I love those old cast-of-millions productions. Nowadays, you can CGI the crowds, but they had to pay thousands of extras in those days. Look, Ludo is stopped up ahead."

"Sophia Loren, that is who they cast. I forget the actor of the day, who was to be ugly, mean Attila the Hun . . . cannot think of his name."

"Do you see why they're stopped?"

"Oh no. I think they hit an animal. We will have to pay a farmer all our money." Mira sighed as she decelerated. "There are bandits here. They block the road, you get out to see, they rob you and drive off with your car—"

Roberto, seeing: "They've hit a person."

Ludo's hands were shaking so badly that he could not light his cigarette. Mira pulled up behind the Audi, for the moment confining herself to the car. Roberto got out and walked around to the front.

A girl, maybe nine or ten, in a colorful vest, a long gray skirt, bracelets on her thin arms, an earring, long black hair pulled back in a scarf. Romani. She lay a full car length from the Audi's bumper.

"She was in the road, bent down," Ludo said, his hand trembling, putting the cigarette to his lips.

Lucrezia had walked ahead ten meters, her back turned. Three apples were in the road, where the girl dropped them when the car hit her. There was no blood.

"We're sure," Roberto said, finding his voice, "she is not able to be saved? Let's take her to the next town?"

Ludo stammered, "We have been here for . . . She is dead. She did the stupidest thing—in the road, she bent down to pick up the apple she dropped . . ." In Italian, he muttered about the mealy, wormy apples, as if that constituted the offense. He cocked his head to the orchard on the hillside, already shorn of its fruit. "What the frutticoltori had left behind."

Mira now joined them to inspect the scene. "And she was in the road . . ."

"She was going to sell them to us, I think," Ludo said. "Make us slow down and hope we would be softhearted to . . . to buy the apples."

"Maybe she is from the family whose orchard this is," said Mira, one hand holding the other to keep herself calm. Roberto looked at Lucrezia, still with her back turned to them. Someone should probably go see how Lucrezia is doing, ameliorate what would likely be a terrible break with reality—or for her, perhaps, a reunion with reality.

"Zingale, a Gypsy," said Ludo.

Mira said, "We must take her . . . The authorities . . ."

Roberto began trembling himself, but knelt beside the girl—

"Be careful what you do," said Ludo.

Underneath the stitched colorful vest was a faded hand-me-down T-shirt with a cartoon cat on it, some manga character that Roberto didn't recognize. Her fingernails were very dirty, and so was her face; her forearms had bruises. Her head was askew on her body; Roberto wondered if her neck was broken. She wore cheap flip-flops, which had been knocked off her in the impact. For something to do, Roberto got up to collect them.

"And there wasn't time to stop?" Mira mumbled her accusation.

Ludo sighed. "Yes, I was going fast. This country road to nowhere. The girl had no reason for to be in the middle of the road, kneeling down."

Roberto felt her wrist. No pulse. "Might we still revive . . ." But he knew the answer to the question.

Mira began, "We must . . . we must . . ."

"What must we do?" Ludo said, barely audible. "Please to tell me that."

Lucrezia was still turned away, standing very still.

Mira put her hand on top of her own head, as if that would bring clarity. "We must tell someone. The family will have to . . ."

And now Lucrezia turned quickly, fire in her eyes. "Are you fucking making a joke here?"

Her traveling companions stared stupidly, not recognizing her.

"*What,*" Lucrezia spat at them, "world of fantasy have you decided for to inhabit?"

She walked toward them, shaking her head, disgusted with her companions. "Your precious Audi," she aimed at Ludo, "the police will take, Ludo. I will be raped. Who do you think is the police here? The men who were making the atrocità only a few years ago. Men who have killed hundreds, raped hundreds. You want to put me into their hands? And Mira—oh they will enjoy our Mira too, what a new treat, yes?"

Roberto saw Mira flinch, staring at the ground now.

Lucrezia went on. "This will be a masterwork, di teatro dei Balcanico, yes? Starring all of us, and the mothers and women screaming in their grief, the men after our blood. And if we survive the mob, what will we have left when they are done with their corrupt local courts and corrupt local officials? How many bribes ahead? That is the end of your career, Ludo, Ludo Marchesini the murderer, in his shiny sports car and his pavement of children, yes? And you, Roberto! They will learn of your father, and they will find a way for a hand into your purse as well."

No one said anything.

"And will it bring her back? No. No! We destroy our lives, we hand over our fortunes—those of us who will not be going to a Kosovo jail for the next few years. What kind of treatment where no one speaks Italian? What do they do to the child killers? Listen to me: we move the little *disgraziata* to the trees," Lucrezia continued quietly as if authorities were listening in, "beyond the trees. Someone will find her, or someone will not find her. Maybe the animals will get her, and that will be that."

"Lucrezia," Mira whispered.

"She is right," Ludo said. "We will be a plaything in the hands of officials and courts. Who is to say soon her family will come looking for her. Are we ready to be stabbed or beaten by the band of Zingale? You want Romani justice? Or the corruptions of Kosovo? Which level del'Inferno do you choose?"

And in the silence of a few seconds, a new noise. A distant hum of a vehicle. Mira walked back to the crest of the hill. Across the valley, on the straightaway, was an old delivery truck. "A truck is coming," she said, though everyone had surmised that. "So soon our decision about what to do will be made for us."

Ludo threw down his cigarette butt. Roberto knelt and picked it up.

"Your DNA's on this," Roberto said simply.

Ludo winced, nodded, and put the butt in his shirt pocket.

Lucrezia charged toward him, not meeting his eyes. "Why don't you wear a sign around your neck—you wish to be caught? I do not wish to spend tonight in a village jail!" Lucrezia knelt before the girl's body. "*Dai!*" she barked. Ludo picked up the girl's legs; Lucrezia put her hands under the shoulders. They lifted her and began walking across a small ditch and into the orchard. In three rows, the farm ended and the forest began. Roberto watched as if it were a film; Lucrezia's thin arms dropped the girl a time or two.

"For the love of God," Mira stammered. "We can't . . ."

Roberto said, "If you want to confess everything tonight, it will not matter that they moved her. But if we wish to escape the consequences, this has to be done."

Moments later, Ludo ran out of the woods without Lucrezia. He hopped in his car and started it. "The car will be remembered!" he cried before speeding off.

Mira looked at Roberto. "Then we must hide ourselves too."

They ran to the Golf, though Roberto looked again into the valley to see that the delivery truck had yet to begin the ascent of the big hill. Mira started the Golf, and they went forward, dodging the rotten apples once clutched by the girl that lay in the road. An odd delicacy, not to run over and crush her apples. At the first dirt lane that presumably went to a farmhouse, they turned. Hoping they would not meet any farmers as they trespassed, they bumped along the rocky trail, the bottom of the Golf slamming against the rustic pathway. Out of the view of the main roadway, they rounded a curve, where they discovered Ludo's car idling. They turned their engines off.

Ludo got out for another cigarette. "Now we wait for the truck to pass."

They waited, it seemed, half of a day.

"Maybe it turned off before the hill," Mira said.

But they waited another ten minutes, and there was the sound of a delivery truck, chugging along, the metallic groans as the driver shifted on the hill. Ludo cautiously smoked a series of cigarettes until the truck passed.

"We go back the way we came," said Ludo, shakily. "Our story is simple. We came to Granita—whatever the fucking place was named. We saw the church. Everybody saw us in town. There is no lying about that. We bought some things. Now on to Macedonia. We were never on this road."

Roberto said, "I know our phones don't work here, but you don't know if some satellite can find us, so we must never turn them on."

"Let's go back for Lucrezia," Mira said, looking like she might cry but holding it together.

The Golf backed out first—there was no space for a road turn. The main road was clear. Lucrezia was back at the accident site and stepped out from behind a tree. Ludo was behind them a moment later; she hopped into the Audi. Ludo then sped around the Golf to lead the way back to the Pristina-Skopje national road—the road they should never have departed in the first place. Roberto noticed the three apples in the road were gone, perhaps kicked into the ditch by Lucrezia.

"Verdomde idioot," Mira spat out. "He drives a hundred kilometers per hour on these country roads, and he is speeding again. Maybe we can kill another child before the afternoon is complete."

Roberto thought with a heavy breath, it would help nobody to do the right thing. Even in a country with laws, like Italy, like Spain, it would be a difficult thing to survive a mob of angry villagers gathered around to mourn an urchin hit by a rich playboy in his sports car, whether she was Romani or not. Then the authorities, the police of the largest village nearby, the national police involving themselves . . . and all along the path, baksheesh, bribes, remunerations. All in a language no one could understand. Roberto had never felt so bad about something. But there was no moral voice of conscience begging him to go to the authorities . . . If that moral voice were in him, surely this would have been the time for it to make itself known.

He also knew with certainty if, hours later, police pulled up behind them, made an arrest, because of some evidence of their presence at the accident, he would sell out Ludovico Marchesini in a minute. And would there still be trouble for him, for the fleeing? For the first time in his life, he felt what thousands of aristocratic scoundrels, cheats, delinquents, rapists, must have felt: *My money will get me out of this.* And *Guys like me never go to jail.* And he despised the thoughts as they struck. But indeed they were his only thoughts, and they had the ring of truth.

Would they meet traffic that would remember them and identify such a memorable sports car? They did not. Fewer than a handful of the denizens of this valley of Kosovo even owned cars. Would there be a band of Romani or a wandering group of orchard workers having a picnic, laughing, passing around a cider-filled wineskin, wondering where little Esmerelda had wandered off to? There was no such scene. All was dead in the midafternoon; the few residents were in their houses sleeping off lunch, saving what energy they had for the cool of the evening.

"That was the old Lucrezia," Roberto said to Mira, "when I first knew her."

"Roberto," Mira began, her hands shaking when they did not grasp the wheel, "we must make a decision, you and me."

"I think I have made mine."

"I think I have made mine too, but . . ." She shook her head slowly. "We must be clear. If we tell the local police what happened, we will be not held responsible. This is all on Ludovico. He will suffer greatly, and Lucrezia, I think, was being dramatic . . . thinking they will rape her."

"Like the nun was being dramatic this morning? Shall I read you some more from my Balkan history, the twentieth-century chapter?"

"Roberto. The thing is, we say something now. Or we can *never*, ever say something. Because so far—you and me—no real crime has been committed by us. Who knows if it can be proven we were ever there with them? But we drive on, we participate in the . . . we say *rookgordijn*. The disguise of the crime. Then we are criminals too."

Finally, they were out of the hills, and Mira shifted to the straightaway.

Roberto thought about the word *rookgordijn*. *Rook* is "smoking"—he knew that from NIET ROKEN signs. *Gordijn* must be "curtain"; *curtain* in Norwegian is *gardin*, also in Danish. A smoke curtain. We say *smoke screen*, but a curtain of smoke makes more sense if you're involved in a cover-up. Maybe this would be a Notebook entry tonight. If they did the right thing and alerted authorities to the accident, there would be no Notebook anymore, no tonight in a hotel, no anything pleasant happening to them for a long, long time.

He finally said, "I do not want to turn Ludo over to the locals."

"Nor do I. To save my wretched self. I shall be honest about my motivation."

"Yes," said Roberto. "It's the one thing we can be honest about today."

Who Are You?

The Macedonian frontier was slow but uneventful. Skopje, the capital, was right ahead, virtually on the border.

As they drove into the heart of Skopje, they saw a wide muddy field where cars had parked haphazardly for a central market. They pulled into a spot; Ludo tipped the attendant to look after the car (it was not clear whether the tipped man was the chief of the parking lot or a beggar, but he looked official).

Mira had been silent with Roberto since the drive from the border, but when he glanced over, he could see her concentrating, plotting, working through scenarios. They felt that their fates were now handcuffed, one life adhered to the others for the rest of their lives. It wouldn't do to let small clashes of personality rise up or blame Ludo endlessly; they were in the serious business of sharing space in a life raft.

They walked into the town, past rough-looking coffeehouses with nothing but older male denizens—the sweet fruit smoke of hookahs, and the stench of tobacco from the eye-wateringly strong cigarettes, an earthen note of the black acid coffee of the region. No place for the women. Lucrezia received stares and comments. She still had her hair in a scarf, and she wore jeans and a man's shirt tucked into it, but there was only so much you could dim the wattage—she was still preposterously beautiful, and the rustic, unshaven men of the cafés hummed in appreciative discernment.

They found a less patronized coffeehouse where some women with hijabs were seated, students with a round coffee table full of schoolbooks. They sat near the street, to be less overheard—young people might speak English, even here. The domes of an ancient hammam were across the

street, a jeweler, a butcher, a lonely carpet shopkeeper who gazed yearn-
ingly in their direction. As they seated themselves, there was the crackle
of the city's loudspeaker, and the Asr, the afternoon call to prayer, filled
the streets.

"We might as well be in Kazakhstan," Mira said. "I cannot believe I'm
still in Europe."

Ludo grumbled, "Are we in Europe? Somewhere after Niš, we crossed
into the Middle East."

Ludo had been the only one to change money at the border, and so he
paid for the four coffees and four almond cookies covered in powdered
sugar, handing the waiter two hundred denar and another hundred for a
tip, waving the amazed young man away.

"What you just did there," Mira said, becoming colder as this day
wound on, "is not good. He might have barely remembered the man with
the pretty woman and the tallest guy in Macedonia, but now it is certain
because you gave him a monster tip. You must strive to be unmemorable.
You," she said, meaning Lucrezia, "become as—I can only think of the
Dutch word—*saai,* as you can. You," she added, meaning Roberto. "Try
to shrink yourself. And you, Ludo, attempt for once in your life to go the
speed limit."

"What is *saai*?" Lucrezia asked.

"Unremarkable to look at," Mira answered.

Lucrezia pursed her lips. "Beh, that will not happen."

"Maybe," Mira continued, "they have found . . . our girl, and they are wondering who moved her to . . ." She glanced around; no one was interested in them. "To where she was moved. So. The police will ask, how will such criminals behave?"

Lucrezia seemed unworried. "That is not where their minds will go."

Roberto ate his cookie morsel by morsel, realizing he was famished. Lucrezia contributed her cookie to him.

"I tell you," Mira posited, "such people who did such a thing would flee. They would get to the nearest ferry with their car and head back to Italy, canceling their reservations, losing their money. We must go on as planned with this vacation. We must send postcards, ring on the phone—every night, three, four, all our friends—telling everyone what fun are our adventures."

Lucrezia sneered, "I don't want to be in this terrible place one more day. Maybe we say I am sick, and I fly back to Milan. I take a cab to the airport here—that is, if the marvelous invention of the airplane has made its way to Skopje."

Ludo reached over to take her hand, but there was no affection in it. "No, you will go nowhere."

Mira: "It is important a detective can say, 'Hmm, look at how they went to the beach, the disco, they do not seem to be troubled like people who have . . . done a very bad thing.' Our friends may be asked by detectives, 'Did they seem worried, strange, upset?' So I will call my Radboud colleagues tonight." She turned to Roberto. "You have a girlfriend to call? Let us start painting a portrait of innocent people on a happy vacation, you see?"

Lucrezia nodded. Ludo sipped from his coffee. Mira was replacing Ludo as the leader of the expedition, but that was good in that she seemed to be thinking clearly.

"These detectives will look at all our media. We need to fill our cameras with us laughing and the clinking on the glasses, and swimming inside the pool. They will look at every email sent, every Myspace, Friendster, Facebook posting, every phone call, every photo taken . . . and there can be nothing but four people enjoying themselves on holiday. Have you posted, Lucrezia, your Cat of Macedonia yet?"

"Of course not, I just got here."

"Maybe you should start on it."

"I wait to the next town. This place *is* merdoso."

Roberto faced Lucrezia. "You were taking selfies in the car. When Ludo stopped a few hours ago at the intersection."

"I was taking pictures of myself crying. If anyone wonders if I have feelings, have a soul—"

Mira: "Ludo, erase them all. In fact, destroy utterly the chip and buy a fresh one."

Lucrezia protested as Ludo wrenched the camera from her bag. "It is my profession," she said, "to look all the different ways. I was feeling sad about the little girl and cried and thought, Lucrezia, you must film yourself, the ravaged beauty, the beauty through tears. That is so hard to fake on a photo shoot."

No one bothered to explain to Lucrezia why this was a dumb thing to have on her trip pictures. Ludo found them and deleted one after the other.

Lucrezia begged, "Do not destroy the cat pictures, please. I will transfer them to somewhere." Lucrezia frowned at her friends. "All of you do not trust me, which is for the making of much laughter, because *I* am the Sicilian. *I* will go to my grave never saying a thing. I cannot betray anyone to the police—it is in my blood. But all of you . . ."

"Yes?" said Mira, her arms crossed now.

"What if Mira needs to tell just one other person? What if she tells her boyfriend after he swears that he will never, never tell? Oh, you will not confess this year, but lying in bed sometime, some winter afternoon when you have forgotten us all. Cuddled with your man, you think, eh, what is the harm? And you tell *everything*." Lucrezia then stood and looked fearsomely at the small door that led to a toilet . . . the long-dreaded pit toilet with the foot pads. "I will use their toilet. I suspect it is still better than the one in the Kosovo prison."

They waited for her to walk away.

Roberto was surprised to hear Mira had boyfriends. But then he focused on who might blab first, saying, "Actually, it is Lucrezia I worry about running her mouth."

Mira agreed. "She loves drama too much."

Ludo thought it not worth discussing. "I will handle her. Do not worry.

The pills she takes erase the highs and the lows. In a few months, she will wonder if this ever happened."

Roberto, speculating as Claudia did, wondered if a plan might be afoot for Ludo to leave Lucrezia for Mira. Roberto said to Ludo, "Let's say you are not always around. She turns thirty-five, forty. No one employs her anymore. She wants attention. I see her on tabloid TV confessing, saying of course you were driving . . . or hell, I was driving, Mira was driving. But now she must confess all. As she pouts to the camera, a celebrity again."

"To which I will say she was driving."

Roberto slowed momentarily. "But she wasn't driving."

"She could have been. Who is to say?"

From Skopje, there was a manicured tollway to the west, followed by a near-deserted two-lane to the only resort in landlocked Macedonia, Ohrid. The sloping medieval town was on its namesake, Lake Ohrid, which may have been no substitute for a corridor to the Adriatic or Ionian Seas, but it was one of the loveliest lakes on earth, and on hazy days, when the far Albanian shore disappeared, you could easily pretend Greek sailing ships, announced by Homeric couplets, might yet approach the harbor.

The foursome arrived after dark, too tired to eat, exhausted emotionally. Ludo and Lucrezia shared a room, Mira and Roberto had separate rooms. Perversely, as he was finally alone, in a lovely several-star hotel with herbaceous starched sheets and sumptuous-smelling soap . . . he couldn't sleep. Too adrenalized, too much Turco-Balkan coffee, too terrified of what was playing out in the woods of Kosovo. If one were facing a life-ruination scenario, he thought coolly, were these the people you would want to face it with?

Ludo was nice enough until cornered. It was already in Ludo's mind to suggest someone else was driving. Well, Roberto couldn't drive a stick, but the court might think he was playacting. Mira would back him up . . . unless she worked with her eventual lover Ludo to support his accusation. Lucrezia would say whatever made the police interview go more quickly. Could the three others plot to let the rich American guy take the fall, figuring he would leave Europe and never see prison thanks to money and quality counsel? Roberto should have, when no one was looking, snapped a photo of the accident for "insurance" purposes. He needed a drink and some air.

Roberto, in a T-shirt and sweatpants (what he was about to sleep in, actually), padded down to the lobby. Though the hotel was modern, it was not great on Wi-Fi. The concierge suggested the guests had better come to the lobby for the office-based signal for best results. The lobby held a motley assortment of Albanians, Greek Orthodox religious, Germans and their detailed travel guides, one lonely-looking American man, who upon hearing Roberto speak English to the front desk, hoped to be talked to—they all were there dividing the bandwidth between them.

The messages on his phone appeared from the last days. Rachel had called many times, his father once.

He texted his sister, I KNOW KNOW KNOW YOU HAVE NOT BEEN TO OHRID, MACEDONIA & BEFORE YOU SAY THERE'S NOTHING THERE, YOU BETTER CHECK YOUR WILFRIED KOCH BIBLE . . .

She did not take the bait. There was a rowdy bar off to the side of the lobby. Roberto fetched himself a plum brandy and went back to wait for his sister to respond. He played solitaire on his phone, waited a half hour. A moment later, there was an incoming call. He stepped outside to the breezy, unoccupied terrace; a cold wind off the lake had cleared the tourists.

Roberto looked at his phone, he saw the name CLAUDIA appear on his screen.

"So," said Claudia. "There you are. So you decided not to join me in Belgrade?"

"Ludo is our leader," he said simply. "He wanted to stop farther south. We'd all been to Belgrade before. Your note suggested you were off to your research, goodbye forever."

"Don't be silly. I didn't wish to endure *the drive* to Belgrade, but I assumed you three would be joining me. I made a point to ask Ludo for the hotel, didn't I? I waited up thinking you would arrive . . . Can you imagine me, naked in the big, luxurious bed? I have come to trust you. So that was the night I would have let you do as you wish to your trashy Claudia of Trastevere, your Gypsy whore."

Roberto winced. He then remembered his fellow conspirators' happy-holiday mission and faked a laugh.

"I even miss Ludo and Mira a little," she added.

It was cold, but Roberto stayed on the porch in his thin T-shirt, finding a bench to sit on. He could see the lake a mile or so down the hill, some village lights on the Albanian side, as Claudia went through a repertoire of breathy, sexy topics to entice him.

"You are not listening to me," Claudia prompted.

"I am falling asleep, I'm sorry to say. Call me again. We can gossip about Mira and Ludo."

"Yes, I've been researching, and I discovered many things as well."

On the way back to his room, he passed the computer set out for guest use in a corner of the now abandoned lobby. He did a search for Pristina, the capital of Kosovo. He searched then for important phone numbers. *Policia,* a pretty obvious cognate for *police.* He copied the number. He could call and leave an anonymous tip in English. Nothing too specific, just that he thought there was an accident ahead of him, a girl in the road. By the time the police figured it out, he would be in Albania, maybe Greece . . . But to call would give the authorities a traceable number. He couldn't use his phone. Maybe he could use a pay phone, say the news, and hang up, but he would have to have scores of Macedonian coins for an international call to Pristina, Kosovo.

He looked for a pay phone. There was one; he would have to ask the receptionist for change—he would be leaving clues aplenty. Besides, no one was at the front desk to provide change, so he should just go on to bed. However, Roberto stood for a moment at the empty reception desk. All the room keys were taken, the hotel was full; the attendant was asleep now that it was after midnight. Was there a camera? He didn't see one. He stepped behind the reception counter and picked up the phone . . . and got a dial tone. If he called the police and left an English message, it would be fairly obvious to trace the call and look through the few English-speaking hotel guests. But that poor girl . . . Someone had to be alerted, right? He would relay the news in German—Germans can be blamed for one more thing.

He pressed nine and, indeed, that was how you got an outside line. He dialed the country code for Kosovo and the nonemergency number for the regional police. Finally, someone picked up.

"Hello. Sprechen Sie Deutsch?"

No. A conversation ensued with neither side understanding. Roberto kept saying he wished to talk with the policia, which they more or less understood. After many voices and a very long pause, a gruff, male German speaker arrived, sounding roused from slumber. "Was ist los?"

Roberto didn't say anything.

"Wer ist das?" And then he oddly asked in English: "Who are you?"

Roberto was silent again.

We will not go forward until I learn who I am talking to, the officer said in German. Who are you?

The question seemed to tower existentially, one of those questions like *If not now, when?* by Hillel the Elder or Pontius Pilate's *What is truth?*

"Nochmals, wer spricht."

Roberto hung up the phone, suddenly very far from being able to answer that question.

Quanta Costa?

And now, Albania.

They sat at a table just inside the door of a small café. After the invariable cucumber-tomato-onion-garlic chopped salad, and plate of fried kaçkavall cheese, they shared slices of a giant tavë kosi, a lamb and egg and yogurt quiche. Roberto was going to do a defense of Albanian food in his Notebook. Turkish goodies like their qofte, Greek phyllo dough veggie pastries and stuffed grape leaves, some dumplings from the Slavs, fried fish the Italian way—it may be the gastronomic crossroads of the continent. Or maybe—Roberto saw a provocative article taking shape—it was the Albanians who invented *everything*!

Gjirokastër was made from right-angled quarried gray stone, and one saw these sharp-edged impermeable stones form walls, cobblestones of the street, doorways and sidewalks, a castle on the nearby mountaintop. Nothing around here soft or Italianate, no baroque swirls or Islamic designs, just knife-edged gray stone and white plaster, presumably over more of the gray stone. With the sun ducked in behind a cloud, Roberto wondered if he had wandered into another Edinburgh or Viterbo, other dark-stone towns, where it was possible to snap a color picture and fool everyone that you had made a black-and-white photograph.

"Why are you taking notes?" Lucrezia asked Roberto.

Roberto had hoped not to be noticed. "Partly to not dwell on things . . . I mean, if we are to act normal, then this is what I would be doing, making notes for my journals. Have you noticed that every country we go to, this tomato-cucumber-onion salad is named after the country we're in? This is the *sallatë shqiptare*, the salad of Albania; the same thing was the *makedon-*

ska salata in Makedonia, and it was the *salata srpska* in Serbia, but in Croatia, at that truck stop, it was called the Bulgarian salad, which—I looked up on the internet—the Bulgars themselves call it the shepherd's salad, *ovcharska salata*. Add feta cheese like the Greeks, and it becomes a Greek salad."

No one had a thing to say about that.

"This," Lucrezia said, almost smiling, "is the fascination we have to look forward to when you publish your Notebooks?"

"Well, you asked what I was writing, and I told you. Do you want to know how it became known as the Bulgarian salad? In the 1950s, the communist government of Bulgaria began a campaign to convince the other Balkan neighbors that they invented it. And it more or less succeeded."

Again, no one had anything to say.

Ludo exercised himself, spearing a garlic clove from his salad on his fork and then putting it down. "Is that it for salad talk?"

Mira piped in, "But why would communist Bulgaria care about claiming this salad common from Trieste to the Caucasus?"

"Because," said Roberto, untroubled that he was actively boring them, "Bulgaria has no good associations. No one thinks of Bulgaria, and if they think of it, they think dark Balkan thoughts. The salad was supposed to make people feel kindly about Bulgaria."

"I do not feel kindly about Bulgaria," said Ludo, "so it seems they have failed."

Mira said, "We should think kindly about Bulgaria because they did not hand over their Jews to the Nazis. Or kill their Romani."

"No," Lucrezia said sullenly, "*we* have resumed that game."

"And here we are back on you-know-what topic," Roberto mumbled.

Lucrezia dumped her *sallatë shqiptare* into Roberto's bowl, giving him the almost-smile again.

"There is always," Mira said, taking charge again, "something more to say on that topic. Listen to me. We feel no one knows we were on that road in Kosovo, yes? But we do not know. There could have been a camera somewhere, a witness."

Or, Roberto thought, *someone feeling guilty at midnight might have called the police in Kosovo, leaving just enough clues to bring this whole thing down upon us.*

"They will not," Lucrezia assured them, "be looking for a car. Their minds will not go there."

Mira, notwithstanding Lucrezia, fixed Ludo with her piercing blond stare. "When you get back to Italy, why don't you trade your sports car for another?"

They talked for a few minutes about switching the bumper, the bumper that struck the girl . . . maybe crunching it up against a post back in Milan, so the fateful dent was invisible under a bigger dent. Then Ludo could trade in the car. The new Audi TT was very stylish—

"Ludo," Mira interrupted, "a *different* car. Something that a witness may not have seen. You saw how they were in riot to touch your car and caress it, worship it. Everyone in Kosovo knows you were there in that car. Go get a Ferrari or something."

Roberto reflected for the hundredth time how Mira and Ludo dealt with each other on a low grade of annoyance, never fondness.

It was next agreed that they had supported the illusion of a murderless, happy-go-lucky Balkan trip long enough. After tonight's stay in Sarandë, Albania, they need not put off the trip home any longer.

"It's on the Adriatic, yes?" Lucrezia asked. "I hope they have running water."

"The next day, we two will drive to Igoumenitsa," Ludo announced, "and get a car ferry back to Italy." He held Lucrezia's hand, then kissed it.

Lucrezia moped. "We drove all this way to sun ourselves on a Greek island and eat Greek food . . . and all we did was the horrible part, driving through these miserable pretend countries, divided and divided again because they can't stop killing each other."

"I for one," Mira said, "will follow through on our original plan and head to a Greek island for some sun, some retsina, some souvlaki, some reading, before my sabbatical is over. And some repentance in a local church."

"Not out loud, I hope," said Ludo.

"Just between me and God and the icons. Anyone want my . . ."

Sallatë shqiptare. Roberto volunteered to take her bowl.

"Now," Mira said, all business. "Roberto, give me your phone and iPod. Ludo, you look at Lucrezia's phone; Lucrezia, you look at Ludo's."

"And the point of this?" Ludo asked.

"Soon, we go our separate ways in Greece needing to know nobody has left a clue to what we have done. Who have you called, who have you texted? No, we must do it, like you did Ludo with Lucrezia's camera."

Roberto congratulated himself on not using his own phone to call Kosovo. He traded phones with Mira. They spent a moment looking at logs and histories.

"Who is this number?" Mira asked.

"My sister." They all looked up at Roberto. Had he told her anything? "My sister barely can stand me; she thinks I owe her money. All right, Mira, you have five calls to someone named Jolijn and someone named Luuk . . ."

"Jolijn is my friend and house sitter. Luuk is someone I am seeing . . . he is probably fucking Jolijn now that I am gone." Everyone chuckled at her joke. "It is not a joke," she informed them without a smile.

They took the best-quality road yet from the inland valleys toward the coast, the resort of Sarandë. When it appeared, the blue Adriatic was incalculably cheering.

"This is not a Greek island, but it will do," Mira said, happy to see the coast and the sunshine. Roberto imagined they all felt a release from being out of the mountainous inner country with its fraught history and bloodletting in every village. But why blame the Balkans for that final body in the woods?

"What is that over there?" Mira said, meaning the island that had followed them for an hour off to the right across a narrow channel.

"That's Corfu, Greece. You requested a Greek island, and there it is."

Probably of all European borders, this was the one most like the United States–Mexico line, where privilege and deprivation could stare at each other across where someone drew a line on a map in the centuries past.

At Sarandë, they were reunited with the canonical Mediterranean resort template—slick skyrise hotels, the marinas, back to the whizzing Jet-Skis, the loud youth, the booming Balkan-chanka-'80s disco pop songs from the storefronts, the pedestrian sea promenade with outdoor bistros with their fried seafood and garlic, of course garlic, the incense of the Albanian air. Roberto temporarily found unity with Ludo in exultation concerning a luxury suite for the equivalent of twenty euros. Roberto showered, stood in his towel on the balcony beholding the crescent of beach, uncrowded, off-season, and then lay down just to shut his eyes . . . to find that hours then disappeared. When he knocked on his friends' doors to ask about dinner, he could find no one in their rooms. Mira had disappeared; Lucrezia, sitting, and Ludo, standing, were out front at the café associated with the hotel, having a coffee.

"Do you want company?" Roberto asked, sitting in the miniscule metallic café chair provided.

"I think," she said, "they have a purge of the cats here. Not one to be found."

Ludo: "I saw a cat in the reception at the hotel. Maybe you can ask to borrow it."

Roberto asked if they wanted dinner.

Lucrezia said she had already eaten. Roberto flashed back on the days when they were a couple, a hundred times, a thousand times—*No, I have already eaten*: Lucrezia's diet of oxygen and light. Ludo, though never rid of the hunted look in his eyes, was sociable. "It is hard to believe," he mused. "This was the most backward communist totalitarian state of them all. What was the dictator's name?"

"Enver Hoxha," Roberto supplied. "He wasn't just *any* communist. He broke with Russia because Stalin had betrayed the true revolution. Then he switched allegiances to China, then broke off there too, because Mao had betrayed the true revolution. Hoxha, for a while, was the only true theoretical communist on earth."

"Driving across Albania," Ludo said, "one can see they are fifty years out of step. Perhaps we should abandon market economies of the West for the donkey cart and the fez, you think?"

Roberto was contrarian. "The thing about these so-called backward nations that haven't cashed in on globalist market capitalism yet is that they are the most unpolluted in Europe. The Albanian coast is clean in a way that Italy can envy."

Ludo: "There is no one left in Albania to pollute the country; they have all illegally immigrated to Italy."

Lucrezia: "Italian women are not sexually harassed on the street *quite* enough. Albanian men have come to Italy to help out, I think."

Roberto had learned Europeans did not like to dwell on the panoply of dictators, monsters, war criminals—there was really nothing to do but forget them. Americans unwittingly came off as scolds to speak of Hitler, Mussolini, Franco, Salazar, Hoxha, et al., as if they held the continent responsible. And it was so easy to be American in this; there was no chance, however inept or corrupt an American president was, that he could ever get away with declaring himself a dictator. America, thought Roberto, was autocracy-proof. The American people wouldn't stand for it.

When Ludo strolled away, Lucrezia reached under the table for Roberto's hand.

"We all good together, do you no think? Mira and you like each other, Ludo and Mira, of course. Me and you, me and Mira." Lucrezia moved her impassive perfect face to look at him. Roberto sensed sedation in her eyes, a recent replenishment of her medicine cabinet.

"Yes, we get along fine," he said.

"Then maybe it is settled," she said mysteriously.

Roberto did not want to dine anywhere fancy; he found a kebab / pizza / Albanian things takeaway place and had a few filling stuffed peppers and a slice of the popular *pica franceze*—pizza featuring gouda and mozzarella, neither of them French. Then back to the solitude of the hotel room.

Roberto, wishing himself an empty mind, searched through every offering on Albanian TV, settling on a preposterously amateur dancing contest on something called TV Klan. (Again, maybe think about a name change when they go global.) When that was over with there was an Albanian-dubbed *Hannah Montana*.

Claudia called. She was in Novi Sad researching the carnage of the 1990s; NATO had punished Serbia by bombing their three bridges over the Danube. But what was any of *that* research besides her investigations into Mira Visser?

"I think our Mira began life very poor," Claudia breathlessly reported. "I have been spying on her Myspace page. A picture of her mother's fiftieth birthday party in a council flat—oh, that's British—how do you say it?"

"Public housing."

"Yes, and not the best. I did not think they had any real poverty in the Netherlands. I thought surely a graduate of Delft University could help her mother upgrade, yes? I went to the architecture school site, and I did find Ludovico Marchesini. Ah, but no trace of Mira Visser. *Visser* is a common Dutch name, like um, Pesci, Fisher—it is the same meaning, 'fisherman.' There were some fellows named Visser and a Mira Janssen and a Mira DeCock. Maybe Visser is her married name from an abandoned marriage? I searched throughout the school database. Perhaps she only pretended to be his classmate? Hoping to get her hooks into a rich man? Be careful that she does not fixate on you. Perhaps everything with her is a fraud. I searched for her current school—she is not in the faculty directory."

Roberto had been clinging to Mira as the normal one of this bunch, but now he wondered if anything that got too near the Ludo-Lucrezia axis was normal.

"Are you in your bedroom alone?" Claudia asked.

"Yes."

"Take all your clothes off so we can both be naked."

He didn't obey, but he rustled the bedsheet around and said he was.

"So," Claudia said, delighting mostly herself, "have you understood the criminal enterprise in which you are involved, my innocent American friend?"

"What . . ."

"The great crime happening before you. You should get free of your present company before it is too late and you are in a world of police and investigations."

Roberto's blood ran cold. How could she . . . ? Had Lucrezia telephoned Claudia and already spoken of . . . ?

"I refer, of course," Claudia continued, "to Ludo and Mira's plan to murder Lucrezia. Ludo is in charge of Lucrezia's medicine cabinet, he told me, and she told me as well. Every morning, he sets out her pills, and she takes them. And at night. So right now, she is probably passed out in her hotel room, sedated, unconscious. If you check the hallway, Ludo will be walking on the tips of his toes to Mira's room for their rendezvous. But how long until they tire of this, hmm? How long before he persuades Lucrezia that she has not taken her pills when she has, and she takes a double dose, or a handful too many . . . or maybe he crushes them into a fine powder for her tea, and the unloved wife does not wake up. And then Ludo and Mira can be together. And no one will suspect."

Roberto didn't know if he should laugh. "You have a very wicked mind."

"I think of dark, twisted things for my profession. But we are in the Balkans, where one's suspicions must work overtime. I think Ludo does not want to give Lucrezia half of his worldly goods in a divorce. He strikes me as very much devoted to his worldly goods."

This morning would be the travelers' last together.

Roberto was eager to break free, but at the same time knew he would miss them and be anxious about what each was experiencing individually. But it was settled: stories had been agreed to, emails and phones and cameras had been inspected, oaths to secrecy had been avowed . . . there was nothing now to do but pursue their lives, go their separate ways, and wait for the knock at the door, the police—if they ever come—with their questions. *How on earth did you find out?* Ludo would ask Interpol as they slipped the cuffs on his wrists, and they would mention their one clue—a midnight call from Ohrid to Pristina. But Roberto had shamefully said nothing. They did appear to have gotten away with it.

A knock on the door, which made Roberto's heart skip a beat. He put a finger to his wrist to see if his rhythm had returned to normal.

It was Lucrezia who knocked. She came to tell him the others were in the breakfast room downstairs. The locals were putting raw garlic paste on toast, she said, shaking her head.

"Did you find your Cat of Albania?"

"No. The receptionist pretended there was not an office cat. I spent all morning wandering around but no cats, but lots of dogs. Maybe that's why there are no cats. Also the men staring, drooling, one old man pawing his crotch for me, how lovely and attractive. It is time to go home." She sat on his bed as he shoved the wad of dirty laundry into a suitcase. After he removed the suitcase from the bed and stood it on its wheels, Lucrezia stretched out on his unmade bed.

"Lie beside me a minute, Roberto. I must to tell you something."

What needed to be told horizontal? He lay beside her. She reached for his hand.

"Ludo and I think you should live with us. Mira too. The four of us. We may add people, if we like them."

"Like a commune?"

"Like people who love each other. You love me still, a little, do you not, cuore mio?"

"Of course," he said too quickly, "but I like being single." That made for a thirty-second silence.

"We have houses, money; you have money too," she went on. "It would be good to stay together. Keep an eye on each other, but that is not the main reason. We make a family of our own design."

Ah, thought Roberto, yet another chance to have a dwelling in Milan. The Mediterranean gods would seem to be insisting.

Lucrezia began again, "It was so sad the little girl we . . ."

"It is sad."

"But what if she brought us all together?"

Roberto could not bear to sentimentalize the girl's accident; it was not good luck or a precious gift or sign of grace or any nonsense like that. He ventured, "You and Ludo have an open marriage, is that it? Is he also with Mira?" Not wanting to assume anything, he added, "Are you with Mira?"

"He is not with Mira yet. He can't be. But in the future, maybe, and I will likely give them the money they want . . ."

Roberto didn't entirely follow.

"And he would permit you to be my friend again." She brought his hand to her lips. "Such long fingers . . . I remember, *mio caro*, how you put them inside me . . ."

At that, Roberto broke off gently and hopped up from the bed. "We have to get going. We will talk about this back in Milan sometime."

The Albanian police had a roadblock ten miles south of town. Passports, driver's licenses . . . There was the travelers' collective terror about the police looking for someone in particular, but it was happily just the police with nothing better to do, checking everyone out, strutting and performing the role of being important personages. Roberto suspected all these policemen were hired during Hoxha's reign and there was no real police work for them once the police state collapsed, but as in Russia, East Germany, Ukraine, the civil servants were not to be agitated, so, cravenly, the make-work jobs were not terminated.

The authorities wanted to talk to Ludo longer than to Mira, and Mira and Roberto in the Golf were given their passports back and waved on. Should they be worried? They drove a mile or two more, and Mira pulled over at the intersection for the trunk road to Greece to wait for their friends.

"Why do you think they're detaining Ludo?"

"It is either," Mira said, "the car, which they have no hope in their lifetime of touching and appreciating, or they wish to stare at Lucrezia, which they have no hope in their lifetime of touching and appreciating also."

"Look," Roberto said, nudging her to notice the smoldering, burnt car in the field on the right. It was a particularly ripe-smelling landfill. Piles of food trash, the feral dogs, the half-destroyed furniture. Like many Albanian villages (like many communities east of the Adriatic Sea, for that matter), once one was outside the city limit, you found horrendous dumping grounds. Unsanitary, vermin-infested . . . and in this case, Roberto was shocked to comprehend, occupied by families. A woman changed a diaper of a child, laid on the back seat of a stripped-down-to-its-chassis junk car; two men smoked cigarettes while breaking up chairs for a fire. Plastic wrap and fertilizer bags had been stretched between rusted auto bodies to keep out the rain.

This was the worst poverty he had ever seen in Europe. A Romani settlement. Probably any closer approach to the town would result in violence, so here the Romani stayed, in the landfill, where no one begrudged them . . . although, over time, when something went missing in town, when they turned up to beg for food scraps, then they would be begrudged and would be ordered to move on. And if the first request was not heeded, then there would be a more forceful request that would assure the Ciganësh would never come back to this county of Albania.

Ludo pulled up behind them. He hopped out of the car to discuss their route; Lucrezia followed. Ludo noticed their neighbors.

"Porca miseria!" he muttered. "Let us to move on quick before they take the tires off the cars, yes?"

Mira sighed. "Twenty more miles and then we're out of Albania, back to Greece, European civilization—or the euro, at least."

"What did the police want?" Roberto asked Ludo.

"To look at my legs and up my dress," Lucrezia answered.

"They kept asking what was the price, *Quanta costa, signore? Quanta costa?*—they spoke that much Italian."

Lucrezia: "It was not clear what price for which they were curious—me or the car."

They all stared at the Romani families. Roberto shook his head, noticing a boy wanting to run toward them to see Ludo's sports car, but an older man called him back, and rewarded him with a slap on the side of his head.

"This is probably how the little girl's family was living," Ludo said.

Lucrezia said, "We probably did her a favor."

The others were momentarily speechless. Because they had a softer variation of the same unforgivable idea but would never have said it.

"She was running into the road," Lucrezia said as if offering a valediction, "to beg from us. You know how they are. They beg and say if you do not give them money that they will be beaten when they get home. And they *will* be beaten. How much sex with the older cousins and brothers and uncles do you think she already had, hmm? *Quanta costa?* What

would her uncles have taken to let a truck driver, a peasant, fuck her, hmm? Living in the landfill with the rats—it smells like sewage and things rotting. If I ever live like that, you have permission to drive over me too."

"Lucrezia," Mira pleaded, wanting an end to this speech.

"Have no fear," she went on, finding the sunglasses on top of her head and putting them on. "If the police ever find her, they will not think an auto accident so far from the road. Their minds will not go there."

"That is the third time you have said that," Roberto said. "That their minds will not go there."

Ludo was finishing a cigarette, and as he snuffed it out, he nodded. "Their minds will not go there." He looked at Lucrezia and bowed his head slightly, as if giving permission for something, then returned to the driver's seat of his Audi.

Mira asked, "And why won't their minds go there?"

Lucrezia brought it out without difficulty, not a ripple of emotion on her face. "Because I dragged her to the bushes. I pulled up her skirt. I pulled down her pants. They will think some brute peasant struck her head and had his way with her."

Roberto and Mira looked at the ground.

"Oh, please, let us not cry boo-hoo, eh? I am Siciliana. I am the one of this group who *will* do what has to be done. No prison today or any day, I promise." She stared at them both, and there was a flash of the old incendiary Lucrezia for a minute, in the violent eyes, the smirk. "But I do not expect either of you to inscribe to your savior the thank-you note. Ciao. Ci vediamo a Milano."

She returned to the Audi, and that was, as it turned out, the last time Roberto ever saw her. Ludovico and Lucrezia sped to the Greek border and took the fork toward the Ionian coast. Mira slipped off her sweatshirt since it was warmer, and she would be driving in her tank top. How would Roberto survive the arms, the lovely, pale, lightly muscled arms for the next three hundred kilometers?

Mira's Golf, slipping gears and choking away in the final hills, reached the sleepy border a half hour later. They added themselves to the back of the line of cars waiting for attention at Greek customs and immigration.

"Greece, at last," said Mira, in her accustomed level tone.

"I want a gyro with real tzatziki sauce. Do you know the galakto-boureko? Phyllo dough and custard and honey . . ."

"I am like the dog of Dr. Pavlov, I think. We northern Europeans head to Spain and Greece to be free with our bodies, to have sex. Holland is too tiny a place; everyone knows everything, but in Mykonos, Ibiza, Torremolinos . . . no inhibitions, no fear. As I told you at Mediana, show me one Greek column and the clothes come off, yeah?"

That prompted Roberto to elaborate on an injustice: A blond woman coming to the Mediterranean could have sex with the local hounds every day, any number, mix and match. For a Greek boy, it must be a rite of passage to bed the northern European / North American / Australian girl on holiday who has traveled to their sun and their sea for that purpose, but it did not work the other way. The local Greek Orthodox maidens did not put out for American men. Only a foreign girl was possible.

Mira said, "Let's hope I have not aged out of consideration." They pulled up a car length closer to customs. "So would *you* look twice?"

Roberto turned to her; she was looking straight ahead without expression. "Um, yes," he said. "But anyone who gets with me needs an instruction manual and about half an hour of explanations."

"It's an hour of explanations for me. It is not to be undertaken lightly."

Now she looked at him. He looked carefully at her. The car behind beeped them, since it was their turn to move up and Mira had neglected to.

Transitions

When the issue of casual sex arose, Roberto amused Mira during the drive across the top of Greece with his well-worn speech, explaining his physical malady and that she would be wise not to expect a particularly vigorous performance from his penis.

To which she'd said, "Nor should you expect much of mine. Lots of female hormones since I was eighteen."

"Oh. Okay, so . . . Wow, I am sorry I didn't pick up on your being trans."

"I would have wasted a lot of money for nothing, hmm, if you had!" She remained her Dutch self, frugal with sensational information.

Roberto took this revelation as a personal failure. "I have great gaydar. And bi-dar, for that matter."

"I guess your trans-dar sucks. I'm glad you did not say, 'Who is that fucking man trying to fool? How pathetic.' There was a phase a few years back where, with justice, you could have thought that."

Roberto was quickly over his surprise; now he was curious. "Did you do the brow surgery thing? Where they shave back the skull . . ."

"Heavens, no. I am a coward before the knife, otherwise . . . otherwise I might have had the bottom surgery already. The top was bad enough." She plumped her chest. "But this is not complicated surgery, as surgeries go."

"It's not on topic," he added, "but I have to have heart surgery one day. It will be a serious procedure. I am scared of hospitals too."

"Maybe we should go into the hospital at the same time, be roommates."

"I may take you up on that."

Mira remained crisp and clinical. "What about taking me up on . . . sharing a bed tonight?"

Roberto decided not to think about it too long. "A hundred percent yes. I like femme guys, larger-than-life, take-charge diva women. I should be seeking the"—he was already stepping wrongly—"attractive people who straddle the spectrum, who rest comfortably in between all the . . . constructed . . ." He stopped. "I have no idea anymore what offends people on these topics."

"You are the best-looking American guy I have ever seen, and you are smart and curious—unlike, forgive me, most of your countrymen, and I cannot believe that you are interested. If you wish to check off the box of male-to-female trans like you checked off Kosovo and Albania, I will not be the one to talk you out of it."

Soon they were preoccupied with the directions as they approached the Thessalonian waterfront. Roberto led them straight to the sea and Aristotelous Square and directed Mira to turn into the first luxury hotel loading-zone parking bay he saw.

"Beautiful, but can we afford—"

"Yes," he said, "this is on me. You wanted an Aegean view, didn't you?"

They checked into the hotel, a smattering of tourist Greek came back to Roberto, and after he tipped a bellman to put the bags in the room, he grabbed Mira by the hand and led her outside, along the square with its big Venetian arcades, which kept the pedestrians out of the direct Aegean sun.

Perpendicular to the big avenues were back alleys stuffed with antique shops, coffeehouses, teahouses, places to smoke everything, from cigars to hookah. You couldn't know Thess if you didn't wander the back alleys and dine on Bulgar delicacies and Greek seafood, and drink—drink like the rowdies who occasioned Saint Paul's letter to the Thessalonians two thousand years ago.

They settled on a restaurant. My God, after the Balkan prison menu of shish kebab, Bulgarian salad, overcooked lamb, the Greek menu (which Roberto would have declared limited compared to most European nations) seemed encyclopedic . . . mussels *saganaki,* taramosalata, dolmades, slow-roasted octopus . . . probably not advisable to have all his favorites at once. But the octopus for sure. Roberto steered them to a sparkling Zitsa, which, on such an empty stomach, would get them drunk and erase any anxiety hanging over the evening's grand finale.

After a bit of loosening up, Roberto asked, "So Ludo is leaving Lucrezia for you?"

"Oh no, not at all. Did Lucrezia not ask you about joining the three of us? We were auditioning you to see if you could be our fourth roommate."

"A big polyamorous arrangement?"

"Before we become old and conservative, why not live a little outside the lines? There is room for the four of us to live in Ludo's Milan apartments, which would include living among his parents' and grandparents' properties. We travel, we drink wine, we eat well. Ludo wanted you to fall in love with Lucrezia again; she would be occupied with you while Ludo and I pursued our resolution . . ."

"I did not encourage her suggestion."

"The idea that you would bring your money into the mix was appealing too—let us not dance about that. But Ludo likes you, Lucrezia regrets disposing of you. And I . . . well, it hardly matters. Say no for now, but think on it. As you travel around, flitting here and there, not belonging anywhere, why not have a home location? You can't forever wander the world as a dilletante."

Ah, that word again. "Does *dilletante*," he asked, "not have a negative connotation in the Netherlands?"

"Just a little. But we all want to be one. But think about it, ja? You have to live somewhere."

"I will think about it," he said, feeling the door crack open to its possibility.

"I am not sure how much money I am bound to have. It's not fair for Ludo to pay for everything."

"Ludo?" She sipped her Zitsa and put down her glass, savoring the sip as she shook her head. "He has no money. We are all adrift on a river of Lucrezia's money—she is the rich one."

Roberto's eyes must have gone wide, because Mira laughed her constrained two-syllable laugh.

"Ludo will be when his parents die, I suppose. But you have seen them—and his nonna—no one is near death. But Lucrezia made a million in her few years of fame. Plus she came from money. It is her theater—aw, look at the simple Sicilian waif—perhaps you believed it? She is from Ragusa. Her father is magnate with, um, *asfalt*—you have the word? She grew up groomed and—what word would you use? We say *ingesmeerd*."

"Smeared, slathered."

"I like that—*slathered*. She was slathered in beauty products and hair treatments, physical trainers and clothes. She arrived to take Milan by storm; it was not a low-budget operation."

"So Ludo is living off her?"

"I am too, a little bit, because Ludo slips me money. My academic appointments are rare, and they do not pay me like our friend Dr. Ciobanu, who is more of a celebrity. I could not figure out you two. But you have sexual issues, and she told me that she has a sexual issue. The thing with her cousin and brother."

Roberto registered yet another Claudia confession.

"She told you, ja? She was molested by her brother and then, through her teenage years, the cousin joined in . . . A disaster."

Roberto nodded solemnly.

"Maybe you can help Ludo and me keep Lucrezia alive."

"How so?"

Mira was getting a little glum on the wine. "She will not be long for the world. The drugs she takes often lead to weight gain in others. She has solved that problem by not eating. I ask you, did you see her put one bite into her mouth this entire trip?"

Roberto thought and then shook his head. "No, not a bite."

"But she drinks quite a bit—also dangerous. I do not think it bothers her to die before she gets old. She was obsessed with supermodel Ruslana

Korshunova, who killed herself this summer. She fantasizes about being Marilyn Monroe. Her death a shock, the covers of magazines. Ludo hoped you joining us might . . . might help for her to live longer."

Roberto wondered how long this recruitment scheme had been contemplated.

"Besides, Ludo does not want me as I am. But let us save this squalid plot from *Goede Tijden, Slechte Tijden* for the hotel room, shall we? He likes that he is married to a model, even one not as famous as she was. It is more respectable than being married to someone who began life as Bartholomew. He cares too much about appearances, but you know that. His clothes, his car . . ."

His phone was buzzing. He begged pardon and looked at it. It was Claudia. He wasn't sure he wanted to gossip about all this with Claudia, for whom the three of them were mere entertainment. He checked the missed calls too that arrived when they were in remote Northern Greece. His sister. His mother, for some reason.

Their hotel room, where their bags were waiting for them, had a harbor-view balcony. It was a warmish night, and the moon shone a path past big international tankers and ferries to the islands and container ships. Not exactly Mira's dream of the creak and splash of small fishing boats in a timeless cove on an off-season Greek island.

"Oh, this will do," she said, a little tipsy. "It is my old friend the Aegean, after all."

Roberto hopped in the shower before Mira and turned down the sheets of the bed. He arranged himself naked, so when she walked out, all was on display. And then a moment later got self-conscious and pulled a corner of the sheet across his lower half, like some Hellenic figure in a modest neoclassical painting.

Mira came out of the shower in a towel. Roberto read from his telephone:

"You are all children of the light and children of the day. We do not belong to the night or to the darkness. So then, let us not be like others, who are asleep, but let us be awake and sober. For those who sleep, sleep at night, and those who get drunk, get drunk at night."

"I grew up Dutch Reformed, believe it or not," Mira said. "Paul berating the Thessalonians, I take it?"

"Right on the first guess."

"I like the sound of those children of the night, sleeping and drinking."

He reached over and yanked her towel away, and Mira seemed to flinch in her eyes, then steadied her breathing, and crawled in beside Roberto to snuggle. Roberto was not sure if she wanted the penis to receive his attentions or not . . .

"I can be your bottom. We can do it that way," she whispered.

"The Dutch may organize a class action lawsuit if you get rid of this, I am afraid." He put his hand on her member. She laughed her two-note laugh. "Of course," Roberto added, "if you go to the porn sites with pre-op trans women, they—"

"They all have tremendous penises—I know—yes! I am a stereotype."

They kissed and rolled around, and she enjoyed Roberto's fleeting but admirable erection; when it began to fade, he looked at her, and she winked. They kept interrupting their engagement with questions, points of similarity.

Roberto said, "I would have been a happier man if I had been born exclusively gay and a bottom. No one would care about my nonperformance; they'd just roll me over and get going."

Mira nodded enthusiastically. "Oh, the same for me! I wonder sometime, if I had just enjoyed passive anal sex, would I have surrendered to the comparatively simpler path for a gay man? I would be Mees back in Amsterdam, the quiet blond sitting in the back of De Trut every Saturday waiting for some guy to commit to my backside." She paused. "I still would have been a woman, but I might have bumbled through as a feminine gay guy."

They both agreed that it was a cruel, ironic fate that they did not relish being penetrated. Roberto mentioned "an Indian friend" and how it was fairly tolerable with him, but for the most part, he only said yes to passive sex out of politeness, and it was rarely wonderful for him.

"Me too," said Mira. "Some guy thinks because my sexuality is not penis-centered that I think of my ass as a vagina. 'Ooh, let me in that pussy' and 'I'm gonna eat your pussy.'" She started laughing, really laughing, which Roberto had never seen. "You can call it what you want, it is still my ass."

Roberto laughed along too. "I will find your vagina," he said after a moment. He reached under the sheet and very slowly wandered with his fingers, carefully placing a finger under the scrotum. He slowly and so sensitively investigated the cavities adjacent and behind the organ, and then patiently began a rhythmic stroking of the perineum. Nothing seemed to light the fuse at first, but then he heard her breathing alter. She began helping herself along, caressing her own circuit of erogenous areas . . . and then an orgasm. Quite a thorough one too.

After which, it was time for the Ludo and Mira story.

Ludovico Marchesini began his *laurea triennale* at the University of Florence. The prestigious architecture school was in the Accademia di Belle Arti, Mira narrated, "where down the hall is Michelangelo's fucking *David*." But he was less than inspired by his studies and spent most nights in his car, cruising the lanes of the Cascine, an unremarkable park by the Arno that had been ceded to prostitutes. Half of these prostitutes were girls from the poorer southern regions of Italy, who were doing sex work to afford their transitions and get that bottom surgery. Yes, the male clients knew the girls had been born men, yes, the clients looked around the fact of the penis (or secretly desired it). College boys, drunk businessmen on a convention, and johns who could not afford cis women made their way to the park for sex in the car or behind a bush, twenty to thirty euros a pop. Ludo could well afford the glamorous cis women who advertised online or in the sex listings in the gazette you could find at discos and cruisy bars. He didn't want those women; he wanted the beautiful, impoverished, desperate boy-girls in their wigs and clumsy makeup who had yet to reform their genitals. He was hardly alone in this compulsion—he recognized the other regulars, men who had the same fascination, businessmen, men of good families amid the drunk twenty-year-olds, priests out of their collars. They were a fraternity who would keep each other's secret but would fight bitterly for possession of the prettiest young *puttana* whose accident of male birth had not diminished a feminine beauty.

"The gay scene," Mira said, "in Italy is miserable. Closeted, shut down, full of shame. There is no law against it, but Italy does not accept it. For every gay man in Italy, there is a mother in a church before the Virgin Mary, asking for the dagger to be removed from her heart, due to her gay son.

"But trans? Italy is the world capital. Poor women come from Africa, from Brazil, from the Caribbean to be trans sex workers there—Italy is the World Cup of she-males—you use that word? Maybe the typical

Italian male needs a pair of tits in order to let himself play with a dick. It is a template in the peculiar sexual psyche of Italy, but also throughout the Mediterranean, the Middle East too. I have a shelf of scholarly books about it in my office if you want to investigate. Anyway."

It was Ludo's dream to keep one of these girls as a mistress, to join in their progress, pass them money for the hormone treatments and eventually the surgery, to watch the evanescent male body slip away to permit the female one, master of the metamorphosis, to be there when they wake up from surgery, to take them home to heal, and then, eventually, to receive their first favors in gratitude. The girls of the Cascine knew him well, competed for his attention. He was like a sultan with a small harem of pre-op women for whom he was cast as future savior.

One night, he was slowing down for a group of prostitutes, as he had done nearly nightly in the wilds of Parco delle Cascine, when behind him the blue lights of the Carabinieri police van exploded, sending the girls scattering. Car prostitution is, bizarrely, against the law, where street prostitution is not. So there was an arrest. Ludo could have called his father, and a string might have been pulled, a criminal file conveniently lost, but he was too ashamed. After his hearing and the levying of a hefty fine, he decided to transfer to Delft University and the architecture program there. Somewhere as far as he could run from his compulsions and the bevy of dependent trans women who counted upon him to complete their dreams. Women who, when their dear Ludovico disappeared, were desolate. (Yes, public health would pay for gender reassignment, but there were thousands of ancillary costs—documents, licenses, new birth certificates, mandatory psychological counseling . . . and none of that was free.)

So to Delft. Claudia's research was correct, there were men named Visser at Delft University when Ludo was there, and one was Bartholomew Visser, with the common nickname Mees, which she jettisoned for Mira. In the last years of *middelbare* (high school), she started accessorizing, wearing earrings, women's blouses rather than boy's T-shirts or button-downs, just a faint acquisition of makeup. There were some rude comments, a few close calls with bullies, but this was the Netherlands, and personal freedom is sacrosanct.

"Not because we Nederlanders are embracing and liberal," Mira felt the need to point out, "but because we are Calvinist. The elect and the damned have been prefigured, so it hardly is worth the effort to correct or improve anyone."

Mira presented as female entirely when she began studying at Delft. Being blond and fair, she was striking, even more so when after her required psychological counseling, she began hormone treatment. How did Ludo identify her? Of course, someone whose every fantasy and erotic urge revolves around his fetish was able to pick her out of a crowd. And so began a long romantic friendship. Ludo was older, graduated sooner, and enjoyed an internship in Rotterdam; he cleverly pushed for Mira to be the next year's intern.

"But I had a real fear about the bottom surgery," Mira said. "I knew some women for whom it had been very painful. And there were horror stories you hear, prolapses, and infection. And a swelling that takes forever to go away—and painful all that time. A friend reports your pee goes in any direction it likes . . ."

Mira was adamant she did not want the assembly-line sex reassignment surgery in the Netherlands. Yes, it was competent and would do the trick, but if one was going to do this—a onetime, irreversible undertaking—then she wanted to go to a private, world-class doctor. She had found one in Switzerland, a clinic where you stayed until healed, apparently with spectacular results. The worst of the prep was the hair removal by electrolysis.

Mira shrugged, saying, "I was not some swarthy Greek man, so it was not so terribly bad but . . . you are not squeamish?"

"Oh, there is no body part or function I do not crave to talk about for hours. You have come to the right American."

"Okay. The estrogen did not make my balls smooth. I may have been a smooth boy up top, but my legs and pubic area were not . . . not cooperative. To remove the hair on the scrotum . . ." She said *scrotum* with a short *o*, which actually suited the scrotum better, Roberto thought. Mira cringed as she narrated, "So you remove the hairs with electrolysis. Pure pain, I tell you, and then you wait because it will grow back or grow back in a different area."

"But the scrotum is going away, isn't it?"

"It will be the tissue of the labia. You do not want long, wiry hairs coming out of the labia, no. Like the beard of a mussel." Mira seemed relieved to be discussing all this with someone. "They have a thing," she said, "I wanted and Ludo did not want. It's called *zero-depth genital conversion*. You have the outer appearance of the vulva, the clitoris from the head of the penis, labia from the scrotum, and yes, you can put a finger a little way in. But not much beyond that, no vaginal passage. I mean, it is with the longer extended cavity where there can be problems. Like I said, I do not like to be penetrated in front or in back—*nee dank u*. So why do I need this deep canyon, hmm?"

"But Ludo . . ."

"Ludo dreamed of a full surgery. For which he would pay, although he did not then make enough for the Switzerland option. I cannot afford anything. So our negotiations stalled out."

Ludo left the Netherlands, began working and living in Milan.

Ludo explained to Mira that he was reformed, told her his obsessions with trans women, cross-dressers, she-males, prostitutes in parks, call girls on TSdates.com had been put behind him. Mira heard that in 2005, Ludo was engaged to a model, a goddess. Mira was invited to the wedding, which was a sumptuous affair amid Milan's fashion scene; Lucrezia may have been the most beautiful, and all around her, the bridesmaids, offered bounteous female perfection . . . and yet Ludo could not stop staring at Mira.

"By that time," she said, "I had had the top surgery. I think my breasts are a touch stiff, don't you think?"

"They feel like soft, beautiful breasts to me," Roberto said, leaning over to kiss one. In truth, they were a little rigid, but he would not say that.

"So I attended their wedding, more visually female than he had ever known me . . . His old obsessions began anew."

"And Lucrezia knows about you two?" Roberto asked.

"Of course. But she also knows that Ludo and I will not sleep together as long as I have my boy parts. But she is close to giving me the money for the bottom surgery, the deluxe one, in Switzerland. She does not make love with Ludo anymore. All she does now is sleep and chase after kitty cats. I think she hoped to add you to our house of crazies, but you are, so far, too sensible."

"I don't know what is offensive or my business to discuss, but . . ."

"Please. Speak freely."

"Women without the bottom surgery, I have the sense, have a bigger dating pool out there. When you get to your Greek island, and get on

Tinder or Grindr or wherever it is best for trans women, you will get a man writing you in no time."

"A man with a fetish who will not regard me as a woman, perhaps."

"But we are talking Greek-island sex, not your choice of husband."

She bowed her head.

He brought their flaccid genitals to touch. "I wish I could have made a better American impression."

"Roberto, please." She took his hand and returned it to her perineum. "You could teach my Nederlander boys."

The next morning.

Roberto walked out to the balcony, where the square was coming to life in the hazy morning light; the cool air from the sea was brisk enough for a T-shirt and a shirt over that. He held a collection of work by Athenian writer Demosthenes Davvetas, whom he had been meaning to get to. In part, because in addition to wonderful tales, fables, poems, Davvetas was a practitioner of the aphorism, a real throwback of a genre.

> *Alone, I am melancholy; with company, I am bored . . . yet I love life.*
> *The best way to kill passion is to begin slowly wrapping it in seemliness.*
> *No love can fail to have blood on its teeth.*

It seemed to Roberto that he needed to up his aphorism game in the Notebooks. People might agree with his insights, but how much better if he could stick the landing on a conclusive passage like an Oscar Wilde or a Dorothy Parker. Davvetas's wisdom about the body spoke to Roberto frequently.

> *The best way to hide is to show your wounds.*
> *A body is a bad liar.*

A room service coffee and pastry arrived. As he sat there reading, his will began deserting him. He thought of Marquis Evrémonde in *A Tale of Two Cities,* who runs over a child and parts the curtain of the carriage to toss a coin to the grieving family. He thought of that Voltaire poem where soldiers riding too recklessly through Paris's streets trample a child, and Voltaire—within the body of the poem—seeks out the child's mother for consolation. Do such people, who have ridden away with a child dead in the road behind them, get to savor Greek aphorisms on a sunny balcony? Contemplate the insouciant qualities of life and fate, over coffee and a bougatsa?

Rachel called, but he did not pick up.

Thess was one of his favorite cities, and if it could not cheer him, then he could not be cheered. Thess was a six-alphabet town! At the turn of the twentieth century when there were more Jews here than Jerusalem, when Bulgaria considered it—even across the Greek border—one of its cultural capitals, when Armenians and the Greeks still living on the coast of Turkey had yet to be ethnically cleansed and considered this city theirs, when this city was another twelfth-century Toledo, a place where Kabalah and Eastern Orthodox mysticism and Sufi chant all mixed in one of the most glorious hodgepodges of the decaying Ottoman Empire, then each sign had to be printed in sextuplicate: Roman, Greek, Hebrew, Arabic (the Turks had not switched to the Roman alphabet yet), Armenian, and Cyrillic. There must be road signs in the civic museum that he might photograph. Perhaps that would be the day's activity.

Mira knocked on the glass of the balcony door and leaned out. "I am going now," she said. "I assume you can transport yourself without the use of my Golf, much as you have enjoyed the torture of fitting inside it."

His phone buzzed again: Rachel. "You are leaving so soon?"

"If I am to get to Thassos and Samothrace and get back to the Netherlands in time, I must start out now. I too have a checklist—I have not been to those islands. There is an ancient convent that only women may enter. A small compensation for my never being able to go to Mount Athos, but I will have a kind of revenge."

"As long as the nuns don't have one of those airport x-ray scanners."

She stepped onto the balcony to kiss Roberto on the forehead. "Think about the offer, our commune of crazies. Milan as your playground."

"I will."

"And if not the four of us, maybe you and me."

Roberto was caught off guard but managed a warm smile about it.

It was bright, and she paused, the milky sun held in the blond of her hair, like some maiden favored of Zeus. "Our biology has made us . . . unique. It would be an open partnership, if you like. I am leaving before that silly chemical begins to saturate my brain, the falling-in-love chemical. I have many decisions to make, and I do not need some . . . doomed romance to complicate it. But if you wish it, to live with each other for a while, I would support the idea." It was like she had a prospectus. He imagined if he, some future day, would ask for more information, a good-natured memo of understanding would arrive by email. Mira was the antidote to his track record of dramatic women. Or perhaps this was drama too, just the officious Dutch variety.

"I will, like the Milan offer, consider it, Mira."

She turned to leave but Roberto called out, and she turned.

"None of my business, really," he said, "but I would skip the bottom surgery. You're good as is."

Through the sunglasses, he had no idea if he had affected her formality, but she nodded as if to accept his editorial comment, and left. From the balcony, ten minutes later, there was her Golf, driving down the boulevard, turning left at the seawall, heading to Kavala and the ferry to Thassos.

The phone buzzed again, this time Mrs. Santos.

He decided to catch up on the latest Dad-shakedown news under the protection of the One True and Orthodox Church. Roberto walked into town and made his way to St. Sophia. This was under restoration last visit, and now it was open, the mosaics cleaned and shining, the shadows of the church the only air-conditioning to be had. Thessaloniki's Agia Sophia was sunken a little below street level since it was a Byzantine-era monument when the city was less built up atop the rubble of itself; he trod some well-worn stairs to the sanctuary of the 700s. It had been a mosque for a while (some of the minaret still stood). There were some beggars, some ragged poor hovering around the front of the church, but they did not pester him for money. Stepping inside the narthex, he saw a giant basket of bread. A Romani woman with her child, both quite dirty, stepped in and helped themselves to the bread because they were hungry. *That may be the most Christian thing I have seen inside a church*, Roberto thought. *Why doesn't every church that professes Christianity do that?*

These were great Byzantine mosaics, Jesus in one dome, Mary in the apse with those all-seeing eyes, who knew your sins before you found the words to confess them. She held the Christ child, just as an impoverished struggling mother once held her little girl in the Kosovar countryside, a little girl killed by a carful of rich tourists, dragged to the bushes, and left with the appearance of defilement, where the vultures and feral dogs could get at her. "Forgive me, Mary," he said aloud, no one around him. Unless someone grew confessional, he and his disreputable friends had gotten away with it. But this groove would be worn into his brain for the rest of his life: *Maybe I should report us . . . but no . . . but it wouldn't change anything . . . and to tell would ruin everyone's life for what was truly an accident . . . and it was only really Ludovico to blame . . . but then we inserted ourselves into his shame.* He was sure they all, even heartless Lucrezia, had some variation of this moral interrogation playing like a rondo in their heads on a loop, starting with the girl's just-sleeping face, the justifications, the excuses, the worldly, sad shrugs . . . To live with it, one had to not dwell on it. Or one might stage a late-in-the-game religious conversion, so that one might be cleansed, restored . . . but one would have to believe in a great many other things to achieve this one redemptive thing.

His phone dinged. Rachel, again. Oh all right—he picked up.

"Okay, Bobby," she said, her voice weak. Whatever transpired with her father earlier that morning had shaken her. "Noon, Paris time, came and went without Dad doing the right thing . . ."

"Jesus, Rach. If you're going to extort your own father, at least don't call his giving you money the 'right thing.'"

"There is something you should have known about Dad—really, Bobby. Only an idiot wouldn't have worked it out . . ." She was hyperventilating. "You remember my work on the trompe l'oeil? Well, here we can see—"

There was some noise, a muffle of voices . . . It sounded like they were wrestling over the phone. Roberto looked up at the Virgin Mary. *Give me strength, Blessed Mother.* And it seemed Merle had emerged from the scrum:

"Bobby, this is Merle."

"My sister can't do her own dirty work?"

"There will come a time when you realize we have done you a favor. You're not Salvador Costa's son. Your mother cheated with Gehrman van Till, and your eventual stepfather was your biological father."

Roberto had a second or two of resistance. He floated for a minute in a limbo in which he might laugh at the pathetic nature of this stratagem. But then the second and third second arrived, and the truth of it was . . . shockingly plausible. Some puzzle piece snapped into place. The tall, blond, WASPy guy was his biological father. But still, he pushed back a little: "My folks didn't even meet Gehrman until he came to Providence to set up . . ." He was having trouble composing sentences. ". . . to set up the bond division—"

"Gehrman van Till was a junior officer with Hightower Wiggins who was sent to Buenos Aires to capitalize on the dictatorship. Personally, I think he and your father were both informants for the CIA and hung together forever after, looking out for each other. Mutually covering their crimes."

"I . . ." Roberto could not find his voice. He wasn't emotional, it seemed, but his voice and body were trembling as if his physical presence couldn't follow his brain's orders.

"We can send you the genetic test, if you aren't convinced."

Back in 2002, Rachel and her box DNA kits. She had sat on this information a long time, waiting to make maximum trouble from it and capitalize.

"Rachel says," Merle continued without inflection, "that your whole family knows, friends of the family know, your uncle and aunt . . ."

Rachel in the background supplied the names of Aunt Bennie and Uncle Vinnie.

"Everyone," Merle said, "in Providence knows. Except you."

Ah, thought Roberto, rough edges and obtuse angles regularizing themselves in his head. Vó Costa's hatred of his mother, her intrafamily reputation as being a harlot . . . *Poor Sal,* they must have been saying. And his mother waiting for decades for Gehrman to get free of Katrin, waiting, they must have calculated, until the Van Till children were older. And also flashes of Gehrman being paternal, his stepfatherly affection, the too-expensive gifts at Christmas, once even venturing to say, "You can call me 'Dad' if you like—you'll have two fathers who'll look after you."

Did Sal always know, or did he work it out? However it began, there was never a moment Bobby wasn't his beloved son . . . Right?

Merle droned on with the items that brought her pleasure. "Because there are some holdings of the Costa family that may have to go to Rachel, of course. Since she has the real Costa blood; I'm thinking about the Providence properties of your great-uncles and great-aunts on the Costa side your father holds in trust."

I'm not a Costa, he thought, debuting the thought.

"And you may consider," Merle was saying, "getting a lawyer and seeing what portion of the Van Till estate you may be eligible to inherit—"

"Put my sister back on, please."

More mufflings. "Um," said Merle, "she can't come to the phone . . ." More whisperings, hissings . . . It was hard to know if Merle was forbidding it or encouraging it.

"She might as well talk to me," Roberto said, his voice refusing to embolden itself. "It's the last time I will be speaking civilly to her."

In time—thirty seconds later—she took the receiver. "What?"

"For a little extra allowance money, you stuck a dagger in your mother, your father, and your brother."

"Half brother."

His father was calling him. He passed on the call. "So you knew from when we were kids I wasn't your full brother?"

"Pretty much."

"Looking back, I suppose, you treated me accordingly. Even so, we were living in the same home. Didn't you ever want a . . . an ally against all the family nonsense?"

"Europe's not big enough for both of us, Bobby. Go on back to America. I'll be over here, and we won't have to deal with each other anymore."

His father was calling him again. "I'm not going anywhere."

He hung up on his sister and connected to his father.

"Bobby?"

"Dad, it doesn't matter to me—it doesn't change anything."

"It doesn't change a goddamn thing!" Sal said, his voice full of passion.

"Right? I mean, you're my dad. You're the dad I love—"

"It doesn't change a goddamn thing! You are the only son I have ever known, and don't you know a thousand ways that I love you to death? Huh?"

"I know you love me to death!"

"Ever since you came into this world. Our little trips when you were a boy, all over Providence, down to the piers for stuffies, down for those winter sunsets where we'd have a coffee milk."

Such relief flooded over Roberto Costa. Nothing had changed. Of course nothing had changed. Roberto felt tears escape, but this wasn't sadness. He was not sad. Nothing had been lost, not really. "We'd swing by and get the hot dogs."

"Olneyville." Roberto heard his father voice falter. "No other reason to go to that part of town."

"But they got the celery salt, don't they, Dad?"

"New York system."

Both men paused here. Roberto heard his father sniff, clear his throat, breathe roughly. And he supposed his father was hearing the same thing from him.

His father recovered first: "We got to get rid of Merle. Just as much as we had to get rid of Michael. They were trying blackmail, pure and simple, said they were going to tell you about Gehrman if I didn't send Rachel thousands of dollars. Then I said if they followed through, then I would alter the trust—and they're about to find out I mean what I say. Mrs. Santos is working on it right now. We had a folder set aside, Plan B, we called it." He laughed his famous cackle. "*B* for *Bobby*. Where you gonna be next Friday? I'll meet you. You gotta sign some things."

"Anywhere you say, Dad."

"Brussels. I have some EU regulatory issues . . . And we can talk about everything then. But I'm gonna give you the short version here, okay? It was clear when I came home from Europe in 1976 that your mom's and my marriage was . . . was going to be a rocky one, let's say."

"When you came home from being a CIA agent," Roberto joked.

"Well, your mother didn't think I was any kind of James Bond, sad to say. We were Catholic enough not to want a divorce, so we put on a show for twenty years. And I even told your mother I wish we'd have run dry after we'd had a son. Always wanted one, of course. So for Providence in 1980, we got—lemme tell ya—downright sophisticated. We were I guess what you kids call 'open,' and the only rule was no embarrassment, no scandals, and no pregnancy. You see how well that worked out." He took a deep breath. "Hey, once I saw you in the hospital, I told Lena, 'Unless you're gonna go marry Gehrman and set up a family, this kid's mine.'"

"I lucked out, I'd say."

"Now Rachel doesn't know any of the details. She just has that DNA test she conned you into taking. What she doesn't know is that I sat down with Gehrman, who was, and remained all his life, a great friend, and we talked about it. He had two kids from marriage number one, and three with Katrin, still in elementary school, and he wasn't looking to start marriage number three and divorce number two and child support payments, all that. But you know what he did do? He set up a trust fund for you, like he did *all his kids.* He was the trustee. And when he died, I was the successor trustee, and I added to what he did. And so next year, I was going to sit you down and tell you, because at thirty, you get the trust free and clear. Rachel, as I said, has no idea."

"Let's keep it that way."

"Oh, my daughter is going to have plenty to occupy her when I follow through on my threat. I'm going to make *you* the trustee of the Raquel and Roberto Costa Revocable Trust."

"Wow. That will . . . That would be . . ."

"And I think you should cut her off cold. You know why?"

"Because . . ."

"Because once the money's gone, then Merle will be gone too."

Roberto felt good to be on the confidential, loving side of his father. He pondered a moment on the word *father.* Did it feel different now? No, no, it didn't at all. "It will be a pleasure to cut Rachel off," Roberto said. "I'm not feeling very charitable about her today, as you might imagine."

"I was weak, Bobby." Again, he heard his father struggle to speak. "Shoulda told you a long time ago. You're gonna have to forgive me. I *knew* I was going to *have* to tell you since you were going to be given the Van Till trust on your thirtieth birthday. I would sit in hotel rooms or in downtime on the CNBC show . . . I mean, once I got a cameraman to film me so I could see how I came off telling you. I just dreaded it. And then I thought after Gehrman died . . . and it's unworthy, I know, but I got to thinking, *Why ever tell Bobby?* Just say Gehrman was a generous guy and left his stepson a bundle. Gehrman was dead; it wouldn't matter to him. I didn't want to lose even one percent of you . . ." His father was quiet again. And he said the next thing with strain. "I didn't want to take a chance that even one small part of you was gonna feel different about . . . about that maluco Salvador Costa."

"C'mon, Dad," was all Roberto could manage, equally tight in his throat.

After they hung up with plans to meet in Brussels ahead, he sat there. He sat there for an hour, occasionally looking up to check on Mary and the Christ child. He wiped his eyes. He would sit there for another hour, under the watchful gaze of the Theotokos, the mother of God, and review his life, the parade of clues he might have seen had he been thinking that way. He considered his mother cleaning up her scandalous adulterous love child by her later marriage with her love child's father, Gehrman van Till. Maybe Roberto's sense of Lena being a fortune hunter should be tempered. Maybe Sal was her ticket out of Fall River but Gehrman was the love of her life.

He had never heard or seen or imagined his father crying. Yet despite their being upset, despite the new information swirling around them both, his father seemed securely in place, the esteemed portrait above the mantel and the warm family fire. But as for Rachel . . . The way she chose to weaponize this information showed true hatred. A real effort to drive the usurper of her entitlement and inheritance, from the family.

He stood. Looked at the blinding light pouring through the doorway as a homeless man gathered up some bread into a dirty handkerchief and committed this bundle to his pocket. And he looked once more skyward to the mosaiced Christ in the dome.

It's honor thy father and mother, right? It doesn't say anything, Roberto decided, *about sisters.*

Chapel of the Miraculous Sacrament

"S o what's this place like?" asked Sal Costa, in a pressed white shirt and tie under a suit coat. He abandoned his signature plaid sports coat and loud tie so his time with his son was not interrupted by the CNBC Costa Nostras.

"Your classic *steak frites* mill. All the animal-fat-fried potatoes you could eat under a dollop of eggy Brussels mayonnaise. Plus an excellent steak. Rich chocolate desserts. Everything Mrs. Santos forbids."

In the arcades aside the Grand-Place of Brussels, Belgium, there were no shortage of traditional restaurants with tile walls and floors, cast-iron tables, linen tablecloths and true polished silverware, a thousand-bottle wine list housed in a cellar belowground, and mountains of meat, potatoes, oysters, and mayonnaise to be offered up in various combinations . . .

"Before we start sloshing wine everywhere . . ." Roberto's father had brought a leather satchel of papers and an aristocratic fountain pen with HIGHTOWER WIGGINS emblazoned on the side. "Let's get this done. I'll send Mrs. Santos a text that the eagle has landed or whatever code phrase we cooked up—can't remember."

"And this . . . ," Roberto began, arranging the stacks of agreements before him.

"This makes you a co-trustee with me for the Raquel and Roberto Costa Revocable Trust."

"And you expect me to cut her off and generally make mischief."

"Yes, I do. For a bit. When Merle is convinced the money has disappeared, my bet is she'll pack her bags and mooch herself along to the next meal ticket. She has to, Bobby. This little power play was a work of pure meanness. I hope your sister isn't really that cruel, that this is all Merle's influence."

Roberto felt Rachel was plenty mean without Merle's help, but he held that thought as the waiter supplied menus and carte des vins. Roberto, feeling rich—well, he *was* rich, it was official—ordered a Margaux from 2005.

His father was happy to leave the wine selection up to his son. "I expect," Sal said, "at first, the girls will strike back when they learn the trust is in your hands . . . Oh, initial that, on that form *there* . . . The sticker fell off, I think. And do the same thing on the next three copies. What was I saying?"

"That Rachel and Merle will make another run at the castle, try to shake you down some other way."

"I'm depending on it. Your sister was taking her trust fund money, and they were hiring researchers to find something on me, private investigators. And I'm pretty uncompromised as executives go, but Hightower Wiggins has *lots* of skeletons in *lots* of closets, just like everyone else on Wall Street. We've got some oligarch clients, whose money derives from some serious international crimes. The Meyerbeer Diamonds, for Christ's sake. Havner's and Dudley's Hightower Wiggins slush fund, which I still can't launder. I don't want her opening those doors before I finish cleaning the house."

The wine arrived in the waiter's hands, but the sommelier himself sped to the waiter's side to conduct this precious business—wines this expensive were not decanted in this brasserie every day. There was much ceremony as he carefully nursed the cork out of the bottle, sniffed it, poured a tiny amount in to his silver cup on his necklace (the tastevin, but Roberto would not demonstrate he knew what that fancy prop was termed). The sommelier then poured a tiny bit in Sal's glass and held it up to the light, then handed it toward Sal to sample. Roberto assumed he might defer to his wine-snob son, but his father sipped the contents himself, swished it around, breathed through it, put on a show with a wink to Roberto . . . and nodded complacently that "it would do."

After the sommelier departed: "Dad, I'm gonna bet you've never had a wine that was one hundred out of one hundred in *Wine Spectator.*"

After a moment. "Hell, even *I know* that's good. Now that's an aftertaste. Bring on the steak!"

"It's not a Del's Shandy, I know—"

"No, no, it isn't. And I bet this joint isn't classy enough for an end-of-the-evening coffee milk."

"You're still drinking Autocrat coffee milk, so I'm not sure you're missing anything. Morning Glory syrup, all the way. Maybe we can ask if the steak comes with some B&M Beans."

"Why have a steak? Get 'em to bring out some Saugy franks and do 'em up like they got at Olneyville."

"New York system," said Roberto, nodding seriously. "Not Paris system."

"Paris—nobody wants a hot dog from Paris. Who ya kidding?"

Roberto smiled finally. "You know who makes a good hot dog? They're even as crazy about them as Americans are. The Norwegians. Every service station is like a 7-Eleven with do-it-yourself hot dog fixings. Actually, I think it's *actually* 7-Eleven who runs the convenience stores up there."

"Never been."

"I may go. Thinking of answering this ad in Svalbard. They need a conversational English teacher. Pays next to nothing."

Sal shrugged happily. "Thought the Scandinavians all spoke English anyway. Better'n we speak it, in fact."

"Yeah. But half the workers up there are Russian or foreign. I want to sort out my Notebook, get writing, see if I can accomplish something."

"Sounds *cold.* Isn't Svalbard way up beyond the Arctic Circle?"

"Northernmost town on earth. A few hundred more miles, you're at the North Pole."

Their steaks arrived, but Sal had settled back in his chair, savoring his glass of wine. "I may have rubbed shoulders with Putin's pals and Providence wiseguys, but at least I can speak to the Providence families like a neighbor, someone who went to their church, drank in their taverns. They're not the worst people on earth. You wanna know who *are* the worst people on earth? Those much-talked-about One Percenters, the richest of the rich, tens of billions, hundreds of billions—one day, that Bezos guy at Amazon, a trillionaire. Inconceivable wealth, unknown since . . . since ever. I have discovered, Bobby, that they are not, big surprise, often very nice people. No amount of money is enough. They don't care if the republic, the Constitution goes in the trash can as long as no goddamn penny rolls off their desk and gets away from them. Or worse, that penny ends up in the hands of the needy. And they got a lot of people on their payroll, Mitch McConnell types who will go and retrieve that runaway penny and bring it back in their teeth and bow their heads before the wealthy, for a pat on the head."

Roberto nodded. He had never heard his father say anything bad about wealth and the wealthy.

At last, his father sat up straight to attack his steak. "Over in my little naive bond division, I didn't see so much of the bad stuff. But now that I'm CEO, I see who runs our country, and this country, the EU, the whole Western Alliance. And I'm worried for your generation that . . ."

"What?"

"I worry about oligarchies and autocracies, which is all there's gonna be one day. A dime's worth of difference between the U.S. and Russia." Sal broke his chain of thought: "Enough! Let's just eat. 'Cause I got an even more important thing to talk about."

And around dessert, Roberto's father started in on the topic that concerned him: "We both have iffy hearts." Sal stared at the silver gravy boat filled with yellowy mayonnaise, the fried potatoes in another platter. "You have an aneurysm growing, an aorta with a bulge, getting bigger each year. I don't have to go over what you know about your condition. At some point, like now, as you reach thirty, you're going to have to have a surgeon do a resection. It's two hours. Some people with a milder case—

and that is likely you—can have a surgery where they go up the artery in the leg; whole thing fixed in no time, you're out of the hospital lickety-split. If they decide they have to crack your ribs and go in . . ."

Roberto's appetite disappeared. "C'mon, let's talk about this another time—"

"We can do it at Presbyterian; they have, like, a zero percent kill rate. It's not complicated surgery. But I got my pacemaker here in Brussels at Saint-Luc's, big, top-rated university hospital, specializing in hearts. Which they'd *better* specialize in if the Flemish are gonna keep up this here mayonnaise business. There's an available appointment tomorrow, Bobby. Let's see the lay of the land, and if surgery is suggested, let's do it. I could stay until you come out of the ICU. We'll pay cash—probably get moved to the front of the line."

"We don't want to do this in the U.S.?"

"I thought . . . the pressurized cabin of an eight-hour flight. You don't want to take the chance."

This was a topic where Roberto found himself speechless. "Can we have this discussion at breakfast tomorrow? This whole thing freaks me out."

"You know what freaks me out? You walking around with a four-centimeter swell in your aorta ready to pop like a balloon. Your chances of surviving that kind of aneurysm tear untreated are not wonderful—"

"Yeah, I know, Dad—"

"But you have the procedure now, before it's dire, you live to a ripe old age."

"C'mon, I'll be lucky to hit seventy. You know the stats for Marfan patients."

"Anything's possible, but hey, let's go for seventy, then." His father stared holes through him. "You want to get it taken care of, Bobby, before the last minute and you're halfway up an alp or somewhere like Albania, where Rachel said you were. I didn't sleep well 'til you got back to civilization."

"Okay, okay."

So the next day, Roberto was off to Saint-Luc's. Some tests and PET scans and x-rays were done by the university interns who got to work on Saturday. Sunday was dreary—in a hospital bed, trying to find something halfway entertaining on Belgian television.

Monday, with Sal in attendance, Dr. De Veuster said he felt the minimal surgical procedure would work—the endovascular option, the apparatus that went in the femoral artery and snaked its way to the aorta. An after-noon procedure, a few more days of observation, and then home to rest. No bench-pressing right away, the doctor joked.

Tuesday was the day. There was the expected fasting, preparation with IVs and drugs, one pill (about an hour before he was wheeled down to the surgical suites) that relaxed him nicely. And then the anesthesia . . . He was in the middle of saying something to the anesthesiologist and wham—he was out midsentence. He was awakened what seemed a second later, and he was in a post-op ward . . . he looked around. His fellow occupants looked like they'd really been through the grinder; there was groaning and ugly bandages and an array of heretofore unsmelled biological odors. And then he was wheeled to the ICU and hooked up to every machine in the building . . . and the doctor was suddenly there with his stethoscope. Roberto was groggy; people were appearing and disappearing at his side.

His father sat by his bedside when he was moved to a private room. "This must be running you a small fortune," Roberto mumbled.

"Guess what?" said Sal with his trademark smile. "Even paying full price might end up being cheaper than how they fleece you back in the States, even with insurance."

"Obama will give the country health care," he said.

"They've been saying that since Teddy Roosevelt."

"Don't you have to go back and do your TV show?"

"Stephanie has got the week." He scooted his chair closer. "One happy headline you probably didn't get a chance to hear about: There's a com-mitment from Treasury to buy up our bad swaps, so Hightower Wiggins will live another day. It's official."

"Thanks to you."

"I just tread water better than the others. I think I told you, me and Mrs. Santos are looking at the exit sign next year. I've watched so many guys get carried out of Hightower Wiggins or Lehman or Goldman, dropping dead at their desks, coronaries and strokes. Don't I get to gallivant around Europe like my son? I'd like to let Mrs. Santos get back to her family; some grandchildren are on the way, and she needs to spoil them. I want to take Rosario to see Europe. And I've been having this hankering for Argentina again. Rosie and I could get hooked up with one of those tango clubs and dance away the nights in Buenos Aires. They got these senior packages."

"You won't be offended if I drift off to sleep, will you, Dad?"

"I'm hoping the sound of my yammering will comfort you and let you go nighty-night. After I leave Hightower Wiggins, I can concentrate on the TV show . . ."

The next morning, Roberto was even better, and more normal the day after that. His father had rented a ground-floor apartment in Woluwe-Saint-Pierre, facing a park. There was an Everest of four brick steps leading up from the street to this ground floor, equipped with a hospital bed and no other furniture. Here was where he would recuperate. They said two weeks of mild activity, walking farther each day—no lifting, no exertions—would bring him back to normal. A nurse, Bregje, was contracted for two weeks to check in on him, cook some nutritious, cleanly prepared meals, check his resting pulse and blood pressure. He felt sorry for Bregje; he had lost all appetite and slept all the time. He was not a fun patient. He would stand with difficulty and feel a heaviness in his chest, which recently had spread to his stomach.

And that stomach thing did not improve. Bregje called Dr. De Veuster. He mentioned his fatigue and stomachaches, and Bregje took the phone and rattled off a few more statistics in Flemish . . . "*Negentig boven de zestig*," she said . . . Ninety above sixty? That doesn't sound good. And soon an ambulance appeared, and men to lift and deposit him on a stretcher, then a wild ride back to Saint-Luc's, emergency room, the ceiling in the presurgical lobby—he recognized that he'd been here before, he thought pleasantly. Regular customer. And then he was parked in a room of blue tile. Roberto recognized the anesthesiologist from last time, though this time, he looked more harried. When they made eye contact, the anesthesiologist nodded, hoping to make his wink and a smile like a casual acknowledgment, two gentlemen on the street passing and recognizing each other.

A mask was attached to his face, and everything withdrew into a terrifying extinction, as if someone had flipped the off switch to his existence.

Still alive?

Yes, still alive. He opened his eyes in that same postsurgical waiting area. There were different people this time . . . this time the postsurgical crowd comprised a better class of survivors. He suspected this time it was he who looked like the survivor of a wreck on the highway. Oh, and here comes some real pain. He gripped the railings of his bed. A nurse adjusted the valve on his IV, and things felt immediately better. *Morphine*, Roberto thought. *I see what the fuss is all about now.*

Then somehow he was back in an ICU room, more machines, more beeps and whirrs, and if he lifted his hand and undid a sensor by accident, then alarm bells and the rush of nurses into his room, panic followed by calm, as something he had unplugged was replugged.

His father, looking concerned. Trying to smile.

Rupesh came by. But maybe he dreamed it. Everyone in ICU wore surgical masks and gowns, and Rupesh was there in his pajama bottom, . . . and Mira came by in her tank top with her alabaster arms. Odd, everyone in flimsy tops in winter.

Then Lucrezia and Ludo, with the little Gypsy girl trying to squeeze between them. His mother? She was hiding out from Rachel, but, yes, she may have checked in on him. Saw that he was going to recover, and ran off. But in time, he decided that was a hallucination too.

Over a week in ICU. He had the strength to control the TV set. Ah, here was the second half of the Belgian cop show cliffhanger he saw last week when he was having the endovascular. It's good to complete things. This second time around, they had cracked open his chest; the mesh artery they constructed originally was leaking. While they were in there, they did something else or other. If he lived through all this, maybe . . . who knows, the fabled sex life, what other men took for granted, would be in his possession again, blood heading to the assigned places. He felt wrung out and deflated, not strong enough to make a real fist . . . although he could change channels—that was something, wasn't it? He tried to follow the Dutch shows.

Like all English speakers, he had an educated guess for what written Dutch meant (sort of German-ish, sort of English-ish), but to speak it . . . impossible, despite cognates being thick on the ground. *De kat sliep normaal in de deuropening.* The cat slept normally in the door opening. But when *they* say it, they have to clear their throat five times. Pairings of vowels, which were pronounced inscrutably from the back of the throat with pursed lips sounding like neither of the vowels featured. He remembered *eu* was like *ayh,* as in Dr. De Veuster . . . *Ik denk dat ik erg ziek ben.* I think that I am very sick. *Ben ik dood?* Am I dead? I am sort of hungry. *Hongerig.* The Dutch world is another of Europe's regions where the potato is the earth apple, *de Aardapfel,* the *pommes de terre* in parts of France, *Erdapfel* in Germany . . . "I think I want some french fries," Roberto said aloud to the empty ICU room, 3:00 a.m.

Sooner than he felt he ought to be moved, he was moved. He was back in Woluwe, same apartment, different nurse. She was Nees.

"Stay in the hospital too long and you'll pick up some bug," his father explained. "Hospitals will kill you. I had the apartment cleaned top to bottom. No one but Nees and you will ever be there. And me for the next day or two."

"So Stephanie's doing the show this week?"

"Yep. Believe me, the pooh-bahs at CNBC are happy she's there. They've been a little upset with me about some of my 'Two Cents.'"

The last five minutes of *Costa: Doing Business!* were devoted to Sal humorously ranting about something; this segment was called "Sal's Two Cents." Apparently, his dad had been excoriating the lions of Wall Street, Congress, Bush, Alan Greenspan . . . "They actually sent me a page of 'notes,' like I'm a newcomer. Essentially, they keep saying, 'We're a capitalist concern, and stop with your Trotskyite harangues.'"

"Well, you can't quit Hightower Wiggins *and* get canned from *Costa: Doing Business!*"

"I'll clean up my act," Sal Costa said, grinning broadly. "Oh, and Lena."

"What about Mom?"

"She's engaged. Got some French Canadian guy on the hook."

"Some multi-zillionaire, I guess."

"Not superrich, but he's well off. Owns a chain of restaurants and a few gourmet establishments in Montreal."

"She's gotta be working some kind of angle."

Sal looked like he was going to make a joke, then his face corrected itself. "In the Christmas spirit, lemme say that maybe the old girl's found love. I wish that for everybody. Even my gadabout vagabond son, Bobby."

Christmas in Brussels. Roberto considered how no one ran around extolling the virtues of that. He had been getting up and walking a bit. Finding his way every few days to the mirror . . . oh, man, was that ever not something he was prepared for. Who was this shriveled-up, skeletal man with lines beginning in his face . . . and gray around the temples? They said they were fixing his heart, but what they really did was cut into him and remove ten years' worth of youth. Something was off with his eyes. He had to squint to resolve his image in the mirror.

It became 2009. Roberto lay in his bed hearing celebration dimly in the streets, firecrackers and shrieks of delight or someone being murdered—it was hard to tell.

One of Roberto's walks took him to the cathedral, not really one of Europe's showstoppers. But there was an eye-opening chapel dedicated to the pogrom of the Jews in 1370 who were accused of stealing the Consecrated Host and sticking pins into it, making Christ bleed again. This anti-Semitic trope was celebrated in the stained glass windows without apology. The Chapel of the Miraculous Sacrament. Some five hundred Jewish quarters around Europe in the 1300s were razed and the people persecuted, executed—Brussels was late to the practice. The Jews and their ritual cleanliness prevented wide-scale death by plague, which looked like witchcraft to the fourteenth century—through what sorcery had they not died like the Christians?

You'd have thought, post-Holocaust, this chapel would have been re-purposed, reconsecrated . . . much like the sweeping under the ecclesiastical rug of all the churches to Saint Hugh and Saint William of Norwich and Saint Simon, all imagined child saints who fell into the clutches of Jewish alchemists—saints quietly decommissioned in the 1960s. He mentioned it to Rupesh, one visit.

"How strange you like to go in so many churches when you hate the institution that built them," Rupesh wondered. And when Roberto didn't say anything, Rupesh pressed on: "Never once, in all the churches, before all the art and architecture, were you not tempted to put up a prayer? Not even to that hot saint, with all the arrows?"

"Saint Sebastian? No, he inspired other yearnings."

"And when you were being put under for your operations? Not one little prayer just in case? No belief in anything extra?"

"I wish I did believe in something," Roberto said. Whatever shams and hypocrisies Christianity peddles, it does offer forgiveness, the slate wiped clean. Roberto did not believe what happened on the road in Kosovo could be wiped clean because there was no God he believed in to do it. But he saw, as he never had, how without the hocus-pocus of a God who forgives, one's past was an ever-expanding boulder to be dragged behind one.

Rupesh was soon taking the train every weekend now. Nees entered the room once and stared coldly at Rupesh, who squinted defiantly at the nurse; they had become officially enemies for life. Rupesh was squeamish about all wounds and bodily sufferings; the sight of the chest incision (which was healing well) about sent Rupesh to the bathroom to be sick and running to the train station to return to Amsterdam, far from the scar. (The chest wound, still hidden by the T-shirt, could yet be exposed to him like Perseus brandishing Medusa's head. The threat of that corrected any number of Rupesh's wayward behaviors.)

"I look old *and* fat," Roberto said, hoping to be contradicted.

Nees was thickening him up with Flemish cuisine. She made a fabulous buoyant gingerbread, crushed under the weight of rich double cream. Blood sausages on a bed of salted pear slices, Stoemp—mashed potatoes and root vegetables with sausage and bacon bits—accompanied by a dense bread softened by a film of bacon grease and butter, meatballs of swine and boar and rabbit, under sauces of cream, sometimes sour cherries . . . He was gaining weight, at last, but it was centering in a little potbelly. The curse of the Thin Man's Weight Gain, the skinny-man gut. This and the white hair at the temples, the gray in the beard when he was too weary to shave . . . Roberto standing in the bathroom, staring at himself, could now see the Dutch looks of Gehrman van Till staring back at him in the mirror.

Brussels was a monument to bureaucracy for its own sake. A *perfect* place for the capital of Europe. It was nineteen separate municipalities with their own bureaucracies and city halls and petty rivalries with each other. And this already in a country where the French and the Flemish barely acknowledged each other. Roberto tried to walk some in each of the nineteen municipalities (with help of the Metro) so he could have an opinion about it all. Roberto was struck by the prevalence of that self-conscious architecture of empire, the excess and insistent stone whimsy, the wealth of their colonial supervillain, Leopold II, king of the Belgians. The Belgians went down to the Congo and took the ivory, the metals, the rubber, the diamonds, everything of value and left the country a shambles it still hasn't recovered from. The academic debate, last time Roberto looked, was whether ten million or fifteen million Congolese died so King Leopold, who micromanaged every operation, could dominate the rubber market.

Roberto sat on a bench, now too tired to get back to the house. Maybe he would flag a taxi. He dreamed of sunnier places to convalesce, like Spain, like Portugal ... when it occurred to him that they too had decorated their cities and cathedrals with the spoils of empire. The gold altar of St. Joseph in Santiago de Compostela, the ocean of gold leaf affixed to the altars of São Francisco in Oporto ... shall we pretend the gold wasn't provided by enslaved indigenous, toiling for short brutal merciless lives in Spanish and Portuguese colonial mines? Potosí in Bolivia—didn't eight million African and indigenous slaves die in that one mine alone? Where were the European treasures without sin? The stately palace of sculpted ceilings, Chippendale furniture, the gardens by Capability Brown ... such serenity at Harewood House in Yorkshire for Lord Harewood and his family—thanks to a fortune derived from plantations in America and slaving. If ill-gotten gains were given to artists, composers, the ballet, architects, may we excuse and separate the resultant work from its funding source? In our own time, is any arts grant or fellowship courtesy of governments (none of whom are without wickedness) or generous donors (all of whose fortunes tie them to exploitation at some point) just as problematic? Roberto had a hankering to call up on Google Images the golden altars of São Francisco Church in Oporto on his smartphone ... that was built in Asia by exploited labor amid a well-documented environmental devastation for the locals.

This was a new turn in Roberto's thoughts. Anywhere wealth had accumulated, there was crime. Maybe not at first, but eventually. Ferdinand and Isabella. The burghers of medieval Brussels. Lord Harewood. Leopold II, king of the Belgians. Salvador Costa. Roberto Costa.

Land of Bolles

Because Norway is so pure and clean and its allotment of the earth looks indestructible and protected, there is an idea that Norwegians are all vegan, recycling, well-behaved, regularly exercising, happy socialists, but every Norwegian friend Roberto ever made would have given the most dissolute trailer park denizen in New Orleans—minus the guns—a run for his/her money on drink, random hookup sex, marijuana, pills, heroin (done by someone in the family, little brother, big sister), and American-style debt up to their eyeballs despite one of the highest wages and standards of living in the world. You'd be in debt too if every beer you had cost twelve dollars. For the craft artisanal beers, take out a mortgage.

"I think it's a perfect country anyway, just about," Roberto said to a full table of acquaintances in Angst (the name of the trendy, overdecorated-on-purpose Oslo bar). Among their number were two certified friends: Emilie, whom he backpacked with around Trollstigen in 2004, and her husband, Karl, who had two kids with her before they finally married. Karl knew that Emilie and Roberto had slept together, but then Emilie had slept with a few of the guys around the table, and Karl had slept with their wives/girlfriends in some long-Norwegian-winter circumstance as well. No one was sweating it. Roberto wasn't sure which names went with which braying Viking boys, all fair-skinned, loud, and red-faced from beer and shots of Aquavit—Lucas, Aksil, Isak, another Lucas, and someone who went to get a pitcher and never came back.

"The sun does not come out," said Emilie. "I am rained on all the time—better that it would snow! But no, the fucking Golfstrømmen keeps it raining in Oslo all the long autumn. There is no light. We are bored. We

294

are also . . ." She seemed to have trouble thinking of anything else to complain about. "Oh yes, full of old people who are prejudiced, against all the Somalis and Middle Eastern people."

"But there are too many of them," said one of the Lucases.

"Welcome to Eurabia," said, possibly, Aksil.

Isak (possibly) said, "I do not mind the beautiful Somalis. But the Poles—I hate the Poles."

"Who would clean your house?" Emilie spat back at him. "We have become like those immobile blob-people in *Wall-E,* who have grown soft from never working. We don't do anything ourselves anymore." With two boys, three and four, Emilie knew every Disney/Pixar cartoon available.

Barely able to find anything seriously wrong with Norway, the attention turned on all the things wrong in Sweden (grimly becoming right wing, they serve cake with shrimp on top, too blond, hygiene issues, worse health care and social programs for the old, who have to steal from stores to eat) and Finland (all alcoholics, most boring country in the world if you don't like ice hockey, moose, mosquitoes, grimly right wing, insisting on speaking their native language, which has too many umlauts and words like *kääntäjää*, and being too close to Russia, who will one day take over Scandinavia).

"Do you really worry about Russia starting a war?" Roberto asked.

Karl said his sister lived in Sweden, and it was all they talked about. There were always Russian submarines in their waters. "First the Baltics, then us," he added.

The group, excepting Roberto, agreed that the major activity each winter in Sweden and Finland was committing suicide.

"Well, if you lived there," a Lucas said with sympathy.

"Yes," Emilie said somberly, nodding, "what choice would you have? You would fucking have to do it."

Her husband discretely pantomimed that she should eat something.

Emilie had been threatening to make a run for bolles and french fries from a food van, one long block away from the bar. But she kept stalling, as she couldn't find a stopping place in the conversation about the inferiority of all peoples beyond the border of Norway, but as this topic dragged on, she nudged Roberto and cocked her head to the door. They collected some ragged kroner from all pockets and slipped out into the frigid night, stomping across the wall of plowed snow slush into the street. At this hour (1:00 a.m.), there wasn't a lot of traffic . . . but there were lines at the food trucks. Look at all the Norwegians in short-sleeve shirts when it's in the thirties Fahrenheit. Burgers, kebabs, something called a *burrito* that wasn't ... but up Torggata was a twenty-four-hour 7-Eleven. Hot dogs! They call it a *pølse;* they are wrapped in bacon, inserted into a long bun, and then there was a world of toppings ...

"This is what I love most about Norway," Roberto said as Emilie loaded up at the pastry case. "And Britain. Lots of comfort food and junk food and no pretentions."

"We make a point to eat every food that is junk from around the world." Emilie felt hot in the overheated 7-Eleven and pulled off her wool cap. Roberto was surprised for just a second. She was bald. Apparently, the alopecia that was bothering her on the back of her head had continued to progress ... He remembered hiking with her, following her on the trail up the troll's mountain; she would often ask, "How bad is it?" and "Can you tell I'm losing hair?" She was, but he told her it was barely noticeable, blond hair, fair skin, et cetera. Maybe now, she had shaved her head rather than having a blond mane that was a patchwork.

He added, "I was a long time this year in France and Belgium. It's exhausting pretending to be civilized about every meal." He sidled up close to be confidential: "So you're shaving? This is the first time I have seen."

She laughed. "I have lived like this so long, I forget it is unusual. That is right, Mr. Roberto—this was beginning when *we* were traveling. Maybe it was you who made for it to fall out."

Roberto leaned in, then kissed the top of her head. "It *was* me. I'm glad you're not mad. I remember you telling me about all the grades of alopecia ..."

For some strange reason, a woman and her five-year-old were up at 1:00 a.m. in the 7-Eleven. The little boy tugged on his mother's skirt and pointed and tugged and kept telling his mother to "*se, mamma, se!*"

Roberto remembered. "There was alopecia totalis, which was no hair on the head. And what was the other one?"

Emilie turned and said, "Universalis," before squatting down at eye level with the five-year-old and bowing her head for it to be rubbed by the fascinated boy. The mother apologized, but Emilie assured her it was all right. Emilie's own boys at home were just as curious. She returned to Roberto's side. "Universalis is no hair anywhere." She batted her nonexistent eyelashes. "Even down below."

"Did it go that far with you?"

"You have to pay to see . . . I charge you for an admission, hmm?"

His phoned pinged. It was, as it always was, Rachel. She texted: WE WILL BE EVICTED. IS THAT WHAT YOU WANT?

I HAVE NEVER WANTED ANYTHING MORE, he texted back.

At the 7-Eleven cash register, Roberto paid for it all: cinnamon bolles, cream-filled bolles, bolles with that addictive fudge-like brown cheese, ready-made sandwiches, and four pølser without buns for the others, all packed up and zipped inside Roberto's coat for warmth-keeping on the trek back to Angst.

Roberto smiled. Even a month ago, he felt this world of the living might be denied him. Confined to live in a hospital bed in Brussels, looking out at a park, Nees feeding him soups and stews, him reduced to watching couples hold hands and children play under the trees while he felt bitterness. But now, he was back to his well-worn ways: people, conversation, clomping about in the snow, the lights of the city and the white ground-cover illuminating the low clouds so it didn't really seem like night, material for his Notebook piling up, and eating deleterious crap after intemperate drinking.

These days, post-surgery, two drinks qualified as intemperate. He had switched to nonalcoholic after two tamer Hansa lagers. When one of the Lucases mocked this temperance, he said he'd just had open heart surgery, which no one believed. "Just say you are a lightweight," said Aksil (maybe). "Why try for our sympathy? Raised on American piss-beer, you cannot keep up with the *norske menn!*"

He had slipped off his sweater, to the rapt attention of the table. Peeled off the Brown University T-shirt he wore for warmth over his dress shirt. Emilie put her hand to her mouth, not wanting to look but sort of wanting to. He unbuttoned his blue dress shirt so they could see a still-pink, livid scar. Instantly, he went from wuss-American lightweight to crazy macho American, staggering straight from the surgical theater to drinking and festing in Oslo—their hero!

Somehow, in the inexplicable ways of drinking nights, the festivities were suddenly over with revelers stumbling off in all directions. Lastly, Emilie and Karl confirmed that he must come by the house and meet the boys. Karl started to the parking lot, and Emilie said privately, "Sometime I will come see you, *okay?*"

Meaning his hotel? His bed in the hotel? Roberto plodded back to his comfortable chain hotel, the Scandia near the train station, not sure what she meant, but, as with life in much of this year, he was willing to let all things transpire. His main objective was to teach conversational English in Svalbard, a place with so little else to do, he might actually finish a draft of his Notebook.

How would he even begin a preface? He would do so tomorrow a.m.

After acquiring tea from the Scandia Hotel lobby, he fashioned an un-nutritious meal of two packs of Kvikk Lunsj (the Norwegian KitKat bar, but better) and some peanuts. Kvikk Lunsj means "quick lunch." *Peanøtter* means "peanuts." Oh, Norwegian, just stop it—when will you *admit the truth to yourself*? That you are merely badly spelled English!

Roberto, in preface mode, made a stab at the Kennedyesque.

> I am American, but *bin ich auch Europäer.*
>
> Yes, I'm one of those foreign language students who stayed too long on his study-abroad program and thinks he belongs in places most North Americans save for vacation. The hassles of foreign language, money exchange, odd toilets, no AC where one needs it most, being fooled or misled by your own incom-prehension of the local language, accidentally eating what you are allergic to, accidentally insulting one's hosts with some phrase you have learned incorrectly ... most Americans enjoy their time in Europe but come running back home to the famil-iar, the ridiculously cheap-to-buy appliances and thoughtlessly great technology, the ease of acquiring drinks with more than one ice cube in them, the open-all-night convenience store that supplies snacks to accompany our collapse before our house-size televisions. Our patriotism is renewed!
>
> But then there's me.
>
> When I went back home, I was sad. The United States was merely a waiting room until I got it together to head back to where life was, where Culture was in the air, where Art was on the walls and the great leaps forward of Architecture were in the main square across from the hotel, next to the medieval church, next to the Roman column, next to the Greek arena.
>
> I know how people see me: the dilletante, the flâneur (even

that is too European a designation), the snob, the annoying American who breaks into French or German and the accent sounds like the locals. If I listened to what my former friends and relatives thought of me when I was stateside, I might be bothered, but I am not bothered because I am never stateside.

Too personal? This would be a preface before thousands of pages—oh, c'mon, Roberto corrected himself, be realistic, *hundreds* of pages of cultural ramble and musings. One should expect an autobiographical preface, casual, friendly, self-effacing.

Having written that iota of text, it was now time to surf the internet.

Favorite music videos, travel videos of Norway (was there something he needed to see this visit? Americans don't go inland to Røres—that looked good), an hour of downloads from the Trondheim Cathedral Boys' Choir, Grieg's traditional hymn arrangements, the current choral-god Ola Gjeilo, whom he had seen in New York City and *who was also a hunk,* work by Alsen, Olsson, a blind what-the-hell download of Emily Crocker, who was known for adapting Sami folk melodies, and modern works from Einojuhani Rautavaara. And some bluegrass Dolly Parton downloads, videos, interviews for no other reason but that the sound of her voice, talking or singing, pleased him totally and connected him with his abandoned America.

With so much writing accomplished, how to waste the rest of the day? He had already seen all the museums. Rupesh had sent him some dirty pictures . . .

But he was saved by his phone dinging; Rachel was contacting him. MERLE IS DISSOLVING OUR PARTNERSHIP. SHE'D LIKE TO SPEAK TO YOU.

Roberto texted back: TELL HER GOODBYE FROM ME.

Another ping, and his email received a picture from Rachel. Were they back at it? The European Treasure Competition?

She texted: THIS 1100S BEAUTY IN URNES IS HARD TO GET TO, BUT TRY. HOW, WITH ALL THE CANDLES AND FIRES INSIDE, DID THIS WOODEN VIKING ROMAN-ESQUE NOT GET BURNED DOWN IN 900 YEARS? THOSE CREATURES THAT LOOK LIKE AFGHAN HOUNDS ARE LIONS. (THEY'D NEVER SEEN ONE.)

He texted back with a photo he had been eager to send her and would have much earlier, if they hadn't been feuding: THIS IS A DOOR OF A CHURCH IN THE NATIONAL MUSEUM FOR SAFEKEEPING. THE VIKING SENSE OF

LIFE IS PHANTASMAGORIC, GOTHIC, CREEPY. REMINDS ME OF THE SET WORK OF H. R. GIGER IN THE "ALIEN" FILMS . . .

Then the phone buzzed. Roberto thought it might be a ruse to connect him to Merle, who no doubt had "an offer," a "compromise," or a shakedown attempt, so he did not pick up. He listened to the message as soon as the voice mail icon appeared on his phone:

"Do you not feel," a serene-sounding Rachel commenced, "that the Vikings had it all *over* the other Romanesque sculptors? Everything is interconnected. From the mythical figures, the griffins and dragons whose tongues and tails and serpent coils tangle and tie and untie themselves . . . how don't you see that this is Life? Some deadbeat dad leaves his wife and kids who can't make the mortgage, and that is the financial straw that leads to some clerk at Hightower Wiggins and Lehman and Bank of America noticing that the subprime house of cards and the whole financial system is wobbling, and soon the banking system of the Western world crumbles down around all of us, the good thing being that Obama got elected, the bad thing being that my trust fund got cut off by my brother. An intemperate punishment my father wishes to enact because *Mom* fucked around thirty years ago and *I* finally said something about it. The CIA and the SEC and the KGB and those CDOs and the Federal Reserve and the Forex international currency exchange—it's all up there in that door, if you look hard enough. Where is God in all this, you ask? He's not there. Only chaos and the entangled confusion of human existence. We all know the Vikings were Team Odin anyway, even if they gave lip service to Yahweh."

And then a second message: "Dad is not taking my calls. Truly, he has paid me back a hundred times over for our little stunt. It is solely on you, Bobby, whether I see a cent of my trust fund. But let me ask you, do you really want to be alone all by yourself in Europe? What will you do without me to compete with? You'll slack off. Let weeks go by without putting anything in your Notebooks. I predict drift and depression."

He texted back one of their familiar mantras: LAST ONE IN EUROPE WINS.

Roberto had been visiting Emilie and Karl the last few nights for dinner and conversation; they assured him they weren't tired of his company. The opposite, in fact—something to break up the identical winter evenings. Roberto could have rented a car and driven out to the tract-house settlement of Grefsen to see Emilie and Karl; he found it strained his chest to hold his arms in the ten-and-two position, and it took a while for the heaviness to subside. Besides, he liked Metros and Trams. This allowed him to ask people, in his almost-serviceable Norwegian, if he was close to so-and-so stop. He knew the answer; the questions were for practice.

Boy, was Norwegian close sometimes! *De sa å si hei til dem.* They said to say hi to them. What is the best way to go to Grefsen? *Hva er den beste veien å gå til Grefsen? Trikk nummer eleve og Metro nummer seks.* Tram number 11 and Metro number 6. And you can tell the Vikings marauded through English at some point. A humid day is muggy, and *mugg* in Norsk is "mildew." You cook pork and you get grease, and *gris* is the Norsk word for "pig." In Latin tongues and Germanic tongues, there is no common root to living and dying; they are different words. But in Portuguese, *ele mora, ele morre*—the distinction between *he lives* and *he dies* rides upon an extra *r.* Norwegian has an oddity too: the grave is *grav,* and to be pregnant is *gravid.* Both being in the ground and being in the womb are burials of sorts, true. The Skor candy bar has toffee buried in chocolate, *karamell begravet I sjokoladen.* Odd in the evolution of the language they would permit giving birth and burying the dead to share an etymology. Beckett wrote that we "give birth astride of a grave, the light gleams an instant, then it's night once more."

Not knowing what the drinking-around-children policy was, Roberto limited his house gifts to flowers, candy, high-powered licorice gummy fish (licorice candy is crack-level potent in Norway), and he saw the dutifulness with which these gifts were put in a drawer. Children were like pets—Roberto could love them for an hour or two at a time. Vidar, the younger, was the sweeter, and if Roberto had to bounce one of the boys on his knee, it was shy, blinking Vidar. Aric was a hitter—the cat, the sofa, Vidar . . . and Roberto feared he might land a blow squarely on his chest wound, and that would be all she wrote . . . As he dandled Vidar and made small talk with Emilie about her job, he felt the summons once more, back to the Notebook. Bill Bryson's *Mother Tongue* was almost twenty years old, so the peculiarities of language were due for another bestselling visit . . . but now John McWhorter was edging closer to his territory; Roberto trembled before his *Our Magnificent Bastard Tongue,* which called to him from the St. Pancras Station bookstore shelves in London last year. He decided not to look at it, but then decided he had better buy it, so as not to overlap material. It was surpassingly good, but there was still room in the world for the Notebook!

As the hour approached where the trams and metros stopped, Roberto would keep looking at his watch, the clock in the hall. Don't worry, his hosts would say, waving away his concerns with knowing smiles—because you could set your watch to the public transportation in Norway. Indeed, he would be released in time to make the ten-minute walk to the tram stop, followed by the tram within two invariable minutes.

His phone pinged to reveal a text from Emilie: WONDERFUL TO SEE YOU. I AM GOING TO COME VISIT YOU TOMORROW.

Again, with the announced "visit."

As he crossed the street to the tram stop, a car idling at the curb rolled down its window.

A figure in a fur hat, scarf, dark glasses was within. She spoke. "Roberto, if I could have a word."

Merle?

"I didn't want to bother you at your friends' house—"

"How do you even know where I'm visiting?"

"I've been tracking you for days in Oslo. Now get in the car, if you would; I will take you to your hotel."

"I'll let you take me to the Metro station. You have until then to say whatever it is you want to say." Roberto understood that the temperature played a part in this concession.

He got in the passenger seat, into the warmth of the rented car. "I have not one little molecule of incentive to return Rachel's money to her," he said immediately.

"I know. Were I you, I wouldn't give her a dime."

Merle set up her GPS to take her to Storo Station.

"You won't persuade me to fund Rachel. No blackmail will work on me," Roberto added, though that was a bluff. One word about Kosovo and he'd have folded.

"You wholly misunderstand me."

"I will consider Rachel paid back when she gets on the plane and goes home. Europe is not big enough for the both of us, as they used to say before Wild West shoot-outs on Main Street."

"I think you're right. You crowd each other, compromise each other's personal communion with Europe."

She must be really up to something, Roberto thought.

"Rachel's and my partnership," she said in stately fashion, "is at an end, though perhaps you think this is a ruse. The truth is Rachel is a dabbler, someone who doesn't finish what she starts. She will never finish the Ph.D. I want to be of service to someone who is a true scholar, who will commit to a serious project. I thought her Romanesque catalog was that project, but the true important work of ambition was before my eyes all along. Your Notebooks."

Roberto had not seen this coming. "What would you know of them?"

"What would I know of them? I've read every word. You mailed all your drafts—some admittedly rough, some polished and brilliant—to Rachel, like clockwork. She had no interest in them, but I devoured them. It's scholarship, but it is also improvisation, whimsy. Your piece on Rome and how the word *romance*, meaning 'adventure,' and *romance*, meaning a 'love story,' became entangled. The fact that *roman* in most European languages, even Russian, is the word for the literary novel. You speculate about the verb *to roam*, which has another root as its etymology, but the other words carry it along in a sublime confusion."

Sublime confusion—that was his phrase. She at least read one chapter, he supposed. Storo Station was in view. She pulled over to park.

"The Notebooks," she proceeded, "have the makings of a great series of volumes where culture, art, music, architecture, literature, and the interlinking skeins of language, to which you are rightly attuned, come together to make a kind of thesis statement for the Western world. Despite its crimes and follies, what you have gathered is an apologia for the West as a high-water mark in human existence. I am interested in all cultures, of course, and value non-European accomplishment, but I plant my flag in Europe, as have you."

"Thank you for the ride," he said, opening the car door. "But I work alone."

He stuck his ticket in the automated gate, and it opened, admitting him. Down the stairs he went to wait for his train. That was close. He was this close to discussing her proposal, which he would have in the morning rejected. But Merle, of all people, seemed to have made a critical assessment of his work—the only person, he suspected, on earth who had done so. He was drawn in and ashamed; his ego thirsted, yearned for some serious appraisal of his Notebooks. Given what he knew of Merle's transatlantic childhood, her Ivy League humanities education followed by a misfire at law school, she was in some ways an ideal reader of his Notebook . . . but no way!

"Bobby, this is my last chance . . ." She had paid for a Metro ticket and was joining him on the platform. "My last chance to speak to you about this. I fear for your project. Rachel said you were up here craving isolation, so you might work on a final draft."

He turned to look at her as she came up to face him.

"I fear," she said solemnly, "you will not do it. Maybe you're going great guns already and my fears aren't founded, but it is vast. Disorganized, unwieldy. You will not be able to make the thing cohere. To find the themes and make for chapters—someone with a certain administrative eye must aid you in that. There are holes in the research, places you have left blank intending to research at a later date."

Roberto should return to the street and hail a taxi back to town, ending this conversation forever. But he said, "It is a mess. I was going to live in a university town for a year. Take an apartment in Paris or Oxford or Edinburgh—"

"That's the place. In Great Britain, they teased out the Indo-European trace, Muller, Lockwood . . . Their notes, their papers. Do you think you will ever finish it? You won't, Bobby. You think you will, but you won't, not under your own steam, not without someone to say stop going down this rabbit hole over there and do the proper diligence on this significant point over here. It is the sort of thing I was . . . I was born to do."

She was distracted by the unusual high-pitched vibration of the distant rails, ethereal, coming in and out of phase. The fast train from Trondheim was approaching at speed; it would not be stopping at the local station platform a few hundred meters away. In the cold night air, it was like someone rubbing the rims on crystal glasses. High E-flat, Roberto thought.

"Thank you for your offer," he said, "but I think it would upset my sister. It would seem as if you abandoned her, in her poverty, for me, in my prosperity."

"I am sure you do not much care for your half sister's hurt feelings any more than she has concerned herself with yours. Or your mother has troubled herself at all to mind your sensibilities. Nor your adoptive father."

He took a step closer to Merle. "My father has been very devoted."

"Devoted," she said lightly, "to his own career. I am asking you to be similarly self-interested."

The headlight of the oncoming high-speed train was now evident; it shimmered above the rails, which sang in advance of the train. "If we were to have a working relationship," said Merle, "we simply have to do away with the haze of sentiment both you and Rachel maintain around your father. Your adoptive father and your real father, Gehrman van Till, met in South America, propping up the despicable Argentine junta, under the direction and seed money provided by the CIA. There were crimes. Money channeled, laundered to the United States—"

"Really, you are the conspiracy theorist par excellence."

"Did you know your father had an affair with Katrin van Till, Gehrman's second wife?"

"There was a time my mother and father were separated. So what?"

"Once Gehrman knocked up your mother with *you*, he and your father made a gentlemen's agreement. I talked to Katrin van Till; she told me all about it. Gehrman could have Lena for keeps, if he got your father out of Providence and to the big leagues in New York. And Gehrman kept his end of the bargain. You really think Hightower Wiggins would look twice at a down-market door-to-door Fuller Brush salesman like Sal Costa? But Katrin, full of mischief, reneged, and wouldn't give Gehrman a divorce—"

Roberto stopped her recital by grabbing her by the shoulders, little Merle Westmore, all five foot four inches in the clutches of Roberto Costa, six foot five, being marched backward, toward the tracks, toward the source of that increasingly deafening pitch. And now here was the headlight and the horn-blare as the train rounded the curve.

"Bobby, let me go."

"I'll tell the police you have been stalking me for years, and as you threatened me, I pushed you away and you lost your balance."

She struggled to escape, and he clamped his arms around her.

Roberto added, "Think of the white-shoe law firm my father will hire."

He backed her toward the edge of the platform. There was the purest fear in her eyes. She tried to scream, but no sound came out and the train was suddenly there in the station, flying through on its way to Oslo's terminal, clattering close by in a deafening howl. One track over.

"You mustn't worry," Roberto said, releasing her, arranging her collar, straightening her hat, her down jacket. "The InterCity lines do not use these Metro tracks."

She moved her mouth, but no speech yet came out.

"The shakedown attempts and the continuous digging into our family, they stop right here, okay, Merle?"

She nodded faintly.

"I would hate to hire someone to provide you and your mother a night-time visit—in Tours, was it? If I hear from you again or my sister does, or if my father hears that someone in France was asking about old South American times or client lists in Providence . . ." He leaned in to whisper: "My father can give me the name of a guy. We're from fucking Providence— you *know* we know a guy. It's done all the time. It's just the people who get caught are poor and give themselves away to undercover policemen, offering some ex-con five thousand for a hit job. But when you have millions and are willing to pay the right price for the right services, as I do . . ."

"I could report you for what you've said, threatening my life."

"There you go being unwise again."

What was this emotion strengthening his heartbeat, almost making his ears ring, this surging circulation pushing against his skin? Was this dangerous for his health? It did not feel dangerous. It felt drug-like, enhancing, a pulse of some latent savage primate mechanism usually, dependably buried.

"Sal Costa has more of a conscience than I do," Roberto added. "Trust me."

She broke into a run.

The train from Trondheim had sped through a 10:16 p.m., just like the nights before. And being the well-oiled machine that Norway was, rumbling into view was the Number 6 Metro at 10:19.

The 7-Eleven in the Oslo Sentralstasjon had American-style doughnuts and would still be open. Roberto felt that he deserved a treat.

Maelstrom

Emilie had a dental appointment in town; her boys were parked at an in-law's, Karl left for work. Emilie did not go to her appointment, which she had secretly canceled out of earshot, and came instead to Roberto's hotel. On the Metro ride in, she texted him a warning, which was enough time—barely—to shower and find something clean in the suitcase to put on (only, he suspected, to take off).

There was a polite knock at the door. He opened it. Emilie had fixed up, including a blond wig that accurately recalled the mane she had lost. "You want to, yes?"

"Yes."

"A question or two, just so I know," Roberto prompted.

She slipped inside, unfurled her headscarf, began unbuttoning her coat.

"Karl doesn't know and will never know, right?"

"We are not exactly 'open.' But we have sworn never to embarrass each other, never to be, how you say, *indiskret.*"

"Our word is the same. As we established the other night, I had to have heart surgery, so my circulation—"

"Yes, please, about that. Can I persuade you to keep your shirt on? Neither of us should expect a return to our early twenties, ja? I have passed two children through the . . ."

Roberto was naked except for his T-shirt. With Emilie's coat flung to the corner with the scarf, the kicked-off shoes, the sweatshirt was next. She was not wearing a brassiere. "Tell me I am still beautiful," she demanded, "not a *husmor* in Grefsen. What is your word?"

"We sometimes say *hausfrau,* from the German. You are beautiful. I'm assuming you did not surgically enhance your . . ."

"No, it was a bonus of having the children. I gained more *bryster—breaster.*"

"Breasts."

"You should kiss them before they go away again."

Roberto started along the side of her neck—from ear to neck was always, it came back to him, her most sensitive, lucrative area. He moved slowly from there to her breasts, and he took his time fondling there too. Married sex, Roberto figured, is comfortable and super-familiar and tender and often uninspired; a person cheats on their spouse for something rude, raw, extravagant, filthy. He pushed her to the bed, and she landed with a bounce next to his suitcase, which he had yet to remove from the bed.

"I missed your smell," she said. "I remember it now."

He scooped up some dirty laundry and pushed it in her face. "Smell me, then. I remember how you taste," he said next, peeling off her jeans. "Have your children changed that too? Are you now milk tea, butter biscuits . . . or . . ." He made a great theatric act of hovering over her sex, savoring its qualities like a fine wine. His breath and his gentlest touchings had her stirring in anticipation. Wonder of wonders . . . he was aware of an erection, a seven out of ten. Personal best for 2009.

"Kiss it, eat it."

He entered her without any preparation. He felt the tumescence was bound to be short-lived, so if he could perform, he would go for it. She wasn't ready and scooted back on the bed. He slowed but did not stop the forward pressure. In a few seconds, with a shudder, she was ready, her own hand helping matters along.

"I remember this ridiculous big thing. Sometimes I thought I had made it up in my mind, but no. It is you who should be in a Scandinavian porn film, I think."

Once inside her, he looked at her lying there until she made eye contact, exposed, sprawled beneath him, her wig crooked but part of the sexiness of the scene. "I see you wear a wig," he said. "You are in disguise. You are not Emilie Jenssen—who are you really?" He began to sway back and forward, ending the forward thrust more abruptly. "Tell me, who are you?"

"I am one of the Russian women you see in the high-priced hotel bars."

"A Russian whore?"

"Det... er perfekt, *keep like that,* ja? I am very high-priced. You cannot afford, I think."

Roberto, inspired, reached over to his suitcase, where he had an inner zipper pocket in which he had a bank envelope of euros, which were no good in Norway. Five hundred in twenties. He took the money and put the stack in her face. "Maybe you would rather I fuck you with this, hmm?" The money went everywhere. "Open your mouth..." She blew the money away, laughing. "You are worth every dollar, euro, kroner..."

"That is not even close to what I charge my clients..."

This and a few other semi-scenarios with campy dirty talk provided what she was looking for, and with Roberto inside, and an assist from her own hand, she found her way easily to orgasm. She always went quick, Roberto remembered, but no, *Take a bow,* he told himself. *This is the first time you have managed to please a woman in the longest time. Contact the historical society to erect a plaque.* He felt warm and prideful—perhaps, at last, he was on the comeback trail.

When they lay there recovering, side by side, she reached over since it was "his turn," but the evanescent circulatory moment had passed.

"It's the blood thinners," he said. "It is a sign of your irresistible sexiness, Emilie, that the slumbering beast rose from its den once more. You had a nickname for it, something Norse, but I've forgotten it."

"Thor's hammer, perhaps."

"Oh, please, since the beginning of time, every Norwegian girlfriend has lied to her mediocre lover and called his cock Thor's hammer. It was a dragon or a serpent..."

"Ja ja ja, it was Jörmungandr, the longest snake on earth. Wrapped around the whole globe, in fact."

They were hungry, and Roberto found that his passion for authentic Norwegian dining—the Matjes herring, the cured fish, the reindeer sausage with lingonberry compote—was deserting him. It was all Norwegian 7-Eleven junk food around the clock.

They bought prepackaged sandwiches and went for a picnic to the just-opened opera house, a wondrous modern temple where slanted planes of white marble allowed people to wander above, beside, around the auditorium, down to the harbor, up to a precipitous knife-edge height to see the futuristic rows of eye-catching skyscrapers designed for contemporary Oslo. The mirrored walls reflecting the planes made it an Escher staircase brought to life, causing one to stare, squint, and attempt to re-solve the true perspectives when seen across the harbor.

Roberto mentioned his plan to teach conversational English in Svalbard.

"Do watch out for the polar bears. They eat one or two people a year."

"I need to get away, isolate myself from my family's money drama."

"I sometimes think," she said, trying to manage a tuna sandwich in which the filling was squirting out both ends, "that you and me should have been . . ." Her English gave out. "Maybe I should have picked you and not Karl."

"I bet Karl has no circulation problems," Roberto said, hoping to keep it light.

"No, he is always ready to go. But if you had married me, we would be in Florida or California, somewhere warm. You would work on your Notebook; I would sleep with hotel bellboys and tourists from around the globe. We would have traveled the world, hiked up every mountain . . . I am like a character in Ibsen, having married wrongly."

"If you're Hedda Gabler, then that means you will put my Notebook in the fireplace."

"And that you must have vine leaves in your hair. Which you do, *metaforisk*—how you say?"

"Metaphorically."

"Would you have had children with me?"

Who could say no to children with this woman, though? Sweet, smiling, maternal, patient Emilie, good genes . . . But why say that to Emilie, who was feeling around for reasons to be happy where she was? "Never," he insisted, a little dramatically. "Do not want kids. And you are a natural mother, so it would be a crime if you ended up with me."

Her phone buzzed. It was a text, and her expression changed. "*Dritt.* Karl has come to get me at the dentist's, and of course I am not there. He may suspect . . ." Her mind worked through a small drama. "If he asks them, they will say I canceled, so I have to explain where . . ."

Roberto stood, and they started walking three blocks to the train station. "I was going to take you and Karl out for dinner this Friday, right?" he asked. "Say I felt bad but will have to leave for Svalbard early; I misjudged the trains and ferries. But I left money to take you both out, and I insisted you come to get it." Roberto reached into his jeans for the big-euro bills he thoughtlessly reassembled and stuffed in his pocket when dressing back at the hotel room. "Take these and say I gave them to you last night, but you had to go to the train station to exchange the bills for kroner. And it was all supposed to be a surprise, but alas, now he has learned. Text him and say you'll meet him at the station."

"Ja, that's . . . that's good. Okay, I will pay you back."

"Don't worry about it."

She kissed his cheek and started for the station, just three blocks away. Waving, smiling, winsome, and Nordic—whoa, she came running back. "Um, take the wig. Karl will know something is up if I went out in the wig."

Roberto took the mass of blond tresses and offered her his wool cap.

"No," she said. "He knows all my caps. But I'll freeze . . ." She pulled it on her head. "I'll say you left it and I was returning it . . . but why didn't I take my own cap?" She handed him back his cap. "It is my punishment to have a cold head—here." She skipped away, now twice as fast to limit her time outside. Only a block away did she turn around and wave, smiling, laughing at herself. It had been a great adulterous one-off adventure. There would be a bit of nerves as she lied several lies in succession but Karl would not notice or if he did he would not pry to learn what he did not want to know and life in Grefsen would continue in its pace. Was this their last visit? Would he look her up again? Probably not, to preserve their fond ending and not invite further sordidness.

How odd it seemed. Here on the threshold of all the money and time and life ahead of him to be with friends and lovers, it felt instead as if he were on some kind of farewell tour, a concert pianist on a retirement series of encores. *Hélène, Lucrezia, Emilie, goodbye, goodbye, remember me fondly as you race with open arms toward middle age and the suburbs. Was I a good memory? Do I warrant a smile when you're standing at your sink some late afternoon?* Goodbye, even, to Rachel and Merle. Rupesh would live on; they were each other's last man standing.

He walked back to the hotel so as not to run into Karl solo or Karl and Emilie together. Particularly carrying her blond wig. He might as well follow his lie and pack up, leave for Svalbard early, working his way up the coast.

If you are a lucky traveler, you will have some excuse to head north up the coast of Norway, where the most comfortable ingenious towns cling to the most spectacular scenery on the planet.

Roberto, earning the resentment of passengers in the forward lounge, would open the door to the cold foredeck of the ferry. Leaning into the chill of the April wind like the figurehead on the prow of the ship, cursing, screaming aloud, enduring the face-numbing agony, Roberto was victorious in getting the photos of these wondrous storybook fishing villages. They were affixed, somehow, to the sharp rocks on this rind of coast, where thousand-meter cliffs plunged to the waterline. These were the wild waters of the Kraken. This was the home of the Maelstrom, the whirlpool that presented itself when the inner bay of the Lofoten Islands contrasted grievously with the outer ocean, and tides, temperatures, and winds collaborated to open a hole in the ocean. Actually, the Maelstrom of Jules Verne and Edgar Allan Poe and *Pirates of the Caribbean,* swallowing ships swirling ever downward to a vortex of a dry, dark ocean floor, does not exist . . . but looking around at the roiling seas, you wouldn't put it past the Norse gods to let it rip on occasion.

Roberto had a cabin for the final leg of the trip, to Tromsø, the last city with a large-enough airport for an escape. He would stay the night there and decide: follow through and head North Pole-ward to Svalbard . . . or bail out, giving health reasons, which would be a plausible excuse, and go back to Oslo, then Amsterdam, then Rupesh's bed.

Tromsø was aglow with interior lights, which gave a muted sheen to the snow on the ground and low fog in the sky, cozy, inviting. The Radisson Hotel (among the pricier chains in the U.S., among the cheaper in Norway) had every human comfort, a still-open restaurant, a bar . . . great Wi-Fi.

He looked over the recent dabblings on his Notebook's preface. So much was dated or immature, unusable. Even an exuberant alternative intro that he had just written in Oslo:

> As I write in 2009, I can't help but think about the long-awaited change of the empowered generations in North America—Justin Trudeau in Canada, Barack Obama in the United States—will be part of the West's further advance beyond the parts of the world organized by tribe or ethnicity or subject peoples passed from dictator-father to dictator-son. Am I wrong to think that a Golden Age of European–UK Commonwealth–American alignment is now imminent? Isn't this the very combination of powers and sensibilities who will rally to defeat climate change? Income equality? World hunger

. . . yeah and cure cancer and give everyone lollipops. He can't just propagandize for the Western world. Merle just maybe had a point. His Notebook's warehouse of notes, of riffs, of musings, was nowhere near becoming a proper consideration of culture.

All right, north to Svalbard! To the pole! Three or four months locked away in the cold, with no social life or love life, writing and refining every day, would do the trick!

And Now, the Police

B ut it did not take any time at all for the old traps and snares to present themselves.

The lovely administrator at the Activity Center (Ragnhild) slipped him a phone number; at least two of his students—the svelte Russians, Natalya and Svetlana—had let it be known he was attractive; the obviously gay guy from Food Services in the university food hall, Dogukan, from Central Asia, with those irresistible Eurasian eyes and golden skin, gave him a second look.

Longyearbyen delivered on that end-of-the-world-outpost sensibility. It was still night most of the time in March; to the north, there was the faint green smudge of the aurora borealis, to the south, there was a turquoise glow as daylight kept getting ever closer to peeking over the horizon. Svalbard's main town was just a few north-south streets, a hotel or two, a bistro or two, a coffeehouse or two, the university at the bottom of the hill, an array of housing built for polar conditions, and the famous Seed Vault plugged into the side of a mountain, where a million seeds are preserved in a chamber five hundred feet under the earth, in the event of doomsday, nuclear exchange, global extinctions. For the longest time, the concept seemed fantastic.

Roberto selected, from his list of rental possibilities, the farthest-away house from town. He hoped he could see polar bears wander down the slopes to look through a trash can or two, then turn around for the interior. Everyone seemed quite alarmed about the polar bears, grateful to go months without seeing one. Roberto wanted to see one, just not face-to-face. If you traveled away from the village, you had to be armed—that was a rule. Another rule: you must make every effort not to die in

Longyearbyen. The original Norwegian settlers of this Arctic isle learned the hard way: the body will not rot in the frozen earth, and the bears will detect the carrion odor and come dig you up for a meal.

His reward for choosing a place so far from the coffee shop in which he conducted the lessons was 1) bad phone service—he would have to buy a local phone and a Norwegian-based service contract to solve that—and 2) some of the coldest walks of his lifetime.

His sister, in their past life, had had another kind of picture-transfer they enjoyed—to find the remotest, most desolate, most underfunded schools, take a picture of the most unloved 1950s building, and send the photo to the other, writing, OH LOOK, I HAVE FOUND THE PLACE WHERE YOU'LL END UP TEACHING! Some snow-covered polytechnic in Slovakia, repurposed from a communist-era compound. An inhumanly Bauhaus series of concrete box buildings in provincial Luxembourg in the rain, and so on. And he had hoped that the university branch in Longyearbyen would top them all: some rusted-out, winter-battered, corrugated metal series of huts, slit windows from which teachers and students looked out longingly, yearning for some kind of Bergman-film death by lying down in the winter drifts . . . But of course not.

This was Norway. The Polar Institute looked warmer, lovelier, and more up-to-date than half the campuses in America. There were computers, a great Wi-Fi signal, banks of outlets for recharging all one's devices. Message boards were exciting—who wanted to run out to the Sassen-Bünsow Land National Park to help resupply the Climate Change Polar Ice Measuring Team? And the students were from central casting—Norwegian could-be Olympians, pink with sun- and windburn, out cross-country skiing, rifles across their torsos (for the bears or maybe target shooting), fit, blond, clad in enviably patterned sweaters, sexy, inspiringly omni-capable.

Word spread that Roberto was halfway entertaining, and he kept gaining students. Two more guys from Ukraine—he combined their tutorial; an older Norwegian woman whose English was just fine, though she felt inadequate (perhaps the lessons were so she might have company); and a few others signed his sheet but did not show. But his intensest focus was on the two Russian women, Natalya and Svetlana, both recent immigrants to Norway, hoping to lose the Russian accents, which Roberto (and anyone interested romantically in women) hoped they would never lose.

"Ve have wery big party at house. You come? Bring wodka?" Svetlana's hour of instruction was devoted mostly to rounding the rough edges of her English; her only topic was Moscow and how much she missed it. He learned her brother-in-law's name was Yuri.

"Not Yuri Yurkov?" he asked as suddenly an ancient name came flooding back to him. How could he have forgotten it? The pale, pouty-lipped Russian model that Lucrezia made him kiss in the disco. It was Yuri Yurkov who told him, "My last name sound like *jerk off* in English, yes?" And indeed, through the years, on some occasional moods, the last name for Roberto had proven prophetic . . .

"Yuri yours friend?"

"*Is Yuri a friend of yours?* you should say."

"Too many words, such clutter! *Is Yuri friend of yours?*"

Eh, close enough. "Yes." And Roberto lied for efficiency, saying he modeled in Milan and Yuri was a colleague there. Did he have a web page? Could they find him on the internet? Svetlana could tear through the Cyrillic pages lightning fast; Roberto was happy to have her perform this service.

"If he was pretty and famous model, he maybe no come home, da?"

But after very little searching of Юрий Юрков and, for good measure, модель (*modeli*), a professional page turned up.

"Ahh," she said. "Too pretty for straight man."

The last round of photos was from 2007, so perhaps Yuri of the pouting lips had moved on to another profession. One photo had him smiling in front of an upscale clothing store in Moscow.

On the third lesson, she had asked him to come to her apartment. The wreckage from her *wery big party* had not entirely been cleaned away. An empty vodka bottle—Finnish, in a lack of Russian patriotism—sat atop the fish tank. After ten minutes about familiarity versus formality, Svetlana said, "We have old proverb. Russians always with proverbs, da*? Romansy sozdayutsya na nebesakh.* 'Couples made in heaven.' Understand meaning? If two people each other are to love, it was first in mind of God."

"We have a venerable philosopher, Dolly Parton, who in her teachings wisely noted, 'If two people are gonna fuck, then they're gonna go ahead and fuck.'"

Svetlana thought about it and then nodded. "Yes." She began unbuttoning her shirt. "I love American music. I know of who Dolly Parton.

With the . . ." She pantomimed bosoms, which she did with a sneer, being so different from her less buxom attributes.

"I need to tell you something, my Sveta."

"Oh." She began buttoning back up. "Dolly Parton–knowing, friend-of-gay-Yuri . . you are no for woman. *Konechno*, prosti, prosti, prosti . . ."

"No! Something else." Roberto pulled down the neck of his Brown University sweatshirt until the heart-operation scar was evident. He explained his heart condition and that things down below might disappoint, but he would assure her pleasure.

"Disappoint?" She laughed, the buttons now recommitted to unfastening. "Russian men after wodka is same."

So this period of isolation, this self-imposed exile of work, a serious draft of his Notebook—this was already giving way to *wery big parties* with new friends, coffee with the Polar Region students in the morning, time-waste with the Wi-Fi at the university, then afternoon lessons leading to sleeping with his conversational English students, the standard pattern worn into the earth like the migration of reindeer herds, just as Roberto had done for the last, oh, nine years. Henry James spoke of his admiration for Byron for moving himself for months to the most boring town in Italy, Ravenna, which was bereft of society in the nineteenth century, so he could finish *Don Juan*. It showed the scoundrel, playboy, rhymester could knuckle down and get to business, after all. Not so, apparently, for Roberto Costa . . . On the other hand, you read about the work habits of Balzac (the rich gourmandizing) and Hugo (the two mistresses) and Maupassant (sex ten times a day with any woman, anywhere), and his own creative methods were comparatively chaste. But then, he wasn't French.

Time for a walk to clear his head . . . somehow today's Kvikk Lunsj didn't hit the spot; he needed some protein, a bacon bolle, maybe. He walked the half mile from the apartment blocks, down the cold dirt streets to the main drag, Hilmar Rekstens vei. He saw the coffee shop he had already made his classroom and second home, lit from within on this sunless afternoon. Didn't Norse mythology have a pig that had the most delicious bacon on earth? And no matter how much you butchered away on this pig, it restored itself so the great bacon would never die? That myth seems more suited to the American South.

"Hey, Maja," he said as the door opened, the bell tinkled, and the wave of warmth hit him in the face. "Eventuelle snacks der?"

"Ja. En sandwich, litt shortbread, et bakverk . . ."

"Hvilken type bakverk?" The pastry—*bakverk*, bake work—was a puff of dough filled with red berries. Roberto pointed to that and the sandwich; he would clean out her late-afternoon survivors.

"Roberto," she said. There were authorities here looking for you. Police, maybe? I did not recognize the man. Your visa is tourist? Maybe that is the problem? You are working, giving lessons, while a tourist.

"I asked about that," he said in English. "I did not think such a small amount of money was of any concern. My lessons take no job away from a Norwegian."

Maja said, I have no idea what this official wanted. I am guessing. "Til i morgen," she said with a small smile, now ready to close her shop and go home to dinner.

Roberto stepped outside and breathed the cold in deeply. Police.

He gnawed absently on the sandwich, though his appetite was now gone. He started back to his apartment. Maybe he could go hide out at Svetlana's . . . no, this wasn't Oslo—they could in a matter of hours check every dwelling and find where he was hiding. As he approached the turn for Vei 230 . . . he saw blue lights at the end of the street, a police car. Not able to help himself from fleeing, he turned back on the main road for the university at the bottom of the hill. If this was what he thought it was, he would need a well-charged phone. Figures. In Svalbard, he had finally lived through the first days that he did not think, dream about, dwell upon Kosovo in quiet hours. So now, the police.

Had Merle reported that he'd threatened her life? Well, that would be a he-said, she-said, and the offense could be swept away. But if it was Kosovo . . . First, he would call his father. He'd make a businesslike confession, but he would insist to all who would listen that he did not commit the accident, just was a shameful party to not reporting it. He was in no way responsible for the accident itself. Unless Ludo and Lucrezia had decided to say he was driving the car. What of Mira? He had not been in contact at all, which she may have taken as a rejection. Would Mira go in on Ludo and Lucrezia's story?

Roberto looked up to the snow-covered hills encompassing the valley. Across the Isfjorden, the high ridges were catching some of the parsimonious light. Soon the sun would peek over the horizon for the village and its inhabitants, but for this long, liminal transition, there would only be traces upon the distant mountaintops, this dead sideways light of the far north, not able yet to conquer the darkness.

He fumbled with his phone. Just 2 percent power; perhaps just enough juice to take a picture. This was his warmest coat, and he usually kept a camera in a lower pocket, in case of polar bear sightings. He hadn't brought his gloves, so his hands felt the arctic breeze as he fumbled with turning his camera on. He would take this shot. That's what Bobby Costa did: he took pictures for his friends to look at; this afternoon would be no different. Life was still normal. See? He was taking a photograph. He would write something in his Notebook. He was not sure if it was beauty he was seeing all alone—not another person on the street—or if this crepuscular almost-dawn was a preview of some Norse afterworld, the dying called to walk toward those distant snows in that purgatorial light that was not light.

Once inside the Norsk Polarinstitutt, he slipped off his shoes; the polished wood floor was treacherous in his socks, like a skating rink. He leaned against the wall near the publicly available chargers and watched as his phone returned to power, 5 percent, 10 percent, at last at 25 percent . . . It pinged as messages loaded. And pinged and pinged. Oh God. Rachel had called. Mrs. Santos. His mother four times. And Mr. Pereira, the lawyer he had consulted when he made his last will and testament, back in Brussels. Jesus, he was in so much trouble his father had directed the family lawyer to get in touch right away?

He put on his shoes again, barely finding the will to tie the laces. He was scared to check his messages. Rachel gloating? He would not waste his battery on checking his messages right away. He would go back to his apartment.

The police car was gone. As he walked up the stairway to his unit, Mrs. Grimsrud leaned out to speak to him. The police had come by; it seemed important. Shall she call the station and have them return?

"Ja, takk," he said, heading on up.

This was an odd three, four, five minutes, however long it would take for them to return and start their questioning. He looked at his preface, reading a little of his praise for the two great acts of Western idealism of the twentieth century, the Marshall Plan—the victors rebuilding the vanquished—and the European Union—a step toward a world-saving government where actions could be multinational and collective and . . .

There was motion in the house, doors, conversations. Footsteps on the staircase. Roberto looked at his too-hopeful words. Someone would inherit the bounty of this coming golden age, but it was unlikely to be Roberto Costa. When the scandal spread, would the rich playboy Costa son be a piñata for the press, batted about for regular tabloid abuse on slow-news days? His dad would be ashamed, have to make a falsely cheery acknowledgment on his TV show . . . if, indeed, that was permitted to continue. Why take life advice from a man who can't even raise his own son properly? Well, they'll say, the hit-and-run party-boy wastrel wasn't *really* his son—

A knock on the door.

The policeman entered gently; his partner waited in the hallway. "Roberto Costa?" he asked. "My English is all right, but I wish it were better for this thing I must tell you. Everyone is calling, even the ambassador from the United States. They want to find you and let you know some bad news. Your father has passed away."

Irrevocable

The shock and numbness that Roberto felt hearing the news of his father's passing never abated. He kept waiting for sadness, for tears, for deep and racking sobs . . . but something emotional had been snuffed out in him. Perhaps during the many memorial services, back in the homey confines of Providence, he would be flooded with sentiment.

He was not. The memorial service, however, at Hightower Wiggins was splendidly done. The speakers told funny stories, recalled what a character his father was, how unique he was for the hallways of a Wall Street institution. Sal's colleagues spoke warmly of his briefly serving as CEO and claimed that his public performances saved Hightower Wiggins—which they did. Sam the Intern, now a junior account manager, was the only shaky and tearful speaker; Roberto felt shame for once hating him so much. A devastated Mrs. Santos was led to the podium, and said, unsurprisingly, how much Sal meant to her, that he was the best boss there ever was, how he set up college funds for all her children and her grandchildren, and then having read her note card, she sat down. This led to a final speaker, an exec Roberto had never met named Gary, who had prepared a humorous performance of Sal's most outrageous quips and pronouncements and tried to do Sal's accent. The service was appropriate and mordant without being flip, though Roberto really felt the class divide between Mrs. Santos and Sal's old cronies in commodities, bonds, futures, and the well-dressed boardroom associates. It was hard to know who was more ill at ease around whom.

Next was another warm lunchtime reception/memorial at CNBC. All the CNBC stars were there, and the big testimonial was from Stephanie, his substitute host. She was emotional but got through her speech.

The funeral mass at St. Joseph's was dreary in a welcome way. The funeral was not designed to be a monster turnout with an array of mayors, ex-mayors, indicted mayors. Just family and a few friends, the modest way Sal would have wanted it. Here, Roberto was thankful for the rote funeral mass and dry homily that the Catholic Church can be depended on to provide. Roberto had a horror of melodramatic showbiz funerals, where every child, spouse, sibling, second cousin, gets up to emote and break down, with the relative who understood the deceased the least hogging the mic.

Some surprises: Katrin van Till, looking chic in a formfitting black dress, came to give Roberto a hug. All the truths were out now, so she could tell Roberto that he had been lucky to have the best two men she ever met as fathers. Roberto thought about whether what his father said about being "open" in the '80s meant, as Merle may have fabricated, that Katrin had been an intimate of Salvador Costa, as well. Her affection for Salvador was genuine, Roberto observed. The other one of Sal's consorts, Rosario with the auburn hair, his tango-partner-to-be, was devastated. She showed up and was unsteady on her feet, helped down the aisle by her sister. Sal had exited her life right before the promised retirement romps and world travel. Roberto gave her a long hug. Rosario was the only one Roberto felt truly sorry for.

When those two women left, only then did Lena appear (was she hiding, waiting for the other women to go?). Lena was there looking like a million bucks that had been gold-plated and set on top of another million bucks. She didn't look a day over forty; slim, sleek in a black mourning dress that was in truth a Chanel little black dress, her hair in a bob, platinum white . . . if she had broken into a Bob Fosse number, slinking past the coffin, letting a bowler hat somersault down her arm, Roberto would not have been surprised. She had her new stepson-to-be, Xavier, in tow but not her new husband, Mr. Comeaux. They would marry this summer.

"I was hoping to meet Stepdad Number Two," Roberto said, lightly hugging his mother, whose assembled visage might not survive a bear hug.

"Bobbikins, the last place I'm bringing a new husband is Providence with these vipers all around, looking to inject their venom . . . Less Sid knows about all of this, the better. God, I suppose Vinnie and Bennie had to make an appearance, but they have some nerve."

The extended family may or may not have known about the shameful Vó Costa rewrite-Sal-out-of-the-will gambit, but Roberto's aunt and uncle slunk into the funeral late as if they were wearing signs advertising their crime, as in Rhode Island's days of Puritan justice. Bennie looked singled out, unhappy, desperate to leave. Their kids, Vinnie Jr. and Margarida, were appropriately sober; Vinnie Jr. came up later and chucked Roberto on the shoulder and said, "So sorry, man. We all liked your dad." But Vinnie Sr. was wretched. His know-it-all brother was gone, his protector, his deep pocket, and his idol whether he wanted to admit it or not. His face was swollen from crying. Vinnie went up to the coffin, nearly collapsed, and left the funeral soon after. Roberto felt bad for Uncle Vinnie, but not bad enough to say something to him; he assumed there wouldn't be another reunion.

It wasn't certain where the Rachel-Roberto relationship stood. She had departed Europe against her will, deprived of funds by Roberto. She had unwittingly been a part of their father's death, talking to him on the phone as he stepped into William Street. Sal did not hear an electric vehicle barreling too fast down the narrow street. The impact did not kill him, just knocked him down. Mrs. Santos was right behind him; she didn't hear the silent car either, which was a private-hire car, tinted windows, no telling who was in it. It backed up to the previous street and turned and fled.

Sal was shaken, thought he'd dislocated a shoulder. Mostly shook up, no big deal, he was telling the small crowd around him in the street—of course, they knew it was Sal, Sal Costa on *Costa: Doing Business!* Mrs. Santos helped Sal to his feet and put him in a taxi for a branch of the big hospital ten little downtown blocks away. She promised to join Sal in the emergency room, but first, she went back to the office, shut down the programs they were running, saved the bookkeeping to a series of memory sticks, before calling CNBC to say that Sal had been in an accident and to contact Stephanie. Then she taxied to the hospital.

"Bobby, remember this," Mrs. Santos had told him, being calmly informative even when it came to delivering the details of Sal Costa's death to his son. "You know the worst place to have a heart attack? In a hospital. No kidding. If you're checked in for something else and have a heart issue, you're three times more likely to die of it. They fill out your charts for some other ailment, they never think about you again."

"Were you with him, Mrs. Santos? I mean, when he had the heart thing."

It wasn't an accusation, but she might have taken it that way. She was Sal's minder, his babysitter, his stopwatch, his human calendar and itinerary. Sal was waiting for an x-ray in a lobby off the emergency room. That's where he had a coronary. By the time Mrs. Santos got there, a gathering of orderlies and nurses had the late Sal Costa on a stretcher; the time of death was thirty minutes before Mrs. Santos had arrived.

Roberto, though it changed nothing, wanted to know all about the car—no license plate gotten, no phone-camera witnesses—but Mrs. Santos assured him that Sal had blundered into the street talking on the phone, just as Roberto had seen him do in cities all over Europe.

"Could it have been a hit job?" Roberto wondered. His father had been concerned in Brussels about the international investors. The Saudi princes, the Central Asian strongmen. The Russian oligarchs.

"A hit job?" Mrs. Santos considered. "They make these electric cars so quiet they don't make any noise. That's who's to blame."

In time, his interest in blaming someone turned to his sister.

"What did Rachel want?" he asked Mrs. Santos. "Was this another shakedown?"

"I'm sure she was asking for money—what else would she be doing? But don't go holding her responsible. This is on Sal. He fucked it up. You look both ways when you step in the street—I tell my own children." Mrs. Santos's patter stopped abruptly as if another wave of grief had broken on the shore. Roberto could hear in her ragged breath that she had said about all she could manage to say.

So here was Rachel at the funeral, looking miserable. Roberto wondered what the last thing she said to her father was. What bratty, accusatory, manipulative thing had she flung at him? And what would Roberto say to her about it? *How awful for you to have been trawling for money and stressing Dad out when he was run over* could not be packaged sympathetically, so he left his sister alone.

The wake in the church's activity hall was catered; some classy stuff but some Sal favorites too: Saugy franks, Del's Shandy, *pasteis de natas* from Silver Star. Mrs. Santos arranged it, and Roberto paid. They could have departed the church for a hotel ballroom for a swank affair fit for a Providence boy made good, but as Mrs. Santos said, "A lot of bottom-feeders in this room. I'm not giving them filet mignon . . ."

Sylvie Bernstein came to Sal's funeral, Lena's smoking buddy. The woman with the voice like an unoiled hinge whose name meant forest amber. And all their East Providence neighbors, some of the guys who never moved on from Merrill Lynch in One Financial Plaza—"Second-tallest skyscraper in Providence, Bobby!"—and he got trapped for a while with dear Mrs. Henriques, a zillion years old, who looked after Roberto and Rachel when they were tiny children, before they moved up and beyond College Hill.

She had the most marvelous story to tell about Whiskers. Whiskers went missing one day, then another, then another after that, and then if you can believe it, another whole day after that, and she thought Whiskers was lost or perhaps run over or maybe he fell into the bay but each day she went to the chapel here at St. Joseph and she prayed to Mary and she prayed to Our Lord and she prayed to Saint Anthony, who finds lost things, and to Saint Francis, who loves all the animals . . . and on the Friday of that week, which was in August . . . or had it turned September—no, no, it was August, she was sure of it, Whiskers came home! Oh, our precious Mary, Blessed Virgin, can she not accomplish all things? Isn't God a wonderful god?

"He certainly is, ma'am," said Roberto, rising, pretending there were catering issues that required his attention.

Lena was making the rounds. "Bobby," Lena said, "this is Xavier." Her eyes were darting in all directions looking for people not to run into, hoping Xavier would be her human shield preventing a little mother-son one-on-one. "He is thinking of doing foreign languages at McGill next year, and I know you're just the person to talk him out of it. Tell him all about how little good it did you, careerwise." And she was off across the room.

"My friends call me 'X,'" he said, shaking hands. He was a lovely boy, Roberto thought, Canadian earnestness meets Gallic smoldering looks. Some young Québécoise is going to have a fine time taking his virginity.

"Well then, X," Roberto began, detailing the career options ahead, translator, scholar of foreign literature, a sometimes instructor like himself in foreign languages or English in foreign lands—

"I'm gonna be like you," X interrupted. "Dad's rich, after all—he said there's no sense pretending it wasn't the case—and he said I don't have to be practical. As long as I do *something*. I can do what makes me happy."

Keeping oneself happy, Roberto thought, *will prove to be a full-time occupation.*

He excused himself to pull Lena aside, since he wasn't sure when, where, or if she would be visible again. "Mom," he said, "if I could have a word."

They wandered to the coatroom of the church's activity building. "I don't know," she said, "precisely what's in Sal's will any more than you do, honey. Do you know?"

"We'll find out next week, I guess. What I wanted to ask is about Milan and that apartment—"

"Oh, Bobbikins, we don't have to visit that again—"

"Mom. This has been bothering me for six months. If you went through with the original plan, where Rachel brought two hundred thousand and I brought two hundred thousand, you'd have scammed us for four hundred thousand."

"Water under the bridge, Bobby. I don't see—"

"But when Rachel and Merle scraped me off the deal, you ended up with three hundred thousand from her, and change from Merle." He paused. Lena fell quiet too. "Since when do you leave a hundred thousand on the table? You could have had four hundred K, and you settled for three hundred K."

Lena was hard to read.

"I thought I knew you," Roberto prompted.

Lena now had a familiar expression; it was one where she went through the lies at hand and took the temperature of the truth to see if it, on this rare occasion, would suffice. "Well. Merle was throwing some of her own money in, and, Bobbikins, it was too good to resist. That *parasita,* that bloodsucker. It seemed more delicious to take her money than beat more out of you. And . . ." This was the pause either before the lie or the truth. It turned out she went with the truth. "You've lived long enough, haven't you, honey? To know that you can fall in love with more than one person, right? At the same time, even. I came to talk to you in that little bedroom, and I looked at you sitting on that child's bed, looking up to me, and you were my little boy, but you were also, swear to God, the spittin' image of Gehrman van Till when I first met him back in the seventies. Sal and Gehrman were the loves of my life, and I know I shoulda picked just one, but I never could quite do it. And you were all I had left of him, and I said, 'Aw, screw it, Lena. It's worth a smaller payday to take from Merle and let your boy win one for a change.'"

Roberto glanced briefly at her eyes. "So you messed up."

"Yeah, did myself out of a hundred K," she said, taking her turn in meeting his eyes then looking away. "I played myself there."

Roberto felt exhausted from the funeral performance (one is crushed, sad, bereft, but one is still performing for all the others, receiving their consolation with some dignity). He had worried, before the service, about being an emotional mess. Now he was worried that he had no emotions at all. He hadn't cried, or pounded the walls, or felt anything but numb. Well, that wasn't precisely true: he had gallons of anger for Rachel. That emotion seemed to renew and recharge itself hourly. Now he wanted nothing more than to go to the Hilton and never leave the hotel room again. The crowd had thinned. He unfolded a napkin and made himself a doggie bag of *pasteis de natas* and chouriços in a blanket.

Waiting next to waylay him was a rumpled man with a lot of pomade (or some kind of product . . . Vitalis? Brylcreem?) in his hair, a hair treatment of another era.

He put out his hand to shake. "I am Georgiye Gorki. I do not know if your father has mentioned me, but—"

"Oh yes! Mr. Gorki! Um, you knew him in Argentina. You . . ." Was this something you could bring up to someone politely? "You, um, defected, right?"

"Yes indeed, I left Soviet Union, true, with your father's help. I was so happy to be in America. Ha, but look, I then went back when Soviets were gone to be a part of Russian glorious rebirth."

Roberto couldn't discern if that was sarcasm.

There was so much to ask! Roberto wanted to learn what his father was like on his bureaucratic assignment in Argentina. Was there danger in such a volatile political situation of rebels, juntas, secret police, resistance? Or was it the usual collection of businessmen in a bar, putting each afternoon in the bin, waiting for news, waiting for some assignment to clarify itself? But before any of that could get mentioned, Mr. Gorki looked at his watch and made a little bow goodbye, clapping Roberto on the shoulder. "I will see you again, perhaps, da? When you come for them."

Georgiye inserted a business card—English one side, Russian in Cyrillic on the other—into Roberto's breast pocket of his black suit. Roberto smiled politely. "Uh, I . . . come for what exactly?"

Georgiye lowered his voice. "The diamonds, of course. The Meyerbeer Diamonds."

Monday, and the reading of the will.

Roberto had been misinformed by movie scenes and Agatha Christie whodunits where families gathered for the reading of the will, dramatic surprises were revealed, and then someone was instantly rich. Salvador Costa's will would disburse some things immediately, but for the fine print, it would take three years to finish probate. True, it was a complicated estate, as any CEO's would be, but it was made more complicated by lawsuits; the lawsuits were perpetual. Some litigants had sued Hightower Wiggins for lost money, and when that failed, they turned to the man they knew from TV and sued Salvador Costa personally, even though he was dead, and this too failed, but it took time to play out. In 2010, 2011, 2012, upon each week, Roberto's liaison with his father's legal team would provide a summary of activities on a PDF attached to an email. He had stopped reading them sometime around 2011, before, at last, they stopped.

His mother sued. Although Salvador left her $250,000—the phrase in his will was "given in expectation that Lena will not bother our children with continuous moneygrubbing"—but she felt entitled to more. Wasn't the whole of her beloved Sal's rise from the grime of Providence to the boardroom of New York accompanied by her marriage? Wasn't she an essential part of his success, a partner, a helpmeet? No, said the courts once again, she was not, particularly after she abandoned her family for her husband's colleague. She didn't fight as in days of yore since she had another rich man in tow now, but you could see she would have liked to have carried on, just to keep her hand in.

Nothing for Uncle Vinnie and Aunt Benita. Good.

Rachel, like Roberto, got $350,000 free and clear from a life insurance policy. But Rachel figured that half of the millions in the trust fund that formerly used to pay her allowance were coming to her too. But a delicious cruelty awaited her: upon Sal's death, the Raquel and Roberto Costa Revocable Trust switched magically to an irrevocable trust, with the surviving trustee, Roberto, as the sole manager.

Rachel sputtered and fumed and went loud and also went quiet: at least half the money in the trust was rightfully hers—why, her name was on it, for God's sake! And she was, after all, the true blood relation of Salvador Costa. It was a short-lived suit because Rachel had to pay for her own lawyers from the dwindling money pile she had inherited, and Mr. Pereira (Sal's lawyer for twenty years) was ruthless and effective (and expensive, but then, Roberto had the money). Was she not able to look up the word *irrevocable*? The terms of their inheritance trust were locked in legal cement forever and ever, with nothing to be done about it.

Rachel tried to rook Mrs. Santos into testifying on her behalf. Roberto was in the New York office and heard Mrs. Santos dress down his sister by phone.

"No, missy, Sal cut you off because you and that Merle character were always trying to extort from him. Remember when you two were going to tell the press about his connection to the mobsters in Providence, right?" Roberto listened intently to one side of the conversation. "If you had played that card, that would have brought me into the scandal too—you ever think about that? I go back to those days and watched those scary men come in and out of the office." More listening. "We have nothing more to say to each other, then. Good luck." Roberto could have pressed Mrs. Santos for more information, but he had all he needed to close the door on the sibling relation and indulge his most vengeful inspiration yet. Two of them, in fact.

Stephanie Velazquez, the alternative guest host for *Costa: Doing Business!*, the always colorfully garbed banker-broker who played up her South Bronx background and accent as she dished out advice on portfolios and the greatness of bonds, was made the permanent host after the sudden passing of Salvador Costa. She was very affecting when she took over the show the Monday after the week when Salvador had his fatal coronary. She praised Sal as her mentor, her friend, her example. He cared about the little guy who had been brave enough to invest, and she would carry on his work. (CNBC would drop the show two years later, but Stephanie eventually became like Suze Orman, one of those TV investment advisors who specialized in normal people's investments, a fixture of the PBS fundraising drive.) She came out to bachata music from her ancestral Dominican Republic; there would always be a framed picture of Sal Costa on the business desk that was her stage prop. That week, Stephanie emceed a showcase of Sal's wackiest interviews and most inspired rants . . . Roberto watched a few minutes and turned the set off—it was like a stab to his own heart. All of this would be on videotape or YouTube and could be pored over later when the wound wasn't raw, but he never asked for that tape and never searched for it on YouTube and the wound was never not raw. He asked to go on Stephanie's show that first week, since he was in New York for Hightower Wiggins's memorial service.

"I loved your father to death," she started their segment.

"And he loved you," Roberto returned. He held a manila folder that had the next round of people that Salvador Costa wished to reimburse.

"I know your dad had the power to reroute the board members' bonuses to his project of making these fine people whole, but you . . ."

"This is my money, Steph. Mine and my sister's. From our inheritance. Both of us—my sister, Rachel, and I—believe so strongly that while we can't reimburse everyone on Dad's list, we can contribute to more than a few."

Stephanie got choked up a little. "Why does this not surprise me that Sal raised such . . . such damn fine kids? It's not all greed and sleaze down here on Wall Street, folks." She reached over to clasp his hand.

Roberto read from his list, just as his father had done in his news conferences: "To Madge Kowalski of Wilkes-Barre, Pennsylvania. Your principle of two hundred thousand—her life savings—will be returned to you with an extra hundred thousand, courtesy of Sal. My dad actually went to see Madge once when he had business in Scranton; she served him hot chocolate . . ."

And after a few other fortunate names were called out, the segment was over. Those quibbling executives on the twenty-third floor had to be loving that segment—it was great TV.

Rachel was waiting for him back at the Costa Manhattan apartment . . . which was in the process of being sold by Mrs. Santos, their executrix.

"Are you suicidal?" she asked. "You're going to give away the whole trust so we'll have nothing to live on?"

"I'm just following in Dad's footsteps. What does it matter if I spend down the trust if I . . ." He theatrically looked saintlike. "If *we* are rewarded by the warm feeling of doing what's right."

"Oh, you're a laugh a minute. Giving away our inheritance."

"I'm giving away *your* onetime *former* inheritance. There is a Van Till trust."

Rachel was momentarily confused . . . whose trust and for whom . . .

"Gehrman, my biological father, left me a trust equal to that of his other children. It's only Sal's money I'm giving away. Truly, Rachel—you mustn't worry about me."

Three weeks into the sorting through Sal's papers and effects, Mrs. Santos patted Roberto's arm. "I need you to hear something. I served your father for almost thirty years. I got to see the world. Japan, Australia, India, everywhere in Europe. It was a good run. But I'm gonna retire, Bobby, and be a grandmother. Those kids are getting school age and need a little spoiling."

"Yes, ma'am."

"You'll wonder about this and that, whether the taxes got paid on the New York apartment for the final year, whether you owe property tax money on his car we're gonna sell . . . and you're gonna want to call me. And I'm good for a question or two every once in a while, you know? But mostly, when this estate is settled, I'm out. Do you understand what I'm saying?"

"I do, Mrs. Santos." One thing, then. "This Russian fellow, Georgiye Gorki, was at the funeral."

Mrs. Santos stood erect, at full attention now. "Georgiye? I didn't see him."

"He was in and out. He said to get in touch if I came to get something called the Meyerbeer Diamonds."

Mrs. Santos took off her glasses, pinched the bridge of her nose. She sat down again and bade Roberto sit too, though there was only the office windowsill. "You don't want a piece of that. Those no-good diamonds. It's a Hightower Wiggins holding, sitting in a safe-deposit box in Russia, in a bank run by some scary, dodgy businessmen—what do they call them?— oligarchs. The jewels have every stain of human wretchedness. Blood diamonds, colonial diamonds, Holocaust diamonds, the SS, Stalin, and the gulags. Bobby, your dad looked into it and threw up his hands. And I am really surprised Georgiye didn't find me to say hello. And I'm surprised additionally that he wants to involve you in that diamond madness. Thought he was a better friend to your dad than that." She stood. "Bobby, you got plenty of money for one lifetime. Call it quits, okay? And again, don't call me from here on out every week, if you get what I mean."

Roberto stood up too. "I won't bother you unless it's something only you would know. Mrs. Santos, I thank you for everything. Not just the will and the estate stuff. I've been coming to you with problems since I was a kid, knowing my mother wasn't around, and I could find you in Dad's office when he was in that strip mall on Wayland Avenue. You put a Band-Aid on my scraped knee a few times. You were more my mother than my mother."

She nodded at this, swallowing hard. Roberto decided that was as much emotion as the stoic Azorean was likely to show. He made the hug brief so things didn't get any schmaltzier.

After the Manhattan apartment was cleaned out—suits given to St. Vincent de Paul, furniture sold off like the kitchen goods—Rachel ambushed him a last time.

"I thought I'd find you here," she said. "At least his will says I get half of the value of this apartment. Your attempts to leave me destitute only go so far, you see."

Roberto sat in the remaining chair. Nothing in this apartment had been loved; nothing had been passed down in the family as in the home back in Providence. This was never anything but a serviceable place to lay their heads. Sal and Lena probably didn't imagine Sal's New York tenure would last; they treated it like a long-term hotel room. First, Lena made her escape and the children, to university, and for years, this must have been their father's all to himself. Where he would come home from his telecast at CNBC and . . . what? Fix a drink, order in food? It was hard to picture Providence's Sal Costa in this Manhattan luxury condo.

"Well," Roberto began again, "I'm not so sure this apartment was a great investment."

"It's listed for three million."

"But Dad didn't own it outright. He'd barely paid down the interest on the mortgage. The money you will split with me is solely the gain in value. You can use that to reimburse the trust."

Rachel stared at him, for once not ahead of him. "Reimburse . . ."

"Do you not remember? When you borrowed against the trust. It was three hundred thousand for that place in Milan. Dad issued you a loan, you signed forms electronically, and you handed the check over to our mother."

"Which she stole."

"Which makes no difference to the trust. Which is owed, by you, three hundred thousand."

"Bobby. I can't pay . . ."

"Under the terms of the will, in that boilerplate language you have no doubt pored over, all debts and liens on the trust must be made right. You owe the trust—well, you owe me—three hundred thousand. Some of your inheritance can't be processed until you clear the debts and liens."

She started to hyperventilate. "I'll get a lawyer . . ."

"You already tried that. Why waste another fifty thousand on fees? When I will, of course, win."

"I . . . When Dad died, I was supposed to be a co-trustee, and I would have forgiven my own loan, which I legally can do."

"Yes, had you been co-trustee, but you are not. I am the sole trustee, I do not forgive the loan, and you owe the trust three hundred thousand. Actually, a little more because of the interest that has accrued on the loan. And I do hope you mentioned this windfall on your 2008 taxes. Better see to that, because it will be in my IRS paperwork. Maybe I can write off your delinquent repayment against my profits. I'm sure you can work out a payment schedule. Fifty K a year, maybe. I'll have Mr. Pereira work up a—"

There was the slam of the door. She had left.

He sat there for a while. The last night in the Manhattan apartment. After a few minutes letting it get dark without the lights on, he made his way to the bedroom (now cleaned out, even of the bed frame), and wondered whether if he waited, if he opened himself to it, would the ghost of Salvador Costa wander the halls again. Why would Sal choose this place to haunt? Roberto thought. If he would haunt anywhere, it would be that grand two-story, porched, gabled mansion on Taber Avenue in Providence. The parking lot of the Olneyville Hot Dogs, maybe; an apparition in the plumes of celery salt . . . Roberto recited his half of the rote formulation, thinking it might sadden him. He still had not cried a tear yet.

Roberto did make his way to the door, still in the dark. One last look back.

"Bye, Dad," he said, his eyes adjusting to the bright lights of the hallway.

PART II:
2019, TEN YEARS LATER

———

Superficial Monster

Roberto had a seat free beside him on the bus. Because he took up the space of two people, he hoped that passersby would look at him wedged into the space and decide not to sit with him, rightly fearing that they would be pressed against one another. Alas, one of the Polish workers who hopped on at the last station, dithered a bit, and then sat down beside him. He spoke to him in Polish, and Roberto said something back in English, hoping to discourage him, but that only delighted his seatmate all the more—the chance to practice English all the way to Kaliningrad!

Roberto's next strategy was to yawn and pretend to be so sleepy— which he should have been, having ridden on all-night buses for a day. But after a fake nap for an hour, Roberto stirred, with his friend waiting giddily, ready again for more talk.

"Why?" asked the man. "Why not hop on a plane for Moscow? You will be three days in a bus this way."

"I like seeing what's between two places," Roberto said, which was truthful enough. And it was how Georgiye Gorki suggested he enter Russia. To come in through Kaliningrad by bus . . . such offices and their officials will not report anything for days, waiting for bus station reports on paper to be logged into computer screens. Perhaps Roberto could conduct his business and be gone before any curious Russian authorities even knew he arrived. At an airport, Roberto would be on the cutting edge of Russia's self-surveillance, captured by dozens of cameras and questioned by cadres of officials.

"Is it a nice city?" Roberto asked of Kaliningrad.

His bus buddy shook his head. "Perhaps Russia has forgotten about their little island." Wedged between Poland and Lithuania, this little land claim got isolated when the Baltics became independent republics, cutting this oblast off from the rest of Mother Russia.

"The bridges are still there? The Seven Bridges of Königsberg?"

His Polish companion smiled, not knowing what he referred to.

The bus across Poland had been crisp, air-conditioned, and modern, but this bus (which appeared after Gdańsk) was ready for the scrapyard. No more first-class tickets for Mr. Roberto Costa. He had come down in the world.

If you had asked him back in 2009, "Hey, Bobby Costa, you have one of the best social lives on the planet and you're going to end up with all your dad's money—so where do you think you'll be in ten years?" His answer would be some moonshine about being the author of *The Notebooks of Roberto Costa*, academic conferences and book fairs, and as for the money, he hoped he would be able to spend it all visiting his unparalleled range of acquaintances, friends, lovers . . . And now ten years later, he was pretty much a recluse, not wanting to connect with people any more than with his uninvited traveling companion on the bus. And the money was nearly gone.

At the time of Salvador Costa's death, March of 2009, the nadir of the financial crisis, the Dow Jones was at 8,000-some and sinking fast. Roberto was informed he could cash out the trust's mutual funds and investment vehicles and not pay capital gains taxes because of the widespread losses. So he did, and he was proud of himself as the market sank to the 7,000s, then 6,000s. But sticking the $1.1 million in his money market and checking account was the folly of his life. Those funds would have made him rich beyond belief had he left everything alone, as the Obama stock market would return to the 19,000s and Trump's anything-goes era would take it to 26,000, with no roof in sight. He would have made millions of dollars and not worked for a penny of it.

As for Hightower Wiggins's stock—a core investment in both Sal's trust fund and Gehrman's trust fund—the death of Sal Costa sank the stock to ten dollars a share. It rose steadily upon the announcement of the new CEO, Franklin Martin. Yes, crawling up from the grave, the guy Sal termed a "buffoon for the ages" was back! And his first order of business was to reinstate all the golden parachutes and payoffs and sweetheart severances, lost bonuses, perquisites, and emoluments that Sal had taken away from the motley assortment of failed executives. The stock climbed up to eighteen dollars, but Roberto was naive about that. People who knew things knew that Martin was going to buy up all the stock so he could dismantle the company unheeded, and the rise in stock price was merely speculation. Roberto did not sell—how could he sell the stock in his dad's company? His father swore they would be coming back strong. Finally, the stock sank to four dollars a share, and before it fell to three dollars, he called Gary—the nice guy at the memorial service, who did a passable Sal Costa imitation—and he kindly oversaw the sale.

As long as all the crooks were getting their spoils, there were some outstanding spoils due Sal Costa, even in death. Roberto pressed Gary, who reported that Sal's salary—he was on some deferred plan—his separate stock plan, life insurance plan, 401-something, 403(k), or was it (b)437 or 457 (whatever), all of that was due to be deposited in the Raquel-and-Roberto trust, in the event of his death . . . but, of course, there were complications.

"We're having quite a liquidity problem," Gary reported, "but I'm pleased to inform you that we can deposit equities of the equivalent value into your trust. Pooled viatical settlements, a good solid investment."

"Pooled viatical settlements," said Roberto, recognizing that term from the roster of garbage his father recited from the first time Hightower Wiggins was facing bankruptcy.

Gary went on, "We have a hundred thousand in promissory notes, these from European banks, so you know that's secure. And I know the idea of getting mortgage swaps sounds poisonous, but, Bobby, they are tied to forward-rate agreements . . ."

This was probably Franklin Martin's payback, to pay himself and all the former board back in truckloads of bullion, while they screwed Sal over with substitute no-value properties that vaporized when the company was dissolved.

And by January of 2010, Hightower Wiggins was no more. The bond division was sold off to Ally Invest; the equities portfolios were assumed by JPMorgan Chase; the William Street 1908 skyscraper was put on the market.

Roberto and Rachel's several hundred thousand shares of Hightower Wiggins, once worth $14 million, were now worth $800,000. That, plus all the stocks that Roberto sold, brought the total figure to $1.9 million. That wasn't nothing, right? Roberto could draw out $60,000 a year for thirty years . . . and with his health issues, maybe that would last to the end.

Ah, blustery, cloudy, cold Kaliningrad.

Roberto and his light suitcase disembarked. The shabby concrete high-rises that only the leaden hand of Soviet social architecture could produce sprawled and slumped in all directions. There were a lot of weed-filled lots and empty blocks too, where the buildings had collapsed or been torn down: Detroit-on-the-Baltic. Königsberg, "the king's city," the great Prussian commercial and intellectual capital, had once been a rich port town of the Hanseatic League, known for its university with its great scholar Immanuel Kant, who was buried in the cathedral. Königsberg was now named Kaliningrad, after Mikhail Kalinin, metalworker turned party hack, who supported Stalin over the other rivals when Lenin died and, for his backing, was elevated to chairman of the Central Executive Committee of the All-Russian Congress of Soviets. The city's name demotion tells you all you need to know about the fortunes of the place.

"The Seven Bridges of Königsberg" was the logic problem of the Enlightenment. The seven bridges over the Pregel River linked two river islands with its two banks: the object of the math problem, famous throughout the academies of Europe, was to cross each bridge once in a continuous trip with no backtracking. Any second grader, with a finger, can trace the puzzle and see it cannot be done; one bridge will have to be repeated. But to mathematically affirm this in a proof constituted a conundrum. The great mathematician Leonhard Euler in 1736 stripped the geography down to four points and seven lines on a graph, then he logically defined a function for each line . . . and as a recross was beyond the definition, the proof was definitive—it could not be done. Roberto could have saved them all a lot of trouble: there are bridges you cannot recross.

Roberto saw the grave of Kant, listened to a lunchtime concert of the cathedral's wonderful organ (Buxtehude, Franck, Brahms, and Widor). Then in honor of Euler, he crossed the old bridges; one bridge's wooden slats were so broken that you could see down into the river. Really, Kaliningrad? Your one tourist attraction and you can't keep the planks intact? Then he tangled with the amber salesmen in the park. Bernstein—remember that? Amber was nowhere on earth more common or in a better location to get a bargain than this run-down outpost. He bought some wonderful necklaces, a bracelet or two . . . But who to give them to? They would end up in the boxes of trinkets and bric-a-brac gleaned from his twenty years in Europe. He had potential Christmas gifts nailed down for the next twenty.

So back on the bus.

He wouldn't be in such money trouble if it hadn't been for Rupesh. There wasn't a day that he didn't miss his friend, but their life together was not sustainable.

They had bought a very upscale flat in the De Pijp district of Amsterdam, right in the center where the fun was. (Another in a series of disastrous financial decisions.) Roberto's $60K a year budget came to $5,000 a month, but he and Rupesh blew through that in no time. Amsterdam was an expensive city in an expensive country with expensive taxes. Roberto thought, *Okay, after we decorate our apartment, the money demands will lessen. If we don't eat out nightly, if we don't cruise the stores alongside the otherwise cheap Albert Cuyp street market, if we don't buy art, if we leave off the high-cover gay club on weeknights, with the ten-euro cocktails . . .*

Eventually, Roberto temporarily raised their monthly stipend to $10,000, with a $5,000 allowance for Rupesh. And somehow still the money vaporized; Roberto continued picking up the tab for everything—he couldn't help but notice—and that led him to wonder what Rupesh was doing with his money. Roop left his bank statement out, and Roberto started playing detective. Online, he called up their accounts to learn that three, sometimes four of the five thousand allowance immediately disappeared the first week of the month. He was sending money to his mother, perhaps? His unmarriable sister? That was at least forgivable, though the secrecy was uncalled for.

More detective work turned up that he was routing the money back to Rachel.

Roberto imagined the scenario of Rachel, back in the States, pleading poverty and hunger and injustice and Rupesh, softening, and sending her the money behind Roberto's back. Two offenses: the lie, and that it was Rachel. Rachel had income; she had begun her teaching at the Walsh Academy in Connecticut. (Roberto imagined with her retirement plans and savings option, the irony would be that she would have more money upon retirement than Roberto!) She was just manipulating Rupesh into giving her the money that she still imagined was rightfully hers. So Roberto revealed that he knew all and cut Rupesh off completely.

"Yes, I suppose you must," Rupesh said stoically.

Roberto was disappointed and cold and sour around Rupesh, yet still he did not conceive that by the end of the month, he would come home to find Rupesh packing up.

"I am the one," Roberto insisted, "who gets to be offended—not you. And why would you leave me over an issue of money? I thought our connection was much deeper than that."

It was now Rupesh's turn to wear the stone countenance. "You think it is the money I am leaving about? It is the other thing we always discuss and for which you never make the right answer."

"I don't need therapy. I admit I am not Mr. Sunshine, but I am rich and all-right-looking and privileged beyond measure. *No one* wants to hear me say woe is me."

"I fell in love with your happiness, your spirit. And it has been a long time since that has been in evidence."

"You fell in love with my big, tall, white blondness and my big dick and big wallet. You have screwed every kind of man, true, but the men you target for your boyfriends have been well-off white men who could provide for you. I was just the first in line."

And that concluded the civil part of that final, hours-long blowout and breakup.

So many bridges, if not exactly burned, then unable to be recrossed.

Rupesh said he fell in love with Roberto's American happiness. Roberto was prompted to think of Hella, packing her bags, leaving Europe for home, in James Baldwin's *Giovanni's Room*: "What's the good of an American who isn't happy? Happiness was all we had." It's an old trope, American luck and happiness and smiling naivete, the unwary hero/heroine offered up to sinister Europeans and doom, the plot of a clutch of Henry James novels. (*Fuck you, Rupesh,* Roberto thought. *I will dwell on Henry James as much as I want to!*)

God, Bismarck quipped, protects fools, drunkards, and the United States of America. Like George W. Bush, America was like a badly behaved scion, careless and amateur beyond belief, falling upward, eluding consequences. There was no neighbor on America's continent to invade them, no twentieth-century war that ever razed the cities of the republic; her post–World War II adventures cost, at worst, tens of thousands of American lives collectively, not millions. (The countries America invaded or overthrew might offer up hundreds of thousands of lives, however.) Compared to Europe and its millennia of strife, the U.S. has skipped smilingly through history. And Emil Cioran, of whom Roberto copied great tracts into his Notebook, felt America was "unlike the other nations which have had to pass through a series of humiliations and defeats, she has known till now only the sterility of uninterrupted good fortune . . . Those who preside over her destiny, those who take her interest to heart, should prepare for bad times, in order to cease being a superficial monster." *This* was the European opinion of Americans: monstrous and superficial. They thought we were Donald Trump before Trump came along and then, terrifyingly, fulfilled their worst projections of us.

And then there was the monstrous, superficial Roberto Costa.

What had he ever accomplished with his money? Not the exalted Notebooks. Years of editing and balling-up drafts and self-disgust had convinced him there was no publishing future for *The Notebooks of Roberto Costa*. He was a diarist. Nothing wrong with that. Maybe, like with Samuel Pepys, someone will find his summation and celebration of the Western world one day and value it for what it is. Perhaps by then, China will run the world and the basket-case West, spent and intellectually exhausted, will let them. *And,* Roberto found himself thinking, *they will read my diaries and* . . . Ah, but there he goes again: thinking any of his labors will amount to anything.

Like the flop of his "Kosovo operation." Back in 2015, he was doing a run of conversational English teaching in Aarhus, Denmark—mostly prodded by loneliness and wanting someone to talk to. Among his students was Muharrem, from Pristina, trying to make his way in construction work up north. Roberto proposed a lucrative operation for Muharrem. He would pay for his student, on his next trip home to Kosovo, to approach the police about the date, which he provided, that the Romani girl was hit in the road. He told Muharrem that he saw the accident years ago and observed the people run away from the scene, but he was scared to report the incident for fear he would be drawn in, maybe accused of the crime. But it had always sat badly with him. He assumed she was found and something was done. What happened to her? Did her body get back to her Romani family? If Muharrem would research this, maybe get a name, a family, perhaps Roberto would give a contribution because he felt so bad.

"You were right not to involve yourself back then," Muharrem confirmed. "Maybe it will still be bad to involve yourself now."

He would pay Muharrem two hundred euros for the chore, three hundred if he turned something up. He found nothing. Muharrem played out a transparent ruse that he thought he *almost* found something, if only there could be another two hundred euros . . . Roberto sent it and never heard from him again. Muharrem did not return to the construction site or Denmark.

Roberto considered his isolation appalling. Roberto Costa had the best social life of anyone he ever met! Acquaintances from all walks of life, all countries, all backgrounds, and—in his younger, more attractive days—all sexual expressions. Money, ironically, dimmed some of that social life.

Except for Ludo and Lucrezia, his backpacking-hostel-holiday gang was very middle class as he used to be in his Brown University backpacking study-abroad days, and that was not so noticeable when they all were in their wild-ass twenties. Liesl, Hélène, Emilie came to lead normally financed lives, with mortgages and loans from parents. To sweep in as the millionaire friend sat less happily than it did before the fortune was conferred on him. He would hear, say, how there was no money for piano lessons for little Yves . . . and so before he left, Roberto would write a check. He left little gifts all over Europe looking up friends who were harried with children, at work most of the day, tired when they got home, Liesl and Jürgen moving to Chemnitz, Hélène and her husband in Lille, growing older and stouter in gray cities where whatever linked them in the first place—their youth, their earlier sexual hookup—was too far over a distant hill to be seen from the present. As if it were a consolation prize, they all were Facebook friends, and Roberto dutifully liked their pets, their gardening, their children with ribbons for some school contest or other, their summer vacations to the same locations . . .

The sex life really hit the skids. The next round of Claudia-smart women who wandered into his sights did not often make it to the third night in Roberto's patented delaying tactic. He was not too terrible-looking in his thirties, but the bloom, alas, was off the rose. He had become a bit drawn, graying, that magnificent flop of dirty blond hair up top thinning, perpetually a little sick-looking as if he was recovering from an operation, which, in truth, he was. Coupled with the inevitable sexual disappointment in the bedroom, he was not able to hold the interest of the women he had interested for long. And that was new for Roberto.

Nor was it cheering that some in his world had subtracted themselves permanently. In 2012, Ludo sent him an email to let him know that Lucrezia had passed away. She did not receive the Marilyn Monroe-style tabloid coverage she would have wished, but there was a suggestion in the Italian papers of pills and booze, which would have pleased her. The more prosaic overmedication with self-starving was not as tabloid-friendly a story. And this was assuming nothing sinister was afoot, as in Claudia's sensational theories. Roberto once dreamed of Lucrezia's bedroom with Ludo stroking her hair as she slept . . . only to press a pillow over her face. When he removed it, it was the dead Romani girl underneath.

Rupesh had promised they would have dinner parties, create a salon. And they did entertain, though most Amsterdam evenings with their bohemian friends ended with too much hash smoking, too much drinking. Mira, just a few towns over, had seemed cool on a reunion, but Roberto invited her and her new partner, who was gender nonbinary, and requested to be referred to as *he,* despite an especially conventional female appearance. Rupesh kept misgendering him; Roberto was better but slipped up after Rupesh slipped up. Mira had changed her public affect. She was very academic now, very critical of everything, festooned with the jargon of the hour, holding life continually up to her doctrinaire gender-studies lens. Maybe this was to get a permanent post, or maybe it was insurance so if they denied her one she could then claim she was the victim of discrimination. The fun individual he had enjoyed in Greece left no trace; but as Mira said, northern Europeans are very different on southern vacations. About the time the evening was at its peak, around dessert, the couple stood and said they had to be off for Nijmegen. The partner went down to warm the car, and Mira hung back.

"It was the wine," Roberto said. "Sorry we were so clumsy about the pronouns—"

"Never mind. I wanted to tell you something, and it would have made for bad dinner conversation. I heard from colleagues at the Politecnico di Milano that Claudia has died. By her own hand. When one thinks about it, it is not such a surprise."

She then departed—the last time Roberto saw Mira. Roberto retreated to the bedroom and cried a little. He hadn't intended to drop Claudia cold, but he had done just that. Because of the accident in Kosovo, which he worried about her divining, *not* because of her complexities and unreliable autobiographical narratives . . . but she could not have known that.

And if those mainstays being removed were not sufficiently depressing, in 2017, Mrs. Santos passed away.

Safira

His last trip to Providence was in 2017, for the funeral of Mrs. Santos. She had eight rich years of grandchild-spoiling, looking after her adult children, establishing herself as the matriarch of the Santos clan, who had connections to half the Portuguese Americans in town, also named Santos. Part of why Roberto, the permanent European, had hopped on the plane was the assurance that Rachel—a committed enemy of Mrs. Santos—would be unlikely to attend.

The commute to Providence stabbed Roberto with nostalgia, one slap of memory after another. Flying into Boston, he decided to take the train to Rhode Island. He was immediately touched by the landmarks of his youthful commute to Brockton Prep . . . he looked out the train window at the Route 128 train stop, where for years, after school holidays, the little ten-seater purple commuter van would wait for him, to whisk the students away to Brockton. It was not waiting there for him this April evening. He had hoped to see boys in their disassembled Brockton uniforms, sneaking cigarettes (well, maybe it's all vaping now) at the chilly bus stop before knuckling under to the housemothers and that Personal Responsibility Contract they signed without reading it. He was surprised at how he found himself wallowing in sentiment about so many survivals from his boyhood.

Then the train groaned into his hometown, Providence, Rhode Island, where he had not been in eight years.

Where Sal's St. Joseph ceremony was just family and friends, the St. Joseph farewell to Safira Leonor Machado Santos was the funeral event of the social season—five hundred people easily, lots of music and hymns, a fado soloist who was a dead ringer for Amália Rodrigues singing "Canção do Mar," which was appropriately elegiac for a Providencian or an Açoriana. Even the happiest fado song sounds right for a funeral, Roberto reckoned. Then there was a parade of Santoses from all the generations who were truly broken, bereft, not at all sure how they would go forward without their matriarch who knew and advised them all. Roberto imagined the ghost of Mrs. Santos appearing beside him for thirty seconds, leaning in, and going, "Shoulda planned something smaller. This is a circus."

"Are you saying that you . . ."

"Oh yeah. Fucked it up big-time."

Surely this would be Roberto's last visit to St. Joseph's—maybe to Providence. When his mother passed away, she wouldn't want a service here. Perhaps he could arrange a solo funeral where just he could attend? No, that's not how funerals worked.

He assumed his mother would outlive him, but that notion was cruelly revised when he saw her in the back of the church. Rachel had brought their mother—haggard, washed-out, withered—supported on her daughter's arm. He squinted to see them, waving. Jesus, she was on a portable oxygen machine she pulled behind her.

As the congregants shuffled up for the endless communion, Roberto's row cleared out, and Rachel and Lena sat beside him. "Didn't expect to see either of you in the mourners' cortege," he said.

"Talk to me before you head out," Rachel said lightly. "I'm happy that bitch is at last in the ground. I'll be out in the car in the parking lot." She waved her phone at him. "Someone should have told me that teaching meant a hundred emails a day . . ." And she slipped away.

"Mom," Roberto began a little stupidly, "are you sick?"

"I lived on cigarettes for forty years so . . . I don't have lots of breath, and I need to use some of it to talk about money."

Sidney Comeaux had Lena sign a prenup, and though she had some line of funding from him, it wasn't likely to cover what was ahead. The $250,000 left to her by Sal eight years ago was long gone. She wasn't yet sixty-five, so Medicare couldn't kick in and meet the big expenses.

"Why didn't you stay in Montreal? You'd have had health care in Canada."

"I never got the paperwork done to be Canadian. Then I had two judgments against me in Rhode Island and I had to come back. My lawyers got the costs down to a few hundred thou."

"Time to declare bankruptcy. Again."

"Some of these debts I do not intend to pay. I'll die before they collect." Lena may have been shrunken with illness, but there was the mother he recognized. She then added, "It's in my lungs. It's cancer, Bobby."

"Oh, Mom." Roberto glanced at her watery eyes, their aquamarine cast. "Can they do anything?"

"Charge me a lot of money, that's what they can do. Forget it. You don't have to do anything for me, if you don't want. But here's my plan, so you'll know where your scrap heap of a mother is headed to. You know my aunt Ines, the nurse."

"She's *still* alive?"

Aunt Ines (great-aunt for Roberto) had worked when he was young at a nursing home in Fall River. She married, late in life, to Uncle Anthony, moved to Arizona, where she worked in care facilities out there.

Lena narrated, measuring her breaths: "She's back from Arizona. Finally left that bum Tony, once the kids were grown. Working in the same care facility in Fall River for the last twenty years; they were happy to take her back. She thinks she can get me in there. You start out in independent living, then, when I cough my remaining lungs out, I get dumped in nursing, then hospice to end up, get shot full of morphine, then *pllfffsbt.* It was a low-rent place when you were young, but it got bought by some corporation and classed up a bit. About as good as I can hope for around here, but it's . . . it's Fall River, whaddya expect?"

"Quite a circular voyage, huh, Mom?" She didn't understand him. "You start out working for nickels and dimes at Fall River, you move up to East Prov, then you marry one rich guy, then another, spend your summers in Europe among the rich folks, then when all is said and done, you're back where you started." He thought when he said this, she would laugh with him, oh, isn't life a kick in the butt, that kind of thing. But a tear escaped down her face.

"Yeah, back where I started, Bobby. Back where I started."

Roberto's heart broke a little; he hadn't meant to be cruel. "Mom. How much is this place?"

It was three thousand a month for independent living—he should come see it, they have a decent cafeteria, a solarium, a nice garden with a few too many saint statues, a Virgin Mary in a niche patrolling each hallway. "I guess," she said, "so you can die in every corner of the place with your last sight being the Blessed Mother. Nursing will be closer to nine or ten thousand a month, but that's just at the end. Years from now, we hope. I'll try to drag it out to sixty-five so Medicare can pay and not you."

"I don't mind," he assured her.

"At the very end, they move you to hospice care." She paused, labored in her breathing. "They ship you to hospice because they want your actual death off the main stage. The old people in nursing don't need to see the bodies taken out, which might encourage the others to kick the bucket too, and how then would this clip joint make any money, huh?"

"Oh, Mom," he said, chuckling at her despite himself.

"Don't come see me when I get to nursing—you're not to visit unless you give me warning and I can fix up like I did today." Geez, Bobby thought, she could not have looked more corpse-like than today. "Nursing's bound to be ghastly," she was saying. "But when I get to hospice and the end is near, I'll give you a call. Rachel can give you progress reports."

"Did you and Rachel patch things up?"

"I gave her back most of the money I stole, got it from Sidney and passed it on. I was a little too free with his savings, and that's probably what did *us* in. Never did pay it all off, but she seems to have forgiven me. You, I'm not sure she'll ever forgive you."

"Can't say I'm interested in forgiving her either."

"Bobbikins . . ." She stopped to hack into a wadded-up ball of tissues. Was there blood? He couldn't bring himself to look. "She tried to hurt you with something, but it was something that was *true*—that Gehrman was your birth father, which you'd have learned anyway. Did she not do you a bit of a favor?" More of her hacking cough, more of the wretched tissue ball. "Excuse me . . . What I'm saying is that Rachel's one of the few people who gets you, and you're one of the few people who gets her. You've put a few decades into this feud. Why not try a different tack for the next few decades?"

As an incentive to entering St. Joseph's, Roberto had promised himself that afterward he could make a culinary journey for the quahogs and the Olneyville hot dogs, to drive by Vó Costa's, if only to see the boat deck and pier to nowhere Vinnie built at great expense, to maybe dine on bacalhau at the Riviera Café. But his earlier nostalgia had fled; the Bobby Costa who treasured these things had expired when his father died. He had been a different person since his father's death—a stranger. And he saw himself as Rupesh saw him, cold, remote, not able to feel things . . .

Were there seven bridges in Providence? Couldn't he find just one to make an unnoticed backtrack over?

Lena said she needed to rest now, so Roberto accompanied his mother to Rachel's (very nice) Hyundai. Rachel was six years into teaching art history at the Walsh Academy in northwest Connecticut. He didn't have to send a spy to know that she had become a Miss Jean Brodie, a cult figure for the girls. And her three-week study-abroad journeys to Europe with twenty rich girls in tow must have been life-changing for the young women. No one would be more thorough, no one would narrate the pageant of Europe better.

Rachel hopped out of her car once Lena was in place, the heat turned on, the radio on a channel she liked. "Just wanted to say one thing," she started. He looked squarely at Rachel. She had found, at last, a good style for herself. She had aged into a quite serviceable, no-nonsense, expert-instructor look.

"I don't wanna fight, Rach."

"Who's fighting? I wanted to say that yes, I dried up on paying back the loan, but before you send me to a collection agency again, let me say—"

"You might be richer than I am now. Borrow against your lovely house and pay me back, sis."

He expected Rachel to explode, to rage . . . but she was different. She sighed, looked amused—she had acquired Sal's wry smile! Roberto was transfixed by this late arrival of the long-lost Sal. "Europe did not make me happy, Bobby. When I was younger, I got that all wrong. Europe was too big, too vast, too much to be seen, too many of Wilfried Koch's dots, right? My every academic article, the best I could ever do, was still Johnny-come-lately; everything had been studied to death, for centuries, and I couldn't live up to what was necessary. My anxieties opened the door for the Michaels and Merles, who were quick to tell me I could do it, that I'd never have to come home, that I could stay in the playground after dark, so to speak.

"So I get back here and I start teaching. I'm nervous these rich girls who go to France every summer will see through me, but . . . they love me." She smiled. "I've found my place. And the Walsh Academy actually pays me for this! I've got a house—I used the insurance Dad left for the down payment. And I get to go to Europe as I please, on the school's dime." She paused. "I invite you to find where you belong. Maybe it's Europe, but just maybe it's not."

"I know it's not in America now. Donald Trump, for Christ's sake."

"Tell me about it. Brexit—that's boneheaded too. Every country over there's got a little fascist pipsqueak trying to take over. Merkel and Macron are just two fingers in the dike. Putin's meddling everywhere. We're entering the Age of the Oligarchs, and we're just along for the ride—and to pay the taxes for the people on top."

"You're channeling Sal, there."

"I find I'm doing that a lot. I envy that you got to spend so much time with him. It was my fault that I never did—you don't have to rub it in. I wanted to . . ." Rachel seemed to melt a little. She slowed but then powered through: "To thank you. Thank you and Dad for helping me clear out Merle. Even thanks for sending me home, where I could find a place I truly belonged. Dad did it to help me, you did it out of meanness, but I was mean to you too, and I have accepted my . . . my financial fate." She concluded with an easy smile—something Roberto was not used to. "You take care."

It was fucking obvious to Roberto that, in their lifelong competition to better the other, Rachel had won clean and undisputed, no need for a recount. And this was as close as Roberto had felt to Sal since Sal was alive. And what would Sal tell him here in the parking lot of St. Joseph's, on a cool, damp Providence evening with the salt-and-fish smell from the sea breeze in the air? He would be saddened that Roberto had let the sibling feud run this long. Sal had only switched the trust to Roberto's control as a means to eliminate Merle and help his daughter, Rachel . . . just as he had run Michael McCord off and subsidized a three-week adventure in Spain for his children. He wanted them to be, if not loving, then at least in solidarity. That had been Sal Costa's role—looking out for the family. And now it occurred to Roberto he could not go on as he had been going, lonely, miserly like Ingegerd Stern, surly in his soul. He needed to take up Sal's purpose and work for the betterment of the Costa Family of Providence, Rhode Island.

And so he would.

The Meyerbeer Diamonds

A night bus to Pskov . . . through rural Vitebsk. (Some seriously un-beautiful names for places.)

As dawn broke, there were hills beyond the bus window; they would present themselves and threaten to rise toward something, hinting at a greater prominence in other geological eras, but then diminish and disappear just as one was beginning to feel acquainted, and the long, grassy weed-and-wildflower-filled plain would reconquer the view to the horizon. No scenery for long stretches, then a small begrimed industrial site arrayed with rusted and sooted trucks that might or might not have been capable of revving to life again, and also towns of no more than one hundred Russian citizens, in which everything and everyone lived in the road—cows, goats, vegetable stands, children, ancient puttering cars spitting exhaust, chickens, kvass sellers, logging trucks (those trucks everywhere, but from what forests?), babushkas, one modern and usually unattractive Russian Orthodox church. Then the valediction, a bereft World War II–era tank upon a crumbling concrete plinth would say farewell to passers-through of the hamlet . . . and then back to the isolation of the steppes. With the sole interruption of the Ural Mountains, there was only five, six thousand more miles of this grassland to go.

Rupesh, before his departure, would annoyingly return to a regular topic, whether Roberto believed in anything as a lifeline, as a higher power.

"Art," Roberto said one time. "Art inspires and redeems, so that is my religion."

"Bobby, let me say that all the art you like is fucking depressing. You need to, at least, change churches!"

Roberto always tried to read the contemporary literature of the countries he traveled in, and he usually passed the books he had read on to Rupesh, if he was reading a translation in English (e.g., Tom Lanoye's *Speechless* [about his charismatic actress mother lessened by strokes, leading to her death] and Philippe Besson's *Lie with Me* [a tragic gay romance starring the closet] and Dag Solstad's *T. Singer* [lonely man marries into a single-mother family; things become even lonelier]).

"Can you not read anything happy by a European writer?" he said upon abandoning *Speechless* a third of the way in.

"There are no happy books by European writers."

The pleasures of reading had dimmed a bit, and so had stepping inside church after church, finishing off Wilfried Koch's dots. His thoughts on religion had been undermined by the thought of Mrs. Henriques and her Miracle of Whiskers the Cat. Through the offices of the Blessed Virgin Mary, God was able to reunite her with Whiskers—that seemed the sort of victory at which God was adept. What played out on the western steppes of Russia overmatched God. Roberto supposed that the ground around the Somme, the Marne, might be a worthy competitor, but he was sure, in terms of blood spilled into the soil, few plains rivaled these plains, the killing fields to end all altars of human sacrifice.

The largest land invasion in history—Hitler, double-crossing his "ally" Stalin, and invading his country, trying his old blitzkrieg idea, from the Baltics to the Crimea, an 1,800-mile wall of soldiers conquering all in their path. Behind them the SS, sorting out the Jews and Romani, the handicapped, the reputedly gay, and—the Germans were thorough— every man, woman, and child in any position of power in the Communist Party. Half a million of these Jews never made it to a death camp; they were shot outright and buried in mass graves. In downtown Kyiv is Babi Yar, a ravine where one hundred thousand bodies, mostly Jewish, were dumped—thought to be a record for a single mass grave of civilians. Rape was rampant, the troops doing anything, anything at all to women and girls, before putting a bullet in their heads. Divide and conquer—let the locals friendly to the Germans have food, let the others starve. This was the Backe Plan, named for SS food minister Herbert Backe, who was to organize the death of twenty to thirty million Russians by tactically depriving these steppes of food.

The Slavic population needed to be thinned so Hitler could establish a greater Germany that would reach to the Russian border, and from here to the Urals. How to enslave the Slavs while eliminating them? The deadliest battle of the deadliest war on the planet was a front for this racialist intrawhite social engineering project. Himmler wanted to turn these Russian provinces into a vast slave state, 14.5 million strong in forced labor, with a calculated death rate of 10 percent of the population each year. The prettier blond women with German qualities could be used for upping the German population back home, used to breed and populate the continent with the superior German seed—a reward for German soldiers.

Stalin sent his police ahead to root out possible traitors, in some cases destroying his own villages before the Germans got there. If you were a Russian soldier captured by the Germans, as the invasion went on, you were simply shot or starved to death: Some 3.3 million Russian soldiers died at German hands; half a million of those in concentration camps. Some 800,000 Russians were forced to fight for the Germans and be cannon fodder, bearing the brunt of their own side's attacks. And there were the medical experiments: exposure of captured Russians to x-rays, radiation, and other sterilization techniques, to better understand how to limit the Untermenschen birth rate in what would be the new German Reich.

Roberto was sure a prayer or two went up to the heavens through all that—Allah beseeched by the Chechens, Yahweh by the Jews, Jesus by the Russians—just as fervent and desperate as Mrs. Henriques's prayers for Whiskers. The God of Abraham seemed to have a customer service issue.

It takes a while to see humanity for what it is, and once you see it, you know the world will not improve for long. If you have been lucky enough to avoid holocaust and totalitarian injustice, then it's ahead, you can depend on it. As a young person, the worst is kept from you, or if you read it, you will not quite believe it, but as you age, the dark reality of incorrigible humankind becomes clear. The only comfort, if you are lucky enough to live your life between the slaughters and medical experiments, lynchings and forced sterilizations, is love, the love such as you have been able to find. Your family, your friends, your beloved.

And, Roberto reckoned as the bus pulled into Veliky Novgorod, *my accomplishment for nearly forty years of life on this planet is that I have estranged family, no friends, and I have no beloved. Good work, Bobby!*

At the family-run hotel, in shop windows, in cozy cottages with a single window, there would hang a poster or an icon itself of the Romanov family, Nicholas and Alexandra, the last czar and czarina, shot by the Bolsheviks, saints of a sort, venerated widely. A hail of bullets ended the reign of the czars, although the four czarevnas did not die immediately; the rich bro-

cading of diamonds and jewels in their dresses blocked some of the bullets. The young girls were run through with bayonets, and later, the whole family was dissipated in acid and thrown into a mine shaft. Roberto bleakly wondered what happened to those diamonds. Maybe he could add those blood diamonds to his pile of blood diamonds.

Once Roberto secured a room and left his suitcase, he began to walk toward the kremlin of Veliky Novgorod, the first in a series of kremlins from the 800s, when the Russians began their ascent as a power, assembling an array of capitals and palaces, fortresses and monasteries, known as the Golden Ring surrounding the final chosen capital, Moscow. But first it was necessary to eliminate all rivals right here: Mongols, Tatars, rival princes, the Swedes, Teutonic Knights sweeping across the steppes. Roberto walked through the gates of the redbrick castle walls, he ambled toward the shiny gold onion domes of St. Sophia.

After some well-done photos of the west-facing doors receiving the sharp afternoon light, he was tempted to send a shot to Rachel, as if they were still lightly battling and the year was 2005 instead of 2019. He shouldn't jump the gun. He would contact her when he got the Meyerbeer Diamonds and split the loot with her—*then*, then they could try to get back on track with each other.

But then he decided to do it, what he had not done in years: he sent a photo of the doors of St. Sophia, texting: MAYBE THE BEST 12TH CENTURY DOORS ARE NOT EVEN IN WESTERN EUROPE.

Roberto had become so inured to bus travel that the drive across the grasslands to the railhead on the Moscow–St. Petersburg line passed in a flash. The fast train—the true showpiece of Russian railroading— did deposit him in Moscow in no time at all. It was only 1:00 p.m. So he stood for a while in the cavernous lobby of Leningradskaya Station, looking for Georgiye, but instead he was approached by another man, Lev.

"Georgiye has sent me," said Lev, offering his hand to be shaken. "Georgiye will join tomorrow. He is setting up deal at bank. Lev was sent"—he meant himself, Roberto figured—"because English spoken best."

Lev drove him into the city. Moscow, Roberto had to remind himself, is Europe's most populous city, twenty whopping million. The drive took the rest of the afternoon to breach the heart of Moscow, with the halfway point being their exit from the Garden Ring beltway, where the traffic and the widespread construction made the passage through some intersections take a half hour, as no more than three cars were able to crawl into the blocked junctions with each green light. Finally, they crossed the Moskva River and found Ulitsa Pyatnitskaya, the main north-south artery. It was an old, venerable neighborhood of faded but stately apartment blocks. Amid this was the Hotel Tretyakovskaya. And, lookee there, across from the hotel was the brutalist, square-columned, stolid Progressbank.

The Tretyakovskaya had a 1920s lobby with heavy, dark furniture of the period; it was not clear if the eye-adjusting dimness was a design choice, attempting an imitation of a gaslit parlor, or mere economizing with low-watt bulbs. Lev told Roberto to wait to check in until Georgiye showed up. Ten, twenty minutes, passed ... Finally, a man, short, mustached, sharing the same hair oil as Georgiye, came in from the street and looked around at everyone in the murk, then seemed to recognize Roberto.

"My name is Ivan," he said, shaking Roberto's hand vigorously. "Georgiye could not be here tonight. But I will check you in."

At the reception desk, Roberto pulled out his passport, but Ivan shook his head, and the woman behind the desk, who was reaching for it, withdrew her hand. In Russian, he said a name the room was booked under and apparently paid for; the key was slid to Roberto, and the woman, as if in a hurry, retreated to the office.

"We must wait," said Ivan, "for Georgiye tonight, and you must meet Dmitry Morozov, who is an officer at the Progressbank. We can do nothing without him."

"I want to make it clear," Roberto said, "that I am here merely to see if the Hightower Wiggins holding is obtainable. If there are complications, perhaps I will have to return with more documents, more support . . ." Roberto trailed off as Ivan stared at him oddly.

"It is complicated to take away the diamonds, and that is why we must speak to Mr. Morozov tonight. And his secretary. At 7:00 p.m."

Roberto's paper sleeve for the electronic key listed the hotel's internet and guest password. But wouldn't his every internet search be known to . . . to whomever was taking an interest? If they could read Hillary Clinton's emails and funnel them to Donald Trump, then hacking the shmuck trying to run off with the Meyerbeer Diamonds would be child's play. *Schmuck*, which is German for "jewelry"; *shmuck*, which is Yiddish for "nincompoop" . . . and the Jews flourish in the jewel trade . . . surely there's an etymological connection worth researching for the Notebook . . . before he remembered he had given up his Notebook. Maybe only a shmuck (idiot) would go to this danger and trouble for shmuck (diamonds).

Moscow was still a city with lots of internet cafés. His guidebook said there was an internet café chain, Café Max, and one was not too far away. With a wool hat and a scarf, he left the hotel. Had he seen too many movies, read too many John le Carré novels? It seemed his walk to the paved-over plaza surrounding the Palladian entrance/exit to Metro Novokuznetskaya was solely populated by himself and the shadowy figures suspiciously lurking. He sat for a while on a bench and watched the Metro riders come and go, then, thinking he had bored to death anyone following him, he made his way to Café Max.

He searched for Progressbank (*progress* was a cognate in Russian, he discovered) and saw a glossy page about its many services. He switched to Wikipedia in English to learn that this was the twelfth-largest bank in Moscow, owned by two brother oligarchs, Dmitry and Alexei Morozov. That was sobering—he was meeting the oligarch who owned the bank, which sounded ominous. He next went to the *Wall Street*

Journal page, paid some kind of use fee, and searched for "Moscow Progressbank." No shortage of articles here, mostly about money laundering, and one about a third brother, whom Putin had imprisoned for something treasonous and trumped up. Putin probably held the third brother as a kind of ransom, hoping to influence the other two.

He checked his emails and saw that Rachel had responded.

SHE WROTE: ST SOPHIA IS GREAT BUT THERE IS A GREATER. ST DMITRI IN VLAD-IMIR, RUSSIA. THE GREATEST 12TH CENTURY SCULPTURAL ORGY OF THEM ALL. I WILL NEVER GET THERE BUT YOU MIGHT. TAKE PLENTY OF PICTURES AND SEND THEM; I'LL USE THEM FOR MY CLASS AND SAY THAT I TOOK THEM, LEST YOUR CURSED NAME BE UTTERED ALOUD.

Well, that seemed to be as civil as their last meeting. Roberto next checked his own Facebook page. He was quite proud of his stealth Facebook presence. He had a site with a false name and a stock photo of a young woman. He never posted, but he got friended by most everyone and was able to follow the adventures of Hélène and Madame Disse, the late Lucrezia and her cats, Rachel and her study-abroad trips for the Walsh Academy, and of course Rupesh, who only posted inept vacation pictures. With Helmut. His new lover. Roberto got out his wallet and unfolded a much-worn piece of paper, courtesy of Svetlana in Longyearbyen . . . and searched for Yuri Yurkov, the Russian boy with the amazing lips. He worked at a men's clothing store on the island in the Moskva River. Not too far away.

Roberto was in the elite men's clothing store for a full five minutes before he put himself in the way of Yuri. Yuri was still model material from the neck up; he had gained a tummy since Roberto had seen him last.

"Mogu ya pomoch' vam koye-chto nayti?" Yuri asked, before making eye contact. "Ah you, the friend of Lucrezia!"

"Yes, Yuri, it's Roberto. We had . . ."

"The beautiful kiss." He looked around to see who was listening.

Small talk ensued, why was Roberto in Moscow, was Yuri still modeling in Moscow, and then a less happy topic, Lucrezia.

"And she is . . ."

Roberto bowed his head. "She is not with us anymore. She always took many, many pills and never ate anything . . . and she fell into a coma and passed away." Or rather, Ludo yanked the plug out of the wall, when the machines were all that was keeping her in this world.

"Ah, *bednyaga*..."

Roberto asked if Yuri got commissions, and he did, but only for the prestige items, otherwise an insultingly low salary. Russia would prefer not to kowtow to China, who dominates the world of silk products, but Kyrgyzstan on its border, on the immemorial Silk Route, had the precious *shelkovitsa* silk, the finest of them all ... but the rich maroon ties were ₽90,500 (or $1,400).

"It is too much," Yuri said, slowing, not wishing to talk the once-kissed American stranger out of a sale. "You know Alena Akhmadullina? It is a designer from her house, Tolya—he goes by one name, gayer than both of us in the same room. But this is ... is the sort of things oligarchs buy to show off. If they have taste, which they usually do not."

Roberto would wear this tie to Progressbank, then. He bought it; Yuri would be walking home with nine thousand rubles. Yuri said he had to make sure the tie was correctly ... hung. He winked at that and took Roberto to a fitting room, pulled the curtain, and bent Roberto's head down for a repeat kiss.

"You are kind," said Roberto. "I have become old and balding."

"And I am fat."

Roberto kissed him once more. "Come see me in the West," Roberto whispered. "I'll pay for your flight."

"I am married," he said. "But, yes, I come anyway."

As Roberto left the store with his beautiful tie in a beautiful custom box placed in a beautiful bag, he noticed a man of no fashion sense whatsoever, shambling, between cigarettes, looking at the socks. When Roberto left, he left. The thing about being followed in Russia is that they wish for you to know that you're being followed.

Back at the lobby of the hotel, Lev and Ivan were there, pacing, still waiting on the others. They asked Roberto to wait for a moment, make himself comfortable, Mr. Morozov would be here any minute. Moscow traffic! Roberto sat in a low chair, the stuffing long beaten out of it, before a coffee table of old magazines. He then noticed the desk clerk disappearing into her office again, that Lev and Ivan were now standing still. The front door slammed open as if kicked. This new figure was an impatient Dmitry Morozov, heavyset in a cashmere tracksuit, leisure wear that retails for thousands; he was thundering to someone on his phone. There was a new personage, the accountant Boris, whose English was excellent.

To Roberto's relief, Georgiye had now rejoined the pack. Roberto had speculated that they had killed Georgiye and were hoping to negotiate for the diamonds without him.

"Here is the man of the hour," said Boris, a dapper man in a business suit, with teeth so blackened and horrible that Roberto had to look askance when talking to him.

"Someone is tailing me," Roberto said pleasantly, "so I figured you knew where I was." Out kissing boys throughout Moscow, in defiance of the state homophobia of Mr. Putin.

"That would not be us." Boris relayed the news to Dmitri. Ivan went to the hotel entrance to see who he might see. "Well, my friend, you have come for the Meyerbeer Diamonds. We have brought you here in such a way that no official, like the customs officer or policeman, would know you had arrived. Perhaps we underestimated . . . well, never mind." He had a folder with information, which he now peered into. "The safe-deposit box was owned first by Gehrman van Till, your stepfather, as an agent for Hightower Wiggins. When he died, it passed to your father, Salvador Costa, still a registered agent for Hightower Wiggins."

"He was the CEO."

"He left you the papers of agency?"

"What he left is in my room. I will go get them."

In the clanging elevator cage, Roberto realized his heart was beating very fast. He would pop a nitro pill once he got to the room. A voice from the back of his head: *You see that fire exit that leads down the stairs and to the street? Take it. Don't come back. First bus out of Moscow, if you know what's good for you.* He entered his room and got the papers from his suitcase. He felt, weirdly, like someone had been in his room. The maid, of course. The bed now had a chocolate on the pillow. He looked at the window. Would he be going out of it to the street below, later this afternoon?

Back downstairs, he presented the documents to Boris. Dmitri, still raging at someone on the phone, looked up to see what Boris made of them. He looked, he perused, he turned pages, he scowled, his eyebrows went up, then down. Boris pulled out his own phone to type something . . . maybe a translation app. "There is no agent anymore, but the rights to the safe-deposit box have been passed to you. I suppose you have the key."

"I do." Attached to his own key ring was the key left in the little envelope in the tranche of documents and papers passed to him by Mrs. Santos. Her words too came back to remind him: *You don't want a piece of this.*

"It might be best if we take the key for now."

"It would be even better if I kept it until we have made some settlement on the diamonds."

Dmitri barked a directive in Russian. Then, surprising Roberto, he spoke in passable English: "You cannot sell the diamonds. You can own them, but to sell is in violation of United Nations. Only international dealer can sell unregistered diamonds, and you are not international dealer. You will get the diamonds from the box, you will sell them to me. I give you many millions, I put them back in the box until day when it is possible for me to make a use of them." He reverted to Russian, speaking to Boris, which Roberto took to mean, "Work out the details," and he and Lev blustered away through the front entrance to a waiting limo.

In the silence of his departure, Boris began quietly again. "There will be issue of how you will get such a sum out of the country. Russia does not like to see millions of rubles make departure—Mr. Putin, I mean. And your country will wish an accounting of how you will arrive millions richer. The limit is ten thousand dollars. Anything beyond that requires immense attention from all tax authorities, not to mention the State Department and our Ministry of Foreign Affairs."

"So how would I . . ."

"We have a plan. It is how we extract money out of Russia for our customers of Progressbank, for Dmitri and his brother Alexei. It is safe, well-made system."

Georgiye was now hovering and taking an interest. "Yes," Georgiye added, "billions leave Russia every year so our well-to-do can spend their own money in Paris, London, New York. Three of Hightower Wiggins clients' accounts are money of this sort. When viewed from a distance, it does not seem . . . not seem legal. But step by step, as we do it, it is not illegal but requires some level of inconvenience. It will require a trip to Cyprus, which has no restrictions about deposits. You will take currency on your trip, and you will deposit it at a bank in Cyprus; I will go with you to make sure no one makes off with your briefcases. You will also bring some of the bank's money too for depositing."

Did Roberto hear this right? He would be transporting his own money and some of the Morozov brothers' money too? Seemed an important detail to be said so lightly. "But," Roberto asked, "there are still customs. How do I get on a plane—"

"A chartered plane. First, to Crimea. Back in Russian hands, as you know. That is of no interest to anyone. Then a charter to Cyprus, under the name of the Morozov brothers. It is the sort of flight that is unexamined, uninspected, and departing from a private airport. And remember, the Russian state knows not that you are here. Who is looking for a man with millions departing Russia who never arrived?"

Boris said they would meet them at 10:00 a.m. at the Progressbank, right across the street. Perhaps he would bring some vodka for the toast, da?

"If the price is not right for the diamonds," Roberto said, his legs weak, his heart rate high again, "then there will be no deal."

"The most they might fetch is twelve million euro," said Boris, "if they could be sold to a merchant; the biggest stone alone is two or three million. But there is no dealer who will buy them. It would be the end, a finish, of any merchant or diamond house in the Low Countries to touch Meyerbeer Diamonds. Who has these diamonds has lawsuits, international tribunals, the interest of your Donald Trump and our Vladimir Putin."

"You mean *your* Donald Trump."

"Yes, ha-ha, we think it is so. Nevertheless, that lowers the price to ten million. It is good pay for something you merely inherited, do you not think?"

Boris gathered up his papers, patted his pocket to assure his phone was there, bowed his head in farewell. Roberto reached to touch the arm of Georgiye, asking, "Will you hold back a minute?"

After Boris left, Georgiye smiled, patient with his American charge. "It is much to take in, but I see you are your father's son—up for all challenges."

"Yes, well, I wanted to ask you about my father. The old days—"

"We will be trapped on a plane together very soon. Crimea, Cyprus, we have all the hours in the world to look back at old times." He patted Roberto on the shoulder and leaned in for the double cheek kiss. "Tomorrow begins a new day in which everyone will be more rich and more happy, da?" And before Roberto could detain him further, he too was out the door.

And now, except for the newspaper reader by the dim lamp in the corner, the lobby was empty. And now even the newspaper reader, folding his *Moskovskij Komsomolets* neatly into a rectangle, which he put in his overcoat pocket, was ready to decamp. Wait—this was the man perusing the socks at Yuri's clothing store. A woman in a maid's uniform appeared at his side.

"It was, um, unwise," the man began, "to announce that you had the safe-deposit box key. If you walk outside tonight, someone will take it from you or go through your hotel room to find it. Once they have it, there will be no need for business transacted at the bank tomorrow. They will have what they want. And you can be safely deposited at the bottom of the Moskva River, where your body will be found full of heroin or krokodil or something terrible . . ." Roberto stared at his new companion. "I am Georgiye Gorki, your father's friend. Great friend, I may say."

"I have already met Georgiye Gorki. He just left."

"The man who convinced you he was Georgiye Gorki just left. Please, he is fifties; I am sixties—think of the calendar. I assure you I am the real one. I knew you were coming—my contacts are still that good. But I could not find your entrance at the airport or through St. Petersburg . . ."

"I don't know who you are."

Mr. Gorki No. 2 pulled out his wallet. There was a library card, a bank card, a driver's license, and government ID with ГЕОРГИЙ ГОРКИ on them all. "Give me your room key, please." Roberto had become supine before these authoritative men, which he despised himself for. The maid took the key and left for his room.

"We must move quickly, I think. You must leave Moscow tonight. They will hunt for you at the main borders—you should fool them by going east, deeper into Russia. In a few days, when they see this deal is not to be made, they will forget about you. If you do as I say, you will be safe."

"I do not believe I am in . . . in real danger."

"Oh, you do not believe it?" Mr. Gorki almost smiled but corrected himself. "I am surprised your father permitted you to even dream of the Meyerbeer Diamonds."

"He told me not to come for them."

"It is good that Safira called me a few years back, said you had asked for the papers, the deposit box key."

368 | *WESTERN ALLIANCES*

It took Roberto a minute. "Mrs. Santos? She let you call her by her first name?"

"I would have married her had she waited for my defection. Alas, she did not. She had a low opinion of Russians; I should have liked the chance to persuade her otherwise. Perhaps when she is a widow."

Roberto decided not to mention that she had passed on. He was beginning to see that this man was, truly, his father's comrade and probably was the sole option to surviving this idiotic choice he made to join his father in the sordid history of the Meyerbeer Diamonds.

The maid returned with Roberto's suitcase, all packed up.

"Out the back door," Georgiye directed. There was a taxi in the service alley, and the maid hopped behind the driver's wheel. Georgiye put Roberto's suitcase in the trunk. And Roberto and Georgiye sat in the back seat. "We are better to be in a crowd than off somewhere isolated—too tempting."

Roberto was hoping he might see Red Square before departure; in fact, he intended to spend the evening, where it never got dark, walking to see Moscow's most famous sight. But Red Square loomed into view, as if conjured up.

Georgiye mused, "Again, I have my contacts, but you got by me at the airports. Perhaps you came by train through Minsk?"

"Bus from Kaliningrad. They told me I would be off the radar, so to speak."

"What patience—the bus."

"I like to see what's between two points."

Georgiye chuckled; the contemplation of a three-day bus ride was inconceivable. "Between here and Kaliningrad, as you now know, is absolutely nothing. But your father was the same way," he added. "Had to see everything for himself."

At the bridge over the Moskva, the driver slowed, and Georgiye hopped out with Roberto sliding over the seat to follow him.

The bridge was full of pedestrians on this crisp late afternoon, and the square ahead was packed with tourists and Muscovites. Georgiye nodded to the piles of flowers halfway across the Bol'shoy Moskvoretskiy Most. "In broad daylight, Putin had his chief critic, a former deputy prime minister, shot four times right here, within view of the Kremlin." Georgiye brought his hands together like a child in celebration. "And how fortunate for us all that Vladimir Putin himself said he would take charge of the investigation personally! After our coffee, we could take a tour of buildings where people just happened to fall out of the windows . . ."

"Seems to be a Slavic propensity, defenestration."

Georgiye smiled at him, sounding out the word. "De-fen-is . . . *de-fenestratsiya*, it is the same word."

"The Thirty Years' War," Roberto mentioned. "I'm not sure if Russia was dragged into that one."

"Oh, quite. The Romanovs were reduced to paying off the Polish king to renounce his claim to being a czar. The Thirty Years' War was a close call—I could be speaking Polish to you and making homage to the pope of Rome. It was a time of muddle in Russia. You remember from Pushkin, Czar False Dmitri I followed by Czar False Dmitri II." Before Roberto could follow up about the czarring of the False Dmitris, Georgiye clapped a hand on Roberto's shoulder, tall as it was.

"Why, young man, would you ever wish to soil yourself with the wretched business of the Meyerbeer Diamonds? There is now the phrase *conflict diamonds*. For the Meyerbeer, there needs to be totally new word: *massacre diamonds, Holocaust diamonds, apocalypse diamonds.* Since they were found in the time of King Leopold II, in a mine disputed between the Germans in the East Congo and the Belgians in the West Congo, the bodies have been making themselves into a pile. A miner, it was thought, stole one of the diamonds and swallowed it or had a fellow villager swallow it to keep it from being found. There was a Belgian officer who followed him to his village and disemboweled him and everyone in his family, hunting for the diamond, which he retrieved. To cover up the crime, the entire village was killed and the village burned . . . and this is just *one* of the diamonds, one of the thirty or so, who all are attached to a tale of horror."

From the north end of the bridge, they began their ascent of Red Square. It was surprising, thought Roberto: from the the historical film clips of the May Day parades where Soviet officials stood in the cold with heavy, stolid faces watching missiles rumble by, the square looked flat as a pancake. But it's actually quite a hill.

"Diamond trading," said Georgiye, clearly expansive, enjoying an excuse to speak English, "can be a deadly business. I carry the diamond to you, but I am killed by you and it is taken. You buy it from me, and you are killed and it is taken. Maybe you kill me rather than pay me. Maybe you pay me, take possession of the diamonds, and as I try to leave the country, you kill me and take your money back. Then the henchmen returns to you triumphant, only to kill you . . . And this is the history of diamonds."

"So I gather."

"Only the Jews have figured out a way around this problem. Their system is nearly incorruptible. I have some Jewish blood, I am proud to say. Only a stateless people with a code of honor could handle diamonds. They might game each other in the arena of bargaining and fixing of price—that was fair. But they would not kill each other. And they did not exchange money. Accounts were kept, money eventually would find its way where it must. Mostly, with Jehovah looking over their shoulders, the diamonds made their way from Africa to Low Countries to Forty-Seventh Street in New York.

"But when you have something this size"—Georgiye reached into his pocket and produced a wrapped cough-drop lozenge—"worth half a million, something this small to be slipped into a pocket . . . there is no way to stop the greed. Only after the Meyerbeer family of Germany, with the aid of organized crime, secured them did the murder and thievery die down . . . in time for the Nazis. The Meyerbeers all died in the camps, and their houses, holdings, art, antiques, first editions, all stolen and hoarded by a trio of SS officers who are part of the eastern offensive against Russia in 1941. They use the mayhem of war to try to kill each other—all three plotting against the other two—and the jewels fell into Russian hands, who dutifully send them up the line to Stalin . . . except, no surprise, they were not to not reach their destination. The Germans seize Smolensk, and the great war criminal Klaus Schurz kills the contingent of Russian officers entrusted with this task—just doing his job, killing all my countrymen he can find, of course—when he bumbles onto the diamonds."

Georgiye directed them to the interior gallery of the GUM department store, abutting Red Square. This used to be the showplace of communist commerce. Brezhnev would walk Nixon through this mall of malls to show that Russia had everything it needed—frumpy, gray, ill-fitting clothes for the women, suits ten years out of fashion for the men. Now it was an oligarch's dream—Prada, Dior, Van Cleef & Arpels, Omega watches, Tiffany, Levi's, and for the home team, a caviar bar. The normal Russian could no more afford anything in here than the average American. So was this the triumph of the West? Dull goods that everyone could afford under communism versus luxury items only affordable by the Ivanka Trumps of the world under capitalism? Roberto felt it would be a short victory lap for capitalism.

"That is where we will sit and have a coffee." Georgiye pointed to an ice cream parlor besieged with squealing kids who ran in and out and up and around the tables like electrons circling uranium-238. "The ambient noise will destroy their directional listening devices."

After the coffees were set down before them, Georgiye picked up his story. "So we come to the seventies; there was still some good Nazi-hunting left to be done in South America. Simon Wiesenthal had found Franz Stangl working for Volkswagen in São Paulo. Nazis everywhere you looked—Erich Priebke ran a Viennese deli in an Andes resort, Rauff was protected in Chile, Schwammberger in Argentina, Barbie in Bolivia, Mengele in Buenos Aires. And Klaus Schurz, under an assumed name, was also in Buenos Aires. Schurz was wanted by the Russians for medical experiments on Russian soldiers, among his other SS tasks of shipping Jews and Gypsies to extermination. The KGB wanted him, Mossad wanted him, the CIA wanted him despite having permitted his escape to Argentina, facilitated by that fanatical Catholic bishop in Austria.

"Right before the Israelis closed in, Schurz tried to secure an international bank account, imagining he would soon flee. I have no idea how he landed on Hightower Wiggins, but he did—walked right into the office and opened an account with your stepfather, Gehrman van Till. Oh, what a treasure trove our Mr. Schurz had gathered onto himself—bearer bonds from German industries, gold coins from the czars back to Alexander—those stolen, of course, from the museum in Smolensk. There were stacks of currency—dollars, pounds, deutschmark, Swiss franc. And a small velvet pouch with thirty-three unpolished diamonds."

Georgiye picked up a sugar cube from the bowl. "A diamond, uncut, this big, maybe five or six carats, is already heading to a million in value. It is rare to have a pure diamond be larger than three karats, not yellow or brown or have seams and fissures throughout the stone. The Meyerbeer, they gleam as if already polished. They must be the purest uncut diamonds at loose upon the world. And one must speak . . . speak of the beauty . . ." Georgiye, dazzled by the mere memory of the diamonds, drifted momentarily. "Even a man who cares not a thing for diamonds is drawn . . . drawn into their labyrinth of light. They are the sort of diamonds where the uncut price is greater than the cut, for the potential is, my friend, *infinite*. The scepter of a czarina, the tiara for the Queen of England, a pendant for a high lady of society. Your father told you all about them?"

"Just that they existed."

"So, let us finish off the despicable Mr. Schurz. Mossad moved upon his mansion on the outskirts of Buenos Aires to arrest him as they had Eichmann; Schurz had a phalanx of Germanic guards ready to do battle. Schurz was shot and killed in the melee. Ha, I suspect he was shot by CIA, since among the secrets he had to tell included who were his Russian informants during World War II, who had turned informants for the Americans in the Cold War—so bye-bye and good riddance to Herr Schurz.

"Given the publicity, the notoriety, Van Till alerts the Russian embassy about the coins, the gold ten-ounce bullion bars with swastikas on them, all the loot. Israel, Germany, and Russia descend upon Buenos Aires to discuss who gets what, what goes where. End of case, one might think."

"But the diamonds?"

"Gehrman—I will never forget the day—was having his usual whiskey and soda, your father, his one and only one pisco sour, and myself, Stoli on the rocks, in our usual booth in the Hotel Carrera bar in Buenos Aires. The Schurz excitement was all that there was to talk about. That's when Gehrman pulled out the velvet pouch. He had not handed over the diamonds to authorities. 'Well, boys,' he said, 'what do we do with these?'

"Understand, we three had no idea of what the diamonds were worth or what their history had been. Eventually, I said, 'There will be a demand for these in Russia, in Germany, by Israel, who had a claim to Jewish assets when a family was wholly exterminated by the Nazis . . . eventually, someone will check Mr. Schurz's Germanic record-keeping and come looking for these.' And that is when your father said, 'Let's each take one. And hand this in to the UN or someone.'"

"Did you do that?"

Georgiye rested more comfortably in his chair, finishing the end of his espresso. "That is what we did. Your father said he knew a *fence*—that is what you still call it? A fence in Providence who would take the jewels, no questions asked, and give good value. Probably not top value, but good enough. So we each picked a jewel. We left the big five-karat monster to the bag; that would be way too obvious."

"How did the diamonds end up in Moscow?"

Georgiye, smacking his lips, was quiet for a moment. "I betrayed everyone. After we pocketed a diamond apiece, I kept the thirty-some other diamonds and did not turn them in. I kept them. Someone must have figured out that I was the last to have them, because twice in the eighties and once in the nineties, my apartment was ransacked, floorboards lifted, plaster broken . . . If they were looking for the diamonds, they did not find them. I buried them deep, in my mother's old farmland. When the Soviets went away, and Yeltsin was in power, banks opened, and I retrieved them and confined them to a deposit box there. A bank that eventually became owned by some disagreeable oligarchs. I put the box in the name of Gehrman van Till, and I sent him the deposit box key. When I defected, I told Salvador and Gehrman what I had done. They did not blame me. There was no selling the other thirty diamonds in the Soviet Union without suspicion, so there they have sat for decades, waiting for a time we might make good our theft. In 1986, off-the-grid diamonds became illegal to trade, so we may have missed our moment. Of course, they still have value to a criminal class, the underworld."

"Do you know what became of my father's and stepfather's diamonds?"

"I most certainly do. I followed the path of their diamonds with great interest. If they fumbled and ended up arrested, I might be arrested as well. Sal used his for a down payment on your home—you remember that lovely house up the high hill in Providence, with the beautiful porch. You were a toddler—you do not remember me coming by the house. You used to take a newspaper, yes, and circle your father's name, I think. And leave it for him to see. I remember what a beautiful boy you were. I never warmed to your sister, sorry to say."

Roberto remembered how Merle had made a big deal out of Sal suddenly having such a fine house for a strip-mall-office Merrill Lynch account manager. Roberto assumed living in a house bigger than his classmates' in public school was because his father was miraculous and successful.

"And Gehrman," Georgiye continued, eyeing Roberto carefully. "He had at last learned, as we all did, about the history of the Meyerbeer Diamonds. That they were an emblem of all that was horrible in the West: colonialism, genocide, rape, brutality, exploitation, imperialism, Holocaust, fascism, police states, the darkest reaches of capitalism. Gehrman was going to buy a small yacht with his hundred thousand, but he became . . . He felt it may be like the treasure trove of Tutankhamen, that maybe the diamonds were cursed, that if he bought a boat, it would sink or take his family and loved ones down into the depths of the sea. So he began an account with it, and when another of his children were born, he set up a trust for the child with that money."

"I am his biological child," Roberto said slowly.

"Yes, I know, but I did not know if you knew."

Roberto looked into his empty cup. "Was I this . . ."

"Yes, he also went to the fence in Providence, took the money, and opened an account for his latest child."

"So the money in the Van Till trust, the house I grew up in . . ."

"Were courtesy of the Meyerbeer Diamonds."

Roberto sank into his chair, deflated, breathing barely.

"You are in danger now. You have no idea what they have planned for you. Come, let us walk."

They returned out into Red Square. Georgiye guided them to an entrance into the Kremlin, or the official exit, rather; streams of Chinese bus tourists were pouring out. There was a line to the right for Lenin's Tomb. "Take my arm like I'm an elderly uncle; we can lean in to talk and not be heard. The bankers will give you money for the diamonds, yes? And you will facilitate getting the brothers Morozov's money out of the country as well?"

"Yes. I am to take my money and their money to Cyprus and make a deposit."

"Private planes?"

"Yes, so no one official sees me leave with so much money."

"The fun will start in Cyprus. The Cypriots will search your luggage. And there will exist a partner on their payroll among the customs agents. All the better for the little drama ahead."

"Drama?" They arrived at the Kremlin entrance; Georgiye showed an ID of some sort, and the guards waved him through. Here within the redbrick fortress walls was a spectacular showcase of the czars' wealth through the centuries. The palatial retreat, the buildings of state (some modern and clashing) but foremost the center of the Russian Orthodox world, the great eastern cathedrals in a cluster.

"You have been," Georgiye asked, "to all the European capitals. This compares, do you think?"

"This is the most magnificent city center of them all," Roberto said. "But you mentioned a drama . . ."

"These oligarchs' henchmen you have befriended," Georgiye said, "used to work for the KGB and then the GRU; the oligarchs pay better, and the graft is more assured. I recognize one of these men. They have a culture, a style of mischief. A poison-tipped umbrella, a dose of polonium in the tea. They would hate everything about you. Tall, good-looking, American, rich . . . They will not hesitate to toy with you; they would like to see you weaken and cry and beg them for your escape. So listen to me. They will give you a good price on the diamonds, to put a piece of sugar in the mouth—a little extra for your trouble, a million more than you thought you were going to get. You will show up in Cyprus, but look, the police are waiting. They open your briefcase and, aww, *nu nifiga sebe*, what have we here? A bag of cocaine . . . some khanka, some Afghan heroin . . ."

"Jesus," Roberto muttered, hopeless.

They made their way to a park on the south side of the Kremlin, a park bench just waiting for them.

Georgiye: "What a familiar story: One more headline of a spoiled aristocrat's son—you can see the *New York Post*, da? That was my favorite of your papers, such clever headlines. They will write an editorial about how this would break Sal Costa's heart. These agents who are so much your friends today will enjoy your distress; they will not let up until you are broken down, begging for mercy. I know these men. I know their sport."

"You think that is what is planned."

"Oh, you will get out of it, of course. You have a briefcase of money to bribe your way through, but there goes your profit. And then officials who have been bribed for their participation will take their cut and return most of the millions to the Morozov brothers, who talked you out of getting your diamonds and begged you to take their money. And you *still* will be on the hook for laundering your new oligarch friends' money too once back in America. And if the Treasury decides to prosecute this obvious laundering operation, it will be you who is in trouble, not the mysterious Russians you will blame everything upon."

A little kiosk nearby sold ice cream and drinks. There was almost no need to talk further; the diamonds could be dropped into the Moskva, for all Roberto now cared. "Would you like something, Georgiye?" Roberto offered.

"No, the coffee was sufficient."

"So your advice is to get out of town, right now, just leave."

Georgiye reached into his pocket and pulled out an envelope that, upon examination, revealed a bus ticket to . . . Roberto sounded out the Cyrillic . . . Ivanovo. "They will be looking at the Western border. As I said, go inland, the opposite direction. Take in the sights, go have a plate of stroganina by the Volga with a shot of polugar, keep a low profile, and then once they have realized there is no transaction for the diamonds to be had, they will cease to care. Although. As long as you are walking around with the key to the box they want, you are not really safe. Tonight, they would have likely visited your hotel room and would have been quite threatening until you handed the key over. But we have outsmarted them."

Georgiye nudged his friend subtly to look up. "Those two men." Mr. Gorki nodded to two men in dark overcoats standing by a historical plaque. "They seem to have taken an interest."

"Are they from the Progressbank brothers?"

"No, those thugs would not dare defile the Kremlin. They are from the government. You can tell by the clothes. If they are just looking at us, it is one kind of afternoon. If they come to speak to me, it is another kind of affair."

"Are you in trouble for helping me?"

"I believe Mr. Putin and his associates would like to see the diamonds stay right where they are, so I believe I am an ally in their eyes. To be an enemy of Mr. Putin is a dangerous thing; but to be a friend is only slightly less dangerous."

Roberto reached into his pocket. He unwound the key to the safe-deposit box from his key chain.

Georgiye Gorki looked at it without emotion.

"I will give it to you. You will be reunited with it after so many years."

Georgiye took it from Roberto and slipped it into his own pocket. "It will not likely be me, myself, but someone, someone from the state will get the diamonds tomorrow and move them somewhere less complicated. Perhaps they will let me do it. I would like to see them again. To see their perfection once more, the play of light . . ."

The men were coming closer now.

"Walk back to the GUM," Georgiye said. "There is a south entrance for taxis, and you will see my assistant who brought us here. She will take you to the bus station at Shchyolkovskaya. There is a bus each hour to the east. The ticket is in no one's name; no one will ask for ID for internal travel. You will be anonymous."

The two men that Georgiye pointed out now hovered near the kiosk, as if they might buy a soda. Yes, it was now clear they were not tourists or uninterested in them. Roberto stared at the ground.

"Georgiye?" Roberto asked.

"Yes?"

"How do I know you and these men are not working together? How do I know, since you stole them once, that your goal is not to have the Meyerbeer Diamonds all to yourself at last? Maybe you only wish to scare me and send me running back to Rhode Island."

Georgiye smiled thinly. "Once you walk through the door to the bank and begin to claim those diamonds, your life, dear Bobby, will never be the same."

"How do I know you are even Georgiye Gorki? Maybe you did your homework very well."

At this, Georgiye broke into a full smile and patted Roberto again on his shoulder. "You do not know, and you will never know. But now I have repaid your dear father, who I miss once a day—I have paid him back for all that he did for me. I have taught his son how to think, how he *must* think in Russia."

The men appeared at Georgiye's side and spoke to him. Georgiye pretended indifference, but one man took out an identification. The other man took him by his upper arm and helped lift him to his feet. "It seems my friends here," he said, bowing absurdly to Roberto, "would like a word. You will give Safira my best, yes?"

They walked toward the modern civil buildings, away from the churches and cannons and bell towers, leaving Roberto on the bench, aware his hand was trembling. He stood up unsurely and walked directly to the exit; not even the melee of the waiting Red Square beyond the thick, fortified walls of the Kremlin allowed him to feel free, unobserved; he felt he was the only man in Moscow with a spotlight, cameras, rifle sights upon him.

Perhaps, at some remove, this whole trip could be reckoned a failure, but Roberto did not feel that was the case. He came to learn about his father—both of his fathers, as it turned out. He came to awaken an old excitement; he came hoping to hear his father's voice in his head again, and now he did. He heard Sal Costa say, *Listen to my friend Georgiye, and get the hell outta there while the getting's good, Bobby!* And now that Sal was back speaking to him, maybe his counsel would abide awhile.

It was an uneasy time in the bus station, waiting for the coach to Ivanovo. He decided in a flash that he would not go all the way to Ivanovo. He would get off in an earlier city so not even Georgiye Gorki could locate him—indeed, he was thinking now the way Mr. Gorki suggested that he *had* to think. In looking over the bus's scheduled stops, there was . . . Vladimir, the city of St. Dmitri, where his sister's beloved church stood. That was a sign, wasn't it?

So Vladimir it was.

The Dilletante

From the checking in at the modest hotel in Vladimir near the bus terminal to Roberto's collapse on the bed, it took all of fifteen minutes, but once his head touched the pillow, he was snuffed out by exhaustion and worry and tension, and slept for twelve hours. He awakened with a small moment of panic—where was he again? And then he was able to replay the choices of the previous day.

Roberto laughed out loud. What a folly.

He grew up thinking his father and mother had a happy conventional marriage, when Sal and Gehrman were apparently wife swapping. He grew up proud of his father for earning so much money that they could live on College Hill above the rest of Providence, when a stolen diamond paid for it all. He and a few million CNBC viewers worldwide admired his father's looking out for his homespun clients, alongsidewhich were dictators, mob bosses, Russian oligarchs, Saudi sheiks, and a parade of white-collar criminals. Sal Costa had a gifted daughter and a handsome son, one of whom tried to extort and blackmail her father, while the other didn't report a hit-and-run of a destitute Romani girl. All money, if it endures long enough, is dirty, touched by corruption and low scheming. Sal tried to make clean what he had piled up, by letting his children get degrees in art history and foreign languages, to roam Europe and learn and celebrate the culture of the West, to do something ennobling with their lives so that he might be proud. Maybe all inheritances are a sort of money laundering, where the shame of the ill-gotten is hushed so that the newer generation can aspire, can do better things for the good of us all.

So. No ten to twelve million for Roberto to share with his mother and

Rachel and Rupesh and various worthwhile charities (the Romani Holocaust Memorial, which he could devote himself to). He had about a hundred thousand left, and that would last for a year or two, but he would have to work. An actual job.

And that was all right. He would get a license from Amsterdam University and get employed properly somewhere and help elucidate a generation of students. Most Dutch spoke English; his classes would be refugees and immigrants, he suspected, Indonesians and Surinamese, people from all over. And no funny business this time, no lecheries, a real teacher who loves the workings of languages, who loves how what the people actually speak pushes and pulls the language to where it wants to go next.

In the central park of Vladimir was a bluff that was home to the ecclesiastical capital of Vladimir Monomakh, prince of the Kyivan Rus', who made a fortification here in the 1100s, long before Moscow was the anointed center of the empire. There were three striking edifices (all UNESCO World Heritage Sites, not surprisingly): the cathedral, a monastery, and sitting by itself, Rachel's dream church, St. Dmitri. As the afternoon light lengthened and through the sculptural façades into higher relief, he walked around it, taking photos. Roberto for once—if he could wave a magic wand—would have conjured his sister to be beside him so he could see her face. He sent a score of photos to her phone.

Now, if he was going to follow Rachel into the teaching profession, there was one long-running expense he had indulged, which had to end immediately. Having waited for it to turn 8:00 a.m. in the States, he sought Rachel with a phone call.

As hoped, she followed up the receipt of the photo by picking up his call. "Ms. Costa," he said, "of the Walsh Academy, I presume?"

"*Envy* is not the word. Look at that motherfuckin' detail!"

"Top to bottom, all four sides. Every saint, every mythical beast . . ."

"I can't believe you went out to Vladimir just to see this thing! Since when do you follow my orders?"

"I've been led around on your leash for some time now."

She cleared her throat. "Ah, you mean the updates about Lena. Well, I was going to write something, but I might as well tell you. I think we're headed to hospice in the next few weeks. I suppose we ought to discuss funeral plans. Not to be blunt." There was a catch in her voice.

"Oh, just throw her ashes in the Seekonk."

"Bobby . . . we have to do some kind of ceremony for her."

"Actually, we could just save ourselves the trouble of her unattended service and flush the ashes down the toilet. Probably end up in the Seekonk anyway."

"Bobby, this isn't funny. I think she'd like to be comforted in knowing what we're going to do for her."

"You mean what *I'm* going to do for her. Presumably, you'll give me the poor-schoolteacher routine, and I'll pick up the tab for some fifty K send-off, fit for a Kennedy."

Rachel was quiet a minute.

Roberto pursued, "Do you drop in each week to have lunch in the cafeteria with her? Pureed vegetables and minced meat before the Styrofoam bowl of vanilla pudding? What a good daughter you are."

"Bobby, you have really become—"

"How are you going to play it? Are you going to call me and say . . . 'Bobby, oh, Bobby . . . Lena's gone.' Will you be going for the tears and strained voice—all that?"

Rachel didn't say anything.

"You've been such a dutiful daughter. Who'd have thought you two, later in life, would find such companionship? Such filial devotion from you . . ."

Roberto could swear he could almost hear Rachel thinking.

"Will there be a miraculous recovery, cancer in remission? Was that the play?"

A full thirty seconds of dead air.

At last, she sighed. "What gave us away?"

"Lena at Mrs. Santos's funeral really had me going for a bit."

A familiar edge returned to Rachel's voice, the voice he had known since childhood, that blend of snark and sneer, the voice he had come to miss. "C'mon, Bobby. Gotta admit, we had a good operation going. What'd we pull off you, one fifty, two hundred thousand dollars?"

Aunt Ines had access to the billing stationery and envelopes—all that. She filled each month's receipt with trips to the doctor, an ambulance ride to the ER, a lobectomy at full cost (thanks to Lena's lapsed insurance), all the equipment, bronchodilators, oxygen tanks. Lena was sixty-four, not on Medicare yet, so everything is top penny. A host of expensive drugs, cisplatin or carboplatin, docetaxel, gemcitabine, paclitaxel, vinorelbine—except here Aunt Ines (who no doubt had a cut in the action for the federal crime she was committing) got greedy. Anyone with the internet would know you wouldn't take *every known* pricey lung cancer drug, but she depended that Roberto wouldn't follow up. Aunt Ines was eighty-six. Of course she wasn't still working, attending to people younger than she was. A trip to the website for Fall River Rest Care also had a photo section where Ines's retirement party, years back, was prominently featured.

"What was your cut?" Roberto asked.

"Fifteen thousand a year, which is the IRS gift limit. I didn't need the money; it was just the pleasure of taking it from you. And just so you know, Lena came away from Montreal with plenty of money from Mr. Comeaux—she doesn't need the money either. Our mother, I regret to report, has got a compulsion. She can't stop herself from scamming."

"How were you guys going to fake her death?"

"Well, Lena felt she could convince you to pay for a big funeral and a bunch of leftover trumped-up medical bills . . . then she'd call you and say, 'Oh, Bobby, there's been a miraculous turnaround! Aren't you thrilled?'" Rachel started laughing and Roberto joined her, and then it opened up, each laughing at each other laughing.

"At least you got that nice cottage out back," Roberto said. "Where the guests stay, where you work on your articles, grade student papers."

"Are you in the States? You been spying on me?"

"You put it all on Facebook. And I take it that your housemate, Florence, is, um, not another Merle. This is a girlfriend, right? Another human who actually touches . . . touches parts of you, mysteriously has some affection for you."

"You and I are not Facebook friends. I made sure of it."

"I have a blandly named female photo connected to a barely used email, no postings, nothing to give me away. I wrote you years ago saying I loved your class so, so much, and your vanity caused you to add me to your twelve hundred friends. I keep track of everyone, Hélène, Rupesh. I also am Xavier Comeaux's Facebook friend. Has he stopped going by 'X'? That was pretty teenage."

"Yeah, he's Xavier again. You must have talked him out of foreign languages. He went to culinary school. So he might work in one of his father's restaurants."

"I remember the graduation pictures."

Rachel was sounding final, ready to wrap it up, the scam uncovered. "So, Bobby. The money spillway is to be dammed up, I take it."

"I would keep going if only to see the deathbed scene you and Lena would cook up. I thought I might stop paying the bills so Aunt Ines and Lena could send me bogus collection agency letters, to which I'd say I had reported them to the Better Business Bureau. Mom would have a few sleepless nights wondering if the Rhode Island DA was coming for her."

"Coming for her *again*." Rachel sounded cheerful, relieved. "Maybe I will switch sides and let you terrorize Lena for a change, as long as you cc me on all the exchanges. And my complicity, as you might expect, will cost."

"She's cute. Florence."

Rachel took a deep breath. "Yeah. I'm punching above my weight."

"You always do."

Roberto took one more walk around St. Dmitri, took another thirty pictures to send Rachel in a ZIP file, giving the dragons and griffins and two-headed, three-headed beasts the pride of place. Like all good monastical conglomerations in Russia, Vladimir's cathedral, monastery, and St. Dmitri stood bone-white and gold-domed atop a bluff above an idling river. There were benches for sitting and gazing out. Roberto figured he would never be back here again, and even if a return was in the cards, never on such a beautiful early summer day. There were kayakers, distant families on a hike to a pilgrimage church of the same vintage as St. Dmitri, ambling their way along a wide trail across the meadows below.

The phone rang and vibrated, Rachel again. "*Hold it,*" she said. "You saw Xavier's graduation pictures? With Lena there looking radiant, and she's giving X the mountain bike with the bow on it, all that?"

"Yeah. It was very sweet."

"Bobby, that's—that's the spring of 2018. We already had you paying the big bucks for her in nursing, near death. How long have you known about the con?"

"Since the parking lot at Mrs. Santos's funeral. I bought it at the time, but the next morning, I started wondering."

At last, Rachel speechless.

"You guys were a fountain of tells. You and Mom *together* making nice, for one thing. Lena wouldn't show up to a Providence wedding, funeral, PTA meeting without looking like a fashion plate—if she were actually dying, she'd look twice as fabulous out of spite. Her dragging the oxygen machine, not wearing makeup . . . it reminded me of all her other malingering mystery-illness scams. She begged me not to come see her all sick and pathetic in nursing. Who doesn't want to be visited in an old folks' home? She's the mother in *Ben-Hur* all of a sudden? Wanting me to remember her as she was . . . Way out of character for Lena. I *should* have visited, just to make Aunt Ines and Mom cook up a phony hospital room scenario. She kept saying how she didn't have health care, was too young for Medicare. So this period in her life was the only time she could work this scam."

"And you knew from 2017 I was part of the scam, and yet you . . ."

He let her dwell on that for a moment. "Sal has been haunting me, and I think he would have wanted me to look out for you guys, so that's what I was doing—in the only way you'd accept it, both of you thinking you were scamming me out of the money." Roberto and Rachel shared a silence, until Roberto said, "Also, the biggest tell. You winning my trust by thanking me, *thanking* me for exiling you to America. Or was there a hint of truth to that?"

"Okay, I was acting in the parking lot, gunning for my Oscar. Then I went home and told Firen . . . um, Florence all about it, and she said I'd spoken the truth after all, if I would only be honest with myself. And, um, she's right."

"I think you just revealed that you call your girlfriend Florence 'Firenze,' which is worth the price of this phone call."

"I'll say what I whispered to your crib the day you came home from the hospital: fuck off and die!"

"When are you over here next?"

"I'm taking the senior girls to Rome, Marseille, then Seville."

"If you stay after the program's over, what if Rupesh and I join you?"

She couldn't help but hum a note in pleasure. "You say that not knowing Rupesh is two years with Helmut now, living in Hanover. I talk to him regularly; you don't. Helmut is not going to let you abduct his partner."

"If I hang up with you and call Rupesh Doshi in the next five minutes and say, 'We're touring in Spain again, so either divorce or get permission to escape from that fat burgher Helmut What's-his-name—'"

"He's gorgeous. You should see him."

"I have seen him on Facebook. He's a shorter *me*. Rupesh will run screaming from that rain-bog capital-of-the-color-gray known as Hanover and fly down to Seville."

"I'm bringing Florence. I've never shown her Andalusia."

"Is she Moroccan? She looks sort of . . ."

"African American. And Jewish. I'm converting, slowly."

They traded a few more logistical details—for example, Rachel would return to her primacy as La Generalísima—before Roberto heard Florence musically informing Rachel she would be late for work in the background. "Gotta go," she said. "Keep those pictures coming. And I hear they're hiring a French instructor at Brockton."

And soon all was serene again; the splashing of the kayakers, the tolling of the 5:00 p.m. church bells, the trees stirring in the mildest of breezes.

He would not be teaching at Brockton. He would not be returning to the United States to live down the street from Rachel, though it was not without a certain pull.

Weil ich Europäer bin.

I am the dilletante. It's true. He thought it without dissatisfaction.

Sitting in a gay bar watching the Eurovision Song Contest and howling at the worst entrants in national dress. The World Cup every four years—when Europe comes to a chaotic costumed standstill. Who will see about Paulina, the ski instructor in Cortina he met two years ago . . . And Veronica, who worked in Brussels at the EU as a translator; her mastery of ten languages was threatening, humbling, but now he would curl up at her feet and learn and bask . . . and she sort of liked him back, he suspected. And Yves, the French West African former minor-league soccer player . . . good God, what bodily perfection. He roomed in Saint-Denis with another closeted black gay ballplayer—not as pretty, sad brown eyes, but what was his name? They both told him at the Bear's Den in Paris that they both were looking for an older white man to "adopt" them and care for them while they went on to football fame and fortune. What American must roll up his sleeves and attend to all these needy Europeans? None of his new plans could be expensive—those days were done—but didn't he once wander the European continent without twenty euros in his pocket and know glorious days, magical days, full of love and revelation?

Who among his fellow expats in Europe—a show of hands, please— intends to live on cheese, on wine, on the contents of the town's boulangerie? To try every bizarre liqueur made from mushroom or garlic or mastic or artichoke? Who will avoid the whir of the modern Laundromat for the grandmotherly art of washing the briefs and T-shirts in the hotel sink with Winni's verbena and setting them on the marble sill to dry in the Mediterranean sun for the next morning? Who will be the old regular at the Paris café who takes his morning coffee and evening brandy at the same table, who watches the owner's child grow to adulthood? Who but the boulevardier? (Oh, he may look useless, but we understand he is an English teacher, he has lived here since he was a teenager on school study-abroad trips.)

I am the flâneur, the wanderer, the curious bachelor of eccentric and refined tastes, Roberto decided. What is Europe, he thought, without one such as I? My Notebooks were admittedly juvenile, written by a man-boy in his twenties . . . but who is to say a mature series of more worldly ramblings might not have an audience? There were blogs now, vlogs even, podcasts—and who better to pontificate than Roberto Costa? And if that too is a flop, if it never comes together any more than my school days' foreign coin collection show-and-tell, if my efforts are generous but ineffective, if such a media maven never comes into being, who is deprived? Do you see my worldly shrug? Europe has been at that shrug for millennia, waiting for my arrival so that I might acquire it.

Who will be the man in the train car who has fallen asleep with the Thomas Mann novel he has put off reading, propped open upon his chest?

Who will be the elderly gentleman—from America, they say—staring upon the horizon for hours in a whitewashed village proffered by a cliff to the cerulean sea? Roberto is not naive about the life expectancy of some Marfan patients. When that day comes, when he is found unresponsive in the pensione, where he had been observed as too slow in coming down the stairs, where his appetite had seemed to desert him, too much of his favorite cassoeula was left in his bowl last night, which upset the signora; when no one can stir him in the tall-ceilinged room with the night-black nineteenth-century dresser and ornate beaux arts mirror on the inner wall, the crucifix centered above the headboard, well, then that is a shame, but he must have been at the end calmed by the fountain in the square, the hourly tolling of the parish bell, summoning its population of widows, its choir who sends the ancient threnody out across the small plaza, beyond the ocher walls and terra-cotta roof tiles, to find release at day's end so that God may, again, take notice. And didn't he dress well? A flower from his morning market stroll in his lapel. What a backward glance was this sort of fellow, an emissary from the time where Europe claimed the hearts of men and women of sensibility, exiles from their newer world of coins and capital, favoring our inscrutable gestures lost in meaning even to us, preferring how slow are our manners, how richly we gave decoration to the passing of the centuries, what a marvelous surprise, the American who loved it here and who spoke our language so especially well.

Acknowledgments

The men and women I dedicated the book to, a few hundred pages back, were my European tour guides, my couches to crash upon, my providers of food, shelter, laundry detergent, interpretation, and wisdom. I wish to thank North Carolina State University, who let me lead a decade of student groups to Europe with plenty of time to spare for my own tourism, which had truly begun back in my days at Oxford, for whom John and Christine Kelly were responsible. My life has never been the same because I met them.

My five perennial traveling companions—Rodger Blum, James Fergusson, Greg Kelly, and Cecilia Straney, and as of late, my niece Brenna Marie Barnhardt—were dragged to every dot in Wilfried Koch's *Baustilkunde*, who with Henry James, was our presiding god. Along with the redoubtable Tom Gidley and Henrietta Miers, we together endured the speeding tickets (Germany!), the breakdowns (Italy), the thefts (again Italy), mistaken arrests (Sweden, Switzerland, and the old East Germany), and numerous close calls with armies and police (Northern Ireland, Russia, the Balkans). There were one or two money crises for which the greatest traveler I have ever known (who upon her death had still been more places than me) saw to my rescue: my mother, Mary Barnhardt. She never once thought I should come home.

A whopping thanks to St. Martin's Press, and George Witte (who smartly supervises my cutting a good deal of literary debris, book after book), and my one and only forever-agent, Henry Dunow (who has stuck with me for thirty-five years), and Tom McCormack, to whom I owe my career and many of the advances blown utterly, to the penny, on travel. They have recklessly allowed me and my typing habit to flourish.